THE BEECHMONT

A Private Hotel for Gentle Ladies

A Private Hotel for Gentle Ladies

Ellen Cooney

Pantheon Books, New York

Copyright © 2005 by Ellen Cooney

*All rights reserved. Published in the United States by Pantheon Books,
a division of Random House, Inc., New York, and in Canada by
Random House of Canada Limited, Toronto.*

Pantheon Books and colophon are registered trademarks of Random House, Inc.

A Private Hotel for Gentle Ladies *is a work of fiction. Names, characters, places, and incidents
are the products of the author's imagination or are used fictitiously. Any resemblance to actual events,
locales, or persons, living or dead, is entirely coincidental.*

Library of Congress Cataloging-in-Publication Data

Cooney, Ellen.
  A private hotel for gentle ladies | Ellen Cooney.
     p.   cm.
   ISBN 0-375-42340-0
   1. Hotels—Fiction.   2. Runaway wives—Fiction.
   3. Boston (Mass.)—Fiction.   4. Male prostitutes—Fiction.
   5. New England—Fiction.   I. Title.

PS3553.O5788P75   2005   2005043135

www.pantheonbooks.com

Printed in the United States of America
First Edition
2   4   6   8   9   7   5   3   1

To Philippa Brewster

A Private Hotel for Gentle Ladies

∞ One ∞

Charlotte Heath was in such a hurry to get to her husband, it took her a while to notice the absence of her bells. If they were there, she would not have seen her husband at the edge of their town's big square, under an elm tree, bending his head toward a young, pretty woman, to kiss her.

It was midafternoon. No one else was out. No one else was watching. Except for Charlotte, her horses, her husband, and the woman, the roads around the square were deserted. All the houses were shuttered against the cold.

If it weren't for the absence of bells . . .

She'd imagine it like a song: If it weren't for the bells, the lack of the bells, if it weren't for the lack of the jingle of bells . . .

Her sleigh in the snow down Mulberry Street should not have been silent. It should have announced itself, as sleighs are supposed to, in a chimey, wild jangle, which the horses would add to with snorting and horsey whistles, just to make noise. They disliked snow.

They missed hearing the rhythm of carriage wheels on uncovered roads, and their own, steady clip-clopping.

If he'd had some warning—and he would have recognized her right away, by the bells—her husband could have thought of good excuses. He could have passed himself off as a man who'd offered his arm to a solitary woman, in a social-decorum sort of way, as if they were headed for a stroll across the park, and never mind that the walkways weren't clear. The big square did not resemble a town green so much as a white, high-banked, North Pole tundra, with whirls of snow blowing everywhere. Hard white sunlight was in the trees, in every branch, like an extra layer of ice.

Who was the woman? Charlotte didn't know.

The snow in the road was deeply packed. The blades of the sleigh ran as smoothly as a child's fast sled. There was a basic unnaturalness about soundless, gliding runners, Charlotte felt, even though she'd grown up in the East and loved winter.

It was the middle of February, 1900. She was supposed to feel glad and optimistic about this new century. It didn't seem enough to be astonished to keep finding herself still alive.

Her husband turned away from the woman in plenty of time for the kiss not to actually happen. You had to know him to know he was saying (with a look, no words), "This is something we have to postpone."

Charlotte remembered that sometime last summer the cook's girl and boy had taken her bells from the stable for some game of theirs in the kitchen. They had not put them back, which was typical of them. Except for Charlotte and the cook, Mrs. Petty, the feeling in the household about those children was this: they were like two red squirrels who'd burrowed in through the walls, and very much needed to be removed.

They were gone now, having moved with their mother into

Boston. Charlotte loved them. She'd been sick. She owed them, in a way, her life.

Her horses were fond of the bells. There were many more than she needed, in many sizes. Some were as small as buttons; some were as large as fists. She was always collecting sleigh bells. She was encouraged by the Heaths to be musical. She had not learned an instrument as a child. She did badly at learning piano, worse at violin, worse still at other strings, and worst of all at woodwinds. She was told she lacked a feel for scales and notes and could barely distinguish a key. She had no patience.

Maybe the horses knew what lay ahead before she did. They were unusually quiet. After the turn onto Mulberry Street, they slowed down a lot more than they had to.

Their town, south of Boston, was settled in the earliest of colonial times. It was a Puritan-prosperous place: big homes, good manners, modern conveniences, gentility, professions, sacred inheritances, nothing out of place. Her husband loved their home like a box he happily fit into. But he was always prepared to burst out of it. Charlotte never traveled with him on business trips.

It was the home he grew up in. It was enormous; it was the only one on the street. A Heath had taken it over in 1820 from a man who'd made a fortune as a sea merchant and who then, having become religious as a result of a near-shipwreck, envisioned the place as a self-sustained college for the training of missionaries, which had not happened.

The house was elegant and austere, with so many added-on wings and hidden rooms you could wander around for hours without sight of another person. Two of her husband's sisters lived there with their husbands, and his two unmarried sisters, and two of his brothers and their wives. And Charlotte's father-in-law. Charlotte's mother-in-law.

A dozen of them. One of her.

The various Heath children—six of them who had parents in the household—lived at their schools now; two were old enough to have established their own homes. Charlotte's husband was the baby of his family.

It never occurred to him to live anywhere else, not even at their summer place—on the coast, in Cape Ann, in the village of Squab Cove—where Charlotte always longed to be, no matter the season. He didn't care for the sea. He tolerated it one weekend a month in the summer because that was what was expected of him. He disliked dampness.

Just now, he was involved in arranging money for the switching of a factory in Ohio. He had been called home unexpectedly for the death of one of his uncles. Had he brought the woman with him?

He did a great deal of work in the Midwest and felt a personal relationship, something like love, with the train he rode to get out there: he'd arranged the money for a part of the track to be laid. That particular factory was in the process of changing from the making of kitchen and parlor stoves to the making of bicycles.

Everyone needed stoves, but everyone wanted new bicycles. That was where the money really was. Her husband didn't ride one himself (as far as she knew), but he'd offered to get her one so she could ride in the lanes at some future point, like his sisters and sisters-in-law. The future point meant, "if someday you're well." There was always an "if." They had thought she'd never get well.

If he brought home a bicycle for her, she'd let it sit in the yard and rust. Or give it to the maids. There was only one kind of riding she was interested in.

She'd given the horses their heads on the way across town; her ears were still ringing with rushing, icy air. Her heart had barely started beating again in its usual way, from that wonderful fisting-up that seized her inside the chest like a good, big hand, then let go.

She wasn't reckless. She knew her way around speed. Before she was sick, people were always telling her husband to make her stop going so fast, and he would say, "Charlotte, you must change the way you carry yourself, you have got to slow down," and she would answer that he was right, they all were right, and then she'd go at a ladylike canter out of town, to gallop through the woods and fields and old logging roads, where no one saw her but God.

No bells. Only a silence.

Her husband and the woman must have just left the house she was heading to. It belonged to her husband's uncle: the man who'd died. A Heath uncle, Owen, of the lawyer branch of the family.

It had happened the morning before; he was eighty. In his house, a high, handsome mansard full of marble and gleaming wood and French furniture, they were holding his wake.

The branch of the family her husband belonged to was the finance branch. "Our Mr. Heath owns money and he arranges things" was how Mrs. Petty explained him to her children. He liked that. "He owns things himself and when other people want to get things, or manufacture things, they give him money and he arranges it."

Charlotte saw the way the woman let go of her husband's arm. Slowly, reluctantly. Confidently. It was the same way people stopped talking about personal things when a servant came into the room.

She pulled back the reins and the two horses stopped. She knew it looked wasteful of her to have brought out the pair for such a light sleigh, but they hated being apart. They were young, handsome chestnuts, high-headed, proud of themselves, healthy. It had been a long time since she'd been out with them and they kept letting her know their joy to have her back, even though they'd never been sepa-rated from her completely: someone from the stable had brought them to her window every day when she was sick.

Her husband took off his hat—a stiff, dark one. A mourning hat. He brushed his hand along the crown, as if a load of snow had settled on it, weighing down on him. But there wasn't any snow; he was procrastinating. He took a long time to put it back on, and he did so with an awkwardness that didn't suit him. He was amazed to see his wife and her horses and sleigh, coming upon him silently. He wasn't in the habit of being stolen up on.

John Hayward Heath. Hays, he was called.

Funny he should speak to the woman first and not to her. But at least he didn't whisper.

"Why, here is Charlotte and her horses." The woman didn't know who Charlotte was—or pretended she didn't. Hays said, "My wife."

The woman wore a fur coat—dark mink—and a matching hat, and stylish leather boot shoes, very narrow and pointed. In spite of the coat, you could tell her corset was steel-lined. Steel-lined corsets had a particular look. The coat had a tightly gathered waist. It was belted, with the ends in a perfect knot, exactly in her middle, pulled tightly.

Charlotte hadn't worn a corset for a long time. She lost a lot of weight when she was sick; she didn't need one. But she'd made up her mind never to put one on again. You don't get up from a sickbed and find that you are the same person you were before. It maddened her to think of herself as a weakling.

Why, here is Charlotte and her horses. Charlotte and her horses. That sounded like a song, too.

She saw the way her husband looked at the woman.

He was soft in the face. She knew that look: serious, naked, with a longing that sooner or later would be satisfied. He had that. He was someone who knew that whatever his longings were, he wouldn't walk away from them unsatisfied.

Until this moment, she had believed that there were only two things to cause that expression: desire for her, in the days before she was sick, and babies, especially when someone showed him a new one, or even mentioned one.

She had no idea how much it was required of her to keep saying she was sorry not to have had a child by now. She knew from other women she should never stop trying, she should not give up hope; she should think of three misses as a rehearsal, or dues you must pay, as if bearing full-term was something she'd eventually get right, something she would have earned. She'd developed the talent, at her time of the month, to never pay attention to the sight of her own blood. She avoided wearing clothes of any red shade.

At the summer place there was a female cat maintained by one of the maids. It was not allowed outdoors because Charlotte's father-in-law, in retirement, was studying birds. There were feeders all over the yards, birdhouses in the trees, particular flowers and shrubs to attract certain types. Cats in this system were murderers.

The summer-place cat must have felt it was in solitary confine-ment. All the maids felt sorry for it; then one day a fisherman brought over a scrawny orange kitten. The cat took the kitten by the neck and walked away with it to a dark corner—either to destroy it or to adopt it. Charlotte happened to be there. She was always turn-ing up in kitchens.

This was the first time in her life she understood what it was like to be shot through her body with pure, stinging, burning envy. The cat came proudly and boastfully back into the light to show off its baby, as if saying to the humans, "I don't recall giving birth, but I suppose I must have done so, and now I am very pleased." Charlotte watched the cat lick every part of the kitten, but after that, until the kitten was grown, she stayed away from that part of the house.

The woman with her husband wasn't maternal-looking. She wore her hat at an angle, very stylishly, in spite of the fact of the wake.

Hays and the woman stepped away from each other. They did a good job. They could have been strangers. They looked as if they were used to being parted when they didn't want to be parted.

There was no guilty look on her husband's face when he realized his wife was in the middle of Mulberry Street.

She wasn't supposed to be out. He looked amazed, but he didn't look guilty. Charlotte thought, He doesn't think he'd be doing something *not all right* in kissing her. He looked like what he was doing was right.

"I was on my way to look at your uncle," called out Charlotte, as if he had asked her. She'd expected to surprise him at the wake: the only husband among all those relatives without a wife at his side, not counting the widowers. He was the Heath whose wife was always absent. She'd thought he minded that. He wasn't particularly fond of Uncle Owen, but that wouldn't have kept him from playing a part he knew well: a man who's doing what he should. A man who gets things right.

A man who gets things.

Heaths took mourning—and all ceremonies—seriously. Uncle Owen had lived much longer than anyone thought he would, and for that alone, Charlotte admired him.

His heart had stopped while he dozed in front of his fire, exactly the way he had wanted to die. He was a competent lawyer, and he was rich, and neither overly greedy nor overly hoardful, which was true of all Heaths. He never denied himself brandy, butter-rich foods, sweets. He was gout-ridden, heart-weak, blood-torpid, and as fat as the Falstaff of Shakespeare, whom in fact he had played. The Town Players were always putting on the history plays in Town Hall, which was built with town money but designed and endowed by Heaths.

The Heaths knew Shakespeare for the histories, and maybe one of them—Hays—knew a couple of things about Hamlet. But Charlotte felt she could say for certain that there was not one Heath who knew anything at all about the greatest of all the great tragic heroines. There were two: Juliet and Cleopatra.

Once at a family Christmas dinner, she made a remark about the Players' theatricals, which she never took part in, beyond donating her horses (and herself to drive them) for the fetching of scenery, built on a farm outside town. The Players disliked stage settings that were not elaborate.

The scenery makers also sent in carvings of birds such as wood pigeons, thrushes, and owls, to be suspended by wires above the stage, for the sake of Charlotte's fatherinlaw, who anyway paid for all the props.

She said at the dinner, wouldn't it be interesting if the Players put on the tragedy of Queen Cleopatra, which was basically history? She concealed the fact that she'd love to play the part of the queen herself. No one thought to ask her, but she believed she might really be able to pull it off: she would have loved to create the illusion of herself as being larger than life, and brave and majestic and uncontainable.

She didn't think the queen a coward, or out of her mind, for being bitten by a snake she knew would kill her.

Put on *Antony and Cleopatra*? The managers of the Players were Heaths, as were many of the actors. In every cast the major roles were played by Heaths. That play? In their town? It was the same as if Charlotte asked them to lie on sofas to eat, and then conduct a Roman orgy.

"But it's *made up,*" said one of her husband's cousins, who was a professional military historian with the Navy.

"It's a purely sensationalist romance," someone else said, "and it's not even English."

The odd thing was that the Heaths themselves had not descended from the English. They were German. The original American

Heaths had a German name lost to history: they'd settled in Pennsylvania and Ohio, where they operated slaughterhouses and sausage
factories, long since sold. The Heath migration east took place years
ago, even before there were railroads. There'd been a Heath bank in
Boston, but that had been sold. They had left the city and settled a
bit to the south; they'd turned their new town into a Heath town, but
the Midwest was where they still were making money.

Hays spoke German and French and some Italian without an
American accent. Men from those countries, in the East on business,
were often turning up at the household for dinners, card games,
musical evenings, billiards and gambling with dice in the games
room, and Sunday afternoons on the lawn, resting off a night-before
of God knew what. Hays had been to college in Michigan, but he'd
spent two years in Paris, which he felt had shaped his core, years
before Charlotte knew him.

In the presence of those visitors, his European alternative self
would emerge in a clear, vivid way, as though he had changed into a
costume, and rearranged the lines of his body, and even, perhaps,
put on some sort of a mask, which resembled his own face, but was
someone else's. This was not something Charlotte had ever found
disturbing, not even when the part he played carried over—after the
guests had left—to their own rooms upstairs.

Hays didn't take part in the Players, partly because he could never
be counted on to be in town for rehearsals and stagings, and partly
because (few people knew this) he suffered from a terrible form of
shyness. He'd go rigid, like a whole other version of himself, changed
into a man-shaped wood block. He could not give speeches at meetings, could not perform anything that required an audience.

In college he was part of the debate club, but only as a coach. The
one time he was called upon to deliver a eulogy at a funeral—of
another Heath uncle, who in fact was childless and a bachelor, and
had left Hays his money—he made it to the pulpit of the church, but

all he could do was bow his head and say, weakly, "I am too filled with feeling to speak what I came here to say." When he returned to his pew, the Heaths said he was just like Antony in Shakespeare's *Caesar,* but a modern-day American one, who'd decided to keep his words to himself. He was a tall man, pole-thin. He was dark-brown haired like all his family, but his skin was fair.

He blushed sometimes like a girl. Spots of pink rose up in his cheeks, out from the ends of his mustache, when he defended Charlotte at that awful Heath dinner. He obviously agreed with his family that *Antony and Cleopatra* was all wrong for them, but he seemed surprised and pleased that his wife even knew who Cleopatra was. "Charlotte has the right to make suggestions and take part in this family as she wishes," he said. Everyone admired him for his loyalty. Everyone thought, Hays loves Charlotte, for some reason unapparent to us. He'd married for love. Everyone said so.

And his lawyer uncle, who now lay dead in state in his elegant, wide front room, had leaned toward Charlotte and patted her hand with his plump, spotty fingers. He wasn't unkind to her; he seemed to feel sorry for her. "Look at it this way, my dear Charlotte." Would she care to know what he was offered to write on years ago for *The Bar?*

The Bar was a national monthly magazine, now defunct, for lawyers. It was not concerned with legal matters only but had articles, stories, anecdotes, drawings, and personal essays and remarks pertaining to the lives of men in law. Uncle Owen had been a regular contributor. He rarely went into the courts himself; his specialty was business law. But for *The Bar* he wrote jokey pieces about unusual details of court proceedings, family backgrounds of criminals, outfits people wore to cheer on disturbers of the peace, and things people ate at afternoon tea in murder trials.

"My dear Charlotte, knowing my interest in Shakespeare, they asked me to write an article speculating on a scene in which Hamlet, the killer of his butler, not to mention his mother and his king, is put on trial for murder, and I, as his lawyer, must defend him. Can you think of anything sillier than that? No wonder that magazine went out of business."

Charlotte had not seen the point. "But how would you do your arguments to defend that poor man?"

"Ha-ha!" Uncle Owen cried. "There could not be a case!"

She felt she would have defended Hamlet on the grounds that, one, he was no murderer, and two, everything he did, he did honestly, thoughtfully, and morally. He was the most honest, thoughtful, moral man she ever heard of. "Charlotte would never stand for anyone speaking badly of her favorite dramatic hero, even if he was insane and hated his mother," her husband said. He seemed to think he was helping her out.

Charlotte said, "Is it out of the question logically to have a defense because, at the end of the play, there could never be a trial, as Hamlet has died?"

And Uncle Owen leaped in with his thrust. "Died or not is immaterial. We're talking about the difference between truth and fabrications. There could be no case against Hamlet because *he wasn't real, he was only a story*."

Well, Falstaff wasn't real, historically, she should have argued. But Uncle Owen had yet to play that role.

She wondered if he'd changed his mind about stories. She wondered if he caught a glimpse of death, like some sort of shapeless, strange thing coming toward him as he sat in his armchair with his ideal last breath gathering up in his old-man's lungs. She wondered if he believed that actual death was something history could prepare you for—or history plays. She would think it would not.

She would think it would resemble ghosts, witches, stories, inventions. Maybe she'd had an ulterior motive when she decided to come out for the wake. Maybe she wanted to be looked at as someone who did a remarkable thing. She was never supposed to get well. She was supposed to have been an invalid, period.

Here is Charlotte and her horses. Charlotte and her horses. My wife, up from a sickbed to go to a wake. Isn't that *odd?*

Hamlet wouldn't have thought so. And Charlotte remembered what it was like to be still in her twenties, newly married, seated at a table in candlelight in her husband's family's dining room, the only one in the house awake, reading Shakespeare for the very first time.

She had sat one night nearly till dawn reading *Hamlet* and for weeks afterward her heart would feel clenched up, at odd moments; and she'd feel a wholly new, powerful, tender affection for her husband.

Maybe she fell in love with Hamlet himself. Or maybe, in her husband, buried somewhere, she saw traces of him. She had told him as much. "You don't have an uncomplicated soul, Hays, although you would like to pretend to." He blushed at that, but he didn't disagree.

Her husband's family's household was at the opposite end of town from the lawyer Heaths. Hays had gone out that morning with one of his brothers-in-law and had not taken his own sleigh.

She'd wanted to bring him home herself. She'd pictured the drive, her husband beside her, in dusky air and mild windblown snow: a ride away from death. She'd thought they might bypass home and turn out into the old roads for a while. She'd thought, I miss my husband, and I'll tell him so.

They had not shared anything for so long. It was as if she'd turned into another of her husband's sisters or the wife of one of his brothers. Or a stranger. One more member of the household who could never be turned out.

You couldn't be a Heath and turn out your wife. Her illness had terrified Hays. She knew this. And she had thought, back at the house, putting on her coat, sending for the sleigh and the horses, that a death in the family would be a reasonable time to try to set things at last on the course they were supposed to have taken.

Death, she'd thought, would have a practical, logical application. But she didn't go into Uncle Owen's house on High Street for his wake. How could she, when Hays had just come out of it with the woman?

She wondered if Hays was trying to remember the last time he'd seen her outdoors. She couldn't even remember herself. A long time ago.

Her length of time in a sickbed was ten months. But it seemed much longer: two years, five years, eight, nine. Her principal doctor felt that what was wrong was some form of brain disease. She had heard that often. "Charlotte, brain disease, it's some form of brain disease, which I expect will go away. Probably."

The consultants, and there were many, believed it was a type of polio. They insisted on the "some type of" aspect, as if rubbing it in that her particular case was abnormal—as if she'd not got it right, as if it were one more thing not right, like not having children.

Or even like the color of her hair, as though she'd had a say in it. She had hair the color of a pumpkin, a ripe one, and it was frizzy and wild and would never stay tucked in. She was no longer para-lyzed from the disease, not in any part of her that showed.

The polio theory was the one that made everyone more nervous; the Heaths didn't want anyone outside the household to hear about it. It seemed less offensive to them to say, "Something is wrong with her brain," which to Charlotte sounded horrible and embarrassing, and was a lie.

The woman with Hays was as fit as Charlotte's horses, all glowing, with that perfect lady's hourglass figure. Perfect. Like a picture in a magazine. She looked like she'd never been sick, from anything, ever.

One good thing that happened in the sickness was this: Charlotte was able to stay out of hospitals. The room she was kept in was off the front hall, at the top of the stairs that went down to the kitchen. The cook's children had stayed close by her.

The girl, Sophy, was nine now, and Momo, the boy, was six. There was also a baby, Edith. When Mrs. Petty came to the house-hold for her interview with Hays's parents, she'd come alone. The Heaths didn't know about the children until they all moved in.

Those children had loved it that Charlotte was still for all those months, with nothing to do, it seemed, but have her muscles rubbed, and talk to them, and allow them to climb all over her and brush her hair and use her bed as their playroom.

The girl heard one of Hays's sisters say that the story of Alice and her adventures in Wonderland was a blotch on the tradition of En-glish culture, and a silly, ridiculous thing, as bad for the mind as a diet of maple candy, and nothing else, for the body. Sophy loved maple candy. She took about a month to have memorized a large portion of the story, and might have completed it all if she had not gone to Boston.

She stole the book from neighbors who had a daughter her age. The neighbors used to let her and her brother play in their yard with their ponies and ducks, but there'd been trouble.

One day Momo Petty went into the neighbors' house by the front door instead of the rear. A child of a servant at a front door! When he was made to see his mistake, Sophy walked into a mud puddle (it was raining), slipped into the house, and allowed herself to place footprints of mud on the neighbors' extremely expensive drawing room carpet. A vase was broken as well.

Charlotte only had to think of Sophy and her brother ducking under her bed to hide from some trouble they'd been in—and the baby curled on a pillow, sometimes fussily, bubbling up oatmeal or milk—and she could hear that voice.

"Alice shall have an adventure. There's a big white rabbit. You must prepare yourself for things you would never expect," she'd begin, as though no one had heard this before.

"She is going to be sitting near a river with her sister, who is a very boring girl and she is going to *run fast and fall down a hole*."

There was a loose eye of pine in one of the floorboards, under a little brown rug, and the boy would lift the rug to reveal it. It would seem they'd fall down that hole just like Alice. Under them was the kitchen with its heat and steam and Mrs. Petty.

The Alice part of their lives was a secret.

People often remarked on the fact that the children did not resemble their mother, or each other; certainly none of them appeared to have shared a father. Mrs. Petty believed in keeping things discreet. She was a genius of a cook. Even Charlotte's father-in-law had to admit she would never be matched in the household, although the new cook, a middle-aged widow, had trained in New York at well-known restaurants. There was no Mr. Petty.

There were no other families they knew who allowed their servants to have children. It could not have lasted. One day Charlotte's mother-in-law said simply, "I want to be rid of that woman," and that was that.

Mrs. Petty hadn't asked for references, which she anyway didn't need; you only had to put her into a kitchen with a chicken or some eggs and cheese, and you'd want never to eat the cooking of anyone else.

Charlotte missed her and the children more than anyone knew. But she knew where they were. Mrs. Petty was the cook now in a private hotel for women, the Beechmont, on the back part of Beacon Hill, behind the Capitol with its glittering dome.

"I'm going there," she decided. "Now."

She didn't know Boston well. She'd been to restaurants near

the Common, the theaters and music halls of Tremont and Washington, the art museum, the library, the shops of Charles Street, the
Garden, Park Street Church and Trinity, and a neighborhood on
Commonwealth Avenue in Back Bay, where her principal doctor
had an office for consultations. Before they were married, Hays had
a Commonwealth Avenue town house, but he'd given it up. Boston
was only thirty miles from their town, but to Charlotte, since her
illness, it could have been a city on the moon.

If only a large talking rabbit would appear in the snow to lead the
way. She would have appreciated it. She would have been grateful
for the chance to tumble down a magic hole and find herself where
she wanted to be, but there were practical matters to deal with. It
was cold; the air was turning more frigid by the minute. It would be
twilight soon enough. She had no lanterns, she had no bells. She
had no money.

She felt no panic, or even fear, but she had images of losing her
way; of the horses complaining and giving her grief because they
wanted to go home; of her limbs, encased as she was in wool and fur,
turning frosty and blue, and hurting worse than they had hurt when
she was sick.

Thinking of the warmth she'd receive from her friends did not
counteract reality. She realized she might not get far.

There was a whole troop of Heaths gathered in one place
nearby—she was not forgetting this. She was sure, at an alarm raised
by her husband, four or five of his rowdy young cousins in their
mourning suits would have been pleased to leave Uncle Owen, leap
on horses like boys in the Wild West, and charge after her and catch
her, although she would have given them a good run.

She had learned the lessons of a sickbed very well. What strength
you have, you are going to be careful of it; you are going to measure
it; you are going to feel nervous about it. She felt that this was the way

people must act when they are being released from jail, and first put on go-outdoors clothes, and feel the air on their faces—the real air, and real sun, and real wind.

You can't believe it's true that you are free, and you're terrified; and you cannot believe it's not going to happen all over again that Fate will conspire against you and lock you up again, as if the worst of your fears is the one thing you can count on to happen.

And meanwhile as you try out your new, out-of-isolation self, on wobbly legs, squinting, squeamish, as pale as white paper, everyone around you is clamoring to know why you don't seem glad. No one knows that the outside of your body—or what can be seen of it—is the same as a container that seems to be made of something durable. But it's no more dependable than a water glass, if the glass were placed in a fire.

Because you know what it's like to be not in charge of yourself. To be at the mercy of confinement. To want out. To stare at a window and wish yourself as thin as a curl of smoke, slipping out through a crack. Get out, get out! And you come to believe that getting out might take place in only one way. And you'd not be afraid of it.

Maybe she had wanted to look at Uncle Owen because she wanted to find out if she envied him, was that it? Because maybe she was afraid of being well?

"Save dark thoughts for bright days." Where did she hear that? Not from Mrs. Petty. Her father-in-law? Standing in her doorway, gazing past her at some robin that pecked at the glass, trying to destroy its own reflection, thinking its reflection was an enemy bird, a perfectly normal thing? Well, she knew what that was like, hating your own reflection.

"Save dark thoughts for bright days." It must have been some-thing from the mouth of some king, at the edge of the Town Hall stage, in some battle or some inner-castle mess, trying to put on a brave front. He would smile at her. An old man's smile. As if he knew what she was thinking. As if it weren't abnormal to want to die, if the alternative was to not be able to live.

The thing was, there were no bright days. For so very, very long.

"I don't wish I was you, Uncle Owen," she suddenly said out loud, quietly, like a prayer, as if he could hear her. Maybe he could. "Listen, Uncle Owen. Wherever you are, I'm glad not to be there."

"Charlotte!" shouted Hays. "Where are you going?"

She had an urge to tell the truth, to just throw back her head and shout out "Boston!" But she didn't answer him. Did her father-in-law know about the woman? Did everyone? She remembered the afternoon she was carried into the front sitting room, the yellow one. It was a consultant who had carried her: a hearty, big doctor; she didn't recall his name. He had picked her up in his arms spontaneously and said, "Time for tea, my dear," and there she was, appearing to a room of Heaths, six or seven of them.

Hays was talking to one of his sisters, bending his head close to hers, gravely, confidingly. He was the last in the room to notice that Charlotte was there, and when his eyes met hers—as she was placed in a chair, as someone ran to get a blanket—she saw that he looked like a man who had a secret. He looked at her as if he thought she was an intruder. He was holding a teacup. He set it down quickly, roughly, and tea splashed out, and two bright spots rose up his cheeks. And he told her, in a shrill, breathy way that wasn't like him at all, he'd spilled his tea because he was so happy she'd got up, what a good surprise. He said that he was only just talking about the excellence of the new shade of paint in the room, now that they'd finally completed it. It was the voice of a man talking to someone who didn't have the right to truly know his thoughts.

The walls were dark yellow. The painting job had been completed a month ago, which Charlotte knew because one of the painters had stopped by her room on the last day to ask, did she want to be carried out to see it? But that hadn't been possible; a maid had been with her, putting up her hair. The new paint was exactly the same shade as the old one. Did Hays think that being sick had rearranged her memory? Did he think she didn't know all the ways to read his face, to understand the tones of his voice, to listen to the things he wasn't saying when he spoke to her?

A maid came in to change the tablecloth. Someone poured Charlotte some tea. Charlotte said, "I like the new color, very much, for the brightness."

And her mother-in-law, tall and stern, with her Queen Victoria hair, in her at-home quilted gown, her bone-ribbed corset laced up like a trap, in a chair by the fire, with coal light flickering on her glasses, glanced up at Charlotte from a magazine she was reading, *The Saturday Evening Post.* And she said to the doctor, because it was not a good idea in the household to do anything without consulting her, "You didn't mention you planned to allow her out of bed."

"She's getting well," he answered. When he left the room, Charlotte felt alone. Her mother-in-law turned back to her magazine. Tea was resumed. That was the first time Charlotte thought, in actual words, Hays gave up on me.

"Charlotte! Charlotte! Charlotte!" His words rang out in the cold. He began to run after her, and his hat fell off into the snow, and the woman bent down to retrieve it. He was wearing his dress shoes, not his boots. He didn't run after her very long.

She flicked to the horses to turn the corner, away from the square. They were glad to start trotting. She didn't doubt, in theory, her basic ability to get to Boston on her own (even though she had never done it before). But she made it seem that she was turning for home. As soon as she was out of her husband's sight, she turned again, and headed toward the one part of town where no one would expect her to go.

"Charlotte," she said to herself, "you have got to get some help."

∾ Two ∾

No one died in the strange epidemic of poisoning last spring. It could have been much, much worse. Charlotte's illness was unconnected. She only ate food from the household's kitchen, and anyway, when it happened, she was already sick.

Her section of town stayed free of it. But suddenly in Big Pond Hollow, the thing broke out wildly. There were dozens of cases of skin rashes that looked like poison ivy, and fever, fainting, intestinal cramps, and terrible stomach disorders. And a constant *rat-ta-tat-tat* aching of the head, which was the worst symptom of all, and felt (people said down there) as if you were a tree, and your head was where the bark was stripped away, and a woodpecker was drum-ming his beak there, without pausing.

Big Pond Hollow was built up along the town side of the pond, with farms opposite, and the pond was a substantial one: big enough to fish in out of small boats and be harvested for ice in the winter.

The neighborhood was made up of some twenty-five or thirty

bungalows, each with its own garden, outhouse, and shed. The more prosperous families also had horses and barns, but there weren't many of them.

Some of the men who lived here were employed at the farms; some worked for taverns and inns on the Boston Road. Some ran gambling enterprises; some made and sold beer and spirits; and some were involved in the collecting of horse droppings in the bigger towns and in Boston, which were carted and sold to a company to the south that operated an enormous flower-growing business: a big part of it was poppies for opium, people said, but that might not have been true. Some were laborers going out on hire for rail work, and some, like their wives, sisters, and mothers, worked in service, and were said (in the other parts of town) to be lucky, as they had their own roofs and did not have to live with the families they worked for.

Besides the houses, there was a small Congregational church, a saloon which was actually a rough cabin built onto someone's house, and Everett Gerson's commercial bakery, which had offered employment to four bakers (who did not reside in the Hollow) and three times as many others (who did) for clerking and general assistance. The building was a reconstructed storage house, brick-made, of one story, originally used for grains in the days when the town had its own mill; there used to be a fast-running creek, but it had dried, and the mill disappeared in a fire.

Bad luck was no new thing in the Hollow, but this was different.

It seemed that a plague had arrived, until the Board of Town Council carried out an investigation, and discovered that it wasn't the water, it wasn't spoiled meat, it wasn't milk, it wasn't some odd malign chemistry in people's coal stoves or fireplaces. It was baked goods.

The Town Council was supposed to contain, as stated in the charter, four elected officials, equal in rank, who should divide up powers and responsibilities, including general supervision of an appointed police officer and the fire brigade. For as long as Charlotte had been married and living there, the Board consisted of one coun- cilor only.

His name was Bertram Davenport—the Colonel, he was called. He had led a battalion in the war, and was wounded at Gettysburg, and had lost his left arm, almost all of it.

The Colonel was nearly seventy, but he didn't believe that grow- ing old was something that applied to himself. Some people felt that the reason he was the whole council was that no one else would asso- ciate with him, and some felt, why use four matches to light a candle when one will do? He was also the police officer, and chief of the fire brigade. For a time, years ago, all four councilors were either Heaths themselves or Heath-married.

Unlike the usual elected officials, the Colonel had not been to college, had never traveled to Europe, had never looked at paintings or listened of his own free will to music that was not fife-and-bugle- and-drum. Some people said he was barely able to read. Most importantly, in terms of the poisonings, he had never studied chem- istry and, if asked, would have said he found the subject of metals boring. Things like compositions and reactions involving inanimate objects were, he felt, esoteric, for the intellectuals who inherited their livings and never did a real day's work.

Metals containing contamination? This would be something that could not be seen. He did not hold faith in intangibilities. Charlotte knew all these things about him because he came to the house often, and would salute her from the doorway, and say, "I've seen men in worse shape get up on their feet when hope was lost." She would thank him: "You cheer me."

He was not a bully. He was large, in a Theodore Roosevelt sort of way, but there was a quietness about him, and an overlying feeling of sorrow—a deep, irrevocable grief—which would seem unexplainable, or out of proportion, in the town, until you remembered where he'd been as a younger man.

He never mentioned the war. If other men from the Union Army happened to gather and talk of their memories, he took no part, and he did not display medals or citations, as others did. He was a bachelor.

Charlotte's father-in-law appeared in the doorway of her sickroom one morning to speak to her about some bird he had observed. He did this almost every day, as he felt that news of a new dove nest, or a cardinal in the apple trees, were the very things she was lying there to hear. He never went all the way into her room. Hardly anyone did, not counting Mrs. Petty and her children.

It was rare for her father-in-law to mention anything but his interest in birds, but that morning he was a worried man. It was the first she heard of the trouble in Big Pond Hollow. He reported the news tersely, just, she thought, to get it off his chest, and he must have thought she might offer some insight, as one who was an expert in illness. She had no insight, at least, not then. Her father-in-law described his confidence in Colonel Davenport, and his trust that word of the problem would not extend out of town.

Little did she know that in just a few days she would become, secretly, behind the scenes, very much involved in the problem.

The Colonel took on the investigation himself. This was what he found in Big Pond Hollow: the one thing everyone stricken had in common was that they had eaten some tarts, cakes, shortbreads, pies, or sugar biscuits from Everett Gerson's new commercial bakery, which had just opened for business.

In honor of the event, and as an act of advertising, Everett Gerson and his wife, Mabel, with their bakers' assistants, maids, and clerks, set up a long table outdoors, right by the pond, under a clear sunny May sky, like a picnic, and they handed out baked goods for free, perhaps a full ton of them, to dozens and dozens of people: baked goods cooked in brand-new pans which Everett Gerson claimed to have purchased from the agent of a high-quality, high-priced, highly reputable manufacturer.

There would not have been a reason to suspect Mr. Gerson of lying about where he got his pans, or what they consisted of.

Charlotte would not call what she formed with the Gersons a friendship, because that would imply terms of affection. There was no affection between them. She helped them and, in doing so, she knew that whatever trouble she might find herself in, she could call on them. They had a debt to her. A business debt.

So she knew what she was doing when she turned up at their house in her sleigh, although she hadn't planned the way she presented herself. It burst out of her.

"My husband is with another woman!" She regretted that, but there was nothing she could do about it. She knew there were tears on her face because she felt them crystallizing into ice.

Everett Gerson was forty. His wife was closer to Charlotte's age, seven or eight years younger. They'd both grown up in the Hollow. They'd gone for a time to New York, where they picked up experience in another commercial bakery; they'd returned to take their chances on a business of their own.

The savings bank had financed them. Hays was not involved directly, but Charlotte knew that you could not do anything involving money or the law without involving a Heath, and Hays was the one who (secretly, behind the scenes) advised the bank not to hold back on its lending.

The place was expected to turn a profit in three or four years, supplying all kinds of shops and restaurants, and in the process, perhaps, as Hays had put it, "The more disreputable elements of the Hollow will go away." Or as one of his brothers-in-law had said, "They can give up that hauling of horseshit."

If there was ever a married couple who did not look the part of their vocation, it was the Gersons, who, as it happened, resembled each other as closely as a brother and sister, although, where Everett was fair and blond, Mabel was as dark as a Gypsy. They were as pinched and thin as if no food, other than the most basic sustenance, ever crossed their lips. Their expressions were stern; they rarely smiled. They reminded Charlotte of horses who have been beaten and know of nothing but whips and harsh words, but perhaps this was something in their favor when it came to the bank. Everett was taken for a man who could be depended upon to work, work, and work.

Their house was next door to the bakery. Mabel came running out first, from the house, when Charlotte arrived, and she must have had some intuitive means of communication with her husband, because he appeared a moment later, gently taking hold of the horses, with a look of relief in his eyes, Charlotte felt, because he had figured immediately that she'd come to collect on the debt.

She had sworn a vow to the Gersons that the money she gave them, indirectly, would never need to be returned.

The relief came from the fact that their obligation to Charlotte would be lifted. The stress of their enormous business problems— and there were many—was a heavy weight on their shoulders, push⁄ing them down and almost physically diminishing them. They'd got into things that were very much bigger than they were.

It wasn't hard for Charlotte to picture the scene, and the Gersons' emotions, when the Colonel revealed to them (privately) that their product was making everyone sick.

The bakery was closed down immediately. The ovens were banked. The doors were secured. Charlotte knew from the talk at home that the Colonel believed there was something rotten in the grains or eggs or butter, or something being done, grossly incorrectly, in the mixture of ingredients.

And meanwhile, at the bank, they were getting nervous, and were thinking of calling in the loan, taking possession of the bakery, and running it with their own people.

No one except Everett and Mabel—and then Charlotte—knew it was the pans.

It happened that one of the Heaths' washerwomen, from the Hollow, had fallen ill. She did much of the washing at her own house, and a great pile of sheets and towels needed to be returned—after Charlotte's father-in-law consulted with doctors, who assured him they would not get sick from laundry. The person who drove up to the house, with an old chestnut pulling a two-wheeler, and the Heath linens, was Mabel Gerson.

Charlotte felt that Mabel must have been a Catholic. Something about delivering those linens made her think of a penitent.

Having entered the back of the house and finding no one downstairs, which was extraordinary, Mabel somehow made her way to Charlotte's room. She must have taken the woman in bed for a victim of the same thing everyone else had.

Charlotte was quick to set her straight. It was the one time she was pleased to say the words, "I am told I have polio."

Who can know what impulse made that woman go in and sit down? When the story of what went wrong was revealed—not in sobs or melodrama but unemotionally, dryly—Charlotte did not feel she had a choice.

Mabel Gerson told her, "Everett bought the pans very cheaply from an agent who called on us, and if they investigate any further they will know he has lied about the quality. If we start up again, we can't use the pans we have. Everett meant no harm. We've no money, and we are done for."

It was the flat, dull voice of someone who has moved past hope. Charlotte knew the sound of it. She recognized it like a memory of her own.

"I don't know why you're sick, and I don't know why you're not getting worse and not getting better. You seem to have given up hope. Under these conditions, I can't promise recovery. I'm beginning to agree with the consultants: you're in a position to remain as an invalid for the rest of your life. I don't see what else I can tell you."

Those were the words of her principal doctor. Her principal doctor was a Heath by marriage and could have been speaking out of personal interest, or even fondness. Hope. It was easy to see that hope was a made-up thing, a delusion.

"I believe that the pans Everett bought are from a shoddy factory and contain certain cheap elements," Mabel said. "Elements that are chemically poisonous. When we were in New York we heard of the very same thing, and there were people who died because of it. I do not remember the different types of materials, but there is an element named antimony they talked about, which I believe can be deadly if used wrong. This agent promised my husband that there was no danger, I swear it. But no one must know. You must keep our secret, now that I have told you."

Antimony, thought Charlotte. For the first time since she had been ill, she began to stir, inside herself. Something—just like a spark—began to flicker in her.

"Antimony!" she said. She knew nothing of chemistry. The actual mixtures of undesirable elements in a less-than-honorable factory was something she didn't need to spend time considering.

Antimony. A marvelous word, even if it was a poison.

"There are manufacturers of the better-quality utensils who want to expose the bakers, you see," said Mabel, "who buy from the unscrupulous agents. It's only a matter of time, if word gets out of these sicknesses, before they send in one of their own representatives. They'll try to send my husband to prison."

"That's not going to happen," said Charlotte. "Go home and tell your husband to hide his pans. He must send to the best maker and purchase new ones, and make them look as though they are the ones that were always in use, and he should pay something extra to the maker, to put a past date on the bill."

Charlotte didn't hesitate when it came to the Colonel. "The Colonel has to remain in charge of the investigation. He's got to be satisfied that it was something in—oh, the flour."

"The flour?" Mabel Gerson looked stupefied. She didn't realize yet that she was going to walk out of Charlotte's room a changed person.

"You should allow him to believe in something evil in the flour, and your husband should throw it all away and start over. And now that I think of it, he should also dismiss your bakers and hire new ones."

"New bakers? But nothing of this is their fault."

"You can hire them back again later."

She must have thought Charlotte was in that room, flat and unmoving, because she was a lunatic, kept out of an asylum because she was married to a Heath. Mabel sighed wearily. If her own situation were not so bleak, her expression said, she would have let Charlotte see that she felt sorry for her.

Charlotte had no means of putting her hands on money, and it was not only due to her being an invalid.

Hays thought of himself as a liberal, progressive man. Yes, he was an ardent backer of an old-fashioned president, but so were all Heaths and all businessmen who believed, as a type of creed, that *democracy* meant that anyone with the correct sort of ambition, who was also a white man, had the democratic right to accumulate wealth and, having done so, had the right to tell everyone else what rights they could and could not have, which seemed to Charlotte to be more like a kingdom with kings and princes and dukes and earls.

This, she felt, was the reason why the Heaths were devoted so fervently to those history plays.

Her husband did not go nearly apoplectic with outrage like his father did when it came to the subject of what he called the Suffrage Women, not that there were any of them in their town; it was a sub-ject that came up now and then, when things were quiet and the old man found the need to be roused.

Women *voting*? You might as well ask your horses to saddle them-selves and hitch themselves to your carriage. You might as well ask a bird to read you your Bible.

Hays would simply say, "Women are not horses or birds, but they have different brains from a man, after all."

He'd talk gravely about the foundations of America, as if describing well-built cellars or walls—of houses that were just like his—but Charlotte had the feeling that something very worried was always behind his words, so different from her father-in-law's. It seemed that Hays was worried because, if women voted, there'd be only one possible result: disaster, as though women would cast their ballots for an earthquake, which would happen, and those founda-tions would rattle and collapse; poor America would fall to pieces.

"But I'm a progressive man," he would say. "Practical but pro-gressive." He had irritated his father by arranging for Charlotte to have her own account at the bank, just for herself (and her horses) in her own name.

Charlotte knew that there were women who negotiated with their husbands the right to maintain control of funds and property they had brought to the marriage from their own families, but she had not brought anything to her marriage except herself. Hays regularly diverted money into her balance, so that, officially, she could draw whatever she wanted, at will, and not be expected to explain it.

However, every time she drew a check or presented herself at the bank for an advance, Hays knew about it. There was no stopping the manager from forwarding to him a report of every transaction, the way a schoolmaster reports to a child's father how the child has performed in a lesson. Hays would tell her he never read these reports. She believed him, as hard as it was to imagine him ignoring information about money.

She had a pair of silver bracelets given to her five or six years ago by her father-in-law, as a birthday gift. One was inlaid with a diamond about the size of a kernel of corn, and the other contained four smaller ones, like glittering orange pips. Her father-in-law told her he had not been able to decide at the jeweler's which one he liked better, so after an hour in the showroom, getting nowhere, he bought them both. This was on a trip to Chicago.

She had noted about the bracelets that her own potential preference did not seem part of the choice, or even to matter, not that she held this against him.

She knew it wasn't true about the showroom. He had traveled that time with a young man employed by the lawyer Heaths as a clerk's assistant and errand runner; he was lent to Hays's father as a valet.

This young man was conducting a love affair, extremely privately, with the upstairs maid of one of Hays's sisters. Mrs. Petty knew all about it, and so did Charlotte. The valet bought the bracelets while the elderly Mr. Heath dozed outside in the hired carriage. They were chosen by price. The two together cost almost exactly what the valet had been told to spend.

Charlotte never wore them. Her jewelry was in a mahogany box on the bureau of her sickroom, which Hays had moved there, along with other things from her real room, to make her feel comforted. They did not make her feel comforted.

She felt she could say later on—because she never knew when her father-in-law might ask about something he'd bought her— that she hadn't seen the bracelets since the summer before she was sick. She happened to have worn them, on a whim, while strolling along the cliffs of Squab Cove when they had suddenly slipped off. They went falling down the rocks into the churning, frothy sea, and she'd decided it would not be wise to go after them. Even before she was sick, her wrists were quite thin.

Everett Gerson did not discharge his bakers, but he managed to send for new utensils. "It was the fault of the sugar, and a new distributor must be got," the Colonel decided mysteriously, and he ordered Everett to pay a fine but suspended it.

The new sugar dealer was arranged by Charlotte's father-in-law, so the Gersons now had a favorable connection to the Heaths, an unplanned bonus. As Hays always said, in business, when you tweak one branch of a tree, you never know how many others will start shaking, potentially dropping their fruit.

Case closed, with all the credit going to the Colonel, who was given a raise in pay at the next Town Meeting. Everyone admired him for excluding the possibility of bringing in outside people. What was the purpose of a town if it couldn't handle its own scandals? But the Town Council might have thought differently if the poisoned people were not Hollow people.

Charlotte thought it was loyal and brave of the people of the Hollow to line up all over again for the bakery's reopening. She had a good idea that, if someone were to dive to the bottom of Big Pond, they would find the at-fault pans, sunk with heavy stones and covered with rust and algae.

"Mrs. Heath! Mrs. Heath! You are up! You're well! We thought of you every day! We prayed for your recovery!"

Mabel Gerson hitched up her skirt and climbed into the sleigh as if she feared Charlotte would tumble out of it. "And here you are!"

She grasped Charlotte's hands and stared at her face. Maybe this was the way people had looked at Lazarus.

"My husband is with another woman. I've only just found out. My marriage is over. I'm on my way to my friend in Boston and you must help me."

"Of course. Come inside at once."

That was how it happened that Charlotte arrived at the Beech‑
mont Hotel on Beacon Hill in a delivery sleigh belonging to Ger‑
son's Fine Pastries and Biscuits, with fifty dollars in cash (which
she'd decided to call a loan) in her purse, and her horses secured
safely in a Hollow stable, under the care of the Gersons' chief clerk's
young brother, a groom she knew was trustworthy because, before
she was sick, she had often gone looking for him in the Hollow, to go
riding in the woods. He liked to race and did not mind being beaten
by a woman. She also had a box of cakes, tarts, and sugar rolls, a
pair of Everett Gerson's wool mittens, and a small valise of clothing
and toiletries lent to her by Mabel Gerson.

And she remembered all over again how she had liked the way it
felt when she had put those bracelets in Mabel's hands.

∞ Three ∞

Copley Square. Boylston Street. Churches, steeples, shop windows. Tremont Street. Park Street along the side of the Common, with trees like stern, dark giants. Beacon Street. The State House, wide and ceremonious and domineering, its dome obscured in snow and darkness and fog.

Charlotte felt she was looking at things in a dream, although she'd never felt so awake. She felt she was seeing Boston for the first time. Two sleighs slid by, with bells wildly ringing, full of boisterous young men in light jackets, hatless, defying the winter air: they called out drunkenly, in a holiday mood, *Race with us!* Their laughter was like music; they were just like a welcoming committee.

The hotel, Mrs. Petty had said, was a wide brick building, four stories high, at the corner of Beech and Eustis, with a maze of stables and alleys beyond it. It did not have a river view. It was not particularly elegant, but it was carefully furnished, it was handsome, it was dependable.

The proprietors were a husband and wife named Alcorn: Harry and Lucy Alcorn, around fifty years of age, both of them Boston-born and bred. Some of the servants were men and boys, but the guests were exclusively women.

A wooden sign on the high iron gate said discreetly, THE BEECH-MONT: A PRIVATE HOTEL FOR GENTLE LADIES.

Mr. Alcorn had an office in the back of the hotel and was always present, with a finger in everything that happened, but his wife was reclusive. They kept an apartment in the next-door building, and Mrs. Alcorn never came into the hotel.

The hotel had been the home of a family of southern cotton growers who came north before the States War but had not lasted long in Boston. They'd found it too dank and depressing. Had they tried to switch sides? Had they foreseen the only way the war would go? It could not have been pleasant for plantation people among Bostonians, especially on Beacon Hill.

The Alcorns were said to have purchased the building for next to nothing. There was a bright, lively tearoom at the front of the hotel, which was open to the public on Monday and Thursday afternoons and was popular with local businessmen, lawyers, and men in town for lectures, or men who were weary of their private clubs, but when Charlotte had asked her husband about it, one afternoon in her sick-room, he said, "A private hotel? The Beechmont? I never heard of it. I believe there's no such place."

"Mrs. Petty has a job as the cook there."

"You must mean the Belmont. There's a Belmont Inn, at Bel-mont Hill."

"No, Boston. She went to Boston. Beech Street, on Beacon Hill."

"There are so many backstreets up there. Do you remember going with me to a dinner on Beacon Street, when everyone was so worried that William would lose his reelection?" William was President McKinley. How could anyone have worried he'd lose, a Midwestern man, when every businessman in the country was behind him? Hays had gone to his first inauguration with his father and two of his brothers, no wives. The second inauguration needed to be missed because nothing would happen, Hays felt, that was new. But there'd been all sorts of fund-raising things. Was the woman with him at those?

"I didn't go with you to that political dinner."

"But I'm sure you got it wrong about your hotel name. I never noticed it listed anywhere."

He'd said nothing more about it. There was something in his denial that had not rung true, and something in his expression that crinkled up, as it did when he considered something unseemly, but why? He wasn't a snob. She had no reason to doubt his estimation of things.

She hadn't pressed. She wasn't supposed to have kept up a correspondence with Mrs. Petty.

Mr. Harry Alcorn held to high standards. He would never fit in anywhere that was not a city and just barely felt at home in Boston. You were not supposed to be an eccentric in Boston, unless you had the money to back yourself up, which apparently he had. He was eccentric in his clothing and food preferences, and would only wear whites and tans, no matter the season. He ate no meat, suffered from problems with his teeth, and would only take food that was yellow or white, or had come from the vegetable gardens kept by his kitchen people in a stone-walled back terrace. He was said to be devoted to his always-behind-the-scenes wife. A wedding photo of them was somewhere on a wall: both in white, young and pale and ethereal, but this was especially true of Mrs. Alcorn, all gauzy in her bridal dress, and very fragile-looking, like someone who could easily break.

That was the extent of Charlotte's knowledge of the Beechmont. Mrs. Petty's letters, smuggled to Charlotte by one of the kitchen maids, were lavish in detail and description. She was a colorful letter writer. Charlotte knew to believe every word. Like all good cooks, Mrs. Petty had a firm, insoluble grounding in Fact.

But the letters didn't come half as often as Charlotte wanted them to. In the latest, a week ago, Mrs. Petty spoke of the children. The baby was nearly ready to start walking but was lazy about it. Sophy was attending a primary class in the Park Street Church, and so was Momo, who was too young for it, but he would not be separated from his sister; they allowed him to sit among the girls like a toy of theirs. And just lately, Mrs. Petty took on a second position, on Tuesdays and Wednesdays, trying out recipes at the Boston Cooking School, under the direction of Miss Fannie Farmer.

Dear God, it was cold. The gas lamps were lit along the hill, casting their lights in a yellow haze through gently falling snow. Everett Gerson was patient, and he didn't complain, but Beacon Hill was like a maze.

It was tricky to negotiate the side streets, but at last, here was Eustis, here was Beech, here was the brick hotel, the Beechmont itself, on the corner behind a handsome iron fence.

A PRIVATE HOTEL FOR GENTLE LADIES. It was just as Mrs. Petty had described, but the words of the sign were elegant, put into the fence in fancy metalwork, with bits of snow clinging to some of the letters, like decorations in a picture book.

Everett Gerson had the long ride home in front of him, but he wanted to tie up his horse and go inside with her. It didn't seem right to just leave her there.

No, she was fine; this was where her friend was; honestly, he had done quite enough. Which way should she enter? The horse through long experience wanted to go and find the back, like this was any other delivery, and perhaps a kitchen maid would come out with some sugar or an apple.

The front. She was a guest. She was a gentle lady. "Good night to you, Mr. Gerson. Tell your wife I feel more well than ever."

Her spirits were singing inside her. Everything was going to be different. She found it amazing to remember she'd ever been sick at all.

The walkway was clear, right down to the smooth granite squares laid carefully in tidy rows; someone must have swept it very recently. A large iron knocker in the shape of an acorn was in the center of the door, and when she rapped it, the door opened at once, so that she nearly fell inside.

She hardly had time to notice right away who was standing in front of her in the vestibule. She had a sense of dark wood, smelling of polish, and shadows and flickering candlelight, and the warm rich colors of the inside walls, and a scent of flowers. There was a vase of hothouse roses on a table.

"You have the wrong place," said a raspy male voice.

"No, I think not."

"Your name."

The voice didn't sound friendly, but still, she felt no sense of fore-boding.

She realized she hadn't been able to tell if the figure was a man or a woman. It was the shape of a person in shadows dressed in a dark hooded cloak and holding a broom, which dripped with melting snow. Then she saw a ruddy face, stubbled at the chin and cheeks with a coarse gray sprinkling of beard, and a very large, bulbous, reddish nose, which looked as if it had been broken more than once.

Somewhere inside someone was playing a piano, stopping and starting again unevenly, playing scales, picking out odd combina-tions of notes, lightly, without skimming off into a tune. She said her name. She said she was the friend of the cook, Mrs. Petty, from the household where Mrs. Petty had been employed; would Mrs. Petty please be told?

A sound of grunting emerged from the man, and dragging his broom behind him he disappeared down the hall.

She stepped farther inside. A door was at the right, and she knew instinctively it led downstairs to the kitchen, like the one at home, where her sickroom was. She liked the symmetry of that: every door toward every downstairs kitchen for the rest of her life, she felt, would remind her she was free.

Do-re-mi, do-re-mi, do-re-mi went the piano: a sound of muffled laughter, a sound of wind at the windowpanes, a sound of creaking furniture overhead, a sound of crumbling logs in the little hall fire-place. Do-re-mi-fa-*so*.

She could picture herself ten years ago at the piano in the long gallerylike room the Heaths called their conservatory. "We would love for you to be musical."

Her sisters-in-law played somber German compositions, hymns, songs about babbling streams and flowers, and lovers dying in moonlight in each other's arms, all boring. Her mother-in-law would stand behind her at a lesson. "Charlotte, you make it seem a piano is an instrument of torture; you behave as though all your fin-gers are thumbs"—she didn't know how accurate she was—while the stuffy fat teacher, beloved of the family, who affected an English accent but came from Vermont and had a mustache like walrus tusks, frowned harder and harder at her and tapped his hand on the piano in time to the horrible metronome, and she'd be filled with the desire to go out to the shed for the ax and chop up the whole thing, and all the furniture too, those pink-and-white chairs from France, those spindly tables, those portraits of dead Heaths in wood frames so thick, they would kill you if they fell on your head. Why had she married Hays Heath?

Because saying no to him would have been like saying no to your own heart, that was why, if your heart could ask if you wanted it to keep ticking.

Do-re-mi, do-re-mi-fa-so-*la*, then the sound of a trill, then a still-ness. She felt that if she listened closely enough she might hear

Sophy or Momo, calling to each other, or the baby crying, even though it was well past time for them to be in bed. A shiver of pleasure went through her: she thought of what their expressions would be like when they saw her. They would have grown, children grew fast; it had been almost six months since they'd left the household.

There had not been an emotional farewell. There had been no leave-taking at all. One morning, late last fall, Charlotte woke from a troubled sleep to something that felt like a blanket thrown over her face: a blanket of stillness.

The kitchen below her was as silent as stone. It was as if she'd gone deaf, as if deafness were one more manifestation of being sick. "I shall send up your breakfast myself, as the cook has been discharged," said her mother-in-law, in the doorway. A bowl of ginger pudding arrived, left over from supper and warmed, with cream. She only ate it because Mrs. Petty had cooked it. She considered going on a fast; she considered stopping eating entirely. She imagined herself shrinking under her bedsheets, like the potion-drinking Alice, getting smaller and smaller and smaller, except that, for her, there would be no marvelous adventure.

Then a note was presented to her, privately, a note left with one of the maids, in Sophy's scrawny printing. "You must not be sad you must be good and you shall have some letters she sed so and goodbye I do not like your family just you and Mr Haze we go to the cittie." At the bottom Mrs. Petty had written, "I shall write very soon."

That was when she made up her mind to get well. She must have been preparing for this reunion all along, without knowing it. The image of her husband at the edge of the square was burned into the backs of her eyes, so that she'd seen almost nothing else all the way to Boston—his look of surprise, his hat dropping to the ground, the woman beside him in her belted coat, her arm on his—all that was gone, as if it had happened a long time ago, as if it were truly meant to be.

The door was flung open. She jumped. Her arms were already extending themselves for the embrace she was certain was coming. She felt her throat clutching up and willed herself not to burst out with emotions, like she'd done with the Gersons.

Then suddenly: "You can't stay here."

This was Mrs. Petty, of course it was: this tall, sturdy, big-bosomed woman, bursting toward Charlotte, panting lightly and patting her chest where her heart was. She had run up the steep flight from the kitchen in shock, it seemed, like someone running away from a fire. She wore her same old tie-in-the-back heavy cloth apron. The ties had come loose and the sides of the apron hung limply at her sides.

"Mrs. Heath, you must leave this place at once."

There was a flagstone path outside the conservatory at home, and one chilly morning, before she was sick, Charlotte was out there; one of her horses had got loose and left a lot of droppings. Not good. She'd put the horse back in the stable and was just returning to the path to clean it up when, rounding the corner of the house, she happened upon a maid who'd got there before her. The maid had a bucket of cold water which she heaved up, in a big expansive gesture, and splashed toward the stones, except that Charlotte was now in the way. The force of the blow was like a punch in the face out of nowhere.

Reeling and dripping, she'd steadied herself on the arm the horrified maid held out to her, and she'd been frightened down to her bones because she saw how simple it was to be knocked over—to have your balance shot out—by something as ordinary as cold water. She had felt as insubstantial in her body as a leaf.

That was how it felt right now with Mrs. Petty. The valise and the baked goods in Charlotte's hands slipped down to the floor; she reached to hold on to the wall. She felt something inside freezing up, as if she'd never move again—was it returning? The paralysis? The empty cave that her own mind turned into?

Mrs. Petty loomed up, larger, with a look of worry, but also of firm resolution. And someone came up behind her, from the hall. A man. All beige and white, in a dressing gown of soft tan cashmere, open at the chest, revealing a crisp white formal shirt; his hair was the color of sand. His trousers were white flannel. He had a staunch muscular compactness, like Napoleon, but there was something about him that was gentle, even delicate. He was fine-featured, with narrow eyes, a narrow nose, and high cheekbones. His face looked recently shaved, and was smooth and pale. He was shorter than Mrs. Petty, so he had to look up to her, but you knew who was the one in charge.

"I was wondering," he said to Mrs. Petty, as though Charlotte weren't there, "what is the progress of the supper for numbers Eight and Eleven?"

Mrs. Petty looked at him. "The progress is zero. The kitchen is closed."

"I see. I was wondering, then, where the tin washing pot is, that very enormous one, the biggest one we have?"

"In the washroom."

"I believe we should lock the door and hide the key. If we don't, Mrs. Lattimer in number Eight and Mrs. Upton in number Eleven plan to fetch it, take it outdoors, fill it with snow to be melted, light a bonfire under it and, having obtained some herbs, they will put me into it, and cook me and eat me. That's how hungry they are. I suppose the police will show up, but I don't think they'll mind to see me boiled. Perhaps you recall that the husbands of those women went to one of those mystical tribal islands below the equator where cannibalism thrives, and they are keen to try it out."

"Tell them I can give them the loan of a long-handled fork to poke you with," said Mrs. Petty.

"I'd prefer to lock the washroom door." And with a crisp, dignified turn of his head, he settled his gaze on Charlotte. "I am Harry

Alcorn," he said, "and this is my hotel." She knew he was sizing her up—all over and in and out, she felt—and she recognized the intelligence of his expression, the interest: this was the way she herself looked at horses. She didn't mind. She allowed her eyes to stare right back at him, while Mrs. Petty grew more and more agitated.

"Charlotte, where is your husband?"

"Not with me."

"Were you hoping for a room?"

"I am, Mrs. Petty, though I hardly know you, like this."

"Rooms're full up," she answered flatly. "There, Harry, say goodbye, she's leaving."

"I want to see the children."

"That would be out of the question," said Harry Alcorn. He smiled warmly. "I didn't mind having them about, but one of our guests took a liking to them, and she is rich and offered to take them, so our Mrs. Petty has gone and sold them. I tried to tell her not to, as I suspect it will come to no good, but she is a woman with her own mind."

"This is *enough*!" sputtered Mrs. Petty. "I've done no such thing. Mrs. Heath can go down to Charles Street if she needs to be put in a room, a very nice one, and Moaxley can take her, or I shall myself."

"You have already met Moaxley," said Harry Alcorn. "Our good-looking, agreeable man at the door, who no doubt welcomed you charmingly, in his attractive cloak. Are your hands quite large, Mrs. Heath, or do you wear a man's mittens?"

"My hands are quite large."

"A good quality."

"Thank you."

"I was told you were ill. You seem well now."

"She is not!" cried Mrs. Petty. "She's mad to be out! In the dead of night! Alone! I can't think what she is up to!"

"Your ride must have been horrid."

"I enjoyed it."

"I was told you were driven in a baker's sledge."

"The baker," said Charlotte, "is my friend."

"She *cannot* stay!"

"Then so shall I be." Harry Alcorn held out both hands to Charlotte. She had the thought to slip off her mittens, but suddenly, just when she was beginning to be proud of herself—her self-possession, the way she was holding her own ground—it seemed that it would be much too complicated to even try. How exactly did one go about taking off mittens?

She dizzied. Was she wobbling, was she looking unbalanced? Did it seem she'd been gulping down brandy from Everett Gerson's flask, against the cold, which she hadn't done, though he had offered it? It mattered to her if this man, Harry Alcorn, considered her a drunkard. It mattered what he thought about when he looked at her.

How could the wall she leaned against be so insubstantial? She had the sense that the wood was dissolving, that she'd been tricked into thinking it solid. She would have liked to push herself away and hold out her hands to the man coming toward her, but she could not think how. He seemed to be moving extremely slowly, loosely, as if walking underwater.

"I don't know what's happening to your wall," she said, and she was surprised that the words came out thickly, and strangely muffled, as if she'd covered her mouth with her hands.

There was definitely something wrong with the carpentry of this place, and it wasn't only the wall; it was the floor as well. It made no sound, but it was giving way under her, like a shiny coating of pond ice, which looked thick, until you stepped on it.

∞ Four ∞

All her life, even though she'd developed the skill of keeping most of her thoughts to herself, people told her she had too much imagination, as if that were an awful thing, like an abnormally thickened, embarrassing muscle, which would bulge below the skin indecently, when muscles were supposed to be hidden, and never thought about.

As a schoolgirl, at Miss Georgeson's Christian Girls' Academy, long ago in her other life, she stood out from her classmates for her wit, and for her quick, daring physical boldness. She was the one to run fastest in little races at recess, the one to roll her hoops on hilly surfaces when everyone else preferred flat, the one who took to riding horses with such a fearless, alarming joy, her teachers felt she must be partly Indian, in spite of the color of her hair and skin; and she was a charity student, after all.

They only had to say, "Charlotte, if you cannot spell your words as God meant them to be, you won't be allowed to the stables for a month," and she'd take up her primer with zeal. She'd been in trouble again and again for not doing copying correctly (but putting in her own phrases), not mastering embroidery in the assigned patterns (but making up patterns of her own, with the brightest threads, which came out all knotted and tangled), and failing to memorize passages for elocution lessons, which came from the Bible or from the pen of the headmistress, Miss Georgeson, who wrote complicated, fervent poems, all odes, about the journey of the life of one's soul, with its terrors and dangers, derived from her favorite English book, *The Pilgrim's Progess from This World to That Which Is to Come.*

"You must not let your imagination get the best of you. You must learn to tame its desires; you must learn to ignore its appetite," Miss Georgeson would say, and Charlotte would look at her wonderingly, not understanding why, in all her speeches like this, those two words—*desires, appetite*—would stand out so prominently, with such emphasis, like sudden blasts of a trumpet, when all you'd been hearing was a monotonous background hum of little flutes, say, played delicately.

It was best to consider one's imagination as one's own private thing.

All those months in bed she had counted on it, lying there imagining the workings of the household around her, or what the horses were up to in the stable, or what her husband was up to in Ohio or Pennsylvania or wherever he was, or what the world might have been like, outside her room, colorful and dramatic, spinning on its axis without her, full of queens, barges, violence, betrayal, heartache, love, passion, resolutions. "At least I still have an imagination," she'd say to herself. She felt proud of it.

But maybe something had happened to it when she was sick.

She didn't wonder where she was, not yet. She felt that, compared to what she was seeing, the facts of her situation were unimportant.

She knew she was lying down somewhere warm, and she was quite still, and blankets were on her.

What she knew most of all was that she was experiencing a delu/ sion. Maybe it was fever-raised, she thought, without actually feeling feverish.

Something had to be wrong with her imagination, because look what it was delivering her.

It was unfair, *unfair,* that of all the possible, infinite forms of hallu/ cinations she could have had, this one took the shape of Aunt Lily Heath, her principal doctor, in a nightgown, standing there like a ghostly phantom, looking down at her.

Charlotte did not believe in ghosts and phantoms as things to come lurking about, unhumanly, from some other realm, although once at the household with the three Irish maids—who had rhyming names, Katie, Braidie, and Sadie—she had put on a séance in the root cellar to conjure the soul of her father-in-law's longtime valet, an elderly man named Willis, who had died of pneumonia. They wanted to talk to him because of a box found (by Braidie) under his bed, containing, among trinkets and coins, a bit of paper in his handwriting, saying, "I am the father of the prettiest nut-haired girl at service in this place, begotten and born in Galway, as God is my witness. I spoke not before this, as her mother was the wife of another."

All three maids had hair of some shade of a nut; all three had come from that part of Ireland. It wasn't as if they could write to their mothers back home and ask what adultery had been commit/ ted. As for the "prettiest" aspect, they left that part alone, at Char/ lotte's command. She had the right to invoke her authority as their mistress: they were all three of them, each in her own way, of equal attractiveness. If they quibbled about it they'd be done for.

So which maid? They'd done everything you were supposed to do to call on the dead. They brought down articles of old Willis's clothing and his pipe and boots. They lit candles, and the maids spoke some Gaelic, and they concentrated hard, and Charlotte felt the back of her neck go clammy and bristly, as if cold fingers were touching her, and one of the maids, in a terror, raised the possibility that, what if the spirit they drew wasn't Willis, but someone else, someone of an evil nature? It did not seem likely that a soul which was burning in hell would escape to the root cellar, but one never knew, so they'd given it up. The maids burned Willis's confession in the kitchen stove and resolved to consider themselves sisters, as if he'd fathered them all. They'd been deeply fond of him.

Maybe, Charlotte thought, hallucinations were like potential visitations of the dead. You simply could not control them. And they could talk.

"Hello, Charlotte," said the phantom of Aunt Lily. "How astonishing to see you."

"Don't try to fool me. You're a specter of my imagination."

"Don't be worried."

"I'm not." She didn't feel worried at all. She felt curious. "Where am I?"

"Not at home, that's for sure. I'd thought you never wanted to leave that bed of yours. I'd thought, you know, you chose to be there for all the rest of your life."

If the phantom weren't dressed like this, it would seem to Charlotte that indeed she was back in her sickroom, and the doctor was with her as usual. The nightdress was lovely: a long white one, muslin, with a ribbon at the collar and some lovely, fine lace around the neckline and wrists, and a scent of lilac that seemed to come from the fabric, but might have been perfume.

This was the best she could get for a hallucination? A talking mirage of Aunt Lily, speaking in that same old doctorly voice— that commanding, I-know-more-than-you-do voice, with its rigid authority, its self-possession, its you-truly-ought-to-listen-to-me conviction?

Stupid brain!

Even the apparition of her old headmistress would have been better, in her old-fashioned bonnet and dark, heavy Sunday dress, with its bustle. Miss Georgeson had believed in wearing a bustle, even after everyone else gave them up.

It protruded from her tailbone like an oddly placed, cushion-soft hump. Charlotte knew how soft it was below the ample folds of the dress because once on a dare, at the age of nine, while Miss Georgeson was occupied with putting books on a shelf, she sneaked up behind her and squeezed it, and got away with it. The older girls had said a bustle was actually human woman-bone, like that was something that happened to you when you passed from wearing girlish dresses that went to your shins, to ladies' dresses that went to your ankles. You had to sit in chairs with cut-out seats to accommodate the growth of your maturity, they said. But it was only a rectangular small pillow, tied on there, for absolutely no purpose at all. Charlotte had never been afraid of Miss Georgeson. Aunt Lily Heath, phantom or otherwise, was another matter.

A voice said quietly, a male voice, "Is she very impossibly ill?"

"She's fine. Weak, but fine. She was, as I began to tell you before, never well understood by the family."

"I can see why."

"I think we shouldn't send for her husband."

"I think, Doctor Heath, that not sending for one's husband is a matter of regulations here."

"I should have sent you away. I hadn't thought she'd wake up until morning. But if you think I'd leave you alone with her, you're mistaken."

Charlotte now saw, in the low dusky light of a gas lamp—a lamp had materialized—a pale young man of maybe nineteen or twenty

whose face was so flawless, and so perfectly smooth, and so *radiant,* it
nearly took away her breath to look at him. He was simply the most
beautiful human she'd ever seen, even in pictures. His butter-yellow
hair was combed damply back off his face, and it seemed that he
shimmered all over with such a marvelous, otherworldly glow, she
was forced to decide that her brain was not a letdown to her after all.
She could not have counted the number of times when she was sick
that she had wished to see such a sight.

He looked like an angel, but an angel in a gray nightshirt, which
had a panel of masculine-pearly buttons from the neck to the waist.

Excellent fabrication! He was high-browed, high-cheekboned,
lofty. His eyelashes were thick like a girl's. He had long fine hands,
delicately fashioned. His lower arms were bare and almost hairless,
but there was nothing of weakness about him: there was something
of such concealed inner strength, she thought, he could probably lift
her up bodily, with the slightest of exertions, and the bed she was
lying on, too.

The nightshirt went just below his knees; his bare legs were
slightly curved outward, like a rider's. She liked that. He did not
seem to mind the way she stared at him. His smile was like looking at
the sun when it moves out, unexpectedly, from a grim, dark cloud.

He said, "I'm cold, suddenly. I think the fire's going out."

There was a fire, burning low in a small fireplace on the other side
of the room, which seemed to appear the very moment it was mentioned. A log snapped, with sparks and a hissing.

These were not made-up things, and neither were the pictures on
the walls, all watercolors, in handsome wood frames: a red sailboat
in a harbor, an old wagon at the edge of a wheat field, a silver jug on
a table with a plate of green grapes. Shadows moved this way and
that along walls which were papered very neatly in pale green and
yellow stripes. A red-and-brown rug was on the floor.

A chair was in the corner. On the chair was a pile of clothes, not folded like laundry, but draped over the seat, dropped there. There was a bureau, a high one, oak. In the other corner was a washstand. All real. The room was small and narrow.

The young man picked up an iron and poked at the fire. "I thought you were an angel," said Charlotte, and he looked over his shoulder, grinning.

"Not even an hour ago someone said very near the same thing to me, having heard me play the piano. Irony was involved. I believe I was being insulted."

"I heard you play! I thought you were wonderful!"

A coat was on a hook by the door. A dark macintosh, wool. A silk scarf dangled from one of the pockets. Charlotte knew that coat. She knew that scarf, with its embroidered initials, L I H.

Lillian Iverson Heath.

Charlotte shifted herself and sat up, leaning on her elbows. She looked up at the doctor, way up, as she was singularly tall: five feet ten, which she carried very well and often joked about, saying that the only way she'd got into medical school with all those men was that a sympathetic bone doctor had taken apart her legs (under ether) and added an extra six inches, like a type of experimental grafting, so there'd be few of her peers or professors to look down on her, at least physically. She favored men's coats for the length, and men's shoes, because her feet were big too. But there was nothing mannish about her.

Charlotte sighed. "Hello, Aunt Lily. You're real."

"I cannot begin to describe how much I wish *you* weren't."

"They called you, I suppose. It must seem I'm not well, but I am. I truly am. Look. Moving."

Charlotte wiggled her legs under the blankets as vigorously as she could; they were moving just fine, she was fine, and there was none of the old aching in her head, just a heaviness. She sank back on the pillow. She had wanted to sit up brightly, she had wanted to muster her defenses, especially as Aunt Lily, now that it was clear that Charlotte was in no mortal danger, was not in a happy mood, not at all.

But Charlotte was only overwhelmingly tired. "I feel I must have had one of those sleeping drafts you used to give me," she managed to say. "Isn't that strange?"

Quietly, at some sort of signal from the doctor, the young man lifted a jacket off the chair, slung it over his shoulders, and slipped out of the room without a word. A murmur of voices rose in the hall. There must have been a small crowd out there, like people at a fire or a wagon wreck. Was one of them Mrs. Petty?

She would never ever say another word to Mrs. Petty. And she felt sorry for herself all over again. She had no friends. Even before she was sick, all the other wives had babies; they were locked in a baby world, speaking only to one another, waving at her when she went by in her carriage, feeling pity for her and not bothering to hide it.

Who were her other friends? Maids, servants, grooms, stable boys. People who were paid. A terrible loneliness began to clutch at her chest, her throat. Now that Mrs. Petty had deserted her, she had only her doctor, who had no choice but to attend to her.

"Why are you wearing nightclothes, Aunt Lily? Why are your clothes on that chair?"

"Because this is my room."

Charlotte tried to look as if that made sense, when Aunt Lily had a town house in Back Bay, where her private consulting office was, and the big house where she lived with Uncle Chester, a lawyer Heath, in Brookline.

Uncle Chester resembled his brother Owen, but not below the surface. Unlike Uncle Owen and the other Heaths, he practiced criminal law and was a Democrat and was said to be famous, having written a textbook on the legal rights of people in America who were not American-born and had found themselves in trouble with American police. *Inalienable Rights of Aliens,* it was called, or something like it. Hays had it on a shelf in his study at home. It was six hundred pages long. He had read it. He was the only Heath who had.

Aunt Lily's expertise was in trauma and diseases of the head, brain, and spine, which seemed like things you would automatically die of, with or without her. Until now, Charlotte never would have thought she'd have a problem with separating the morbid stresses of her profession from her personal life. But Aunt Lily looked as pinched-up and knotted as if she'd caught something from one of her patients, some nerve disease.

"This is your *room*?" said Charlotte.

"It was, and it's now become yours. For tonight. I'll have to find somewhere else to put myself. And no more talking. You should sleep now."

There was something that needed to be remembered—she racked her brain—some family thing, Uncle Chester, Uncle Owen. It was hard to try to think. Uncle Owen had died. The wake in the house she'd not gone into, a funeral coming; had Aunt Lily been at the wake? Oh! The woman!

"Uncle Owen died, Aunt Lily."

"I know."

"There was a wake."

"I had patients."

"There's going to be a funeral."

"I'm aware of that."

It was like trying to talk to a stranger. What about Aunt Lily's husband? Uncle Chester was supposed to be made a judge, she remembered. Her father-in-law said it never would happen because Chester was an intelligence-deficient, backbone-deprived, sentimental, radical oddball.

"Did Uncle Chessy get to be a judge?"

"He did, and that's enough with family chatting."

"He's my favorite Heath," said Charlotte.

Everything was beginning to go fuzzy, which was lucky, because she felt she would not be able to bear much more of Aunt Lily's displeasure—no, worse than displeasure: controlled, contained, silent indignation, judgelike, as if Charlotte had committed a crime. What had she done?

All she'd done was come into the city to Mrs. Petty. Had she asked to be put in this room? Had she sent for her doctor? She was innocent! And anyway, wasn't a physician supposed to act kindly, especially with a niece, who was also, she had thought, a friend to her, after all those months of Aunt Lily coming three or four times a week to the household, sitting with her, bringing things—books, magazines, lotions, oranges, warmth, a press of her fingers in Charlotte's, a cool hand across her forehead—and talking to her, not like this, not stern, forbidding, with daggers of disfavor, directed, it seemed, straight at Charlotte's heart?

It wasn't fair, and her husband didn't love her, and she'd been out in the freezing cold in a bakery sleigh that took hours and hours, and she had been terrified and had to conceal it, which made it worse, and Mrs. Petty!

Mrs. Petty had been horrible, and now Aunt Lily didn't care about Charlotte at all. Cold poured out of her with the daggers. Awful doctor! They should take away her license, they should take away her practice, they should take away her privileges at the hospital. So what if she was in charge of a department, so what if people thought she was highly skilled? She wasn't, even though she looked nice with her hair down like that, her dark curly hair, masses of it, with strands of gray, not a lot, tinsel-like. Charlotte realized she'd never seen Aunt Lily with her hair down.

"I think you're going to be all right," said the doctor softly.

Maybe she wasn't so much of a monster.

"Go to sleep, Charlotte, and I'll think of a way to send a letter home that you're with me, but I shall not say where. They can think I took you in at the apartment."

What was she talking about?

"You look nice with your hair down," said Charlotte. "But I don't know why you're so mad at me, and I don't know what you're talking about, and I don't understand why you told me this is your room."

"Don't worry."

"You already told me that."

"But that was when you thought I wasn't real."

No more daggers. Charlotte was fading out; she couldn't stop it. Everything was slowly fading. The lamp appeared to have been turned down, although no one had touched it. The fire was nearly out, but she held on stubbornly for one instant longer, because she remembered something she needed to say to Aunt Lily.

"I got well, and you said I never would. You said I had to resign myself and be accepting and be *diseased*."

"The one who said so was you, Charlotte," came the answer, from somewhere high up, near the ceiling, as if Aunt Lily had grown even taller—which she probably had, Charlotte thought—as if all the confusions of this situation, gathered together, had stretched her. Now she'd have to go around for the rest of her life banging her head on doorframes, which was, objectively, sad.

Poor Aunt Lily. It seemed to take half an hour for her to bend all the way down to Charlotte to touch her forehead, lightly, the way she used to, as if her fingers, by themselves, delivered sleep.

∞ Five ∞

A fire was burning, a fresh one; the logs were piled high in the grate. A maid had come in, a small shy girl, barely half through her teens. She went straight to the window and drew back the heavy dark curtains. Whiteness. Hardly any sunlight came through.

It was morning. There would have to be sunlight. Her life could not have got so odd that she would wake in a strange bed to a day with no sun. Charlotte was dressed in the same clothes she'd put on the day before, a black and brown wool shirtwaist, with a matching vest and short jacket. It was a good thing all her clothes were so loose on her. She had never before spent a night fully dressed.

"Excuse me, missus," said the maid nervously, cautiously.

The glass was completely frosted in every pane, from top to bottom. "Frost," Charlotte said to herself. "Something natural." She had thought that, in the instant she looked from the fire to the window, something had gone wrong with her eyes, a sort of white blindness, as happened to people struck by lightning. You go through your life seeing nothing but the same white flash that hit you.

That was what happened to her mother-in-law's private maid, Miss Stanfield, as elderly as a prune, and everyone had seen it happen. It was summer, at the summer place, and she'd gone out in the rain, at the age of about eighty, which seemed crazy, but she was leather-tough and fanatically healthy; she ate nothing but lettuce and beans. She had lost the little key to her possessions box, which was metal, and which she was carrying with her, tucked under one arm. She thought she'd dropped the key in the grass by the broken elm in the middle of the yard, which had been hit by lightning years before and no longer had leaves or even branches, just a split-in-the-midsection dissipating trunk. Miss Stanfield liked to have her lunches there, picnic-style, alone, on a bench used only by herself.

The box was where she kept her personal diary. She didn't know as she carried it that it was empty. The three Irish maids had the diary, and Charlotte, too; they were reading it in the kitchen. A lot of it was addressed to Jesus, as in, "Jesus I am mindful of my faults that are legion," and a lot of it was made up of reminders to herself concerning chores. "My missus said put out the green dress for airing that's the green with the blue not the gold. She said the brushes and combs want polishing on Thursday."

It was a big disappointment. They'd just read, "Mr Heath what is her husband had five days go by with no activity of his bowels, & we discussed to send this time for the doctor, to be drained, tho' he swore to not submit & to jump off the cliff instead," when one of the yard-work boys, who was Irish, and who knew what they were up to, rushed in to say that Miss Stanfield was on her hands and knees in the grass by that tree, in what had now become a thunderstorm, and they all jumped up to run out to her; they weren't sadistic.

A general alarm had gone up in the main house and all the cottages around it; everyone had gone to a window or doorway or the wide side porch, calling to her. Charlotte was just coming out of the kitchen door, with the three maids behind her, when the lightning came. Miss Stanfield must have been worried by the first few small flashes, bristling and bright: she held up the box in front of her face like a shield.

It was the third or fourth strike that hit her, and afterward, through the summer and fall, she wore a black satin cloth tied over her eyes like a blindfold, which was supposed to restore her sight, but it didn't. There was only the whiteness, and then she went to live with a cousin, somewhere far away.

The diary was put back, the key was put back, Miss Stanfield never knew. The three Irish maids had Confession to go to, they had Penance, they were Catholics. But what, Charlotte thought, about me?

She was told back in school that if you swallowed an acorn—she was always casting about outdoors for things to eat, having never been satisfied with the skimpy little meals—a tree would take root in your intestines, and it would grow through your lungs, through your throat, with branches poking out from your ears, obliterating you, like girls in the old Greek stories who did not obey the gods and were enchanted.

Guilt was like that. Guilt was like an acorn.

Charlotte hadn't thought about Miss Stanfield since the day she left the house with all her things in one trunk, but now she could think of nothing else, with a burning rush of remorse. She found herself trying to pray, which she hadn't done since school; she'd completely lost the ability. She couldn't remember the words to a single prayer. The hotel maid was bearing in on her, edging toward the bed.

I wish I didn't have a conscience, thought Charlotte, and she remembered the black blindfold, and how Miss Stanfield sat so rigidly in a chair by the parlor fire, relieved of all duties, and saying,

"Please will someone tell me why I must have a white bandage on my eyes when I would so much prefer a dark one."

"Excuse me, missus, please."

"I am very, hugely sorry," said Charlotte. She had bowed her head, without meaning to. She looked up at the little maid. "What's your name?"

"Eunice, missus."

"You're very young."

"Sixteen last summer."

"You made an excellent fire."

"Thank you, but please, they want to know."

Charlotte held up a hand to interrupt her. The chair that had been piled with clothing last night was bare.

"I want my aunt."

"Would that be the doctor?"

"It would."

"She has left. Someone from the hospital came with a wide-runner sleigh early on, like what they use for dire-straits patients, as it's bad out."

"Do you know if she left for a funeral?"

"I believe she was meant to, as I had seen them in the drying room, putting the iron to a dress for her what was black, for mourning. But it may happen she will stay at the hospital today and go nowhere."

"Is my aunt here often?"

"Please, we're not to answer questions such as that from a guest."

"There was a man in this room last night and I wonder, who might he be?"

The maid showed no sign of emotion or hesitance; young as she was, she'd been carefully trained. "We're not to answer questions."

"But he could not be a guest, as I know the guests are ladies, and he is a male."

"We're not to answer questions of who would visit."

"Surely he was not visiting. He was wearing bedclothes."

"We are not to answer questions of who works here."

"He *works* here?"

"I didn't say so, missus. I was only saying what the rules are."

"He works here doing what?" It couldn't be playing piano, as a hired musician for the guests' entertainment. Even though she'd complimented him, it was obvious that he didn't know the first thing about actual music.

"Please," said the maid, "if I can say what I am meant to, they want to know in the morning room. It snowed something terrible in the night, and Mr. Alcorn said, at the stable, they will not let out the horses, and would you mind going home in the Moberly sleigh, as Mrs. Moberly likes the weather and has a dog at home she is attached to, a spaniel, she said, very prized, which is to have its litter, its first one, and she said—Mrs. Moberly—she couldn't live with herself if she missed it. She wouldn't mind the company though you're strangers to each other, but your towns are side by side, and please hurry, as she is anxious to go."

The maid paused, flushed with exertion, and Charlotte said, "Is this room near the top of the house?"

She had a sense of being high up. The wind was blowing hard, with a whistling, and the windowpanes seemed to sigh and turn even whiter. She was used to sleeping a lot closer to the ground.

"This is the third story," said the maid, as if a guest of the hotel would not be thought odd if she didn't know where she was.

"Is there food downstairs?"

"Breakfast, in the morning room," said the maid. "Bread and jam, boiled eggs, some rashers and potatoes, from what was in the kitchen already, as there's to be no deliveries today, with the snow."

"Is Mrs. Petty in the kitchen?"

"I have not seen her this morning."

"Then please come back with a tray for me," said Charlotte.

"But there is no time, please."

"There is always time for eating alone in one's room if one desires. Is there water?"

"What we have. There's none running in the pipes as they are froze. What will I say to Mrs. Moberly by way of answer?"

"Tell her thank you very much, but I never ride with strangers," said Charlotte.

"They won't like that. She is well high thought of."

Well, so am I, Charlotte thought, going prickly all over, with a haughty and dangerous crankiness, which, she liked to think, was something picked up from the Heaths, but it wasn't; it was all her own. She threw off the blankets and, carefully, warily, because she still wasn't sure her legs would hold her up, she swung herself out of the bed and stood upright, wobbling a bit, but not falling. The little maid forgot about her errand and smiled in a cheering way, as if congratulating her; someone must have told her about the illness.

"I had a cousin fourteen years old what had the paralysis," said the maid. "He took down with a fever and his legs went stiff in one night, like two wood boards, then both his arms the next day."

"What happened to him?"

"It was polio. He died."

The knock on the door was so gentle—a light tapping, with the tips of someone's fingers—Charlotte might have missed it, but the maid jumped, startled, and opened the door and peered out.

"Is she dressed?" Charlotte recognized the voice, though she'd only heard it once.

"She is, Mr. Alcorn."

"Please ask if I may be allowed inside to speak with her."

Charlotte put her back up straight and allowed herself to consider that, whatever the morning room was, and whatever one did there, and whoever Mrs. Moberly was, they were trying to get rid of her. She needed to relieve herself—her bladder was nearly bursting—and she spotted a chamber pot under the bed. This must not have been the first time the plumbing had frozen.

"Please ask Mr. Alcorn to give me a moment," said Charlotte, and then added, tipping her head in the correct direction, "and yourself as well." She was not about to pull down her drawers in front of a strange maid.

"Oh," said the maid. She went out to the hall, but first looked anxiously over her shoulder as if Charlotte, left alone, might try to escape out the cold white window. And when Harry Alcorn came in, he looked at her in much the same way. She hadn't brushed her hair; she had never before presented herself to someone who wasn't her husband or a maid, first thing in the morning, unwashed, but there was nothing to be done about it.

You'd never know it was a snowstorm, or even winter, by the way he was dressed. His linen suit, the color of cream, was perfectly shaped; his white shirt was as crisp as paper. His necktie, silk, was a soft light tan, like milky tea, and just as liquidy. The vest beneath the jacket was his only concession to the weather; it was of fine white wool and fit him so elegantly—even with, Charlotte noticed, a slight bit of paunch in his stomach—it looked like an extra coating of skin, and she thought, as if this were the reason she'd run away, Now, why didn't Hays take a little bit of interest in how he dressed, instead of covering himself, day in and day out, in dark, dreary things, all grays and blacks and browns, all shapeless, all dull, and as interesting to look at as mud?

There wasn't any good morning or how-did-you-sleep from Harry Alcorn, as one would expect from a hotelkeeper. He didn't even ask her to sit down, as a gentleman would. She felt she knew what he was going to say. He was going to evict her, as one would evict a pauper.

"I can afford to pay for this room," said Charlotte.

"Please, Mrs. Heath, do not misunderstand me."

Her defenses went up at once. Except for the one time her mother-in-law had required her to leave the summerhouse kitchen, and the three or four times she was banished from the stable at Miss Georgeson's as punishment for minor offenses—which wasn't so bad for someone who'd been there straight through for thirteen years—she had never in her life been required to leave a place she didn't want to leave.

It wasn't so much that she liked the room or even the hotel. She couldn't think where else to go. And she wanted a bath. And she was hungry. And she wanted to change her clothes, even though the clothes she'd change into were someone else's, and would fit her even more loosely than her own.

What had she done that time in the summer kitchen? Oh, that was when the father of the three Irish maids was still alive. He had wanted some of the sherry-soaked jam cakes being saved for a tea with some visiting politician or some banker; the cakes were locked in the pantry.

People were always going to Charlotte for keys to things. One thing had led to another, the old man told some story or other, he was always telling stories, and the entire batch of cakes was disposed of, Charlotte having wolfed down the greater portion, so that—they were extremely heavy on the sherry—it ended with his attempting to teach her an Irish song, something about waiting by a gate in the mist for a lover who'd never come. She didn't remember the words. It was her baying of the song (she lacked a melodic singing voice) that brought in her mother-in-law. "Get out." She could hear the words still. She had a good idea her mother-in-law had not only meant the kitchen.

"I have no interest in meeting the lady whose dog is whelping," said Charlotte.

"I'm not surprised. I have a great favor to ask of you," said Harry Alcorn.

"I have no interest in being taken home."

"That would not be the favor."

The little maid had not come back. Should Charlotte find it alarming to be alone behind a closed door with a man she hardly knew? She did not feel alarmed.

She said, "If you would like me to try my hand at changing the climate, as I'm told there was a storm and much snow, I warn you, I may try, but I should probably fail."

He was somber, serious. "What I would ask you for, you can suc⁄ceed at, Mrs. Heath. There is a man downstairs who would like to interview a guest of mine. It is you who came to mind. You're asked to do nothing but answer his questions honestly unless—and I apol⁄ogize for the need to appear as if I insult you—you sense that the course of his questions would require you to be, shall I say, in aid of myself, circumspective."

"Circumspective," said Charlotte. She felt about twenty years younger, as if that were what she really was like inside, as if she were stunted, as if she were being asked again by Miss Georgeson to spell a word she was bound to get wrong. To her horror—and she gave herself no credit for having just woken up, and for everything else that had happened to her since yesterday—she could not think what circumspective could possibly mean. I am a woman of more than thirty! she thought quickly. More than thirty! This was some⁄thing she'd done all her life, as taught by Miss Georgeson: whenever you doubt yourself, say your age, remind yourself of your age, and then *be* it.

Funny she should remember that and not the prayers.

"Are you asking me to have a conversation with someone that may include a lie?" said Charlotte.

"Not a lie, exactly."

"Why, if you can tell me?"

"As a favor."

"I'm not insulted. And who would the man be?"

"It would be," said Harry slowly, "a member of the Boston Police."

She held her breath for an instant to make sure he wasn't joking. He wasn't.

"But the maid told me, Mr. Alcorn, there'd be no one going outside today, absolutely no one, almost."

"He walked here."

Oh, no! Her heart thudded hard in her chest. Had he been sent by a Heath? Had Aunt Lily sent him, as preposterous as that seemed? Well, she'd not been in a good mood.

And what about Mrs. Petty? Had she bundled herself up to go out in the snow, as much as she hated snow, to a police station, bursting in to say, "Go pick up Mrs. Heath and take her into custody?"

Had she been tracked down like a criminal? Would she be placed under arrest? Could a husband have his wife arrested? Could his mother, could his father? Desertion, they called it.

This was the favor? To go quietly into custody? Politely, even?

"This is of no concern to your own situation," said Harry. He seemed to be reading her thoughts, or maybe he'd expected her to be worried personally, given the way she'd arrived. "It's not my business why you would have chosen to leave your home."

"Someone who would ask another for circumspection," she said, "might not be counted on to be entirely truthful himself. I say so as only a fact."

"I would like to have your trust, Mrs. Heath."

"I don't give it lightly."

"And you should not. It's strictly a hotel matter."

Charlotte looked him directly in the eyes. He had said last night he'd be her friend. She had not taken that lightly, either.

What choice did she have? It would probably be better, whatever it was, than sledding back home in the snow with a woman who was

likely to be one of those matrons her mother-in-law was always planning charitable affairs with, women who wore enormous hats with
flowers and feathers, and corsets of whalebone, and bustles too, and
hothouse flowers in their bosoms, and belonged to organizations like
Ladies Against Suffrage, because they believed that women who
went to college and had money should not waste their time on things
like voting, when it was better to simply tell your husband what
ballot to cast and devote your attentions to the Poor, and the Temperance Movement, and Ills of Society in General. They were always
talking about these things in capital letters. It would make sense that
the behind-the-scenes Mrs. Moberly, as generous as she might have
been to offer a ride—no, to command it—would be exactly such a
person. She was probably a friend of her mother-in-law, who knew
everyone.

And so Charlotte made up her mind. "May I have something to
eat first, and some tea?"

"But of course. The detective inspector is in the front sitting
room, and I will have a tray brought there for you, at once."

"Then excuse me for a moment and let me brush my hair,
Mr. Alcorn."

He moved to open the door, shaking his head. "There is no time.
I've kept him waiting long enough, and Moaxley is hovering down
there, quite near him, which, I assure you, is not a wise idea for too
long, as Moaxley in his very person invites suspicion, not that he was
ever in trouble with the law, not seriously."

"What sort of interview will this be?"

"Oh, general. I expect he will ask you general things."

"Because something is under suspicion?" She tried to think what.
There was an innkeeper outside town, a friend of her father-in-law,
who was under suspicion with some sort of investigators, due to
some type of financial fraud. Was it something like that? Her father-
in-law had testified in court as a character voucher. Maybe it was

something like that, or something in the building. A restaurant Hays had told her about had been in trouble for failing to pay the men who put in their electricity. The Beechmont had not been wired, but it could have been something similar.

Another thought struck her. Oh, no! The antimony! The Gersons! Had they been *caught*? She was one of the conspirators! She'd been seen in the bakery sleigh! Had the criminal cooking pots floated up to the top of the pond? Had someone found them?

No, wait, the pond was frozen. The case was closed. It was the Colonel's case anyway, not Boston's. This was Boston.

"I've only been here the one night," she said, "and late at that, and we can't forget I was brought upstairs in such a way that, I'm not embarrassed to remind you, I do not even know."

"Moaxley carried you."

"I'll remember to thank him. But I would like your promise that no one else needs to know about that."

"We've already forgotten it. You're thought to have walked up the stairs in the normal manner, I assure you."

"All right, then."

"I'm in your debt, Mrs. Heath."

Charlotte felt a rising, wonderful sort of tension, a wonderful clenching. It had been so very long since her body felt taut like this, taut and excited, all though her, the way it felt out riding, in that exquisite, grand moment when a fallen tree must be suddenly hurdled, or a stream must be jumped, as both her horses hated putting their legs into water, especially when it was cold, and would rather, like her, go airborne. She allowed Harry to see the full expression of her face as she took his arm. A detective inspector!

They went out in the hall, into a hush that was deep and enveloping and would have been eerie if she didn't have more than thirty years of winters behind her. She recognized the feel of the inside of a house waiting out a blizzard, hunkered down in a great deal of snow. The gas lamps were on with a glow that was much more yellow than usual.

No one was about. The doors were all closed, eight rooms to a floor. Her mother-in-law had told her that the way to distinguish a house of real distinction from a house that would only pretend to have it was to look at the staircases of the upper floors—that is, in a private house—where invited guests wouldn't venture. If they were only for show, the upper stairs would be narrow, uncarpeted, and of less-than-high-quality wood. This had once been a private house.

All the stairways were as wide and generous as what you saw when you first walked inside, and the pale green carpet looked hardly used, as if people walked on it with their shoes off. Hays had told her that when he'd traveled to Italy—before he married her—he'd seen palaces, three hundred years old, with interior staircases, all marble, built amazingly wide, in gentle, low-stepped inclinations, going up maybe ten or eleven stories, like marble steps a midget could walk with no effort, or a child, and these were for the horses. Why should a duke or a prince climb his stairs when he could ride? Servants had followed to clean up the droppings. "That's vanity and laziness and corruption in its essence," Hays had said.

His sympathies were with the servants, as if there weren't any people in America who spent their whole lives going around picking up manure from other people's animals. "Horseback inside!" He'd been shocked. She hadn't told him how much she would have liked to try it, even though it would be very bad on the horses. Did they have a special type of shoe, to be able to handle the marble? Hays had laughed when she asked that question.

"Good morning, ma'am." Moaxley, near the bottom landing, gave the impression of a man whose knees don't quite unbend. He seemed always to be just in the act of standing up from a chair, which probably came from swelled, worn-out joints (like the head groom back home and the Irish maids' father). This earned him Charlotte's full, immediate sympathies.

"Thank you for seeing to it I got to my room last night, Mr. Moaxley."

"My pleasure, ma'am." Maybe if his nose weren't so awkwardly misshapen, if his face didn't look so fixed into a scowl, and if his eyes weren't so pinkened in the whites—permanently, not just from a night of heavy drinking—he wouldn't have seemed so daunting, like a gargoyle in the wall of a cathedral. He wasn't wearing the dark cloak, just a simple house suit, ordinary. His upper body was barrel-like, powerful, like a boxer's.

"Small bit of slightly unfortunate weather, I would say." He turned to Harry. Reporting on events was obviously something he did, hundreds of times a week, or even a day, automatically and naturally. "The lady with the pups on the way has left in spite of being warned against it, so I sent along that girl what we hired last month for the washroom and told her stay the night, or as long as the snow goes, and she'll be fetched when we get to it, and she didn't mind and thought it a holiday. The back way's shut in with the drifting but the coal'll hold up a couple days. Rooms're all watered, they've all got their pitchers and washbowls, with what we had, and the gentleman with the questions—"

Moaxley casually pointed a thumb down the hall. His eyes narrowed. "Is getting fidgety, like."

"Has he tried to wander around?" said Harry.

"Not a chance. Seems he's playing by the book, so to speak. Official-like."

"Then we'll do the same."

On the wall—Charlotte saw it in passing—was the framed photograph Mrs. Petty had mentioned in one of her letters, the former Mrs. Petty who'd been her friend. It was exactly as she had said, a wedding photo of a pale young Harry Alcorn, in white linen, against a blurry gray-white background, like fog or mist above a lake, and beside him was a bride in such a gauzy swirl of a gown, it seemed she wore nothing but a mixture of pure white smoke and fog and cloud. No corset; you could tell. The white silky wide-brimmed hat on her head obscured her face, as if casting shadows the camera hadn't quite picked up.

"Lucy," said Harry Alcorn. "My wife."

"I should like to meet her."

"She does not receive."

Charlotte looked at him. "But I should like to, all the same."

He only smiled, tightly, professionally. "I'll be right out here in the hall," said Moaxley quickly, "should you want me for any assistance."

Charlotte paused, as this seemed a good enough time to be making requests of her host. "I would like to see Mrs. Petty's children, as well."

"They're not here. But I'm sure we can arrange something."

And stepping in front of her, Harry Alcorn opened the door of the sitting room, gave her a light pat on the arm, and saw her into a small room with white walls filled with pictures—the same sort of watercolors as her room upstairs—boats, wagons, a trolley car, a goat cart, a sled propped up against a barn with weeds growing all around it, a high-wheeled bicycle on its side in a dusty road, a baby's perambulator in tall pale grass. Every one of them contained an astonishing stillness, an inertness; you had the idea that these were things that would never move again. The windows here were not quite as frost-coated as upstairs, but were dripping with melting ice, with heaps of snow piled up against them, and they seemed to be paintings, too. Charlotte wondered why it was that in the galleries and the Boston Museum she had never taken the trouble to look at pictures the way she found herself looking at these. It was the first time she had really paid attention.

So it took her eyes a moment to fix on the tall lanky man of about her own age who stood with his back to the fire, his legs out-stretched, as if every fiber of his clothing and body had been soaked and partially frozen. He'd been preoccupied with warming his hands.

Their eyes met, and Charlotte cried, "Dickie! Oh, my! Dickie!"

"Charlotte Kemple! Why, hello, Charlotte, is it really you?"

"It's Heath now."

"Ah, so you married him."

"I did. Dickie Lang! And they told me a police inspector was here! I think I've been played a joke on, but it's lovely to see you."

He came toward her, and she took hold of both his hands and squeezed them, and would have kissed his cheek if she hadn't sud-denly realized it might be inappropriate.

The last time she'd seen Dickie Lang he was fifteen years old and was being put into the back of a wagon to be transported to a hospi-tal. "I've changed since you knew me, but not that much," he said. He wore no uniform, he carried no weapon (that she could see), but she realized that he was very much an officer.

He'd been a factory boy, in a horrible, foul-smelling tannery, just down the road from Miss Georgeson's, in the center of the Black-stone Valley, where the hills were lovely, the fields were wide, the creeks were frothy and lively, the river was mighty and beautiful, the waterfalls were strong and inspiring, the outlying woods were lush and almost magical, and all these things did not add up to one moment of pleasure if you were sent into one of the factories at the age of eight, and expected to remain there until you turned your face to a wall and stopped eating, at the age of sixty or seventy, and found it a blessing to get to die—which was pretty much the way he'd once put it to her.

He had worked on the tannery's top floor, six ugly stories up, doing things with piles of hides. She'd forgotten the exact details of his accident: an iron contraption of some sort, some tanning machine, had come undone, and had trapped him beneath it. He had not been expected to live.

On Sundays before his accident he'd been allowed by Miss Georgeson to visit the stable, with free use of the horses, as long as he first attended chapel, which took all morning. In chapel the only girl he sat near was Charlotte, because she was the only girl who would speak to him; he smelled like cows and awful chemicals, even when he'd bathed.

"Do you still ride, Charlotte? As we used to?"

She smiled. "Yes, but not lately. I often wondered what happened to you. I saw you when they took you away. I was looking for you. I had permission to go into the shop for a new harness for Betsy."

"The spotted mare."

"Yes."

"I recovered."

"I can see that, Dickie. You look well." As he did not say the same to her in answer, she supplied an answer herself. "I've been sick."

The door opened and the little maid, Eunice, came in with a tray. There looked to be enough breakfast for four large people, and a teapot, and two cups. She set it on a table by a window. "I'm told to tell you, Mr. Policeman, it's a bad storm you have to go back out in, and please to indulge, courtesy-like."

"Thank you."

She fussed about the fire, clearly not wanting to leave, and when she finally did, Charlotte went straight to the plate of toast, already spread with jam and butter; she didn't care if she looked less than graceful, pressing slices into sandwiches and gobbling them down. She poured tea for both of them. He would take nothing, but sat down across from her and got right to the point. "Are you a guest here often, Charlotte?"

She found herself nodding yes. There was a plate of lemon tarts that she recognized as the work of Mrs. Petty, and decided to have nothing to do with them, then changed her mind one second later. Dickie Lang! Everyone at school had thought he was her sweet‑heart. Perhaps he would have been, had he stayed in the Valley. Had she stayed, too.

Their Sunday rides had not been supervised. A picture of him on the spotted mare rose up in her mind, but as he was now, not as he was at fifteen—an angry, sullen boy, given to long bursts of talking, in words and phrases that seemed like explosions, followed by longer spells of brooding silence, which matched, she had felt, what it was like for her within her own self.

The lemon tarts were just the right balance of sour and sweet. The crust was buttery, light, delicious. Maybe Mrs. Petty hadn't made them. They'd never tasted this good back home.

"I have to be official with you, Charlotte," Dickie said, and she responded so quickly, bits of crust spilled out; she brushed them off her chin with her fingers instead of reaching for a napkin, although fine linen napkins were on the tray.

"Be official! Pretend you never saw me before. I was someone else then, anyway."

"Are you happy, Charlotte?"

"Extremely!"

"Are you well?"

"Completely!"

"Is your husband with you here?"

She had finished one tart and was reaching for another; she paused. "This is a hotel for ladies only."

"Can you swear to that, if you had to?"

"Well, there's Mr. Alcorn and the manservant, Moaxley."

"Others. In the rooms."

"Is that a question?"

He reached into his waistcoat pocket, took out a small white call-ing card, and laid it on the table, facedown. "There've been rumors, so I was sent to interview guests. But it seems the only guest at present is yourself, which would appear odd, in a blizzard, but it won't seem odd if you tell me it's so."

"There were two women setting off earlier. You can check with the stable, as one of them must have lodged her horses there."

"Only two? I was under the impression the rooms are often full."

"Well, it's winter. And yes, only two."

"And now only you?"

She nodded. It wasn't lying; every door she'd passed upstairs was closed tight; every room was silent. He turned the card over. It was a business card, not a personal one. It said, in a fancy, printed scroll, *Boston Society for the Suppression & Prevention of Vice*.

"Can you suggest to me why I am looking at this, Dickie?"

"Because I'm showing it to you."

"Vice," said Charlotte. It occurred to her that she'd never had the chance before to say the word out loud as a grown-up. It had a ring to it. "Well," she said, "I can tell you, you'd probably find more vice in a church than in here. You'd probably find more in a graveyard."

"But they didn't send me to those places."

"What sort of vice exactly?"

Gambling, she thought, some secret gambling den? Opium? Was Harry Alcorn running one of those opium places, somewhere in a hidden hotel chamber?

What were the other vices? She tried to run through the list of sins she'd been taught at Miss Georgeson's. Weren't there supposed to be seven? She couldn't think of one.

Liquor? Was there a secret room of drunken binges? The Vice Society and the Temperance Movement people were likely to be the same people. And what about so-called indecent profanity of the written word, like what happened to the poems of Walter Whitman?

She knew about it because Hays owned a book of them which he'd bought in France; he had wanted her to read them, which she would have done, but the poems were in French, which her lessons had not prepared her for, not that she'd tried to master them with any diligence. No, not Walter, she remembered; his name was just Walt. He was the very reason the Vice Society was organized in the first place: to ban him. Fifty years ago, or something.

She remembered Hays telling her that. He was always trying to tell her about things that went on before she was born. He was older than Charlotte by eight years, but sometimes it felt like twenty. The poems were all about the poet himself, Hays had told her: things like lying naked in the sun outdoors, as naked as Adam, and praising old Indians, and being vigorous, and being happy and strong, and not giving a damn what anyone thought of him, which had not, except for the naked part, seemed worthy of being viceful; but the Vice Society had prevailed, the imbeciles, Hays had said. He believed that the American Constitution gave you the right to express your-self, for one thing, and for another, the poems were beautiful. "But don't tell Mother or Father I said so," he had told her, and why would she? She knew how to keep secrets.

Was Harry Alcorn a poet like Walt Whitman? One could sup-pose so, although it was hard to imagine a man like him letting people outdoors see him naked; he seemed much too fond of nice clothes. Maybe he had an alternate self which only came out in verses. Or maybe it was his wife! "She doesn't receive." The woman in that photo could certainly be a poet. She had a dreamy, pensive air. But it might have been the dress. Was there a secret printing press in the hotel basement and they were turning out pages and pages of vice? What sort? Pictures? Books of photographs? Stories?

No, it couldn't be. She would have smelled the ink and the solutions, even if they were locked away behind a thick door.

"Charlotte, are you listening to me?"

She realized he'd been talking and she hadn't paid attention. "Perhaps," he said patiently, "you can tell me the names of the two ladies who left already today."

She was about to say, "Someone named Mrs. Moberly, and my aunt," when something stopped her: the dimly recalled words of Aunt Lily, which didn't come back exactly, but were significant in their hint at secrecy. The family. "I'll let them know you're with me at my apartment."

Something else had been nagging at her, too, and now she got it. "Dickie," she said, "why did you say, when I told you I'm Mrs. Heath now, Oh, so you married him?"

"We're to be official."

"This is official."

"Because," he answered, carefully picking his words, and shifting around on the chair, and looking out the window at the snow, as if he'd only now seen that it was storming, "I saw you one day with him, here." He pointed out the window vaguely. "Walking in the Garden, by the Pond. It was summer and your dress was blue. You were watching the swans."

"You know my husband?"

"I don't, personally, but I would know who he was because an uncle of his had an office above one of the banks. I was in private security then. I was twenty."

"If you saw me, why not speak?"

"Because," he said, "I thought I would have embarrassed you."

"Dickie! You would not!"

"Then I saw an announcement of your marriage somewhere."

"Are you married, Dickie?"

"I am."

"Do you have children?"

"Two. Two sons. Babies still, the pair of them. And you?"

She shook her head no, dismissively, with no explanation, and he said, "Odd that there would have been rumors of men as guests here, don't you think?"

"The tearoom is open to the public," said Charlotte. She suddenly remembered that fact, from Mrs. Petty's letters.

"This would be at night."

"There're servants," said Charlotte. She forced herself to not think for even one second about the angelic young man of last night in his nightshirt. She willed her brain to conclude she must have dreamed him, and this was not a good time to remember a dream, as much as she would have loved to, just to picture his face, his hair, his skin. If she didn't think about him as an actual person, it wasn't a lie.

"These men didn't strike anyone as servants. Have you ever seen a young man or two upstairs, which truthfully, Charlotte, is no crime? The quicker I get rid of this business, the quicker I'll be happy. A woman in a hotel has the perfect right to have visitors. This is not the Middle Ages."

"This is Boston, though," said Charlotte quickly.

"Do you know the city well?"

"Moderately."

"Odd I've not seen you before, as you say you're a regular visitor here, and I live . . ." Again he gestured out the window, again vaguely. "Close by, on Lilac Street, in the direction of the Dome. Surely as a regular guest, you've been by it."

"Lilac Street," she said. "I don't know it. I don't know names of streets."

He sat forward, eagerly, smiling at her. "But I'm sure you must have passed my house, without my noticing. Passing by each other unawares seems to be something we have in common."

She felt bad about disappointing him. He seemed to want so badly to establish this other connection with her—an image to take away of her, out for a stroll on Beacon Hill, glancing up at window that was his. It was a nice thing to think about, but she knew, as a rule, that if you wanted to get away with a lie, or a circumspection, the way to do it was to tell no lie you didn't absolutely have to, even if not to do it was making you want to burst. It would have been so easy to agree with him, yes, I know that street, isn't it nice our paths are crossing?

"Surely on your visits you go walking, especially in the spring when things are at their best. The houses on Lilac Street aren't quite so close to the road as most others, and people have gardens, in a competitive way. The flowers are quite spectacular. I'm sure you would have noticed them."

"If I came to Boston to look at flowers, I would not come to Boston. They're quite spectacular at home."

"I remember at the bank, they had a joke about the name of your town, and called it Heathtown."

"It's not completely a joke," said Charlotte.

"I'm sorry I didn't know you were near when I was injured."

"You weren't conscious, and it was a long time ago, so I can't hold it against you. They said you'd broken a great many of your bones."

"Did you worry?"

"I did, Dickie. Did they send you home?" His family, she remembered, lived somewhere in the west, near the Berkshires, working someone else's farm, someone else's orchards; they had sent him to the Blackstone Valley in order to receive his paychecks, which were mailed to them and which he never saw. He was to wait until the age of eighteen before he could keep any part of his earnings, she now remembered.

"I was sent to a hospital here and, afterward, to a sanatorium at

Dorchester Heights. Bones heal, you know, eventually. Would it be out of the question for you to mention the names of the ladies who went out this morning?"

"It would, Dickie."

"Because you feel you should be loyal?"

"Because I don't know the names of guests here, any more than I know the streets."

"I don't remember you being shabby with your memory."

"Oh, I always was. You only ever saw me around horses."

"And in church."

"I was shabby in church. I seem to remember people saying, and I don't want to offend you, that you might have caused that thing at the tannery to fall on you, you know. I just suddenly remembered that."

"It was a stretching machine for hides. Deerskin, cows," he said. "In the Middle Ages, it was the kind of thing they tortured people on. It was attached to a wall with iron bolts."

"Miss Georgeson said you were a nice, decent boy and people were awful to whisper about you."

"Miss Georgeson only saw me in church. The tannery paid my parents a hundred dollars for the loss of my wages," he said. "And in my profession, believe me, I know exactly how awful people can be."

She liked the way he said "can be" instead of "are." Like there were exceptions to being awful.

"Are you an inspector of vice, if there's such a thing?"

"Not actually. My usual stuff is something different than stuff based on rumors."

"Murders, Dickie? Things like that?"

"All sorts of things. I'm still a junior."

"So they sent you here because you live in the neighborhood, is that it?" Well, Harry had said he walked here. It didn't have to be from a police station. Did he think, at the first opportunity, she'd head straight toward the Capitol and find his street, and he'd be there in a window himself, waving at her, his babies in his arms?

"What about Myrtle Street?" he said.

"What of it?"

"Do you know it?"

"Is that the one with the green door at the end with the knocker in the shape of a lion's head, and a lamp to keep it visible?" She had passed it last night, and Everett Gerson had said, "That is the biggest door knocker I ever saw."

"That's on Joy Street."

"Is Myrtle the very long one, like three or four others put together?" They'd been on it, looking for the Beechmont, and Everett had said, "Mabel's mother's name is Myrtle, I have to remember to tell her there's a street named for her."

"Yes. Do you ever go into that tearoom, a genuine English one with completely imported goods, about smack in the middle?"

"I didn't notice a tearoom. The one here is just fine."

"Have you noticed anything taking place in this hotel you would call unusual?"

"I would call it unusual to be sitting here talking to you."

"Have you noticed anything, in all your visits, that might compromise someone's sense of what is decent?"

"Had I done so, I would swear never to return."

"And will you?"

"In all probability," said Charlotte.

He said, abruptly, "Did you think I caused the thing to come out of the wall and topple on me?"

"I'm not going to answer that. I don't remember what I thought."

"I think you do."

"I think, then, if you press me, I could never have thought so for one reason. I would never be able to bear it if you had looked at yourself as something you would choose to destroy. I don't think you would have intended to have bones broken and survive it. I don't think I wanted to know how much hopelessness you must have felt."

"I told you of it often."

"But we would go riding, and that made it seem all right."

"Thank you, Charlotte."

"You're welcome."

The interview was over. He gave a glance out the window once more, but this time it was to prepare himself to go out into the storm. "There'll be no roads cleared, and I expect to be pushing myself through drifts to my knees."

"Goodbye, Dickie. Maybe all the criminals will stay inside today."

"That might make it worse. I had my coat with me, and my boots, when I came in here, but the maid came to take them. I would like to find the coatroom. Where might that be?"

Charlotte didn't know. How should she know that? "The coatroom? Dickie, there are servants. How would I know, when there are servants? Tell the man in the hall you want your coat and he'll get it."

"I suppose you're correct," he said. Then he said, "I believe you don't realize how much I trust your opinion."

"You're paid to have suspicions."

"But one knows."

"And how do you? Because we were friends from before?"

"Because, Charlotte, I live in Dorchester Heights, near the sanatorium. I married one of my nurses. We could never afford this neighborhood. I sometimes spend the night at the station when it's too hard to make it home. There is no such place as Lilac Street," he said simply, and stood up, pocketing the card of the Vice Society.

"Dickie!" She jumped up, nearly knocking over her chair. "You *tested* me?"

"It's all right. You passed."

∽ Six ∽

Charlotte holed up in her room—Aunt Lily's room—and stayed put for four days.

Harry Alcorn knocked on her door now and then. Did she want some company? Was she looking out the window at the hell-forsaken snow? Did she know the city was as stopped as a clock? Did she mind the blandness of the tedious meals, from what they had in the larder, just squash, potatoes, turnips, celery, applesauce, and cakes with no eggs? Would she like to come downstairs for a card game with other guests, would she like to listen to the gramophone, would she like to hear some piano? They had a very good pianist, as it happened, a New York lady who had played three times in concert on Washington Street, was married to a cellist with the Boston Symphony, and was a whiz at those sublime German sonatas, plus the new modern rowdy stuff.

She answered, to everything, "I wish not to speak to you, Mr. Alcorn, or to anyone else."

She hadn't been out of her room except to bathe once, in the lavatory down the hall. Every floor had its own, with expensive new
ceramic bathtubs fixed with shower heads, which distributed water
from a bucket that was nearly as large as the tub.

The showers were not in use this week. There was still no running water but there was coal, gas, and wood; the little maid,
Eunice, had been instructed to carry up pails of snow to be melted
for Mrs. Heath.

It amazed Charlotte how much snow it took to get two inches of
water in a bathtub. And the boiled snow from the fireplace had to be
blended with a fresh bucket, or her skin would have probably peeled
off her. She hadn't washed her hair since five or six days before she'd
left home, and it was starting to get oppressively sticky and too heavy
on her head, but she was used to that. At home when she was sick
they'd bring a portable washtub into her room, filling it out of
kettles. Often it was just too much trouble to do her hair as well.

In the summer when it rained—the sweet soft rain of July, when
the sun kept shining through it—she'd stick her head out the window and soak it, having first made sure no one was observing that
part of the house, which they usually weren't, because her horses
were always hanging around that window.

In the early days of her illness, her husband was the one to help
her bathe, and he was gentle and affectionate about it, even though it
was not certain, yet, that whatever she had was not contagious.

He turned her baths over to maids when Aunt Lily decided on a
brain disease. "If you're going to make anyone sick, I suppose it
ought to be me," seemed to have been his feeling. He never talked
about it. People said you could catch polio just by standing near
someone who had it, or even touching their bedsheets or clothes,
including things they weren't lying on or wearing, which hadn't
been washed yet, in hard lye soap.

Was that why Aunt Lily said brain disease? So no one would

look at her like a modern-day carrier of some old historical plague, like the smallpox, or that really bad one they had in Europe, in the Middle Ages, like an instrument of torture: the Black Death?

Even the biggest worrier-of-catching-diseases would not be able to say that something in someone's brain could get out and infect others, because how would it get past the skull?

It seemed reassuring to speak of it in this manner, as her sisters-in-law did, in her sickroom doorway, in a general, polite way: Oh, let's not say polio, let's say brain disease, not catching. They were trying to be friendly when they said things like, "It's interesting that the human skull is like a fortress—how excellent of God to have done that." Charlotte's skull was often a matter of discussion, but at the mention of the word she'd think of nothing but Hamlet, melancholy and handsome and hugely, tragically misunderstood. Lines of the play floated through her head.

But they didn't drown out memories of Aunt Lily's voice. "It's in her brain and nowhere else, I assure you."

Aunt Lily, Charlotte decided, treated her like a child. And she hadn't even introduced the man in bedclothes who looked like an angel. Charlotte wasn't supposed to have seen him. Maybe it was getting to be a pattern, seeing things she wasn't supposed to.

The passing of time was not a burden. If there was anyone who had experience in staying still—and not complaining about it, or wasting energy by squirming with boredom, and thinking of things you missed out on—it was her. She felt that if you didn't count riding, staying still in a room by herself was the one thing in which she had a genuine level of expertise.

Maybe this was what it was like to be old, sitting quietly, your eyes on the play of a fire, and looking at scenes in your mind, selectively, as if the living of life was for the gathering up of memories. When you watched them unfold in your head you were free to change anything you wanted, then convince yourself the new way was the way it really happened.

But she did nothing about changing the moment when she first caught sight of her husband embracing the woman at the edge of the square. She saw it over and over again. Like a painting. "Interrupted Kiss," it would be called. Where were his hands? On the woman's shoulders.

Where were hers? At his waist, one at either side.

Was her face tipped up toward his, expecting the kiss, in the cold? It was. Did it seem that this was the first time it was happening? Was it some sort of innocent, spontaneous thing, as if they'd met at Uncle Owen's wake, two long-lost relatives? Was it grief that threw them together, simple grief, which always made people do strange things, for which they had to be forgiven?

Well, no, no, and no, and the woman wasn't dressed in the type of mourning clothes suggesting a relative. Were those hands on his waist the hands of a woman who would look at him and say "mine"? They were.

On the morning of the fourth day of her self-imposed confine-ment, Charlotte began to criticize herself for falling for Hays in the first place, back at Miss Georgeson's, when she was the most senior of the boarding girls.

She pictured the grounds of the academy and the locations of the biggest trees, the vegetable garden, the chapel, the tea patio with its roses on a trellis that never stayed put because the wind would knock it over, and everyone anyway picked the roses as buds: in the middle grades they believed you could put a brand-new baby rose under your pillow, and your wildest wish would be granted if, in the morn-ing, the bud emerged as a full-blown flower. She'd done so herself dozens of times.

Her wish was always the same: to find a way to get out of the

Valley and live—on her own, if she had to, as solitary as an owl—in a city, any city, anywhere, as long as the people in it spoke English. She'd never been to a city, but she would picture high buildings, crowds, shops, movement, stories everywhere, pickpockets slipping their hands in people's coat pockets, theaters, music halls, galleries, restaurants, hotels.

"What do you want for your life, Charlotte?" Miss Georgeson would say.

She'd known enough not to answer, "I want it to take place in a city." Miss Georgeson had come from Manhattan, and said cities were full of filth in every possible configuration, filth and degrada-tion and injustice. The rich were filthy rich and the poor were filthy poor and if there was anyone in between with any sense, they would move somewhere else.

There was an enormous ballroom near Fifth Avenue, she'd told Charlotte, where every year at Easter poor people from the tenements were gathered for a meal on the dance floor, where tables were set up, little round tea tables, about one hundred of them, and white cloths were put on them, very elegantly. They were people in raggy, dirty clothes who had not had a bath for months; perhaps they'd never had one at all, how could they, there was no plumbing in those horrible buildings, crowded together, firetraps every one of them.

These people sat down to eat free spit-cooked mutton, roasted chickens, boiled fruits, vegetables, and Easter cakes, with expensive silver, and with policemen watching so nothing would be stolen. Above, in alcoves, along an extended balcony, gold-rimmed, where people usually sat to watch the ballroom action—couples lavishly waltzing, introductions being made, an orchestra playing, people strolling about in their best clothes—there sat, watching the poor eat their meals, the one hundred richest men of New York City, with their wives.

They were up there like the people in ancient Rome, Miss Georgeson said, watching to see if Christians would be eaten by lions or saved, like Daniel, by their God. And this took place every year on the very day of the Resurrection. If Jesus walked among them, at whose side would he have pulled up a chair? Not the Romans. They were the ones who killed him.

What did she want for her life? "I want to be a good Christian, Miss Georgeson," Charlotte would say. But all the same, she crossed New York City off her list of possible places.

Oh, it was easy to picture the academy: the gray, gritty smoke in the air from the Blackstone factories, the school, the little writing tablets, the generous back folds of Miss Georgeson's dresses over her bustles, the worn copy of *The Pilgrim's Progress* that was always somewhere nearby, the faces of other teachers, other girls, servants, horses.

It was autumn. A day in late autumn, beginning like any other day. She remembered the task she was assigned that morning. She was past all lessons herself, and was living in a fuzzy, undefined state of being somewhat still a pupil and somewhat a member of the staff.

She was supposed to conduct a schoolroom lesson with four French girls whose fathers—they were two pairs of sisters—were setting up a glass factory somewhere in the Valley. She was sent to teach them pronunciation. She had a list of English-for-foreigners phrases and sentences to be recited, elocution-lesson style. She remembered some of them still. "The, thee, the, thee, the, thee."

"Did you read in the reeds what I had read in my bed?"

"Aitch, huh, ha, ho, hard, half, wholesome, who, handle, whistle, her, aitch."

"Don't you know that the bow of the boat lies low in the water, brought down by the laughter of daughters?"

It was all ridiculous; Charlotte carried no weight of authority. The girls' chirpy voices rolled over the sounds melodically, trilling *r*'s, running everything together, dissolving into giggling, into rapid French chatter. The lesson was in chaos when the classroom door opened to reveal the girls' fathers, with Miss Georgeson.

And with them too was the young American businessman— with high spots of color in his face—who was helping to broker their financing.

The girls rushed to their fathers to complain. The businessman turned to Charlotte and said, in a condescending, high-handed way, "Your pupils are appalled by what Americans do with the first letter of the alphabet. And *ow* is a sound that horrifies them, and they're horrified by our *t* and our *h* put together, especially with an almost-silent *e,* after them, which sounds depressing and so much like a thud. They feel sorry for English itself for having words that look the same but are spoken so differently—which, by the way, they feel, demonstrates a deficiency of intelligence."

He looked directly at Charlotte for those last five words. Just to show off, he said everything all over in French, which took such a long time, she knew he was making fun of her. She immediately imagined this awful American up in the balcony of that ballroom, making sport of watching paupers at a feast.

What a Roman! What a pagan! What an awful, self-satisfied man! The girls knew him, and you'd think he was a prince, or a French girl's idea of a god, the way they marveled at him. "Mess-yure 'Eet! Mess-yure 'Eet! Vuze ett tray jo-lee!"

Charlotte had fled the schoolroom. She had thought his name was Eet, until he was presented to her more formally the next day, when she was called to Miss Georgeson's reception parlor, and found him standing there in a tweedy gray suit, with his hat in his hands.

"Forgive me, Miss Kemple, if I had seemed, yesterday, to be somewhat repulsive to you," and she answered, "Forgiveness would be too strong a word, as I believe your repulsiveness, as you put it, was based on rudeness and not in sin."

He seemed to be encouraged by the fact she didn't take him for a sinner. "Then forgive me for the rottenness of my manners."

"I've no reason not to."

And then suddenly ten minutes later, when she was walking outside, he was beside her. "May I walk with you?"

She was on her way to the stables. She didn't want to say yes to him, because she couldn't think of a reason why she'd want to have his company. She couldn't say no to him because she couldn't think of a reason why she needed to send him away. He walked with her that day, without speaking. He watched her ride off, but when she came back he wasn't there.

When she was just over eighteen, she was given a position at another academy, in southern New Hampshire. He came to call on her. Her job was as a lady riding master, teaching tiny girls to handle a pony with a goat cart on a dusty little oval of a track, around and around all day.

Now, sitting by the fire, she wished he hadn't done that. She wished she'd seen the last of him back at Miss Georgeson's. She wished he hadn't taken her driving with him in his carriage. She wished he hadn't looked in her eyes the way he did, and she wished she hadn't looked back, the same way.

The first time he kissed her was at the edge of a potato field. She wished she hadn't liked it. She wished she hadn't felt those astonishing powers of *desire* and *appetite,* every time he was near her.

"Charlotte! Let me in! Let me in at once!"

Aunt Lily. Here she was, on the afternoon of the fourth day, as if Charlotte had been waiting for her.

"Charlotte, let me inside. I want to come in. This is the first time I had a chance to get back here, and this *was* my room, and if you'd care to know who's paying for it, I am."

The door was locked with the inside bolt, but what was a locked door to a physician?

"If you don't let me in, I'll get Moaxley to come up here with an ax. The cost of a new door can be put on the bill—I can afford it—and I'd expect he would enjoy very much the breaking of this one, especially if I tell him you're in the throes of a fit, Charlotte, an epileptic fit. I can say that's what you have, and dishonest as it is, no one will doubt me."

Charlotte opened the door. Her aunt smelled like snow and cold and wind and the hospital.

"You've lost even more weight, Charlotte. They said you've been eating well, but now I doubt it."

"These aren't my clothes."

Mrs. Gerson's plain wool dress was big enough to have fit almost two Charlottes. The jacket over it, brought up by Eunice, had been left by some guest, who'd been obviously on the stout side.

"Whose are they?"

"I'm not telling you."

Aunt Lily bustled in and sat down on the side of the bed. She had a letter. "I have a letter," she said.

"From the people against vice?"

"I heard about your friend the policeman."

"He didn't come here," said Charlotte, "as my friend."

The letter was put into Charlotte's hands. Aunt Lily hadn't opened it. It was addressed to her, at Aunt Lily's apartment. It was from Hays.

"My darling, dearest Charlotte,

"The mail is going out again by horseback & I write in haste as they are waiting. Aunt Lily sends word you are safely at home in Back Bay with her, so I will not for the present be as frantic with worry as I was. The thought of your having traveled into Boston on your own fills me with disbelief and great anxiety, and I have never in my life been so anxious as I am now, to be told in your own words if you are all right. What has been in your mind? I have not, I realize, done well as a husband. Only you and I can possibly know that. As for the family, they think you were upset by Uncle Owen's dying. Had you not gone to Aunt Lily I would be tormented even more than I am. I will come to Boston as soon as you send for me. I shall not impose myself, as much as I want to. Telephone to me at the Colonel's office and he shall let me know, or telephone to the bank, and likewise. Send for me, Charlotte, I beg you, I won't mind the weather, I shall come. H."

"Your hands are shaking," pointed out Aunt Lily.

"They are not." Charlotte went over to the fire and tossed the letter in, and watched it curl in on itself and burn.

"A roof collapsed last night under weight of the snow, near the harbor," said her aunt. "It was a fish-processing plant. Three men were killed, and there are some dozen trapped in the wreck. As we sit here, a rescue operation is taking place. What wasn't destroyed in the cave-in was destroyed by explosions from the gas they'd had stored there."

"I'm sorry for them."

"Sixteen people, four of them children, from the Italian tene-ments on Hanover Street, were brought into the hospital in a state of near death from the cold. I don't expect we can revive them. I expect there to be plenty of work for the surgeons in removing fingers and toes of people who, as we sit here, are suffering from exposure. I don't suppose you've been to Hanover Street. Do you wonder why I'm telling you this?"

"It crossed my mind."

"Because, Charlotte, the world is going on, and I can't be alarmed about you. If you don't want to go home to your husband, that's none of my concern, but you're to move to my rooms in Back Bay."

Charlotte looked at her. "Who was that man with you, the night I came in here?"

"A friend."

"He *works* here."

"That's not your concern."

"But I can put things together."

"Sometimes when one puts things together, the pieces may not fit in quite the way one wants them to, or they may be fitted together incorrectly. Or the pieces may be better off remaining just that, unconnected."

"I like connections. Where is Uncle Chester?"

"At home in Brookline."

"Does he know you come here?"

Aunt Lily didn't answer.

Charlotte said, lightly, "I wonder what the Boston Society for the Suppression and Prevention of Vice would think of our conversation."

"They're of no concern. They are people who want to stir up trouble where none exists."

"Like the witches in *Macbeth*," said Charlotte.

"Not at all. Real life isn't quite so melodramatic."

"You sound like a Heath, not counting Uncle Chessy."

"There's nothing Shakespearean in people suffering because they haven't got heat, they haven't got suitable clothing, their roofs are falling, their shelves have no food."

"Well, what I want to know is, why was Mrs. Petty so horrid to me?"

"You would have to take that up with Mrs. Petty."

"Where are her children?"

"I don't know anything about that."

"Are you in this hotel often?"

"As often as I have the chance."

"You lied for me so they wouldn't know at home where I am."

"I don't want to do so again."

"All right, then. I don't want to make you distressed, you've been good to me." Charlotte sat down at the edge of the bed. She nodded her head, meekly, and thought of the way a young, newly broken-in horse, realizing the odds against it, bows its head and lets its jaw go slack, in submission, with its tongue gently licking at air, or its own teeth, as though it just had been born.

She realized that she'd built up some experience back at Miss Georgeson's: practical experience to draw from. It was just like that, the same sort of situation, more or less, as if saying, "I want to be a good Christian."

"Should I tell Harry you'll be moving to my rooms, Charlotte? I know he'll fix a sleigh for you. As it's not very far, and as Tremont Street and Boylston Street are passable, it won't be quite as treacherous as it may seem, from looking out the window."

"I'll tell him myself, Aunt Lily. Thank you."

"Remember you're still very weak."

"I'll be careful."

"You'll go at once?"

"I'd like to change back into my own clothes, and give some money to the maid, and perhaps have some tea."

"And we won't speak of this," said Aunt Lily.

"I'll say I was at your rooms all along."

"I'll trust you. The woman who looks after the apartment will be there. She'll see to anything you need."

"Thank you."

"I'll come to you as soon as I can. In a couple of hours I am going to be assisting at a surgery for a man who was shot by a storekeeper. There's been looting, something terrible. This man took a bullet in the back of his neck."

"Oh! Will he be conscious?"

"We have ether."

"I'll pray for him. Thank you, Aunt Lily. I'm sorry for the trouble I've given you."

"It's not trouble. It's a question of preventing it."

"I understand. You're right, and I'm grateful to have your help."

"I can't think what might have happened if I hadn't been here that night."

"I was so very incredibly fortunate."

"You don't want to tell me anything of what's happened between you and my nephew?"

"I would not, no more than you seem willing to talk to me about the things I most want to know about."

"Fair enough. You haven't had an easy time of it. I know what it was like for you to be ill."

"No, actually, you don't."

"I must be going."

"I wish I could give some help to the people who are suffering."

"You go to my rooms and stay put."

"I will."

Just for good measure, Charlotte took off the top layer of her borrowed clothes, got up and went over to the bureau, and picked up the borrowed hairbrush, as if already in the act of mobilization, of obedience.

Aunt Lily patted her and kissed her cheek, and when she was gone, Charlotte waited a few minutes before securing the door with the bolt; she didn't want her aunt to hear it. All was quiet. She took a blanket off the bed, wrapped it around her, and sat down by the fire once more, to wait.

She could do that, wait. She was good at it, even though she didn't know what she was actually waiting for. The uncertainty didn't bother her. The unanswered questions didn't bother her.

Who could know what it was like to be sick? Not a physician, that was for sure. She felt a twinge of remorse, a very small one, for behaving so churlishly with her aunt—but not for being less than honest with her, which didn't count, as Aunt Lily herself had set a standard for choosing to be less than forthright.

Charlotte hated it, *hated* it, when people who never spent a long stretch of time in a sickbed said, Oh, I know what it was like for you. No one knew. It was like walking by a restaurant and looking in at diners at tables, lifting forkfuls of roasted meat to their lips, and saying, "I was hungry a moment ago, but now that I've watched someone eating, my own belly is full." Or like the men who were digging at the cave-in of the fish plant, if they called out to the trapped men inside, "Anything you're feeling, so am I."

She would always have a sort of pocket in her mind to contain what it felt like that moment, long ago last year, when she knew, really knew, that something was very wrong with her: it was in Aunt Lily's office. How could she ever go back to Aunt Lily's?

There was a big oak desk, a couple of leather chairs, framed certificates and diplomas on the wall, a vase of flowers on a table by a window, shelves holding bottles and vials and shelves filled with books. Aunt Lily's coat on a hook. Aunt Lily herself in a white muslin dress and a white muslin jacket. "Charlotte, that swelling of your glands I noticed before has increased, does it hurt very badly for you to swallow?"

No, it didn't hurt at all, nothing hurt; there were only these swellings around her neck and just under her arms, and this tingling sensation in both her legs, now and then, and this small, annoying fever, which came and went, sometimes as mild as a hot wet towel held to her forehead, sometimes as hot as if her blood had been set to a boil. She blamed it on going out to ride in bad weather.

She'd only come to the office because Hays was involved in a business meeting at a bank. She would visit with Aunt Lily and meet Hays afterward for a play.

They had planned to see a play on Washington Street—not Shakespeare, but a thrilling drama of a malevolent sawmill owner who wanted to marry a woman engaged to his foreman. First he would tie up the woman with a horse rope and hide her in a closet, and then he would overpower his foreman and place him, like a log, on a table that held the giant wheel of an high-powered, steel-toothed saw, which would turn as in real life. Head first, the foreman would be slid toward it. The woman in the closet was supposed to undo her rope just in time.

Charlotte knew the plot because everyone did; it was in all the papers. Hays had bought tickets secretly. They'd told everyone at home they were going to a recital of some boring soprano.

There would always be a part of her in a state of excited suspension—which a fever could have resulted from, a tingling. A part of her that was waiting to be thrilled. A part of her that was all seized up in an act of expectation.

How had it happened that she felt herself in an act of submission instead? It had happened very quickly. Her aunt was behind her. She had placed her hands on the sides of Charlotte's neck, gently pushing down on the collar of the high-necked dress she was wearing. Then she touched Charlotte's shoulders and, in the mirror—there was an oval mirror on the wall, in a smooth, blond-wood frame—Charlotte saw that the hands which should have been flat were instead quite raised, as if she wore, tucked in the fabric of the dress, two bustlelike cushions, like shoulder humps. And then it seemed that such a hump was inside her throat.

"Swallow as if you've just had a drink of water," said Aunt Lily, and it couldn't be done. Charlotte felt herself gagging, being choked. Aunt Lily did something—some sort of patting—and it relaxed a little, she was fine; she thought with a little giggle that she must have empathized with the heroine of the play without realizing it: there'd been mention in the papers of a choking scene, in which the heroine was first subdued.

After the play there'd be a hotel, on Tremont Street, a night in the city! And dinner at a small table just for the two of them, herself and her husband, no Heaths, and maybe she could tell him what she wanted, what she'd kept putting off.

"I want to have a house of our own."

There'd be a bottle of wine, the fruity Spanish wine he liked. There'd be the leftover thrill of the play, the rising tension, the buzz and whir of the saw, the sold-out audience holding its breath as one person—and then the relief, the flood of relief washing everywhere. The heroine would undo her ropes and save her beloved, and wasn't life *grand*? As for the mill owner, the police would rush in and nab him. Hays would be pleased in the core of himself to see order restored, and he would sip his glowing glass of wine, and be glowing himself, and she would say, "Or if not a house, then an apartment, Hays, right here, perhaps on Beacon Street, or Boylston. And I should like to hurry and buy furniture." And he would say, "Why, of course, Charlotte, of course," and that would have been that; they'd go to see a buildings agent the next day, as they'd be in town anyway.

In the mirror her aunt's eyes were clouded. It was funny, Charlotte thought, how your mind can be churning away with plans, with anticipations, with scenes being played, with *hope,* but your body can go off in quite another direction, as though your own being is a villain turning against you, with the terrible force of its own irrefutable will.

"You're ill, Charlotte."

And it seemed that her illness—that hostile, powerful thing—was coiled up inside her, hidden, and had only been waiting to be summoned to the surface, to take her over. She knew. She knew it wasn't going to go away.

She knew how deeply it was hidden because she'd hidden it herself, way down, the unknown knowledge of it, the unbearable fact. She felt her cheeks grow hot, her shoulder humps begin to throb, her legs go tingly. A dull ache took hold of both of her knees, then a cramping in her shins, as if she'd been running. Maybe this was what it was like in stories of enchantment, when someone was putting you under a spell. "I feel you're putting me under a spell," Charlotte said.

"Don't be frightened. I'm likely to be the one who'll make sure it gets removed."

"Something is wrong with me." There it was. She looked away from the mirror. "Something bad."

"Yes."

"I want to go to the theater with my husband."

"You are going," said Aunt Lily, "to bed."

What was the submission like? It was like trying not to fall off a cliff when you are already in the act of falling, and saying, "Maybe it won't be so terrible," when rocks are rising up right in front of you and your mouth is gulping air, upside down.

Aunt Lily had sent someone to fetch Hays. Charlotte was sitting in one of the leather chairs when he arrived. He went over to her and leaned over her and took hold of both her hands, squeezing hard, as if all she had was a chill that needed warming, as if his touch would make it all go away.

At which point did he give up on her? Last spring, on a trip to Ohio which took longer than usual? Instead of being gone ten days, he stretched it to two weeks, three. Then again, again.

He'd return late at night and come into her room so quietly, she wouldn't know if he was real, or a part of a dream. There was always a lamp burning low in the sickroom, and sometimes she'd half wake in the night and not know if it was her husband looking down at her, or a shadow. A husband-size shadow on the wall. "I am married to a shadow," she would think.

His hands were on the woman's shoulders. The woman's hands were at his waist.

She pictured Hays staring into the woman's eyes, and the wintry, dark, snow-laced branches over their heads, and now she thought, Some of those branches over their heads were actually very heavy with snow. She removed the fact of herself in her sleigh. She took herself out of the scene completely, as if she were watching it like a ghost, incapable of corporeal interference. She pictured a great heavy limb breaking off from the tree at the edge of the square, silently, so they didn't see it coming. Off went Hays's hat into the road, and the woman's hat, too.

Bad luck! They'd be knocked unconscious. They'd be buried in snow like the men at the fish plant.

It really was just like a painting. The kiss was interrupted by the branch. They weren't to die, though; she wasn't malicious.

Suddenly, late that afternoon, a note was slid under her door. She waited a long moment before picking it up, because she didn't want it to seem—if someone was out in the hall—that she was idle, or that she was sitting around waiting for Harry Alcorn to make another try at involving her in some activity.

She didn't know the writing, but it appeared to be a woman's and she thought at first it had come from Mrs. Petty, ready to make amends.

It wasn't from Mrs. Petty.

"I am told you were seen admiring my pictures. Please don't be overly shy, as shyness is no quality I set faith in. Do come upstairs, one flight up, to call on me this evening, at Numbers 21, 22, 23, and 24. It will not matter which one you choose, Mrs. Heath, as all belong to me. If you happen to have any of those cakes which were carried with you on the night you arrived on our premises, do be a thoughtful girl and bring them, as I've not had sweets for an age. I shall provide the tea. Until then, I am yours most indulgently."

There was a florid, complicated signature and it took a while to decipher it. Bernice—no, there was another *e,* between the center consonants—Berenice. Berenice Eloise Singleton (Mrs. Andrew Enright).

An invitation to tea!

She'd forgotten all about the baked goods the Gersons had given her, and when the little maid brought in her supper tray—something different tonight, tinned herrings on crackers and a nice creamed celery soup—Charlotte asked about them.

A guilty, worried expression took hold of Eunice; she stammered and nearly dropped the tray. The cakes? Well, Mrs. Petty had said to put them in the garbage, as they'd come from a bad baker, someone who was a known though unconvicted purveyor of foods that could poison you.

No, the maids had not got rid of them. They'd thought, if they ate just a bit at a time, nothing dangerous would come of it; it was so seldom they had treats, and what with the snow-in and everything stopped, it wasn't so wicked of a thing. There was still a small jelly roll, half of a lemon pound cake, and some chocolate-fig tarts, all of which were in an oilskin bag and hanging out a window at the top of the house, quite frozen, which was the best way to preserve such things.

Charlotte asked for them to be fetched, and the little maid came back a few minutes later with just the tarts, wrapped in paper. Unfortunately for the rest of it, the cakes, there were two maids upstairs just now in the act of thawing them at the fire, and the edges were already quite nibbled at, as it was the birthday of one of them, so please, would Mrs. Heath mind terribly not forcing the taking away?

She smiled warmly at little Eunice. Her heart felt expansive and glowing.

The maid had aired out Charlotte's clothes. She was glad to be back in her own dress, with her hair brushed. She said nothing to the maid of her mysterious invitation, but only said she needed help with putting her hair up; the maid was good with hair and didn't pull too hard or make the knot too tight.

It clearly did not seem strange to Eunice that a lady of the hotel would want to fix herself up for an evening alone in her room. At a little after eight o'clock, nervously, with her pastries, Charlotte tip-toed out into the hall.

A muffled sound of laughter came from the room at the far end. From far below, as if coming up from a cave, she heard piano music, but this time it must have been that actual musician Harry Alcorn had mentioned: it was a slow, melancholy tune—not a funeral-like one, but just sad—with the kind of pausing between notes that made you think something lively would come next, but it didn't.

Which door of the four? Numbers 21, 22, 23, and 24 were in a row at her left as she cleared the top of the stairs; 21 was first, but she disliked that number because of a game—some card game, she never got them straight—that her husband played late at night in his room with his sisters and brothers-in-law. There were always Heaths turning up in his room. For the rest of her life, she felt, she'd recall the loneliness that struck her every time one of them cried out, "Twenty-one!"

Twenty-one was the number of points you had to score to win a hand. They never invited her to join them; she was sick.

So she knocked politely on 22. The door opened at once, and she stepped into an enormous room that was blazing with light: there must have been twenty gas lamps going, and candles along the three mantels, and three fires burning brightly; the windows didn't have curtains or shutters but were bare, except for a pair at the farthest end. The window glass was streaming with melting snow, and there seemed something very bright about the darkness on the other side, as if the night were festive and shiny.

Directly in front of her was a young man, barefoot, wearing nothing but a tight white jersey and a pair of loose white flannel trousers with the legs rolled up, as if he were walking on a beach.

He was not the same man as that night with Aunt Lily, and he was nowhere near as lovely, but still, he was fine-looking, about twenty, with the finest, best-shaped chest she'd ever seen on a male that was not a statue in a museum. Was he posing for a picture? To Charlotte's left was the painter herself, at a large canvas on an easel. A brush was in her hand. The color of paint on the brush was white.

"Hullo!" called out the man. His hands were on his hips; his head was cocked slightly to one side. "I'm Terence."

Maybe she'd already grown accustomed to the small, narrow room with the walls around her so closely. The man's voice seemed to echo, as if in a wide-open space. And it *was* wide open.

There was a screen set up at the other end: a lady's dressing screen, made of dark silk in a thin wood frame. That was where the windows were draped. That must have been the painter's sleeping area, which looked to be made up of one half of one room. All the rest of the place, the other three and a half rooms, was undivided.

Canvases were stacked everywhere against the walls, backs out. There was a long table filled with jars, brushes, tubes of paint, rags, and a round, dining-style table with four chairs; there were armchairs here and there, too, and a shiny maple wardrobe, and a pair of matching, high, many-drawer cabinets, but the walls were bare. So was the hardwood floor.

Suddenly someone darted toward Charlotte—the person who'd opened the door, she realized. She had a sense of a smallish, almost elflike person, in a bright green jacket that seemed misshapen at one shoulder.

It was another young man, and this one seemed to carry himself awkwardly, in a tilt. Charlotte felt her sympathies aroused instantly at the sight of him. He wasn't exactly a hunchback, as the deformity only seemed to be centered on one shoulder, but there was definitely a hump. He didn't appear to be bothered by it. Maybe he'd been born with it, instead of having had it grow in a glandular way. Maybe he was even proud of it; he didn't have that cringing, feel-sorry-for-me manner you saw sometimes in cripples.

His eyes were large, wonderful. Deep-brown eyes, as dark as the centers of a certain kind of daisy that grew wild in the fields back in town, her favorite flower, although no one would ever believe this was so, as the Heaths said daisies were common and childish.

Without a word, this hump man grabbed the little package of tarts right out of her hands, dashed off with it toward the nearest of the fireplaces, and threw it in. The paper caught fire at once, but the tarts sounded like rocks landing hard on the logs—had he known they were frozen? Was this his idea of a thaw? Was he a nasty little brute?

The man named Terence—who still, it seemed, was posing—did not alter his expression, and seemed to speak without moving his lips. "Don't mind Arthur. She can't have sugar. It affects her nerves the same way cocaine affects lesser mortals, not that I have experienced that glittering drug myself."

Arthur: his name was Arthur, like the king. The only not-Shakespeare play ever put on by Heaths at Town Hall was *The Story of the Round Table.*

Charlotte's father-in-law had played Arthur, but he had got it all wrong: he'd done it like a businessman conducting a meeting, all serious and overly controlled, as if the famous knights were only talking about which manufacturing plant to back, which real estate to buy next. Charlotte's mother-in-law was Queen Guinevere, and that was all wrong, too. The man who played Lancelot was Hays's oldest sister's husband, and she had not pulled off the way that, historically, the queen simply could not take her eyes off her lover, even though her husband was right beside her—and anyway she was too old for the part. There hadn't even been a romantic kiss, not even a theatrical suggestion of one. Hays's oldest sister kept saying, "This is all so filled with perversions."

This Arthur had the right sort of—well, dignity, Charlotte thought. Self-composure. Deep, intelligent eyes. Depths. Long, strong hands. A suggestion of complexities.

"Pym," he called out to Charlotte. He gave his head a little bow. "Arthur Pym."

And he undid the buttons of the green jacket, reached up inside, and removed what looked to be a very small cushion, a cushion for a tiny child's chair. He tossed it onto one of the armchairs; his back straightened up.

In the stories of the boy Arthur, which were taught at Miss Georgeson's—with a focus on the holy, pilgrimlike quest for the Grail—Arthur was always up to some prank. He was always using his smarts to get himself out of trouble.

But pretending to be a humpback wasn't pranklike. "I don't think that's funny," said Charlotte.

"I was terribly bored," he answered. "I thought she might like a troll for her garden. I thought I'd pose for her in that capacity. But you're right. I was an oaf. It's not my usual condition."

The painter said, in a strong, clear voice, "Damn you, Arthur, and damn you, too, Terence. Damn both your entire lives and well-being."

Charlotte looked at the picture. It seemed nearly complete. It was being done in oils—that was the overwhelming smell in here, she realized. She'd never been in a painter's studio before, but she did not find it unpleasant.

In spite of the posing young man, there was no young man in the painting. It was a garden scene, a still life—extremely still. There were raspberry and blackberry bushes, tall, spiky gladiolus and irises, plump begonias, delicate bluebells, and elegant, stately lilies. Every one of them—every bud, every stalk, every berry, every leaf—was covered with ice and frost, as if winter had stolen up on a beautiful summer day, and had seized what was vibrant and alive, and had encapsulated it all.

There was no yellow sunshine, but a moonish white glow instead. Some of the flowers were bent close to the ground under their ice coatings; some were more defiant, stronger, but you knew that, if that ice ever melted, which it showed no sign of being able to do, they'd collapse, extinguished.

The picture showed the same hand, the same stillness, the same tragic, nothing-is-ever-going-to-move-again rigidity as the pictures in Charlotte's room and in the room downstairs where she'd had her interview with Dickie. A boat, a wagon, a carriage, a field of wheat, it didn't matter what it was: all of it was utterly struck through with absolute motionlessness.

She had never seen anything so sad. "It's beautiful, like the others I've seen, but more so," said Charlotte.

"Ah, an expert," said the man called Terence.

Was he making fun of her? Was he teasing her because he knew, with some instinctive ability for judgment, some deft inner faculty that art people had, to use like a weapon against people who only went to places like Miss Georgeson's, and always felt so intimidated in galleries? And felt moved by a painting in a way that wasn't sophisticated, wasn't correct? The look of the ice made her want to cry.

"I am Berenice Singleton," the woman said. She held out her left hand, the one that wasn't holding a brush, and Charlotte went over to her and clasped it.

Berenice Eloise Singleton was somewhere around the age of fifty or sixty; it was hard to tell. Her hair was fully gray, done up in a perfectly shaped oval on top of her head. She wore spectacles with thin gold frames. Her face was as smooth as a child's, except for ribbon-like wrinkles around her mouth and at the sides of her eyes; her eyes were such a pale shade of blue, they looked as if they were colored with chalk. She wore a gray flannel smock, frayed at the edges and stained all over with paint. Under the smock was a light paisley housedress with the sleeves rolled up.

She had the thinnest arms Charlotte had ever seen on a grown-up. And her face was thin, too, in an unsettling way, as if you thought you were looking at her in profile. Her hand in Charlotte's was dry and cool, but not icy, not as if the blood weren't circulating properly. The fingers were not returning any pressure.

Because of the smock and the dress, it took a moment for Charlotte to realize that the chair she was sitting on was wheeled: it was the same wood as the beams, and the chair was made to look as if it belonged on a porch or in a yard, somewhere rustic. The two wheels were like a slightly thicker version of bicycle wheels, with rubber edging. The back of the chair had protruding smooth rounded handles.

"Thank you for inviting me, Miss Singleton," said Charlotte. The stillness of the woman, except for the hand that held the brush, could not be ignored. "I'm pleased to be here. You have polio."

It wasn't a question, and it didn't get an answer. Charlotte was looked at with reproach and she felt herself blushing—it was the same way Heaths looked at servants who did something stupid, like dropping things, or spilling ash on the carpets. God! How could she have blurted it out like that? They probably thought she was a— what did her mother-in-law call it, when talking about people on the other side of town? A yokel. A local yokel. It was written all over their faces that this was how they'd already sized her up.

"I think I had polio myself. That was why I mentioned it," Charlotte said. The woman touched the brush to the canvas and frowned at it. "Do you have paintings in museums and galleries?"

This seemed like the right question to ask a painter, but obviously it was not. The woman said, in a chilly, flat way, "Harry Alcorn takes most of them for himself." Charlotte couldn't tell if this was a good thing, or not.

"But at least you've got your good hand," said Charlotte.

"If the next thing you plan to say is to congratulate me on still having eyes in my head to see with, believe me, I lately have been wishing I did not."

"But then you wouldn't be able to paint."

"Precisely. If you've finished with discussing my condition, I must tell you, I'm most very disappointed about my sweets," said Miss Singleton. "What were they?"

"Tarts. But they were old." There was no sign of the promised tea.

"Stale," said Arthur Pym. "Hard as rocks."

"I'm very, very tired. Forgive me for what may seem impoliteness. I'm not in a mood for company after all."

And Miss Singleton gave the picture in front of her, with its glassy, glossy silence, a withering, disapproving glance. She placed the paintbrush on her lap, tipped back her head, closed her eyes, and seemed to fall asleep instantly. When the posing man broke the pose and stretched himself, he made as if to go and look at the picture, but changed his mind and dropped himself languidly into one of the armchairs.

Charlotte didn't know what to do. "Is she really asleep?" she whispered.

"Fast, and you don't need to modulate your voice, it won't wake her. Not even a tornado would, when she's like this. We were talking about the war, just before you came in," said Arthur Pym. "Terence reads politics at Harvard. Do sit down."

Charlotte went over to the table and sat down, as if tea would be served after all. "And do you also?"

"He's medicine," Terence put in. "If you really want to know why the hump, he's studying deformities." There was a liquidy casualness about this young man Terence: Charlotte found herself wondering what would happen at the household if he sat in a Heath armchair in this way, sideways, with his legs dangling over an arm. "Arthur the future wonder physician."

Charlotte feared that the subject would go at once to her aunt, so she thought of the Colonel back in town, the war. "I know a man who commanded a regiment," she said.

Arthur Pym remained standing by the fire. "Her husband, the late Commander Enright, was on the ship blown up in the harbor, the very explosion, of dubious cause, that started everything. He's said to be a hero. What was the name of that boat? It escapes me. For a state."

"The *Maine*." Terence waved an arm as if the air were incredibly heavy. "Poof. But don't let's start talking of Spanish mines and the Navy."

Charlotte had never heard about any blown-up ships; what harbor? She looked at the sleeping painter with a surge of sympathy. A widow! All those years ago, a husband killed in war. Thirty, thirty-five years as a widow. She was probably the same age as the Colonel.

"All those years, it must have been hard for her," said Charlotte.

"Well, it's only been two, actually, and she did take it rough," said Terence.

Arthur shuddered. "Don't please let's start talking about Rough Riders charging into Cuba."

"Then don't let's start talking about Spain," said Terence. "And don't please start talking about Mr. Roosevelt or my blood will boil and I will have to get up and go and lie down."

"I never said it wasn't hideous about suddenly being imperial and taking over Hawaii, and then going for poor old Cuba, and now Manila. Do you know how many soldiers have the yellow fever?" said Arthur.

Charlotte had the sense that they were talking another language. Spain, Hawaii, Cuba, Manila: what did any of those places have to do with the North and the South?

"The war with Spain is what we always end up talking about," said Terence, in a bored voice. It didn't seem his blood would boil at all; he seemed ready to launch into a speech he must have delivered before, and Charlotte said, "There was a war with Spain?"

Terence looked at her. "My dear woman, where have you been?"

"I thought you meant the one of the States."

"Two years ago, just. The war of 1898, with *Spain*. Cuba? And Manila? And heroic Teddy, our now-most-glorious vice president, warlording it up among the natives? In all the papers, headlines as big as your hand?" said Arthur helpfully, but Charlotte shook her head.

"I never picked up the habit of looking at news in the papers."

A light sound of snoring emanated from Miss Singleton.

"I want some rum," said Terence. "I feel we're in for a night of it, explaining things to this lady. Rum and perhaps something more interesting."

"A blank slate," said Arthur.

"Pure as snow."

"I don't want explaining!" said Charlotte. Her cheeks grew hot. She felt she'd been right; they were mocking her. Why should they be mocking her? Why was she up here anyway? It was as mad as an asylum.

She felt ready to burst into tears. And at the same time, it seemed that the stillness of the icy garden in the picture was pushing itself off the canvas, somehow, and getting inside her. She could almost understand why someone would have living, breathing models right in front of her and then paint a scene that was, in a way, the very opposite of those models.

It was as though she could peer into the painter's secret self. Miss Singleton must have wanted the models to inspire her, the same way a match would be struck. The flame of inspiration would then be put to use, and the painter was free to put on the canvas what she truly felt, and truly saw: a drama of something frozen. It must have been as powerful an inner thing as a storm. And she was a widow on top of it. No wonder she'd wish to be blind.

Well, thought Charlotte, that's polio. And the thought came to her that if she stayed any longer up here, she'd never move again.

She made it to the door, the one she'd come in. But she couldn't allow herself to sink to their level of bad behavior, so she turned and said, "Good night. I want to be back in my room. This was not what I expected. And I think it was nasty to put my tarts in the fire, when someone else could have had them."

Arthur Pym was beside her in the hall before she knew he'd followed her.

"Please," he said gently. "Let me go with you."

⚜ Seven ⚜

Y ou'd think that the one flight of stairs down to Charlotte's room was loaded with dangers, like a dark, unfamiliar road in the middle of the night, where robbers hid behind bushes, and all sorts of wild animals: that was how closely and protectively Arthur Pym stuck to her, although who was the protector of whom was hard to tell. She could no more get away from him than she'd be able to get away from her own shadow.

She didn't find this disturbing. She found it interesting.

Maybe he thought she was modest because she tried to keep her face turned away from him. She didn't want him to know that tears—silent ones; she was experienced at crying without a sound—were streaming down her face in exactly the same way as the melting snow on the windows, but she didn't feel that anything inside her was melting.

She felt a terrible, hard coldness. It reminded her of all those nights in her sickroom when she felt she'd do anything, she'd give up anything she had, for five minutes of cool relief from the fevers. She had called on God and all her doctors, in every way she could think of, to make her feel chilled and solid and hard.

Maybe this was what happened if you were religious. Charlotte's mother-in-law had an active, fervent, personal relationship with her own view of a Heavenly Father, an American-Protestant one, who was busy but dependable, and conducted earthly affairs, of course, like a businessman. She was always telling Charlotte how much she believed in the power of prayer, but she'd also point out the fact that something you asked for in prayer might not be granted immediately, but might take some time, like an overdue shipment of goods from a factory, delayed by a problem with a train, or the weather.

Charlotte envied her for her cleverness. Her mother-in-law was a woman who knew a few things about coping with disappointments. Maybe that was something that happened naturally to people who were born rich, very rich, and then married into a family even richer. If you prayed for something and didn't get it, you could call it a prayer God hadn't yet answered, not "I never get what I want when I need it."

And then you'd never feel sorry for yourself like a low-class senti-mental girl with no faith or backbone, crying like a child and never being able to learn skills of proper control, not that Charlotte's mother-in-law had ever put it quite exactly like that; she wouldn't have said "low-class" out loud.

Once at the household, in one of the back sitting rooms, a dark one, rarely used, Charlotte had come upon Hays alone, sitting by the window, doing nothing, just sitting there, in a gloomy way, which was something he never did. She'd already reached the point in her marriage where she accepted the fact that she would never be able to know what was in her husband's mind by simply looking at him. She'd once thought that married people could do this, naturally, as an abstract sort of marital bonus. She always had the sense that, if she asked Hays what he was thinking, he'd invent an answer which had nothing to do with an actual thing in his head.

Why was he so melancholy that day? She didn't know. She went over to the chair, hitched up her skirt, and climbed onto his lap, facing him.

She'd just simply felt like doing it. "Why, Charlotte, it's the middle of the day. This is a family room, it's not right." She put his hands on her breasts. His quick look of pleasure gave way in one second to pure horror. His mother was in the doorway.

You'd think they were naked, the way she reacted. Hays had pushed Charlotte off him, as if he'd never in his life touched her breasts. And his mother had said, "Charlotte, dismount him at once." *Dismount* him.

They never mentioned the incident, but afterward, almost every time her husband came near her "like a husband," as he put it, Charlotte had a nagging sense of feeling humiliated: it would seem that the desires of her body were things to be ashamed of. She wondered if other wives felt this way. There was no way to know.

Now and then in her sickroom she had wanted her husband to make love to her, even during the seven nightmarelike weeks when the paralysis of her legs was fully present. Hadn't Aunt Lily told her to do everything she could think of to inspire the muscles to unfreeze?

Maybe it would have been like that spark of inspiration Miss Singleton required to make a picture. Maybe the paralysis would not have lasted so long if she'd had the courage or the confidence to speak her mind.

"Close the door and make a child with me," she could have said. Instead of maids coming in to rub her with all kinds of liniments, four, five, six times a day. And she'd lie there imagining herself outdoors, on the back roads, in the woods, in the fields, with her hair down and blowing wildly behind her, riding her heart out.

"Making a child" was what he called it. Maybe he'd given up on her because making a baby hadn't worked. He liked things that worked; he couldn't help it, he was a Heath. "I've lost three," she'd remind herself, and another swell of shame and humiliation would rise up inside her. What was wrong with her? That was what everyone always wanted to know, even before she was sick.

She thought he would have turned crimson, blushed all over, at the idea of getting into the sickbed with her and making love to her. Making love to a paralyzed wife!

It sounded wicked. He would have thought it a sin of a huge indescribable magnitude. He might have compared her to one of those Old Testament women who had relations in tents with whole crowds of men-who-were-not-their-husbands. What was it that was said about such women in church? Unclean. "Unclean women." That was what her husband called it when it was her time of the month. "Are you unclean this week, Charlotte?" Was she supposed to feel her body was dirty and his was not?

Right now, all she was was cold.

She'd been right about the mysterious strength of that ice garden. It really had got inside her, so much so that as she stood outside her door beside Arthur Pym in his green jacket, with his deep-brown eyes upon her, she had the thought that if she ran back up to Miss Singleton's, she would find the canvas absolutely blank.

She looked at Arthur Pym. She didn't care after all if he knew about the tears. She almost said out loud, "My skin is like those leaves coated over with frost." If she did, or if she simply said, "I'm very cold, like it's coming from inside out," would he touch her, would he put his hands on her arms, her shoulders, her hair, the sides of her waist?

That would be preposterous. One didn't go around imagining a just-met man in the act of warming one's skin.

She opened her door without having made up her mind if she'd let him inside, or not. The tears on her face were the coldest-feeling tears she'd ever had. It felt that someone had taken up two icicles and pressed them against her cheeks, drawing on the tears, painterlike, frigid: they were so cold, they burned.

She felt that if Arthur Pym touched her, she would not be able to stand it, but would scream to drive him away, and she felt, at the same time, if he didn't touch her, at all, ever, she would never be happy again.

"You're crying," he said.

"I know."

The decision on whether or not to allow him in was made for her. There came rushing at Charlotte such a commotion, such a crowd—and it really seemed to be a crowd, in that tiny room—she nearly went backward, to go back into the hall, without fear of being knocked over. Mrs. Petty and her children were flinging themselves upon her, girl and boy and baby, who was dangling off one of Mrs. Petty's hips and grabbing air with her plump pink hands.

"Arthur Pym!" cried Mrs. Petty, looking over Charlotte's shoulder. "You go back upstairs! What is the matter with her? What have you done? What have you told her? Go away! Don't you come into this room! You leave this lady alone!"

Too late: he was already inside. He'd just slipped right in.

"Glorious to see you, as ever," he said. "Amazing what you do in the kitchen with things out of tins. You have a gift, and when I get around to having my own practice, I will want to hire you to come cook for me."

"Don't you speak to me!" cried Mrs. Petty.

"Here we are for a visit! Here we are for a visit! And so are you! And so are you!" screamed Sophy, whose words were repeated by Momo, louder.

"Hello, you angelic, well-behaved children," said Arthur, brightly; they ignored him. They attached themselves to Charlotte, one at each leg, and she leaned down and patted and kissed them, and patted and kissed the baby, and looked at the baby's new teeth, and a newly missing baby tooth of Momo's, and a new ribbon in Sophy's hair; she told them she had missed them, she had longed for them. Then, to their amazement, she said, "Let's have the visit tomorrow."

A hush fell over them. The children had never seen this version of her. They'd never even seen her out of her sickroom.

"There's no roads open into town, so you can't go home, and they can't get in here, but I've got a sleigh ready, to take you down Beacon Street to the doctor's rooms at her office," said Mrs. Petty.

"I promise," Charlotte said to the children. "Come tomorrow."

"They cannot," said Mrs. Petty.

"We can! We can!"

"Are you tired?" said Momo. He was a gentle, thoughtful boy; he'd grown at least two inches.

"Are you still sick?" said his sister.

"I'm tired, not sick."

Charlotte smiled at the wonderful, shiny Sophy, who saw her chance to take a deep breath and plunge into the many subjects she'd been saving.

"I don't like school. Everyone in it is horrible, and the teacher says I am going to go to hell, and so is Momo, and they say he's not to be called Momo because it isn't a proper name, so we told them his proper name was the same as his papa's, who was hanged for robbery and murder, so it's very bad luck. We said Momo is a magic word for good-luck spells, and it shouldn't be taken away. If it's taken away, he will die," Sophy said, and her brother nodded solemnly, and added, "Except that we haven't got a papa."

"No one was hanged!" cried Mrs. Petty.

"Tell me about it tomorrow," said Charlotte.

"We have to go to school."

"Afterward."

"Will you be here?"

"Yes."

"She will not!"

Mrs. Petty picked up Charlotte's coat and held it out to her. Charlotte hung it on the hook on the door. Arthur Pym picked up the poker and jabbed at some logs in the fire, causing sparks, which hadn't needed to be done as the fire was burning very nicely. He seemed to want to have something weaponlike in his hands, which, Charlotte felt, was not a good idea.

But he didn't raise it up like a sword in the direction of Mrs. Petty. "Mrs. Heath and I," he said pleasantly, "made each other's acquaintance just a few minutes ago, and I escorted her back to her room."

"And now you are leaving, Arthur."

"No, I invited him to sit and talk with me," said Charlotte.

"That poor woman upstairs in her chair! Her nurses can't get through to her!" Mrs. Petty shook all over; perhaps she could not believe that, once again, like the night Charlotte had arrived, she wasn't being listened to.

"Terence is with her, and the maid will be in," said Arthur calmly.

"Terence!" said Mrs. Petty.

"He and Mrs. Heath had an interesting conversation about politics."

"And what else?"

"Please," said Charlotte. She took hold of the doorknob. The door was wide open, and she placed herself beside it like a hostess at the end of a party, seeing off her guests.

"Why is your face all wet?" said Momo.

"Because I opened a window and snow went onto it."

"You'll have the polio all over again! Charlotte! You've gone mad!"

"Are you mad?" said Sophy.

"I promise you, there's nothing wrong with my brain." She reached out a hand to touch the baby again. "See you tomorrow, Edith."

"She doesn't understand what tomorrow is," said her brother.

"Well, that's when I'll see you. You don't always have to understand about things ahead of time."

Somehow Charlotte managed to herd them all out. Just down the hall, near the lamp, casting a hulking, overlarge shadow, was Moaxley, in that huge dark cloak. She waved to him as if she'd known him all her life.

"Things all right?"

"They most certainly are not," said Mrs. Petty, going past him.

"I was asking Mrs. Heath."

"Things are all right," said Charlotte. Sophy and Momo went charging down the stairs, as though stairs existed to make noise on. Maybe some of the ladies who were guests here, behind their closed doors—maybe many of them—were mothers, and didn't mind the racket.

She closed the door and shot the bolt. The maid had left a towel on the bureau by the washbowl, and Charlotte seized it and wiped her face as if she'd just washed it. Arthur Pym had sat down in the only chair.

No warmth was coming at her from the fire. The children hadn't warmed her—or perhaps they had, a little, and Mrs. Petty had undone it. Charlotte said, "I am so very, very . . ." Arthur looked up at her.

"Sad," she said. She'd wanted to say "cold." What, could she now not even trust her own voice?

He said, "Have you left your husband?"

"I have, and I wish everyone would stop asking me that."

"Left him forever?"

"I have no way of knowing that."

"Was he cruel to you?"

She paused. What was "cruel"? Her second-eldest sister-in-law was married to a man who once, in front of everyone, at the dinner table, in a fit of temper, annoyed by something she'd said, took hold of her hand; he was sitting beside her. She'd been reaching for a spoon, which she never got hold of. He squeezed her hand so hard, her face contorted with the effort not to cry; and then repulsively—cruelly—he let go, as if to say he was sorry; and then he gently ran his fingers up and down the finger on which she wore her wedding ring. Just when it looked like she was relaxing, and was ready to forgive him, and trust him again, he calmly squeezed the finger by the bones at the top, and bent it so hard, her hand looked like a fork with a bent-back tine when he let go. She rushed away from the table, but he did not, and the dinner went on. Charlotte's father-in-law said, "I won't have you being harsh with my daughter," and he said, "I apologize," and maybe no one was watching closely what had happened, except Charlotte, or maybe they pretended not to have seen it. She was taken into Boston the next day to see Aunt Lily, who put the finger into a splint. It had come out of its joint and was broken. She'd told Aunt Lily that a maid had accidentally slammed a door on it.

That was cruelty. And Charlotte knew—they all knew—it wasn't the first time, and it wasn't going to be the last. Hays never said a word about it. That was cruelty, too. She was his sister. What if Sophy, a grown-up Sophy, was the wife of a man who would strike her? Momo would go after the man. If a man broke one bone of his sister's, he'd want to break ten of the man's, or all of them.

Cruelty, Charlotte decided, was of a greater degree when you looked the other way while a cruel thing took place.

Hays had *looked the other way*. Being sick was a cruelty. But giving

up on her was like his brother-in-law sitting at the table and bending
a woman's finger right out of its joint.

"I don't wish to talk about my husband," she said to Arthur Pym.

"Then your silence answers my question."

She sat down on the edge of the bed. The tears had stopped. She
had the idea she couldn't possibly feel worse than she did; what did
she have to lose by speaking her mind to this man?

"Would you like a glass of brandy or sherry?" he said. "It would
take me just a minute to go downstairs and bring up a bottle."

"I don't want spirits. I want to have a clear mind."

"Then so do I."

It was odd, she thought, that when you're ready to say out loud
what you already know inside yourself, inarticulately, the words just
manage to present themselves. She leaned forward and, as she did, he
pulled the chair closer, so that their knees were nearly touching.

Charlotte said, in almost a whisper, "Tell me what goes on in this
hotel, please, Mr. Pym."

"I would imagine you have a fairly good idea by now," he
answered. "It's not everyone who has the chance of an interview
with a policeman."

"Are you the student you claimed to be, upstairs?"

"I am."

"Are you planning to have a practice, as you said to Mrs. Petty?"

"If it weren't for this snow, I would be watching a tutor of mine,
out in a town to the west, perform a dissection on a . . ." His voice
trailed off.

"Mr. Pym, I don't require censoring. I was nearly a year in a
sickbed." She looked at his expression carefully, then said, with a
sigh, "You know my aunt."

"I do."

"I suppose she told you of my condition."

"The night you arrived."

"Then you must know medical information doesn't alarm me."

He said, "All right, a dissection on a man who drowned in a bog, so his body is remarkably well-preserved. I should have left early this morning. I'm hoping they've waited for me, and I will try to make it out there as soon as possible."

"What town?"

"Halfway between here and the Berkshire Mountains. My tutor is one of the founders of a hospital for people who don't, as a regular rule, have faith in doctors or the means to afford one."

"There are lots of towns between here and the mountains. Cranfield, Morton Falls, Bigelow Mills Village," said Charlotte. "Chetterdon, Oakville, Blackstone, North Blackstone, Blackstone Junction. Fairfield, Derby River, East Derby. Foxbridge, Allenburg, Wachusetts, Forge Landing."

"Oakville," he said. "You know the area."

"I used to."

"Tell me about where you come from."

"I never talk about that subject, if you don't mind. I had asked if you're planning on a practice."

"If I don't succeed, it will only be because I've died."

"Are you planning to be dead?"

"Not for a very long time. And yourself?"

"I would think it's a subject one would avoid. It makes people so very nervous."

"But not you."

"No."

"But you would talk of an idea of death, and avoid the subject of your past."

"Only because it's past, and the other has been closer to me."

"I would say you are very much alive, Mrs. Heath."

She felt herself blushing. No one had said that to her for a long, long time. After a moment, she said, "Are you often in this hotel?"

"Now and then."

"Are you employed by Mr. Alcorn?"

"I am."

"There was a man in this room with my aunt. Do you know him?"

He nodded. "Martin Wallace. He left the hotel that same night."

"You say that as if I would hope he were somewhere nearby, Mr. Pym."

"No, I said it because Wallace, as it happens, is one of my tutors."

"The man doing the body?"

"No. Wallace is in mathematics. It's my weak point."

"He doesn't look the part."

"No, I suppose not. Do I?"

"That depends which part you end up having. And Terence?"

"There are actually quite a few of us."

"I would imagine your college bills are steep, Mr. Pym."

"They are, for those of us who weren't born to, shall I say, certain families. But you'd be surprised how one's debts can build up."

"By certain families you mean, such as Heaths," said Charlotte. "I was not born a Heath."

"Neither was I."

"Does Mr. Alcorn pay you or does someone else?"

"Harry does."

"Are you well paid, or would it be indelicate of me to ask?"

"Delicacy is a matter of snobbery. Let's not be snobs, Mrs. Heath. Harry is generous with his staff. I don't suppose you made yourself familiar with the cost of one of these rooms."

"Is that something I would need to have explained, like the Spanish war? Or, perhaps, the Vice Society?"

"No need," he said. "Do you look at me and think of that word?"

"War?"

"Vice."

"I look at you and think, Mr. Pym, I didn't like being upstairs at Miss Singleton's and made sport of."

"There was no sport in it. I swear."

"When you said you would come down to my room with me, had you looked at me as a . . . as a . . . ?" She didn't know what to call it. What should one call it? A customer, like someone going into a shop? A customer of a man earning money in a very private way in a very private hotel? A *customer*?

"I looked at you as I look at you now. As a woman I do not want to walk away from, unless you insist on it, and then I would only do so under protest."

"What kind of protest?"

"I don't know. I'm sure I would think of something. I would like to stay here with you tonight, Mrs. Heath."

"Then what about Miss Singleton?"

"She lives here."

"I should like to have that painting," said Charlotte. "Does she sell them?"

"She would give it to you. She would enjoy being asked. You liked it?"

"It made me want to cry."

"All that ice."

"Yes."

"You would know what it means to be frozen. Am I right?"

"Do you ask me that as someone learning medicine, or as a person?"

"Actually, both." He looked at her for what felt like a long, long moment. She didn't mind the way her eyes met his. I would like to stay here with you tonight. He'd actually said that. Had he, actually? He had. He really had.

And he'd said the room was expensive. She thought, in a practi-cal way, because she couldn't turn off the part of herself that was practical, not entirely, I only have fifty dollars, and no hope of getting more.

She said, "I don't have access to my banking account, not at the present."

"That could just as well have gone unsaid."

"I think not."

"This room," he said, "was taken by your aunt for the week, and there are still two days left to it. And I would imagine, for good reason, Harry would not be inclined to present you with a bill, however long you want to stay here. You have, shall we say, a fairly strong personal credit, with him."

"You mean I've put him in my debt."

"Yes."

"Is my aunt here often?"

"Now and then."

"What if she returns?" gasped Charlotte.

"The door," he said, "is bolted."

She tried hard to think of more questions. "Are all the young men who work here, as you do, students?"

"Some of us. Not quite half, I suppose."

"I don't suppose Harvard would be happy to know of your . . . your job. Yours and the others."

"Oh, we're not all Harvard. But you know, it's common to go out to earn some pay—for example, in a restaurant or hotel, as a waiter. Fellows do it all the time. And they're assistants in hospital wards, and on the trolleys, and all sorts of things."

"But you didn't choose a hospital ward."

"I imagine I'll have my fill of them soon enough."

"Are you said to be a waiter?"

"A second assistant cook, actually."

"And would you tell me the—ah, inner workings of this hotel are private, very private, to the extent that, one is able to maintain secrecy?"

"We're careful, Mrs. Heath. The ladies who are guests here would be willing to go to a great deal of trouble to keep things as they are."

"Perhaps you should have come and told that to the police inspector."

"His visit was unusual."

"But another one could return."

"And he'll leave in the same state of ignorance."

"Can you cook, Mr. Pym?"

"Not a bit."

"Doesn't your, ah, job, interfere with your studies?"

"I've fallen asleep in lectures."

"And have you been working for Mr. Alcorn the entire time you've been a student?"

"Only this year."

"Hamlet was a student."

"Yes. The energetic, well-adjusted Hamlet, prince of action and joy."

"You are mocking me. Again."

"I am not. I prefer," he said, "as a man, Othello."

Charlotte didn't know who that was. She hadn't got to that play yet. She didn't want to admit this. She said, "Because you are a man, or because Othello is?"

"Both. And because he has the bad luck to have trusted the wrong person. And he does not believe that a woman could love him as honestly as his wife. He just can't get that into his head, that someone loved him, his own wife, who has one of the kindest, gentlest natures ever put into a heroine. And his clever enemy, you know, whom he loved as a friend, turns him against her, and he murders her. That, Mrs. Heath, is what I would call vice."

"Oh!" said Charlotte. "So would I!"

She couldn't think of anything else to say. But just when her eyes were perfectly dry, just when she thought she was past the point of tears, here they were again, and this time there was no chance of being completely quiet about it.

She didn't try to hide it; you can't hide crying when it's coming out uncontrollably, as water pours from a broken dam. It felt good. A dam had been in her, and it was broken. At least this time the tears were not quite so icy.

Cool, but not ice. Cool tears, almost at the point of being warmer. She thought, Maybe I am melting, after all.

She sat there and tears poured down her face. Her neck and the high collar of her dress were getting all wet. He didn't seem to be worried. Was this *normal*? Was this *all right*?

He said, "May I take off my jacket?"

"I don't mind."

This was all right. Through her sobs and sniffling, she asked him to please pass her the towel; she'd put it back on the bureau. She meant to cover her face and weep into it, with whatever tears were left, and then she'd try to do a little mopping up of herself. She closed her eyes and held out her hand to take it from him, but then she realized that it wasn't a towel he pressed against her cheeks. "Here," he said. It was his own two hands. Warm.

∽ Eight ∽

Arthur Pym's mother, Florence, was a schoolteacher, the type of teacher who was born that way and never gave a thought to doing anything else. This was in Hartford, Connecticut.

Florence, explained Arthur, had come to America as a teenager, from an industrial town somewhere in the north of England. She never lost her very British accent, and never had wanted to. She taught her first class when she was eighteen. She married at twenty, had Arthur the following year, and by the time he was finished with his primary grades she was not only a headmistress, but a consultant to some ten other schools on issues of curriculum and classroom protocol; she taught a class at a teachers' college, and wrote papers on educational reform, and spoke at meetings, and was never, ever at home, except Sundays, when the house had to be silent so she could sleep, which she did, nearly all the day.

As a mother she was a failure, but at least she was honest about it. "As a mother, I've no hope of being up to snuff. I'll simply have to trust that you're like me, and you'll sooner or later be an adult who's utterly, absolutely, in your case, Arthur, himself."

Arthur never wondered if she loved him or even cared about him. She loved him. She cared about him. There was always food on the table, his clothes were always washed, his needs attended to. The family had a live-out housekeeper—a Mrs. Briggs from down the road, who also was English—and a housemaid and a washerwoman, and a cleaning maid. Their house was a comfortable one, two stories, good clapboard, solid, on a quiet, wide, leafy street. There were dogs, cats. He was provided with books whenever he asked for them, which was often, although his parents themselves weren't readers. There were plenty of children in the neighborhood to play with, and they regularly took him home with them when he wanted company besides servants. He was healthy and thriving, like a weed: a weed with no interest in trying to become, say, a proper flower.

His father, Ralph, was Hartford-born. He had managed a small men's clothing store, which never did well, and he minded the pressures and responsibilities. When he was approached by that giant Midwestern supply house, Sears, Roebuck & Company, and was invited to become one of their eastern agents, he was pleased to give up the store. He welcomed the regular salary. He was not a tall or heavy-boned man, but he'd always been mightily prone to excessive amounts of weight, which he tried to compensate for by walking wherever he went; he wasn't comfortable with horses and carriages anyway.

Ralph Pym opened a Sears, Roebuck office in central Hartford, and it was much more successful than anyone expected. People from all over Connecticut, and parts of New York and Rhode Island, and southern Massachusetts, used the office as a middleman-communication device, between their own desires for the cheaper

goods from a catalog, and their suspicions of long-distance negotia-
tions, as it was hard to trust what was, to New Englanders, a foreign
power. People in the rural towns and on isolated farms had their
orders shipped to Ralph: he would bulk individual orders into
groups to cut the cost of shipping, and when you came to Hartford
to pick up your goods, it felt friendly and pleasant. Ralph was a
sociable man. He hired commission-based representatives to stir up
more sales; he had his own phones and telegraph system; he made
deep, lasting friendships with the people who handled the mail and
the delivery system of the trains. He joined a downtown club of
Hartford businessmen, which had a building across from the office.
He had most of his meals there—lavish many-course affairs. There
was morning tea in the office, furnished by a shop next door, and
afternoon sherry and cakes. He grew fatter and wider.

His life was conducted like a clock. He worshiped routine. He
went around in his weekday schedule from home to the office to the
club, and on Sundays, while his wife shut herself up in an isolated
cocoon of rest, he either spent the whole day at the club, or shut himself up in a cocoon of his own in the front parlor, drinking brandy
and being called on by his friends from downtown who wanted to
escape from their families, as if the parlor were an extension of the
club.

Into this format a child did not fit. Ralph was indulgent of his son
and never refused him anything, but he would always seem amazingly distant, in an unfocused, baffling way. He lacked, Arthur felt,
a basic capacity to understand the first thing of being aware of other
people with whom he was not performing his job; and in a personal
way, his entire universe began and ended with his own self, and
especially with the requirements of his girth. He would become anxious of what his next meal would be before he'd finished the one he
was having. His body became a demanding machine that needed

constant attention, and if he hadn't been a very plump man when he married Florence, it would have seemed to his son that his obesity could be squarely placed on Florence's shoulders, for neglecting him, in every way.

But somehow they seemed suited to each other, especially as neither one of them was interested in any sort of intimacy. They had it in common that they were consumed by their professions and wished to be left alone. It was not an unhappy household. Arthur never bothered to ask himself if his father liked or disliked him. It would have been like asking the question of the grandfather clock in the front hall.

It seemed that life would always go on the way it was. Arthur started thinking about college when he was very young; when he was still in primary school his mother told him that she wanted to know, before his tenth birthday, what profession he'd choose, because she felt that this was something one ought to know as soon as possible. Early on the morning of his last day as a nine-year-old he got hold of his mother as she was cramming books and papers into a satchel, preparing to rush out for a day's work. He asked her for some help on his decision and she said, "How would I know?" He pressed, and she finally advised him to think of the one person whose work he admired beyond all others; then he should set about emulating that person.

She knew he wouldn't pick Sears, Roebuck, but she had probably expected him to pick her, to pick "education." She seemed a little disappointed the next day when he told her he wanted to be like the elderly Mr. Gudjohnson, two streets over, who had a medical practice in the bottom half of his house. Arthur was playmates with children in the family next door to the doctor, and though he rarely saw the doctor himself, except when he was hurrying off to some childbirth or sickbed or death, he had observed that of the many people who went into his office every day, there were people who actually looked better, walking away, than they had looked when they arrived on his doorstep. "My son, a physician," Florence said gamely, trying it out. She felt it was a pretty good second choice. She felt it was understandable. She felt he had the independence for doctoring, the self-confidence, the stamina, and the smarts, all inherited from herself, plus his father's dependable, highly developed social skills.

She bought him books on physiology and chemistry and a wooden model of a human skeleton with all the bones labeled. His father was very pleased and said, "I suppose my poor ticker might give me trouble around the time you open a practice, so count me your first patient, Son."

Arthur felt he had no problems. Then one night, around midnight, when he was thirteen, his father and mother came into his room and woke him. His father was in his nightshirt, but his mother was fully dressed, and she was wearing her coat. The fact that they were both in his room, together, at the same time—or any room at all, for that matter—was so extraordinary, it almost seemed an anticlimax when he learned why.

His father said, "Arthur, your mother is going to go away, not because she wants to, but because she feels she has no choice, and it is very, very likely that she will never come back."

"It's true," said his mother.

"What about me?" he had asked.

"Up to you, Son," said his father.

Arthur had spent the day, a Sunday, outside the city with a school friend whose father studied geology: they'd gone out to a quarry, and it had involved a great deal of climbing. He was exhausted. And at nine in the morning he was scheduled for a grilling from his Latin teacher on Caesar, which he had not read as thoroughly as he should have; he was not a natural at translations, and thought Caesar's *Gallic War* was the most dreadful, boring thing ever put on paper, in any language. He was planning to cram at breakfast.

So at the single most important event in his life so far—perhaps in the whole of his life—he rolled over and went soundly, deeply back to sleep.

"Mother walked out of our lives that night, and then everything fell to pieces, more or less," said Arthur, like this was the end of the story.

"It wasn't your fault," said Charlotte.

Arthur was sitting beside her in her bed. There was only one pillow, and they had placed it between them at the small of their backs. Arthur leaned his head against the headboard with his chin pointed up, and Charlotte touched a finger at a tiny cleft there, tracing a line from it down his throat and down his chest, stopping about halfway and pressing lightly. "What's this?"

"Sternum," he said.

He had taken his shirt off, and his trousers, too, and his stockings, but not his drawers, which were winter underwear, wool, dark blue. His chest was downy with light brown hair, all tufted and curly. It was a narrower chest than her husband's, and paler. She liked it. Hays was starting to have a rounded little indication of an extra bulge around his middle, not that she'd seen him, for over a year, with any of his clothes off. She had taken off her stockings and vest. Her hair was down. All the blankets were on them, to their waists. The fire was out. There were no more logs.

"Are you cold, Charlotte?"

"No."

"I was thinking I could bust up the chair and we could burn it."

"I don't think Harry would appreciate that."

"Then I won't."

"Are you tired now?" she said.

"No."

"Neither am I." It was somewhere between the darkest part of the night and the moment when the first gray sheen of wintry dawn begins appearing.

She leaned her head on his shoulder. It was thin, on the bony side, but she found a softer spot just below it. She had never been in a bed for a whole night with a man before. Hays didn't believe in a man and woman sleeping side by side.

Falling asleep after making love was acceptable, but he'd always wake up and pad softly away to his own bed. They always made love in Charlotte's bed. He insisted on it. Their separate rooms were side by side with connecting inner doors, without locks. Separating their rooms was his dressing room and his private washroom, each of which had doors, and he kept them closed. To get to his wife's bed from his, he had to open three doors.

Her own washroom and dressing room were on the other side and ended at an outer wall; they could only be entered through her bedroom. Hays's rooms all had doors to the hall, to the rest of the house.

"I had to go through three doors to reach you," he would say to her solemnly, as if he'd crossed a desert in burning sunlight, without water.

"Honestly, I feel that I just crossed a desert to be with you, Charlotte," he'd say, which was his way of telling her he wanted to make love to her as much as he'd want a drink of water. Sometimes he'd check with her secretly, at dinner, to see if a visit was a good idea. "Would you mind if I was very thirsty tonight?"

That was his way of asking her, first, if it was her time of the month, and second, what her mood was. If she said, "I wouldn't mind," it meant she was *clean,* and if she added, "Please don't take a long time along the way," it meant she was inclined to be in an excellent mood indeed.

For all three times she'd been pregnant, he never came in. He'd felt her body was as sacred as a shrine.

Once, in Italy, Hays had gone to a chapel in a giant cathedral which had a life-size statue of some saint, a woman, and there were two workmen in there, doing something with trowels and clay, repairing something; they were sweaty and filthy and they had stripped to their undershirts. One of them had thrown his dirty jacket on the statue's head. One arm of the statue was held outward and a workman's lunch bucket, empty, had been hung on the hand. Cheese rinds were on the floor. An empty bottle of wine was on its side by the statue's feet, and the workmen were humming the tune of a peasant song from Naples that described—well, Hays's knowledge of dialect wasn't good, but it described unspeakable things a man with an olive grove wanted to do to the wife of his overseer.

In other words, he'd gone into the chapel to be close to something sacred and it was rendered disgusting, although it hadn't sounded disgusting to Charlotte; anyway, Hays wasn't a Catholic.

"They were only doing their jobs," she pointed out, but he felt very strongly that you just don't do unsacred things in a church.

Her pregnant body was a church? She didn't feel holy when she was pregnant. She felt sick all the time, and kept vomiting, every morning.

Each time she'd failed to stay with child, he stayed away a little longer. First a month, then five weeks, then six or seven. It began to be a way for her of counting the passing of time, as if time were a vast, dark, wide-open space, in the outer reaches of things, where there weren't even any planets or stars, just space; all the nights she was alone were like that. And that was before she'd got sick and was set up downstairs.

Maybe he never should have married—not just he shouldn't have married her, but he never should have married at all. He loved the company of his family, although he denied it when she said so. Maybe it was because, as the youngest, and as the one who turned out to be, objectively, the best off, in terms of how much money he made and how successful his career was, it was important to him to be able to have, at last, the upper hand: his brothers and sisters had treated him for so long as a baby, as a toy, as an underdog, as a much-abused pet, as the receiver of all their roughhousing. He had a hundred ways of describing how horrible they'd been to him. If she never bore children, the bulk of his estate would eventually go to his eldest nephew.

He didn't want that to happen. His eldest nephew was not particularly bright, but he was a promising enough boy, and he'd probably take up with the lawyer branch, not the business one, which, Hays felt, would be a tragedy. "What if I were to die without a son, Charlotte?" he'd say. "How would I be able to stand it?"

He didn't talk like this when they were first married, but who ever thinks in their first few years, with visions of pink, smiling infant faces, and parties and holidays and raptures of affection, they'll go a decade with just one bad thing happening after another?

For Hays, not having a child was like living in a deep hole that someone else had dug for him.

That someone would be her.

Funny that she should be sitting here with Arthur Pym—with his clothes off!—with the story of his mother and father in her head, and feeling a little bit sorry for Hays. She couldn't help it. Maybe it was because, not counting professions, body size, personality, temperament, education, income, and background, Hays was a bit like Arthur Pym's father.

Sometimes when she'd settled into bed, she'd hear the door handle of his dressing room turning, clicking open, and just when her body began to tense up, as if she'd been lightly tickled on bare skin, it would be closed, very quickly. The handle would click shut, and she would hear through the walls the muffled voices of whatever Heath, or whichever group of them, had felt like calling on him, after hours. He had one of the biggest bedrooms in the house. He had a card table, lots of chairs, and a cabinet full of brandies and wine, and multiple copies of plays in case it was Town Hall Theatricals time and someone needed to practice lines. It was just like a club in there.

Charlotte said, "It would be all right if you kissed me, Arthur," and he did, brushing her lips like a tickle. Then a long, long kiss. He had a nice mouth.

At the end of the kiss she said, "I feel like Juliet Capulet."

"Juliet Capulet when?"

"When she was in, you know, her bed, with her brand-new lover, and she didn't want the morning birds to be singing. She wanted it to be night birds. She wanted night to go on forever."

"But Juliet wasn't in her bed that night simply talking and kissing."

"I wasn't being literal. I was only telling you something I'd felt."

"Then that would make me Romeo."

"Not exactly. You're much more sensible. Romeo could never have been a doctor. He probably never could have had any profession at all. Or maybe he'd be a poet."

"Making love to Juliet would be a profession, I would think. I wouldn't think his poetry would be any good."

"No one will know. All that happened to him was that he died. And so did she."

"Charlotte," Arthur said, adjusting himself, and putting an arm around her, "do you think we could have a moratorium on mentioning *die*?"

"I want to know the rest about your mother. Tell me what happened after she said she was going away and you only worried about yourself and went right back to sleep."

"I never saw her again. My father went about in his usual way for a couple of months, and so did I. As odd as it sounds, we carried on. I suppose we were expecting every day she'd turn up again. I didn't ask him any questions, not because I didn't want to, but because I knew my father, and he didn't talk to me. The servants looked after us. Of course there was plenty of talk. Everyone knew she'd left, and I suppose there must have been all sorts of speculations. I had them myself, with my limited awareness of the world. Did she have a lover? Was she somewhere having an illegitimate child? Had she committed a crime? Had she done something disastrous profession-ally? I'd go around like an eavesdropper trying to pick up signals. But I never picked up anything. If there were people who knew where she was and why—and there must have been, as she had many good friends in the schools and the college—they were keep-ing quiet about it. My father started—oh, deteriorating. He'd have an extra glass of brandy on a Sunday, then every night, extra glasses. He couldn't concentrate. He was let go by Sears, Roebuck about a year after she'd left, and he never went to his club again, or anywhere in the city at all. He'd been right about his heart making trouble for him. He died in a Hartford hospital when I was fifteen. After he was buried, a man I'd never seen before came to the house one day and gave me a slip of paper with an address on it. He told me that if I wanted my mother, I must write to the address, with no indication of my identity on the envelope, and I must leave the envelope blank. I should wait some two or three weeks, and a message would be sent to me from her, telling me where I could go to see her, which I would have to do in some sort of disguise. And I should tell no one, absolutely no one."

"If you're going to tell me you never went to see her, I will put up my hair, and I will put my stockings back on, and I will ask you to leave this room, Arthur."

"I almost didn't try to go. I was mad at her, you see. I didn't even know what country she was in, and I often drove myself wild think-ing she'd gone home to England, or she'd gone to God knew what place. She'd been connected with teachers who went off starting schools in Africa, all over the place, South America, everywhere, and on those days when I wasn't busy judging her with some heinous thing, I thought of her in a saintly, heroic way, giving up everything to go teach natives somewhere how to read."

"Is that the truth?"

"Yes. It was arranged that I would take a train to New York. The Hartford station was a long walk from the house, and I asked a friend of mine to drive me there in his buggy." He paused. "My friend's name was Paul. He was like a brother to me. We'd been growing up together all along. I did something I never should have, I told him everything. It had never occurred to me not to trust him with my very life."

"What did he do!"

"He took me to the station. We said goodbye outside. The train was leaving in a couple of minutes. I was just about to step onto it when I was grabbed from behind by two very large men, who told me they had pistols, and they were going with me to meet my mother, and if I didn't cooperate, I would be—well, hurt very badly. I think we were to travel all together like a nephew with his two uncles, very cozy."

"Oh!" said Charlotte.

Her body was tense. Part of her was thinking—because she wanted so very much to put up some new sort of dam or line of defense against sadness, against sorrow, against all the rotten things that kept happening, all the stories of all the rotten things—"I wish I never asked him to tell me about his past." She'd mostly done so because she'd got in the habit of never, absolutely never, saying anything about her own. And she'd actually wanted to know things about Arthur Pym. Things such as, everything.

And part of her was thinking, Worse things have happened to him than to me.

"Arthur! What happened?" she said.

"I'm not sure. Do you believe in God?"

No one had ever asked her that question, not even at Miss Georgeson's, where it was assumed that a stern and fatherly God was as present in life as air. "I've tried, especially when I could have used some help, but if you really want to know, I never had any reason to think that all those stories in the Bible had an actual basis in anything real," she said.

"I agree," he said. "But somehow I was able to get away from those two men before we got onto the train. Something must have distracted them, I don't know. I was small for my age and I was nimble. I saw an opening and, without thinking or being afraid, I dodged them, and went running off the platform and out of the station. My friend of course had already gone. I hid for a few hours in a stable near the station. I didn't think it was safe to go home, so I went to the doctor's house, Mr. Gudjohnson's. He didn't know me except as a neighbor child, but I had estimated that a doctor is someone accustomed to taking people in, whether they like it or not. In just a couple of minutes with him, I realized that whatever had happened with my mother, and wherever she was, he knew, not that he was telling me anything. He seemed to have been waiting, in a way, for my appearance, and I believe my mother must have told him about my choice of profession and his part in it. He was kind to me. He wasn't a trained medical man, but he'd been a medic in the war, in the—uh, States War. It was he who arranged for me to go to Cambridge, to Harvard."

"But the two men," said Charlotte. "With the pistols."

"I don't know. I wrote once more to the address I'd been given, and this time I put in a note saying, 'Dear Mother, I cannot come to you because I am being followed and I believe someone would want to harm you.' "

"But who were they?"

"I don't know. They looked ordinary enough. Big, but ordinary."

"What did you do about your friend who betrayed you?"

There wasn't an answer for a long moment. Then he said, "I haven't taken care of that yet."

"Where is he?"

"In the army. He is an officer."

"What are you going to do to him, Arthur?"

"I would rather," he said, "not talk about that."

"Othello," said Charlotte.

"Perhaps."

"So it's all a mystery?"

"There's more. I went to a lawyer friend of Mr. Gudjohnson's to sell my parents' house and take charge of their finances. I had expected at least to have one bright spot in my otherwise dreary situation, the bright spot of having some money. But my parents' estates had been seized. My father had left no will, and as it was not determined if my mother was dead or alive, the bank said that nothing could happen. It was all very shady, very sinister. Then the lawyer explained to me that my parents in fact had sold the house already, to whom, I wasn't able to know. There were masses of papers, documents. All forged, but I was a minor, and had no way of proving it. I believe the house is still sitting there, empty. I've never gone back to Hartford. In my first year in Cambridge, I met a fellow who's the son of a private detective with Pinkerton's. He told me if I came up with the cash, it would be possible for me to hire someone to help take care of the—as you put it—mystery."

"I know a detective," said Charlotte.

"Ah, the man sent by the Vice people."

"We were school friends, in a way."

"In your mysterious towns between here and the mountains."

"I could ask him to help you."

"I don't need," said Arthur, "a Boston man. Pinkerton's is a widespread agency."

"Is it horribly expensive?"

"Not horribly."

"Is that one of the things you meant when you talked about how one's debts can mount up?"

"Yes."

"Oh!" said Charlotte.

Then she said, "Can I ask you a question, not connected to what you've just told me? A delicate one?"

"We said we wouldn't be delicate."

"Did you ever father a child?"

"No," he said. "When you've been with your husband, did he ever, Charlotte, use a sheath?"

She didn't even pretend to know what he was talking about. "On the man," he said. "So that the stuff to conceive doesn't go where it wanted to go."

"It goes into the sheath?"

"It does."

Amazing! And she suddenly lifted her head and moved away from him, bristling. A terrible thought had come to her.

Was this part of the—ah, routine? Did Harry Alcorn's staff—the young men like Arthur—do this sort of thing as a type of *seduction,* as a spider would lure an unwary bug? She wasn't calling herself "unwary" but still, had he been sitting there all along just playing on her sympathies, which were fully, actively aroused?

Who could fail to be melted like butter at such a tale? He could have invented it anyway, he was clever enough; it might have been part of the scheme. "I work here because I want to hire a private detective to find my mother." He'd just about said so. He might have told a different story about his mother and father every time he . . .

Charlotte didn't want to think about the "every time he" part.

"I'm cold," he said.

"Pull up the blankets," she said.

"Come closer to me."

She looked at him. Later on, she thought, when she figured out how to get hold of her bank account, she could hire a Pinkerton detective herself and order an investigation. And while she was at it she might also have her husband investigated. "Who is the woman with whom he is having a liaison?" she'd ask. Something like that. Was there a Florence Pym of Hartford who vanished, twelve or thirteen years ago, with a husband who had died? People were always hiring private detectives for things like that.

The possibilities of her own future suddenly opened up. What an astonishing thing that was, a future.

"Charlotte? Come closer to me."

And she did. How she got out of her dress while in bed, she didn't know; she'd never undressed this way before. It just seemed to come away of its own accord, although Arthur was helping.

Her underblouse slipped right off her. "You wear no corset!" he said, and she felt proud of herself for that, like it was one less thing to be removed, like that was really the reason, all along, she had stopped wearing corsets.

She said, "Are you going to take off your drawers?"

"Do you want me to?"

"I do. May I touch you—there?"

"In what way?"

What did he mean, what way? "With my hands," she said.

"You need to ask?"

She had never put her hands on a man's private parts before. Hays would never allow it, not even when she said, "Oh, just for one second, just to know what it feels like, because I'm so curious."

One of the Irish maids had told her that it felt like a sort of sausage, and sort of like the precooked neck of a turkey—well, she hadn't said so directly to Charlotte, but Charlotte was always eavesdropping on the maids. That was the only time she'd ever heard anyone say anything about it. She wanted to know what it felt like soft, and what it felt like hard. Arthur's was hard, but it would be soft later on; she didn't mind waiting, although she would have preferred soft first.

"Charlotte, have you ever touched a man before?"

She shook her head. She said, "Why did you ask me, in what way?"

"You could have meant your lips."

"My *lips*?"

"And your mouth."

"My *mouth*?"

"And I you."

Incredible! It was just like the night she'd arrived, when the wall in the front hall gave way, and then the floor, and everything went dark and she didn't know what was happening. But now nothing was going all dark. Somewhere in the sky the sun was starting to rise. Gray light was creeping in. It was a wonderful, beautiful dawn, in spite of being wintry-shadowy.

She knew exactly what was happening to her. She had never seen a sunrise look so good.

∞ Nine ∞

The water was running in the pipes again and Charlotte didn't care that it was only coming in trickles. She was going to wash her hair.

The big washroom had a brand-new coal stove and it was thrumming with heat. An iron kettle on top of it was heating extra water; two large pots of water were already on the floor beside the stove, sitting nicely at a lukewarm temperature for her rinsing.

The walls and window were steamy, glistening. The plug was in the drain and the tub contained a luxury height of warmed water, waiting for her. The rug on the floor was an oval of fleecy sheepskin. Charlotte had nothing on except the white cotton shirt Arthur Pym had been wearing, long ago last evening. It covered her to her thighs.

On a little white table were a bottle of Pears' Hair Soap, a box of talcum powder, some fluffy white powder puffs, a set of combs in different sizes, and four jars in four shades of pink, filled with lotions. The little maid had left to get some towels.

Out in the streets things were moving again—slowly, but things were moving. The storm had dumped some fourteen, fifteen inches of snow. Charlotte didn't care about the outside world, as she hadn't done when she was sick. But this was different.

Suddenly the door opened and revealed a dark-haired woman of fifty or so, in a pretty paisley dressing gown and purple slippers. Her hair was thick and there was a lot of it, but it wasn't pinned up. She'd bunched it up with one hand and was holding it in a mound at the top of her head, as if it were a hat, and a fierce wind were blowing; loose strands were streaming out through her fingers. She must have been as eager to clean her hair as Charlotte was.

She had an appealing, horsey face, and spoke at a brisk clip. "Hello," she said brightly, as if they'd come upon each other in someone's sitting room. She did not react in any way to what Charlotte was wearing. Wasn't it interesting how quickly something so extraordinary became normal? "I see you've got in here before me. I'll come back! Are you the new woman who's the wife of the senator?"

"No, I'm the new woman who . . . well, I'm just new," said Charlotte.

"Heavy stuff," said the woman, indicating her hair and furrowing her brow to indicate a headache. "I may have overdone it on the bourbon last night, but it was marvelous all the same, from a lady from Kentucky—have you met her, a photographer, going all over, on her own, to take pictures of cities in their very worst aspects? She's very good at it."

"I met Miss Singleton," said Charlotte.

"Ah. Did you look at her pictures of Mr. and Mrs. Alcorn?"

"I looked at her ice garden."

"Haven't seen that. She invite you up there?"

"She wanted some sweets I had. But they were thrown in the fire instead. Is it true she can't have sugar?"

"It's her blood. Can't abide the least bit. Last time she got hold of a confection she went into a shock and, for days, couldn't even use the one good hand she's got. Are you the woman who came in last Sunday from Rhode Island, the one who's got a hat shop?"

"No."

"Are you the doctor's niece who's not supposed to be here?"

Charlotte sighed and nodded meekly.

"Had your lunch?" said the woman.

"Is it afternoon?"

The woman smiled at her broadly, showing all her teeth, nice teeth, very white, very square. "Like that, is it? Lovely when one doesn't know. I'm in the same boat myself. I should have left two days ago and I suppose at home they're thinking me suffering deprivations, but I have to tell you, I've no complaints of this snow."

"Neither do I."

"P'rhaps I'll see you downstairs later on, and mind you don't use up all the coal."

"See you!" said Charlotte.

"And mind you don't use up the Pears'."

"I won't!"

The door was shut. Charlotte slipped off the shirt, let it fall to the floor, then picked it up, bundled it, and held it up to her face. It smelled like Arthur. She folded it and placed it on the table and stepped into the tub. A cake of soap was in the water already, making frothy bubbles, smelling like lilacs.

What was that song the Irish maids used to sing? About the rover in the clover?

> *Oh, I'll meet you in the clover, you rover,*
> *The clover is where I will be,*
> *Over in the clover, the sweet summer clover,*
> *My rover, you'll come soon to me.*

She didn't remember the other words, but it was a wonderful, buoyant tune and she hummed it. She pictured the summer place by the cliffs, in the heat of August, with the glare of yellow sunlight all around, so strong it made you feel like you'd been drinking too much wine. She pictured the big main house and the little cottages, and in one of the doorways, his eyes squinting up in the light, stood Arthur Pym, she imagined, waving to her, and wearing a bathing costume; he'd just been swimming; his hair was slicked back; his head was as smooth as a seal's.

She pictured fishing boats in the harbor, one of which came in close to the rocks. In real life there was an old iron mooring ring lodged fast in the stone, for boats that needed to come and go surreptitiously: it used to be a colonial smuggler's cove, and probably, when Heaths weren't there to oversee it, it still was.

There were no Heaths in the picture. Charlotte saw the captain of the boat waving for her to come aboard with Arthur, and they did; they went right down the cliffs as if the rocks were a staircase. Arthur told the captain, "I'll take care of it from here," and the captain jumped over the side and swam away, and off went Charlotte and Arthur. The boat would be a dory and they'd each take an oar. "Charlotte, you can row, how clever of you." She'd prove herself as strong as he was, maybe stronger. In real life she'd once paddled a tiny sailing dinghy with another girl from Miss Georgeson's, on a picnic excursion at a tiny lake in the Valley: there had not been wind to bring them back; the boat had turned over; they would have drowned if the water wasn't only as high as their knees, and she'd never done anything like it again. "We'll row to a foreign country, eventually," Arthur would tell her.

Everything she did, he approved of it. Up would rise the horizon like a prize she could reach out and touch.

She had a small pewter pitcher. She scooped tub water into it and poured it over her hair. She could feel the tangles relaxing; she felt as relieved as if she hadn't soaked her head for a year. "Over in the clover, over in the clover, the sweet summer clover, my rover, my rover," she sang. She didn't know any boat songs.

The door opened, and once again, it wasn't little Eunice. Arthur Pym himself walked in, with two big, clean towels and a terribly worried expression. Here he was!

She instantly sank down into the water, embarrassed, like she had something to hide. She didn't mind her nakedness half as much as the fact that she didn't want him to know she'd been lolling around in the water daydreaming of him. But then she thought, if there was ever a man who had the right to enter a lady's bathing room, it was him, and the lady was her.

She wondered what she looked like to him with wet hair. She would have enjoyed having him tell her what the wet-dark redness of it was like, as if he'd make up a little poem about it, spontaneously. Maybe he'd get into the tub with her. Was that allowed?

"Arthur," she said, "I thought you were leaving for your journey to go and cut up that poor bog man's body."

"You have my shirt."

"I'd think you'd have another, somewhere."

"I don't."

"If you want it back, you'll have to wait until I'm finished here, as I've not brought anything else to put on for going back to my room."

He was fully dressed except for his shirt. His green jacket looked sweet, with just his undershirt below it. But he just looked down at Charlotte and shrugged, grimly. "I reached my tutor by the telephone. The dissection's been postponed for at least another two days. There's too much for them to do in the hospital. And the roads out there are still blocked, anyway, as they'd got far more snow than we did."

Her heart felt cold as she finally realized the gravity of his expression. He came over to the side of the tub. "Charlotte, I've come to tell you there's a woman downstairs by the name of Mabel Gerson. She says she's your friend, and she must speak to you at once. Harry has her in the public tearoom, which, by the by, is still closed, but he can't get anything out of her."

She wasn't new at knowing her way around coping with some-thing someone said to her that she didn't want to hear. "I am going to wash my hair now, Arthur, and if you'd like to bring over the kettle, please do. The maid has abandoned me."

"It's urgent."

"I don't know anyone named Mabel."

"Charlotte, you do. She's from the bakery that delivered you here." He'd started sweating as soon as he entered; beads of sweat were all over his forehead. In another few minutes his hair would be damp, and if he pushed it back, he really would look sleek, like a seal. Daydreams can come true!

"The kettle, please," said Charlotte.

"I think it would best for you to see this woman at once. You'll need to know what she has to say."

"I think, Arthur, I'll wash my hair."

"Well, be quick about it."

"It's so warm, take off your jacket."

"Not a wise idea, at the moment," he said. He touched the kettle before bringing it over and first splashed some water onto his own hand to check the degree. He reminded Charlotte of stories about kings who had food tasters, who would suffer and die of whatever was meant to kill the king. He leaned down and poured water on her hair very slowly, although she'd expected it to all come out in a rush, as he was supposed to be making her hurry. He reached for the hair soap and was just about to hand it to her when Mrs. Petty came in.

"Why didn't you lock the door?" cried Charlotte. Even with her eyes partly blinded by water, she knew who it was.

In Mrs. Petty's hands were Charlotte's dress, underwear, stock/ings, shoes, vest, and jacket, and the hairbrush that was actually Mabel's, and the small heavy/cloth purse in which Charlotte kept her money, which had been lying anyway in plain sight on her bureau.

"We have to get her out of here," Mrs. Petty said to Arthur, like they were a two/person conspiracy.

"Is that woman determined to come upstairs looking for her?"

"Harry wouldn't let that happen, but it's worse. Lily's coming to take a nap, in *her* room. She was all night at the wards with the men from that fish place where the roof fell in, and she had three births where there was no one else to attend—they're always putting her on the births—and she was running around like a chicken, as if I didn't know what that's like. She is going to have a fit if she gets here and finds out *who's still here*. She cannot be allowed to do that. And I know what that woman downstairs wants to say because I gave her a cream cake and she never had anything like it, and her husband has the bakery. She wants to say"—and here Mrs. Petty raised her voice, extremely stridently—"Charlotte, your husband knows how you got to town *long ago* the other night, because you left your horses with the bakers and one got away and went home, to your window, and then it left to go back and get the other one and your husband fol/lowed it. Your baker friends swore to God Almighty you were only driven to the trolley and God is with you on that because no one stopped to remember it wasn't running, and I am up to my throat in deliveries coming in, my kitchen is acting like a lunatic, I have got to go down to the cooking school for a consultation with Miss Farmer, who does not take tardiness kindly, and the children are going to be expelled from their school, I think, and the baby's with that maid Georgina who has sniffles and she is going to catch them, and I could *spit*."

"Expelled for what reason?" said Arthur.

"What do you mean, what reason? They don't need a reason," said Mrs. Petty. "My girl told another girl that Jesus didn't rise from the dead, because he wouldn't be strong enough to push out of the tomb, as he'd been tortured and nailed, and, to begin with, he was never any Hercules. That's a reason."

"I thought the tomb got opened by an angel," said Arthur.

"That's the same thing the girl my girl spoke to said. My girl says angels are only bigger fairies and they haven't got muscles."

"Terence has a lady friend who's got a little academy, near Charlestown. You should speak to him."

"Is the lady one of those Christians?"

"I don't think so. I mean, I wouldn't know, but the way Terence met her was here."

"That might be a good idea," said Mrs. Petty. "Do you think she'd take them in as boarders, the girl and the boy?"

"You could ask."

"Good. Every time I tell them I am going to give them away, they start acting like they're not in training to be criminals."

Would they ever stop talking? Why were they talking? The water was getting less warm. Arthur said, "I wonder if anyone followed that woman here."

Mrs. Petty grinned when she got to this part; she seemed to admire Mabel Gerson. They hadn't known each other personally back in the town, but obviously, they did now. "Mrs. Gerson came in at dawn with a milk truck and went to some shops. They're all open again. She's got packages. And she stopped in the tearoom on Charles Street, and came in the back way. They think at home Charlotte's at Lily's and God is with her on that, too."

"We could get her next door, before Lily gets here, and tell the woman she's not here, which is going to be the truth," said Arthur.

"That's what Harry said. I just talked to him. But next door is not going to be happy," said Mrs. Petty.

"I'll go too," said Arthur.

"I could give Mrs. Gerson more cream cakes, and Harry can spring for a hansom so she doesn't go back with the milk cans."

"Give me the *soap*," said Charlotte.

She reached out a wet hand and grabbed it from Arthur and lathered up her head and sank down so she was underwater, just barely. She liked the way her hair floated out around her. She imagined that the dory she and Arthur were rowing was swamped by a wave— a huge gray wall of a wave—and they were capsized.

Down she went, seaweed everywhere, fishes, salt. She wasn't panicking. Calmly, because Arthur was drowning, she grabbed hold of him and shot to the surface, saving him, a heroine.

She shook out her head so her ears could unblock and she hoped that they were both splashed hugely, which they weren't.

"What's Miss Fannie Farmer like, anyway?" Arthur was saying.

"You'll never see her in here, and that's a thing for sure," said Mrs. Petty.

"I meant in general."

"She's like . . ." Mrs. Petty thought about it. This seemed to be a subject she took seriously. "She's like a lady who put out a cookbook that could only have been made by a lady with the character of a general in the army, in wartime, and that is complimentary."

"I heard she'd been ill," said Arthur, and Charlotte paused in the act of massaging her scalp, which she very much wished he was doing, instead of herself. She had developed the habit of listening carefully when people talked about a sickness, especially when the sufferer recovered; it was like belonging to a secret society.

"It was a stroke, they say," said Mrs. Petty, "when Miss Farmer was only fifteen. She's all right, but she drags one leg something terrible, and must sometimes be aided."

"I should like to meet her."

"We haven't got time to stand here chattering about Miss Farmer, Arthur, but I assure you, you never will meet her, unless you ever finish your degrees and become her doctor."

It was Mrs. Petty who brought over some of the water from the side of the stove. First she thrust Charlotte's clothes and purse and the hairbrush at Arthur, then she seized a pot and heaved it up; but, like Arthur, she didn't pour it roughly or too fast, as much as she must have wanted to.

"There, you're rinsed," she said.

The water had cooled considerably, and Charlotte gasped and shivered and thought how unfair it was that she was at the disadvantage of being naked, but at least this wasn't the first time; Mrs. Petty had sometimes filled in at the household when there weren't any nurses or maids available to wash and change an invalid.

She gave her the towels as Charlotte climbed out of the tub. Charlotte knew that Arthur was looking at her but she didn't dare meet his gaze in front of Mrs. Petty.

"You're so thin," said Mrs. Petty.

"I was sick."

"I know, Charlotte."

"Where are you taking me?"

"Next door," said Arthur. "Why don't you, Mrs. Petty, tell Moaxley or one of the maids to go over and sound the warning about there's going to be some company."

"I'll stay right here with the two of you until she's dressed, thank you very much. And I would put my money on Moaxley being over there ahead of you already, as I happen to know he's been right outside the door hearing everything."

"I'll want my coat," said Charlotte, and Arthur said quickly—making a very pointed effort to not look at her—"you won't need it. We're not going outdoors, and it's warm inside there, quite warm."

"Where is my coat, and my other things?"

"Moaxley put everything else of yours in a closet, his own," said Mrs. Petty.

"Is Lily's room being cleaned?" said Arthur, and Mrs. Petty glared at him.

"It is, and everything changed, which wasn't going to be done today, but they're doing it, and if you think I'm saying another word about Lily's room, I am not. I said everything I wanted to, and it's not my business. I'm not the housekeeper."

If Charlotte hadn't been accustomed to being dressed by other people—from her illness, not from real life, as she had vowed to herself she'd never have maids to put her clothes on, like her mother-in-law and Hays's sisters, who anyway needed the help for their corsets—she would have minded being so quickly, efficiently clothed. Maybe they'd thought if she did it herself she'd take an hour, which she would have tried to do, even though the friendly woman with the horse face was waiting.

"What did you come into this room wearing?" said Mrs. Petty, and Charlotte said, "I'm not telling you."

It didn't matter. Mrs. Petty had already found the shirt. "Put your shirt on, Arthur, for the love of God."

Obediently he did, and then buttoned up all the buttons of his jacket on top of it.

When Charlotte's dress was put over her head and pulled down, she had a question for Mrs. Petty. "Which horse of mine was the one to go home to my window?"

"How should I know? They look exactly the same."

"They do not," said Charlotte.

"Well, Mrs. Gerson didn't say which one."

That was a disappointment. Charlotte sat on the edge of the tub for the putting on of her stockings, and Mrs. Petty was the one who did that, too. "What about your cut-up with your tutor some-where?" she said to Arthur.

"It was postponed."

"You must come straight back here after you've brought her."

"What for?" cried Charlotte.

"He has to go to the lecture he was going to miss if he went out for a day-long ride to see the cut-up," said Mrs. Petty. "Harry said to tell you, Arthur, go to school."

Then Charlotte's shoes were on; everything was on. Her hair was soaking wet and no one cared. Mrs. Petty handed her the hairbrush and Charlotte said, "I would prefer a comb," so Mrs. Petty gave her one, off the table. At least they were letting her do that.

"What happened with your husband, Charlotte?"

"I won't speak of it."

"Has he hurt you?"

"In what way?"

"In any way."

"Yes," she said simply.

"Do you want to go home?"

"I do not."

"All right then. We'll hide you, for now. Where're your hair pins?" said Mrs. Petty.

"In the pocket of my other dress."

"Well, never mind, I'll braid it."

She was quick about it, and knotted up the braid and took a few pins out of her own hair and got it secured. "Came as a surprise to me, Charlotte," she said, "to see how great you'd got with the bakers, back in the town, in terms of a personal friendship."

"I'm free to have whatever friends I want."

"And, you know, I'd never forgotten about that unpleasant busi-ness of the food poisonings."

"That has nothing to do with it."

"I'm sure."

"Did your friend poison someone?" said Arthur.

"Half the town," said Mrs. Petty.

"Not half! It wasn't on purpose!"

"We have to go."

Mrs. Petty gave Charlotte a nudge out the door. The hall was empty. The hotel seemed silent. Arthur was sticking closely to Charlotte, like last evening on the way down from Miss Singleton's. "Don't worry," he whispered.

"I won't unless you tell me to start doing so."

Mrs. Petty went with them to the top of the stairs, peering down cautiously, and a voice said, in a whisper, from who knew where, "All clear."

"Thank you, Moaxley," whispered Mrs. Petty.

Charlotte said, "I am not going another step until you tell me where you're bringing me."

"To Mrs. Alcorn," said Arthur.

"Mrs. Alcorn! I'd said I wanted to call on her! I was told she didn't receive!"

"Keep your voice down," said Mrs. Petty, and Arthur whispered, "She doesn't, ordinarily. But she knows what to do when someone needs to be over there."

"Needs to be over there for what?" whispered Charlotte.

"You're not the first person to be hidden," said Mrs. Petty.

"Was my aunt ever hidden?"

"Oh, no, she wouldn't have the need, not with your uncle never going out of Brookline except to the courts, and then, he hasn't got anything on his mind but the courts, him being a judge now. Also, your aunt doesn't need to know *everything*."

Charlotte was hurried down the stairs. At the end of the hall— this was the second floor—there was a panel of a slightly darker wood than the rest of the wall. There were no fewer rooms on this floor than the others, but this was the only such panel Charlotte had seen. There was no handle to it. Arthur pressed against it, and it swung open like a door, which it was.

"This is where I'm going?"

"It is, don't be worried. It's a way into the next house."

"A way because of what reason, Arthur?"

"Harry thinks the first owners of the two buildings shared servants, but everyone else thinks it was probably something less innocent."

"Such as what?"

"Charlotte, I don't know, but it's really just a hallway and it's perfectly safe. Harry keeps it in top shape, because the maids are always using it and they wouldn't if they were frightened."

"I am not," said Charlotte, "frightened."

"I'm going downstairs to my kitchen, God help me," said Mrs. Petty, and a moment later Charlotte found herself being led by Arthur—a different-mooded Arthur, intent on his task, quite serious—down a dim passageway with whitewashed walls, and with many turns and slopes; it seemed to go on forever, mazelike. But having made the decision to submit to being led, which she did because she had no choice, she hardly took notice of where she was, except to see that it was not as dark as one would have expected; there weren't any lamps. There weren't any windows. It should have been as black as the bottom of a cave.

"Arthur, why isn't it pitch-dark in here?"

After they'd gone a few more yards he pointed up at a shaft, which went up in a boxy hole through the building, ending in a flat glassed window, obviously on the roof; daylight was coming in.

"What about nights?" said Charlotte.

"Candles."

"Can people get out through that window?"

"It doesn't open," said Arthur. "And the glass is as thick as you can get."

"It could be smashed, still."

"But you couldn't get up there from here unless you turned yourself into a bird and flew up it."

"Or a bat," said Charlotte.

"But you'd be trapped. You'd flap your wings until they gave out, and then you'd drop down hard to the floor, and the maid would trip over you, while carrying Mrs. Alcorn's dinner tray, say, and it will drop and be ruined, and if the fall didn't kill you, the teapot landing on top of you would, and the maid will have to scream."

"We said no subject of *die*, Arthur."

"I was being hypothetical."

She sniffed at that, but felt a little relieved. She'd thought he was going to say something about, when he'd said no subject of "die," it was last night, and it covered last night only, like a wholly separate thing, *last night*, sealed and intact on its own, and completely lacking the possibility of ever taking place again.

Which was not what he was saying. She knew that there were ladies who stayed in the hotel who did not turn up just one time, and Miss Singleton *lived* here; but still, she did not appreciate this mood.

"Tell me about Mrs. Alcorn."

"Did you see the portrait of her upstairs at Berry's?"

"Berry's?"

"Miss Singleton. Berenice."

"Oh. I did not. Everything that wasn't the ice garden was turned to the wall and I thought you were horrid to me."

"I was not horrid. Did you see the photograph of her and Harry at their wedding?"

"I did. She's all gauzy."

"She's said to be not gauzy now, but except that she's older, she's the same."

"You're not telling me anything useful."

"Actually, I've never seen her myself."

"Lucy."

"Oh, you wouldn't want to call her by that."

"I know what to do, Arthur. Do you think my aunt will stay the night in her room?"

"She wants some sleep today, so that means she'll be at the hospital all night."

Charlotte said, "But if she wants her room for the night, what will my options be?"

"Harry will arrange something. He always does."

"How long am I to be hidden?"

"I don't know. Someone will come to fetch you."

"Do you think you could turn around and look at me when you speak to me?"

"I've got to get back to Cambridge. The roads here to there are open, but it will take me an age with all the snow. I wish I didn't have to, but I do."

"For a lecture on what?"

"Greeks. Statues and things."

"But that's not medical."

"I am trying," he said, "to be well rounded."

"Then how far am I to keep going, just following you, with wet hair?"

A low beam emerged down the hall—it wasn't actually a hall, it was more like a tunnel—and just after it was a proper door. Low, but proper.

"There, Charlotte, it's just ahead." But at least he forgot for a moment about delivering her like a package, to who knew what sort of place, and rushing off. He stopped and turned around. "I want to kiss you," he said.

"Is it allowed, or must it only happen in private rooms?"

"Oh, it's absolutely forbidden, anywhere but in the rooms," he said.

"Then that's why you didn't before, when I was bathing."

"Mrs. Petty was there."

"Before she came in."

"I had to tell you about the woman from your town."

"I shouldn't like you to break rules."

"Charlotte, there aren't rules like that. I was teasing. You looked so very grim."

"I'm not grim," she said. In what position exactly had Hays been, at the edge of the square, behind the tree?

She pictured it all over again, as if it were a painting she'd looked at a hundred times. The snow, the tree, the shuttered-up houses, the nearby uncle laid out for his wake, the silence, her horses in front of her, with their heads up high, snorting and glowing and happy. The gray winter light. The heaped-up banks of the square.

The thrill in her heart from having given the horses free rein. The snow-covered branches. The cold. The feel of the runners of her sleigh beneath her, like extensions of her own two legs, which were working again, which could hold her as legs were supposed to, not just be weirdly attached to her like two dead heavy things.

Hays's hat on his head, black, about to fall off. His head bending down. His hands on the sides of the woman's coat, one hand at each hip.

His body leaning toward hers, like a dancing partner. You could always tell, Charlotte's mother-in-law said, when you see two people on a dance floor, even if they're strangers to you, which category of relationship they belong to: married a long time; married recently; engaged to be married; on the verge of being engaged; unromantic friends who want to dance with each other because they want to be close to the people they wish they were with, who were dancing with someone else; first- or second-timers; and a man and a woman who should not have been dancing together, but did it anyway.

Hays's hands were on the woman in the manner of the last of the categories.

Arthur didn't have a coat on, just the green jacket, and no hat, and she didn't need to lean toward him to kiss him; he was taller than she was, although not by much, just a couple of inches.

She put her hands at the sides of Arthur's waist, at his hips. Then she kissed him, and he kissed her back, and she kissed him again, and he did, too. The pale white of the walls, and the feeble gray light from the rooftop windows—they'd just passed another shaft, where the glass was covered with snow—were very nice, she decided, very ethereal, like the look and the light of a made-up place in a story or a picture, probably not even on earth.

"The roof windows are very snowy," she said, as if that were the reason she didn't want to let go of him.

∞ Ten ∞

Mrs. Alcorn had her own housekeeper, Miss Blanchette. The dominant impression one had of Miss Blanchette was that she was as sturdy and hardy as a tree.

She was as solid as a trunk, and her skin had a coarse, barklike texture. Her hair was tightly pulled back. The knot of it at the back of her neck was like a tree knot. Her simple, high-collared wool dress—without a bustle, although she seemed to be the age for it— had no seam or fold that wasn't absolutely necessary. It was so long that it not only covered her ankles but her shoes as well, so that it seemed she had no feet, but moved about in a rolling, sliding way, as if the hem of the dress propelled her. The dress was exactly the shade of her hair: dull bronze-brown, like an oak leaf.

She was a very large woman. She was so broad and so muscular, and so simply big, it would seem that she suffered from a glandular problem; or it would seem that her parents must have both been giants. Her body had no excess flesh. You had the idea that every part of her was designed for practicality, and for low, no-fuss maintenance.

Maybe she was to Mrs. Alcorn what Moaxley was to her husband, but it was hard to tell what her functions were. She didn't appear to be doing anything at all. The meals at 340 Eustis—that was how Miss Blanchette referred to it—were sent over from the hotel kitchen; the hotel maids took care of the cleaning, the fires and coal supply, and whatever rough work needed doing. That much was evident, as two maids went scurrying past Charlotte, as soon as she'd come, to go back to the hotel through the maze, with empty coal buckets in their hands and canvas bags of dirty laundry.

Being quiet seemed to be the one thing Miss Blanchette was interested in, as in, "We live quietly here at Three-forty Eustis, Mrs. Heath, singularly quietly." And, "Three-forty Eustis has already had lunch, but we can quietly ring for something for you." She said the address as if it were a person, and Mrs. Alcorn's second-floor rooms were the only ones in the building, and perhaps in all of Boston; but then of course, to Miss Blanchette, they were.

Charlotte liked her immediately, but she could understand why Arthur hadn't mentioned her existence, and why he'd physically shrunk from any contact with her. She was definitely an intimidating lady. Arthur was quick about leaving, and never looked twice at Charlotte, and acted as though she really were a package and he'd delivered it.

There was no sign of Lucy Alcorn. "Three-forty Eustis is in the act of resting," said Miss Blanchette by way of explanation, as if Charlotte should rest, too, while Miss Blanchette kept up a sort of vigil. That seemed to be her job, Charlotte decided: to stand vigil between the hush and heat of this apartment and all the chaos of the outside world.

You had the idea that the slightest provocation was the same as an assault to the senses—a sleigh going by in the road, with a driver's muffled shouts to his horse; the din of exuberant schoolboys heading to the Common with sleds; a boy hawking newspapers; the ringing of church bells; piano music coming over through the walls from the hotel, as the lady pianist was practicing; sounds of clattering and thumping from below, in kitchens and sculleries, rising up through the shafts, as if the pulleyed dumbwaiter mechanisms for sending and receiving things from the depths of the building were only there to carry noise.

The way Miss Blanchette glided about was sentrylike. She didn't seem to be waiting for anything. She wasn't nervous or anxious. She was doing her job.

The maid Georgina—Mrs. Petty's assistant—came over with a fresh warm meat pie for Charlotte's lunch, and with Mrs. Petty's Edith riding her hip. The baby was fast asleep, her head tucked into the hollow between the maid's fleshy shoulder and her breast. One fat pink hand was splayed out on Georgina's ample bosom. When Edith sighed and wiggled in sleep, her fingers worked at a breast as if it were bread dough, but the maid didn't seem to notice.

"Mrs. Petty said you have sniffles," said Charlotte, although in fact Georgina looked glowing with health. "I hope they don't turn into something awful."

"It wasn't sniffles. It was me holding back my temper so as not to let loose in the kitchen at how sometimes she's so . . . so . . ."

Charlotte finished the sentence. "Horrible," she said. "A tyrant. You don't have to tell me. I used to live with her."

The meat pie was stupendous: chunks of roasted chicken and beef in a rich dark sauce, in a thick, buttery crust, with onions and celery and potatoes. Maybe Mrs. Petty was Charlotte's friend after all. Back at the household it had been her favorite meal, and when she'd got sick, she was given pies whenever she asked, sometimes three times a day, ham, rabbit, lamb, whatever she wanted, all sized-down into tarts because she really hadn't much of an appetite, and would often let Sophy and Momo have them, or her horses at the window.

There was enough of this meat pie for two or three people and Charlotte ate it all, at the oblong, highly polished table in the big front room of 340 Eustis. The maid had been careful to spread out a cloth to put Charlotte's plate on, and she told Charlotte, with a look, to treat the surface of the table as if it would be destroyed forever if she dropped one crumb on it or left one mark or smear. Charlotte got the message. She knew how to eat like a lady.

The floor was carpeted extensively by a thick and subdued Oriental rug. The draperies, opened but not completely, were the same dark heavy stuff that hung at the hotel windows. There were six pictures on the walls and they were all Miss Singleton's and not a one of them had anything it in that was breathing and alive: a glass of milk on a windowsill, and you knew from the color the milk was sour; a bunch of flowers well past their prime, scattered on a table that was much like the one where Charlotte sat; an ink drawing of a hand, just a hand, with the fingers curling as if to pick something up; another brown wagon in a grain field, harvested and cut to the stubble; a chalky, beige-and-black drawing of a tall, lean pine tree that didn't have any branches; and a small oil of a man's black overcoat on a hook on a dark-green wall, which was probably inspired by Moaxley.

"You like the pictures?" said Miss Blanchette. Even when she wasn't whispering, the tone of her voice made you think she was, but the apartment was so quiet, it wasn't necessary to strain to hear anything she said.

"I like them very much."

"I find them," said Miss Blanchette, "annoying."

Charlotte wondered what Miss Singleton would think of that. She would probably agree. "Annoying because there's no people?"

"No people I don't get bothered about. They are just too plain. Too bare."

Miss Singleton would agree with that, too, and she might add, "That's the point."

It was a comfortable room, if overly warm. There was a coal fire-place and two stoves, at maximum heat. The ceiling was high, and had been fitted with those panels of metal-lined wood that were said to be useful for insulation. Charlotte's father-in-law had arranged to have them in the conservatory and in his study. There hung overhead such a heavy layer of risen, trapped heat, you had the sense it might burst, like a thundercloud, disastrously.

"I was wondering," whispered Miss Blanchette, turning from the window that looked out on the street, "if that man outside, across the road, watching the hotel, is connected in any way to the fact that you are here at Three-forty."

There was nothing to do but go and look.

Dickie! Even if you didn't know he was a policeman, in his coat and boots and felt hat, you would know. "Policeman" was written all over him.

"That's a detective inspector with the Boston Police," Charlotte said. "I don't know if he has anything to do with me, or not. I knew him a long time ago, when I was still at school. I only just saw him again accidentally, when Mr. Alcorn asked me to speak to him the other day, as a guest."

"Oh, you're the lady he put out against the Suppressionists. Nasty bunch, those. Full of bile and as narrow in their minds as a splinter. I'd give my teeth to have them marched off the face of the earth."

It was strange to hear that from someone who looked like Miss Blanchette, the very embodiment, it would seem, of a person who was a member, a founding member, even, of the Boston Society for the Suppression of Vice, or whatever it was they called themselves. Charlotte's respect for Miss Blanchette shot up a little higher. Miss Blanchette seemed to feel that a detective across the road, now stomping his feet and shaking himself from the cold, and putting his hands in his pockets—poor Dickie—was not something to be worried about.

"If the Suppressionists think they'll get a case against Mr. Alcorn," said Miss Blanchette, "they have another thing coming. It's not as though the hotel is a book they can condemn from the stores, and the libraries, like something sinful, so no one reads it, when everyone should."

"Like that poet Walter. Or, Walt."

Miss Blanchette brightened. "Actually, and this is no important detail, it's customary to speak of a poet by using the surname, that is, if one knows it."

Charlotte didn't feel embarrassed at the correction. "Like that poet Whitman," she said.

"Yes. But I suppose if he were here with us, in spite of what's standard, he would very much want us to call him Walt. *Leaves of Grass.*"

Charlotte didn't know if that was the actual title of Walt's book. It didn't matter. She'd only seen it in French, but it made sense that Miss Blanchette would be familiar with anything ever written that had to do with leaves, not that Hays had said there were trees in those poems.

Miss Blanchette knew Walt well and began quoting, and her voice with its built-in hush made the words sound even more thrilling than they were. Had someone told her how Charlotte felt about horses? How could that be? Maybe she was one of those people who had the ability to sense things that are not said out loud, or maybe it was just a coincidence.

" 'A gigantic beauty of a stallion,' " said Miss Blanchette. " 'Fresh and responsive to my caresses.' "

"Oh!" said Charlotte, fixated.

Head high in the forehead, wide between the ears,
Limbs glossy and supple, tail dusting the ground,
Eyes full of sparkling wickedness, ears finely cut, flexibly moving.
His nostrils dilate as my heels embrace him,
His well-built limbs tremble with pleasure as we race around.

This was Walt? Why hadn't she read those lines before? Why hadn't Hays read them to her? He wouldn't have done half so well as Miss Blanchette, but still. Charlotte wouldn't have cared if a poem was in French: if it was about horses, she'd have got the meaning just fine.

"Oh!" said Charlotte again. "That was beautiful, and it doesn't even rhyme."

Miss Blanchette smiled. "Maybe that was why they banned it. Would you like to hear some more?"

"Did you memorize a lot of it?"

"It's a very great favorite of Three-forty Eustis."

"Yes, please."

"Have you any particular favorite?"

"Are there any about trees?"

Miss Blanchette looked down for a moment, thinking, then said, "How about the one about the oak in Louisiana?"

"That would be lovely."

She took a deep breath, as a singer would. And then the door at the other end of the room was slowly being opened, and the woman who was Lucy Alcorn appeared at last, and Miss Blanchette forgot about the poem.

The change in her was so vivid, and so instantaneous, it was like looking at a brown old tree-fallen leaf on the ground, which was being transformed to a spring-green one, and leaping back onto a branch. When she glided across the room to Mrs. Alcorn, which she did at once, it was as if a whole tree sprouted new leaves. It was as if that naked pine tree in Miss Singleton's painting took on branches, and those poor wilted flowers sprang back to life, and the milk in that glass had just one second ago been poured, and that hand started moving, and that wagon went rolling down the field, and that coat jumped off the hook onto someone's back.

"This is Mrs. Heath, who Harry told you about, dear," said Miss Blanchette, and Charlotte, standing there, felt a silly urge to curtsy, as if she were being presented to some royal member of some European court.

Mrs. Alcorn was a beautiful woman, the way a beautiful actress or singer is, on a stage, but even more so, because it wasn't a stage, she wasn't made up for a part: she was beautiful in her bones and her skin the way a flower is, on a stem.

She stood lower in height than Charlotte, but it seemed she was much, much taller. She carried herself with her back straight up and held her own beside Miss Blanchette, when you'd think Miss Blanchette would have dwarfed her. Arthur had said she wasn't all gauzy, and she wasn't: she was luminous, in a white dress and a pale yellow shawl. Her hair was thin and white-blond, crinkly and curly, neither pulled back nor hanging freely, but tied loosely off her face with a ribbon at the back of her neck.

She had a china-cup delicacy and pale blue eyes, so pale they were almost gray, and her skin, what was showing of it—which was really only her face, for her dress was as high-collared, and as long on her, as Miss Blanchette's was on her—had a pearly, moony translucence, without a line or a wrinkle, just purely smooth.

It wasn't until she spoke that you knew something was wrong. It wasn't so much that her words came out slurred, or that she was hard to understand, or that she couldn't get her tongue around pronunciations. It was more that you had the sense of a sleepwalker. Sleepwalkers don't know they're asleep, or what they sound like.

Mrs. Alcorn took no notice of Charlotte, or of what Miss Blanchette had said, but continued out loud on some thought of her own. "I remembered I was wishing for the green one," she said woodenly, in a monotone.

Her lips were pale. Those two blue-gray eyes did not seem to be looking at anything that was actually there: bright eyes, with an overgloss of brightness like an eerie, waxy polish. The pupils should not have been enlarged like that. There was a slackness in her jaw, as if she had to keep reminding herself to keep her mouth closed. That was the impression.

Miss Blanchette knew what she meant, or pretended to. "What about the orange?"

The eyes made an effort to focus. The sleepwalker was coming to the awareness of standing upright. There was nothing about her that was drowsy or groggy in a normal way. Instead, you saw that this was her usual state. "I don't like oranges."

"Oh, but only yesterday we had a letter from the lady in Florida who says when she comes back to next door, she'll bring you a bag of them, fresh off the trees."

"I don't want them. I don't like orange."

"What about the blue, then?"

"Blue is for winter."

"It's winter now, dear. Would you like to look out the window at the snow? It's so lovely today and the sun is shining."

"I don't like windows," said Mrs. Alcorn, and Charlotte said to herself, with a flash of recognition, "Morphine. That's morphine."

"Would you like to go and rest?"

Mrs. Alcorn looked up at Miss Blanchette, wordlessly, and closed her eyes as if the act of keeping them open was too much for her. She went back to her room that way, like a blind person. Miss Blanchette went with her, holding up an arm in the air, in a curve, near Mrs. Alcorn's back, not quite touching it, but ready in case she faltered, as if Mrs. Alcorn were a tiny child just starting to learn to walk on her own.

Miss Blanchette turned her head to whisper across the room to Charlotte. "She wasn't supposed to have come out. Please. There are only a few who know how things are at Three-forty." She said this as if she feared that Charlotte might run back through the tunnel to next door and tell every hotel guest she came upon, "Mr. Alcorn's wife is an addict of drugs."

"I'm dependable," whispered Charlotte.

Murmuring sounds came from the other room, all Miss Blanchette's. Mrs. Alcorn was a shell. There was no other way to think of her. A beautiful white translucent shell.

Where was the woman in the wedding picture? Gone. A great wave of pity rose up in Charlotte.

Morphine. Charlotte wondered what Aunt Lily thought about this. It must have distressed her. Or maybe she didn't know about it.

She could hear Aunt Lily's voice. "If any of the consultants try giving you morphine, ever again, and I don't care what reasons they have, and I don't care if your husband and his parents and the whole lot of them disagree with me, and I don't care how much pain you're in, you're to tell them all, I will personally make very great trouble for them," and Charlotte had answered, "But I like it."

Well, she did. The first few times, only nausea and sickness, like being pregnant, but then came that sweet, lulling, sublime, shadowy pleasure: that stillness and joy, both at once, that softening of everything that had ever been harsh, that deep, deep sense of being safe and sheltered and whole.

"I don't believe in Satan," Aunt Lily had said, "and I don't have to, as long as there is morphine going into the bodies of people who don't require it, and Charlotte, you do not require it, you're not dying."

"But I am," she'd answered, and Aunt Lily had put down her foot. What were those stories of addicts? There'd been many: gripping stories in terrible detail. Charlotte didn't recall any of them, but she remembered listening to them as if they were tales of shipwrecks, of horrible things, people losing their reason, people being buried alive, people being boiled in oil, people being subjected to suffering beyond description. You wouldn't think Lillian Iverson Heath had a gift for that type of narration, but she did, sitting at the side of Charlotte's bed, conjuring every demon there could be, as if all the hosts of hell were gathered right there in the shadows.

She'd probably refused more morphine because, if she hadn't, her aunt would have thought up more stories. Hays had wanted to tell her to stop attending Charlotte. He'd tried to, on the grounds that it wasn't appropriate to have a relation as one's principal doctor.

Aunt Lily had told Hays that, if he blocked her, she'd arrange to have a certificate issued to put Charlotte into an asylum or something. She'd have people from Boston come out and take her away, and how would that look for the Heaths?

Once again, Charlotte looked out the window at Dickie, who never once looked up at anything that wasn't part of the Beechmont. She thought that Miss Blanchette would have been a truly great detective. If Miss Blanchette were the one down there, nothing on the entire street would escape her eyes, and probably nothing going on behind her, either. She certainly had the size to cope with anything that came her way.

I wish I was big, thought Charlotte. She realized she had never felt, around any other person, so . . . so what? So safe, she decided. Why didn't any of the Heaths make her feel that way? Not even Hays did.

Oh, he stood up for her now and then, but not that often, and not dependably, and he never, ever took her side against his sisters and their husbands and his brothers and their wives.

Miss Georgeson at the academy was a little bit like Miss Blanchette, but was a pale comparison in every way, and anyway, it was different then; Charlotte had been a child. There were plenty of things to want to feel safe from when you're young, but when you're older, Charlotte thought, it feels good to stand close to someone who would be willing to take your side, no matter what, and have the size and the conviction to really stick to it.

The apartment was even more silent than before. It was Dickie who was down there in the cold, not Hays.

It's Hays, she had thought, when Miss Blanchette had suggested that she look out the window. Her words rose up at Charlotte, and would not be ignored. I wonder if the man across the road is connected to you.

Crossing that room had been the same as walking through mud. Her legs went all weak. They kept doing that. She'd thought that Hays must have followed Mabel Gerson, as he'd followed the horse; and she had pictured that, although she didn't want to admit it. Hays in the snow, going across town to the Hollow, where he'd never been before.

He must have made one of the stable boys fix up a sleigh for him; he didn't ride. Down he went to the bakery. He hated the cold. He would have taken the big fur wrap. Which horse was the one who went home looking for her?

If it was the mare, Windy, she would have allowed Hays to follow gently. He might even have hitched her to the sleigh. If it was the male, Mercury, it would have been a little more intricate, because he would have known that Hays was someone Charlotte had fled from and would think he needed to do the same. Mercury would have noticed the woman at the edge of the square with Hays. Windy never noticed anything except how fast she was being allowed to go.

Charlotte asked herself, "If that was my husband out there, what would I do?"

And the answer was, the truth, as awful an answer as it seemed to her: "I would go to him."

She'd been almost too afraid to look. She didn't want to go to him. She wanted to. She didn't. She did. She didn't know. She would go to him to tell him she wanted to never see him again, she was going to unmarry him, she decided, and she decided, too, at the same time, to go to him and tell him the same thing she was going to tell him when she didn't meet him at Uncle Owen's wake as she planned, as if nothing else had happened in between, and she would say, "Hays, I'm well now, and I miss you."

She didn't want to be married to Hays. She wanted to. She didn't. She might be able to forgive him, for the woman, for the fact that he gave up on her. She couldn't. She could. She could forgive him for the woman but not for giving up on her. She could forgive him for giving up on her depending on what he had to say. No, she could not.

What about last night? What about Arthur in the washroom, the white tunnel, what she'd done? Was she going to tell him about Arthur? The truth, all of it? What about a part of it? She could almost hear Miss Blanchette's voice speaking her own thoughts out loud. Was she stark raving mad?

The last thing in the world she wanted was to go back to the household. The thing she wanted most was to be with Hays. No, the thing she wanted most was to not go back to Hays and not go back to the household, and let all the Heaths (except Aunt Lily and Uncle Chessy, and a few of Hays's nieces and nephews, who weren't old enough to have caused her trouble) disappear into history, into the mists and unreality of history, like those godforsaken plays of theirs.

Oh, the relief when it was Dickie was enormous. But there was a tiny thud of disappointment inside her, or perhaps it wasn't tiny and she wanted to wish it away.

Why hadn't Hays come after her? Why hadn't he followed Mabel? He thought she was at Aunt Lily's, for one thing, and for another, he'd stated his intentions in that boring, stupid letter, and she was glad she'd burned it in the fire because she didn't want to ever see it again. He would wait until she sent for him. He knew his own guilt. He knew that for the last year or so he'd been lousy as a husband. He knew what she'd seen, with the woman. Clear. Like a business transaction. He never strayed from his intentions once he had made up his mind.

Or maybe he didn't want her back. She hadn't considered that possibility.

That would make everything easy. "That would make everything so easy," she said to herself. It would. Would it? Good God, she thought, how could she ever be with Hays again when he was with her like a husband? That would be, in a way, like saying, "I loved being sick and not being able to move my legs or even stand on them, and now I'm anxious to do it again."

Maybe her marriage was like polio or some brain disease, and maybe it wasn't. How could she lie there in her bed again, waiting while he went through three doors, across a desert, hoping he wouldn't change his mind along the way? If she wanted to, she would have to take those tranquilizing nerve pills that her mother-in-law and Hays's sisters were always talking about: "I am nervy today; I must take one of those pills."

Or morphine.

Then here was Miss Blanchette again, coming up beside Charlotte, silent, intractable, brown, a tree. Neither one of them said anything for a very long moment. Some snow fell off an overhead ledge or a sill, and cascaded like a powdery waterfall. Everything outside was sparkly, glittering, white, a world of white and light. Charlotte thought of Mrs. Alcorn burrowing into her bed like a creature at the bottom of the sea.

"It's morphine," said Miss Blanchette, as if Charlotte had asked.

"I pity her."

"Yes."

"How does she get it?"

"In the beginning, it was a doctor. She'd had trouble with an arm that was broken very badly, in a fall down some stairs. There was a tower she'd much wanted to go up, at a little town in Mexico. She'd gone there with Harry. He hadn't done the climb, he has trouble with heights. She slipped on a wet spot. The stairs were stone. He brought her back home with her arm in a splint, but the pain was worse. That was years and years ago. But it wasn't just the arm. She was lost, I think, from the time she was a young girl."

"How does she get it now?"

"Her husband has a great deal of money from the hotel, Mrs. Heath."

"But money can be spent for a cure."

"Don't you think it was?"

"I don't know."

"Money was spent for a cure, Mrs. Heath," she said. "And now . . ." Miss Blanchette listlessly held up a hand and made an arc in the air, indicating, in its sweep, everything. "We take care of her."

"Does my aunt know about her?"

"And who would your aunt be?"

"A doctor. She's sometimes a guest next door."

"Three-forty knows a lady physician from Watertown who has a skill with digestive problems and has been called for consultations."

"That's not my aunt."

"We don't mingle, Mrs. Heath, on a regular basis, with next door."

"But you know a lady from Florida bringing oranges."

"She's a friend."

"Do you ever go over there?"

"Not once, except to go and find Mr. Alcorn if a crisis arises."

"He must be a sad man."

"Oh, but he knows how it could have been. She had made an effort, before, to stop, you see, not once but several times," said Miss

Blanchette. "But now she's lost the will for it, which has to be counted as good fortune."

"To be cured, you mean."

"Yes, if you consider that a cure would mean no longer to be part of this world."

"She isn't!"

"I mean to be gone from it in a physical sense, forever."

"To die?" said Charlotte. "By her own hand?"

"I wish not to speak of this anymore. I've said more than I wanted to. I don't mind your company, though. You may return here whenever you wish. You're an uncommonly perspicacious lady."

Charlotte didn't know what that meant. She hadn't minded being corrected about what to call a poet, customarily, but this was different. She was afraid to ask about the word because she didn't want to know if she was being uncomplimented, like at the household, where Hays's brothers and sisters—before she was sick—were always flinging extravagant words and phrases at her, in that way they had of making fun of her indirectly. They could sound all flowery, but it was only to sweeten the thorns. How many times had they mentioned to Hays he'd made a mistake in marrying her? One million. But after she'd got sick it really was flowers. Maybe they'd felt guilty.

"Perspicacious," said Miss Blanchette, "means you're not silly. It means you're astute."

Well, she should have realized Miss Blanchette was someone to be trusted. Astute! No one had ever said that to her before. "Then I suppose it's all right they had to hide me. Don't you want to know why?"

"The business of next door has got to be kept to itself."

"The man who came here with me, Arthur—do you know him well?"

"I don't."

"He's very nice."

Miss Blanchette gave Charlotte a long serious look. "May I give you advice?"

"Oh, yes, please."

"It would be a very mistaken, very unsatisfactory thing for you if you were to develop an affection for any of Mr. Alcorn's private staff. It has happened before and it's never pleasant."

"There's no danger of that," said Charlotte quickly. Then she said to herself, "Affection." It sounded like having a disease. Affected, afflicted. Affliction. Bad! To change the subject she said, "Have you been here at Three-forty very long?"

"Years and years."

"What did you do before?"

"I've lived in Boston all my life, in different areas."

"But what did you do?"

"I was," said Miss Blanchette, "unhappy."

"How did you come to be here?"

"I answered an advertisement Mr. Alcorn had placed in the newspaper. He had wanted a housekeeper for next door, but when I came to discover what . . ."

There was a catch in her voice. In the pause, Charlotte said encouragingly, "What goes on there, you mean. You don't like the Vice people but you disapprove."

"I was going to say, when I came to discover the condition of Mr. Alcorn's wife, I asked to be here at Three-forty."

"Oh. Are you unhappy still?"

"I am," said Miss Blanchette, "uncomplaining."

"Mrs. Alcorn is so beautiful."

"Yes."

"Tell me the poem about the tree."

"I'm not in a mood any longer."

"Please."

"I don't remember the words."

"I think you do."

Miss Blanchette sighed and drew into herself for such a long time, Charlotte thought she'd need to press a little harder, but then up came that hushed, steady voice. " 'I saw in Louisiana a live-oak growing,' " said Miss Blanchette.

You could tell the tree poem was special to her. And it was easy to see why.

I saw in Louisiana a live-oak growing,
All alone stood it and the moss hung down from the branches,
Without any companion it grew there uttering joyous leaves of dark green,
And its look, rude, unbending, lusty, made me think of myself,
But I wonder'd how it could utter joyous leaves standing alone there
    without its friend near, for I knew I could not,
And I broke off a twig with a certain number of leaves upon it, and
    twined around it a little moss,
And brought it away, and I have placed it in sight, in my room.

The words sounded so right, Charlotte felt that if she were to be invited into Miss Blanchette's room, she would see that a leafy twig, with some moss tied around it, was in fact there, on a bureau, perhaps, in a glass of water to keep it alive. When Miss Blanchette turned away from the window, and said, "The detective is going away," her eyes, as brown as the rest of her, were filling up with tears, which did not spill down her face, but just sat there, pool-like, unmoving, like something Miss Singleton drew, and it seemed they would stay there and stay there, just like that.

∽ Eleven ∽

The little maid Eunice came to fetch her near dusk, with candles in both hands and two more in the pocket of her apron for Charlotte. She was terrified of the tunnel and made Charlotte go first, which she did, not bothering to light her two candles; she led the way as if she'd been through it every day of her life.

Every question she asked Eunice brought a negative response.

She wanted to speak to Mr. Alcorn, could she? No, he was out; he'd said he would go to a boxing match. Was he a follower of boxing? No, this seemed to be his first time. Had Mr. Pym come back? No, he hadn't. Had Mr. Pym left word he would come back that evening? No, there was no word from Mr. Pym. Had the lady who came looking for her, Mrs. Gerson, been upset, been distraught, even, to know Charlotte wouldn't see her? No, she was fine, she was happy to have talked with Mrs. Petty, and she was happy to be offered a drive back home in a hansom.

Was she being brought back to the same room? No. Had her aunt gone back to the hospital? No, not yet. Had Eunice seen her aunt, to speak to? No, but the managing housekeeper, Mrs. Fox, whom Charlotte hadn't met, and was likely not to ever, had spoken to her briefly, and said to all the maids to leave the doctor alone, as she was down and low and was run off her feet.

Did the managing housekeeper have a standard of never wanting to meet guests? No, not particularly, it was only this time. Did the managing housekeeper say the reason? No, it would have to be inferred, it was maybe something to do with displeasure of the attention from the Law: that, and the irritating, stick-your-nose-in-private-business arrival of Mrs. Gerson, with her demands.

Oh! Did the managing housekeeper think the detective and Mrs. Gerson were Charlotte's fault, on purpose, as if she'd brought in malevolent forces, as if she carried bad luck with her, bad luck and a world of trouble, which wasn't a fair suspicion? No, well, not actually, not in so many words. Did everyone hate her, hate Charlotte, was there a poison-air cloud of resentment waiting for her at the other end of the tunnel? No, of course there wasn't, no one ever hated a guest; it wasn't allowed.

Was anyone with the doctor? Was that a question that could be answered? No. It couldn't be answered; there were rules. What about Charlotte's things, her coat, her satchel, would she be able to get her things from Moaxley? No, no need to; everything was in the new room already.

Would she be put in a room on the same floor as Miss Singleton? No, she was going to the second floor, at the very end, number 6, and she was not to venture out, please, except to go and see Mrs. Petty, who wanted her, and please would she use the back stairs to get to the kitchen.

The children! She had promised Sophy and Momo she'd see them today. She'd forgotten all about them, and now she forgot about everything else.

She came out through the panel door in great haste, thrust the unlighted candles back at Eunice, found the correct door, and went down to the kitchen right away, running down the stairs as if her feet barely touched them, so that it felt as if she were flying. It was only when she got to the bottom that she realized this was the first time she'd run down a staircase—or that she'd done any running at all—in a very, very long time. It seemed amazing that her legs still knew how to do it.

She paused in self-absorption to wait for the trembling, angered response of her thighs and lower muscles, which she assumed would come: trembling and unreliability, with cramps and then a general cave-in. This did not happen. It was as if the muscles were saying to her, "More, please; do it again," as if they were just getting primed. She hadn't felt this way since she was back at Miss Georgeson's.

The kitchen was enormous, with sweaty stone walls; a high, long, smooth-wood preparation table; pots dangling from the ceiling on hooks; a pair of storage bureaus, multidrawered and massive; a sink that was almost as large as a tub; an open back door to the washroom that let in hot, soapy steam; another open door, of the drying room, showing sheets on lines in ghostly stillness; a gigantic black cooking stove in full operation; an open hearth with brick inner side shelves for baking, and cooking pots on a bar above the fire; two maids scurrying about; and Mrs. Petty and another, unfamiliar woman, near the table.

"I ran!" Charlotte expected Mrs. Petty to drop everything she was doing to register, and appreciate, this news. There was only the slightest look, the slightest cognizance of her, as if her appearance were nothing more than a distraction, an unwelcome one. What was she doing, anyway?

Mrs. Petty had her coat on. She was stuffing things into a wooden box: knives, pans, mixing bowls, aprons, cloths, long-handled spoons. Charlotte recognized them all from the kitchen back at the household.

Now the box was passed over to a maid, who took it and rushed to the outer door. She opened it to the dusky cold, and some snow blew in, with the sound of a whinnying, restless horse. Mrs. Petty busied herself going through drawers of the storage bureaus and putting things into her coat pockets and into the quilted bag that hung off her arm, the same one she had when she'd left the household. The maid returned empty-handed, leaving the outside door partly open, but not through irresponsibility. It was a door left open because someone was about to hurry through it.

"Where are you going? What is happening?" cried Charlotte.

"She's leaving," said the other woman, who all the while just stood there placidly: a small, slightly stout, matronly pillar of calmness and strength, in a dark wool coat. Her neck was bundled with a scarf; her hands were gloved; her hat was a dark, wide-rimmed, felt turban, oversized and pulled down low on her head, shieldlike. Even though this was a woman, you thought right away of a soldier, a commander.

"Are you Mrs. Fox?"

"I am Fannie Farmer," the woman answered. "Mrs. Petty's friend."

"But I'm her friend, too, and I want to know what is happening."

Miss Farmer smiled at Charlotte sadly, as if she felt sorry for her. There was another set of stairs to the kitchen, which led from the hotel's front hall, the same stairs Mrs. Petty had hurried on the night—so very long ago, it now seemed—when Charlotte was deposited at the Beechmont by Everett Gerson. The treads of these stairs were partly obscured by half walls, on which hung more cooking implements; it was possible for someone, in the act of coming down, to pause out of sight and peer into the kitchen below.

Down those stairs came a young man dressed up most elegantly, like someone going to an opera, in a fancy English suit, with a very tight coat and handsome striped trousers. A beautiful winter coat was on his shoulders with the arms dangling; he was wearing it like a cape, and Charlotte knew it was sealskin because her father-in-law had one just like it.

This was the man she'd seen that night with Aunt Lily, and in the heat and closeness of the kitchen, appearing as suddenly as he did, he looked even more splendid than he had looked in feeble gaslight, in his nightshirt.

The math tutor who looked like an angel! He barely took note of Charlotte and went straight to Miss Farmer, offering her his arm, and a slight sound of scuffled feet above on the stairs made Charlotte look up.

Arthur was there, peering down, ready to duck out of sight. Charlotte saw him nose-first, then his chin, then the rest of his face; she knew by the way he glanced about that the only person he wanted to see was herself, and he looked *worried*.

Her eyes met his. The worry went away. His lips formed sound-less words which she understood as clearly as if he said them, as if he shouted them. "I'll be waiting for you upstairs. Second floor."

She gave her head one quick nod, and Mrs. Petty found it within herself to speak to Charlotte. "Who are you looking at?"

"No one," said Charlotte.

Mrs. Petty's back was to the stairs, and when she wheeled around, Arthur was gone.

The way Charlotte's heart fisted up in her chest, as if it would burst, was exactly the way it behaved when she was riding, or driving a sleigh or a carriage, with the wind at her face and in her hair, *fast*.

It was all she could do to keep herself where she was and not go dashing after him. She felt she had absolutely no say in the matter of wanting to be with him, not in a logical, thinking-apparatus way. She reminded herself of her horses, who would glare at her with resentment, the mare especially, as if she were the stupidest, cruelest creature on earth, when they were dying to run and she held them back; and they'd shake their heads and try to bite at the reins to be free of her. "Head high in the forehead, wide between the ears," thought Charlotte. Miss Blanchette's voice was in her head. *Limbs glossy and supple, tail dusting the ground, eyes full of sparkling wickedness, ears finely cut, flexibly moving.*

"Come with us, Charlotte," said Mrs. Petty.

She was buttoning up her coat. The elegant, beautiful tutor was going out with Miss Farmer, and they looked at Charlotte over their shoulders and smiled at her as though Mrs. Petty's invitation needed their corroboration. Charlotte remembered Arthur and Mrs. Petty talking about the fact that Miss Farmer had suffered from a stroke, or was it polio? She looked in excellent health, although she did drag one leg a little bit, and she leaned on her escort a bit more forcefully than a fully able-bodied woman would have done.

"My mother-in-law says your cookbook is a work of genius, and she never says anything nice about anyone, or anything at all, unless she absolutely has to," called out Charlotte.

"Why, thank you," said Miss Farmer.

Charlotte turned to Mrs. Petty. "Going! Where?"

"We're taking the steamboat to New Hampshire. Miss Farmer has a friend from the cooking school with an inn that's got a very successful public kitchen she wants help with."

"It'll be freezing cold on a boat, Mrs. Petty."

"They have a heated cabin."

"There'll be icebergs!"

"There are no icebergs on the New England coast."

"It's getting dark!"

"There are lanterns. Charlotte, come. The children have left for the boat already, with Georgina. What's happened with you and your husband, I'm not asking about, but I can see where it's deep. And I am not surprised. You'll not be the first woman to leave a husband she's got the need of being away from."

"Not surprised why?"

Mrs. Petty sighed heavily and spoke in a tone that implied she thought of Charlotte as an imbecilic child. "Not surprised because I'm not surprised. You can have your own room at Miss Farmer's friend's inn for as long as you like. And an ordinary inn it is, not like here. A normal, normal inn. I'm told it's a pretty town, Portsmouth, on the sea, and you love the sea. Don't deny it."

"But you're not saying why this is happening."

"The children were expelled from their school."

"Arthur said Terence knows of another one."

"It only takes girls. My girl and my boy won't be separated."

There was something Mrs. Petty wasn't saying. Charlotte eyed her warily and said, "And what else?"

"That's all you need to know."

"And what else!"

"All right. The Vice people. Miss Farmer had a letter—an anonymous one, I have to add—from someone who was one of her helpers on the cookbook, and feels an allegiance to the school, but had to be careful of her position. She's in a house where a Vice lady lives. There's talk of taking the children away from me, taking them into the Children's Benevolent Association."

"And what's that?"

"Another society. If there's a mother gone to the drink, or, shall we say, to loose morality, that's a mother that's having her children seized up by the Benevolents. It seems that they feel a hotel is not a nice place to have them, and also, Charlotte, not that you ever asked me, which I appreciate, I do not, as you're sure to have noticed, have a husband."

Charlotte made a move to postpone the inevitable. "You wouldn't have told me anything if I'd asked."

"Perhaps not, not before you came here. It was comfortable when I was with the Heaths to seem I'd not had an eventful life before, in spite of having three children with me."

"What about Mr. Alcorn?"

"I've given notice, effective right now. He went with them to the boat to say goodbye. He's fond of them, you know. And you'll see him again, for he'll be coming to visit soon enough."

Charlotte's ears picked up a different tone in Mrs. Petty's voice. She'd had the impression all along that Harry Alcorn and Mrs. Petty detested each other personally, while respecting each other professionally. Wrong! And there was no mistaking her look.

"How fond of the children is he exactly?"

"I have to go now, Charlotte."

"And what about his wife?"

"Lucy," said Mrs. Petty, "has days and days when she would not know if her husband is beside her in a chair, or if he's gone over the other side of the moon."

"I met her."

"Well, then you know."

They were calling to her from outside. "Mrs. Petty! Come! Come!"

"Mrs. Petty," said Charlotte. "Before you came to the Heaths, where were you?"

"Why, I can tell you, I was here," she answered. "I only left because the children wanted to be in the country, or a town, as the girl was thrown out of the school she was in before this one."

"And were the Benevolents after you then as well?"

"Not as energetically. Lily thought the Heath place would be all right for us, and you especially, and she thought the children would be good for you, if not for the family, which of course, they weren't."

Aunt Lily, thought Charlotte, with a groan. Everywhere one went, at every turn, there she was.

"Go upstairs quickly, Charlotte, and get your coat and whatever else you've got with you, or I'll send up a maid."

"Is Georgina going with you?"

"No, she'll be back here to run things. She'll do well enough without me."

"New Hampshire," said Charlotte.

She leaned back against the long wood table to bolster herself, in case she weakened. In the back of her mind she was picturing Arthur on his way to the second floor. She pictured the slope of his shoulders, the small of his back, the bends of his knees, the downy-hairy fuzz of his shins, his chest, his jaw. She pictured him going into a room, a different room, hers, not handed down temporarily by Aunt Lily, and she pictured him taking off his jacket, his vest, his shirt. She pictured him poking at the fire and closing the curtains, if they weren't closed already.

"I already went to New Hampshire," Charlotte said. It was, she knew, a ridiculous reason to offer, but it was the only one she could think of. "After I graduated from the academy I went to, I had a position at a school there, briefly, and as I'd left the state once, Mrs. Petty, I can't see myself with a view to go back."

Everything went silent: the clattering of the maids, who'd gone into the scullery; the fires; the things that were cooking in pots; the drip-drip-drip of the sink faucet, which seemed suddenly to halt in mid-drip. Even the clock on the wall seemed to stop its ticking.

"Rowena!" called a voice from outside. "Rowena, come out here this very instant, or we'll go to the steamboat without you and your children will think they are orphans!"

"That's Miss Farmer," said Mrs. Petty.

"You'd said she was very commanding, like a general," said Charlotte. "Rowena. I didn't know your name."

"Then now you do, and I'll say goodbye for now, and when we see each other again, you won't need to bother with a Mrs., which I anyway am not," said Mrs. Petty stiffly, without betraying how she felt. She pulled Charlotte to her and embraced her and kissed her. "Come later. Harry will have the address."

"Wait," said Charlotte. Mrs. Petty turned her head. "Which of the children would be his?"

"The girl."

"And Momo and Edith?"

"That," said Mrs. Petty, "is known only to God."

"Thank you for telling me that. Goodbye. Tell the children—"

But Mrs. Petty was already through the door. "Tell the children I envy them their mother, and I will miss them all over again, and her, too," Charlotte whispered.

She stood against the table for a long moment, listening to the sounds of a sleigh and its horses, with bells jingling wildly as it pulled away. She waited until she couldn't hear them any longer; then she gave herself a shake and went to the back stairs, and ran up them even faster than she'd gone down.

∞ Twelve ∞

Arthur had brought supper, not from the kitchen but from a shop in Cambridge at Harvard Square: crisp-crusted, hearty, tart-sized meat pies, very masculine, all beef. Charlotte didn't say they weren't as good as Mrs. Petty's. She didn't say she'd had a meat pie for lunch, and she didn't say she minded eating one cold. She didn't say there was too much salt, or that half as much bay leaf should have been used. They ate them sitting on the bed.

He also brought a bottle of wine, not the fruity stuff Hays liked, but something dry, thin. It tasted bitter until she had a bit more and got used to it, and liked it very much. The room was stocked with wineglasses and napkins, but no plates or silver. She'd never eaten a meal before with her hands, crumbs falling down her chin, onto her breasts, into her lap, on the bed. Even at picnics, the Heaths insisted on the good silver.

"Arthur," she said, when he'd finished two pies and was reaching for a third, "how many ladies have you, you know, here, been with?"

"Five thousand."

"I want to know."

He said, "It's not something that needs talking about."

"Is that a rule?"

"Actually, it is."

"Twenty?" said Charlotte. "One hundred?"

"What if I told you that you were the first?"

"I wouldn't believe you."

"Then I won't."

The first time they'd made love, last night, it was slow and tender. Cautious, even, like walking in the woods and coming upon a log bridge someone had erected across a stream that was too deep and too cold to just take off your shoes and wade across. You didn't know if the logs were rotted, if the lashings that held them together would hold. You put down each foot with trepidation, not daring to scamper across.

The second time, also last night, was more like the act of coming to the bridge in a great burst of steam and running across it. The third time was pretty much the same.

The fourth, which began the very instant Charlotte had entered the room just now and found him waiting in bed for her, without his clothes on, not a single stitch, was based on not bothering with the bridge, but going to the stream at a higher level—where it was frothiest, all churning and agitated—and plunging in. Arthur wore his sheaths for the first three times but not for the fourth. He told her there were ways to make sure, without one, that stuff didn't get inside her. That was how he'd put it.

Stuff. It sounded like something that belonged inside a pillow or a sausage, or a drawer in a cupboard, where you put things that had no other place to be put. After the second and third times, he used a towel to wipe the stuff off her belly—liquidy jellylike stuff, which felt, to the touch of her fingers, like something obnoxiously oozy.

"There are theorists in England and Germany," he told her, "who believe that the origins of humans are in slime at the bottom of swamps, probably deposited by rocks, which fell from other planets, full of bacteria, and broke apart upon landing."

That sounded demoralizing. No wonder whoever wrote the Bible came up with the story of Adam, where all it took was God's breath, blown on a clean lump of clay.

Arthur didn't know about the three times there was supposed to have been a child, hers and Hays's. But she wanted to mention it. "I conceived three times with my husband and they all came to nothing," she told him. "I can't bear."

"It must have been horrible for you."

"It was bloody, and I'm not embarrassed to say so. Each time, it was worse. Then afterward no one wanted to look at me."

"I'll look at you," he said. He didn't want to hear about Hays.

Now the fire in the fireplace was burning away; the coal supply was low, but not too much so. There was a pitcher of drinking water and water glasses. The room was even smaller than Aunt Lily's, and there weren't any pictures of Miss Singleton's, just a few large water-colors of people in different types of weather, with scenes that were Boston places: Tremont Street along the Common, where a man in black clothes struggled with the big black umbrella he was holding over his head, for it was pouring rain; a lady picking a flower at the Public Garden by the swan pond, which was illegal, in sunshine; a lady and a girl on the steps of the Public Library, and they must have been inside a long time, because they were dressed for autumn and it was a snowstorm, the steps banked high with snow.

The people in the pictures looked dull, as if they weren't having lives where anything ever happened to them, as if they only existed for the pictures, but maybe the point was the landmarks, and what the sky was doing. Anyway, it came as a respite, not to have to look at Miss Singleton's. Her pictures wouldn't give themselves up to being things in a background. They would hang there and demand to be accepted as the most important things in the room.

Charlotte said to herself, with conviction, like this was something she was trying to talk herself into, "If he was with two hundred, or a dozen, or two, I don't care, I won't think about it."

The wine! It was making her head feel tickled from the inside out. The last time she drank wine was at Uncle Chessy and Aunt Lily's house in Brookline, for some family event, some anniversary or birthday. After her second glass, Hays said, in front of everyone, "Charlotte, that's quite enough for you."

Uncle Chessy must have noticed, by the look on her face, that she was ready to pick up the nearest thing—a bowl of applesauce, it would have been, for the roast—and then go over to her husband and dump it on his head.

It was unthinkable that a Heath, especially the host of a dinner, would get up from the table and wander off, but this was what Chester Heath, defender of criminals, author of a book on the rights of aliens, and now a judge, did.

"Come with me, Charlotte, I want to show you something." They went down to his big, booky, leathery study, which was a mess: the untidiest room she'd ever seen in a house that had servants. Cigar ash everywhere; the air like the inside of a cigar. Papers thrown around, unwashed teacups, books stacked in heaps on the floor, window draperies that had not been washed for half a century. Uncle Chessy was famous for not letting anyone in there. He went over to a cabinet and took out a bottle of wine exactly like the one on the table.

He put it into her hands. "Would you like to go back and set this at your place, and we'll have the waiter open it for you? And you can say to my nephew, who perhaps gets a bit stuffy, God bless him, 'This is Chester's house, and this is a gift from him to me, and I'll do as I please with it'?"

"I want to bash him on the head with it."

"Besides that."

"No, thank you. I didn't want any more anyway."

And that was when he made his promise to her, well, a renewal of the one he'd made on her wedding day, when he alone of the all the Heaths came to her quietly and took her hands and looked into her eyes—this bear of a man, black-gray bearded, with a beard covering so much of his face, his small dark eyes and small nose and lips, round and reddish, looked like afterthoughts, as if they played only a minor role.

He told her that he would love her as a niece, that he welcomed her, that it pleased him right down to the blood in his veins to see that Hays, for a change, had done something unexpectedly remark-able by marrying her; and he, Chester, could be called upon by Charlotte at any time, in any way, and whatever service she would need him to render, he would do it, as he would for a child of his own, which he and Lily didn't have, not that he was complaining about it.

She'd been moved, but it was her wedding day and her head was spinning the whole time: there'd been so much else to pay attention to. In the study, she paid attention.

He reminded her of what he'd said; he told her she could count on him as a friend. It was a solemn moment, and she squeezed his hands and thanked him, and let him kiss her on the cheek, with a chafing—the beard was rough, prickly; poor Aunt Lily. And a moment later she'd forgotten all about Hays giving her commands across the table, and monitoring her the way he did, and always tak-ing a position of being in charge of her, when she was telling him all the time, "Stop watching me, Hays."

"What are you thinking about?" said Arthur.

"An uncle of mine," said Charlotte.

"In what way?"

Charlotte thought of Chester Heath at his desk, in his study that looked disaster-stricken. Maybe he was sitting there at this moment, alone in that big house. Who was to say what was what between a husband and wife? When he'd married Aunt Lily she was already established, with her practice, her own rooms, her own reputation, friends. There'd been a scandal about it because the Heaths were pushing for another match, all of them except for Hays, who could take an independent stand when he wanted to; he really could, and not just about having married Charlotte.

Chester was supposed to have given himself to a much-younger lady from a nearby town whose father was involved with railroads: the lady was porcelain-figurine pretty, corseted up to her neck, with a brain, Hays said, like the inside of a candy box, which was harsh of him, Charlotte had thought, until she found out (from him) that the first choice of the family, for a bride for Hays, was that lady.

Anyway, the marriage of Lily and Chester was hugely opposed by everyone, Hays included, because, first, no one liked Lily, who was tall and strident and professional and unfeminine; it was nice to have a doctor in the family, but lady doctors should still be ladies, it was felt, not go charging into people's houses and sickbeds as rough and bold and conceited as a man who worked on docks or herded cattle.

And everyone was used to thinking of Chester Heath as a bache-lor, a man who preferred the company of men and, more specifically, of other lawyers, or men whose whole existence was taken up in some way with courts and trials and defenses, or in writing about them. Uncle Chessy said that if you couldn't think of anything else to say to a legal man in Boston, at a party or a dance, you could safely launch a conversation by asking him, "How are you making out with your book?"

Maybe Aunt Lily's husband knew about the hotel and maybe he didn't. It was no one's business, really, except their own. Why should it be anyone else's business?

A doctor would need to maintain respectability, but when you needed one, you wouldn't care if it was the worst-morality person on earth, as long as you knew they weren't a murderer; you'd want your doctor to get rid of your pain. A judge was a different matter. Charlotte wondered what the Vice people would think of a judge who had things in his life that truly needed to be hidden.

But wasn't that a natural thing? Why should someone's life seem obvious and plain, and fully surfaced, like an enormous boulder in the middle of a flat, empty field, visible for miles, when it was so much closer to the truth that—if one's life were like a giant rock—three-fourths of the rock, maybe more, would have to be underneath, invisibly connected to cores of things, for good reason?

"It's an uncle of mine I would trust with my life. I'm thinking, actually," said Charlotte, "of writing a letter to him."

"Now?"

"Yes." It didn't seem right to compose one without anything on, so she reached for Arthur's shirt, a different one, a soft, striped flannel. "Ladies should be able to wear clothes like this," she said.

"You can if you like."

"I doubt I'd get away with it, outside of this building."

"It's from Sears, Roebuck," said Arthur. "After my father died I was given a lifetime account to make purchases at discount."

Charlotte was putting one arm in a sleeve when he said this. She paused to look for a label. She looked inside the collar, inside each cuff, and in the stripes, in case the name of the maker was inscribed in threads, which was a stupid thing to think; but she couldn't help it. "What are you doing, Charlotte?"

"Checking." She didn't know anyone who wore clothes from Sears, Roebuck. "Do you cut off labels?"

"Sometimes, if they irritate me."

"Well, I need some paper. And an envelope, and ink and something to write with."

Modestly, or perhaps because drafts were coming in through the window in spite of the closed curtains, Arthur wrapped a blanket around himself when he got up. He went rummaging through the one drawer of the little night table and came up with a leather portfolio embossed in fancy gold letters with the words THE BEECHMONT: A PRIVATE HOTEL FOR GENTLE LADIES.

"I can't use paper with a name on it, Arthur."

"The paper's blank. Harry Alcorn's a very careful man, I told you."

He was right, and there were also stamps, and a handsome, expensive pen, and a new bottle of ink. She sat at the edge of the bed and used the little table as a desk.

"Are you going to tell me who you're writing to?"

"You can read it yourself when I'm through."

"I don't believe in reading other people's letters."

She addressed the letter to Chester Heath at his house in Brookline, and put no indication of where she was.

"Dear Uncle Chessy,

"I want to say first that I regret not having been able to go to Uncle Owen's funeral. It was not that I played truant on purpose. I am sorry for his passing. When I think of him in the future, which I shall do, I shall think of him as Falstaff, his best role, a Falstaff of America but wiser—and richer, I might add. I'm sure you understand my sentiment.

"My true reason for writing besides that is to say: You have offered your willingness to help me in some trouble, if I should need you. I do. Don't worry about my safety or well-being. I am stopping at an undisclosed location, for how long I don't yet know. I am safe. I am well. My illness is a thing of the past.

"Please will you do the following. I give you my trust, as you had pledged me yours. No one can know of this.

"I wish for you to engage a detective. I'm told Pinkerton is an excellent agency. You will need to put up payment in my place, at least, for the time being. I don't have the means just now to have access to my own funds. When I do I shall not mind the expense, however large it may be.

"There was a married couple in Hartford, Connecticut, by the names of Ralph and Florence Pym. Mr. Pym was a New England representative of Sears, Roebuck, with a Hartford office. He died some—"

Charlotte looked up at Arthur. He was standing by the fire, idly waving an edge of the blanket in its direction, as if Charlotte had annoyed him so much, and now he was so utterly bored, he was willing to catch himself on fire.

"Oh, stop that," she said, "and tell me how many years ago your father died."

"My father? What are you talking about? Who're you writing to and what about?"

"I'll read it to you when it's finished."

"I'm not telling you anything else about my family, or about anything."

"You sound like me, talking to Mrs. Petty."

"I feel it. She's left. She wanted you to go with her."

"I didn't."

"Why?"

"Because," said Charlotte. She couldn't say why. "Because I want to write this letter."

"He died when I was fifteen."

She realized she didn't know his age. "How old are you?"

"Twenty-seven."

"Isn't that old to be in college?"

"I'm combining it with my medical studies."

"But still."

"All right, I admit it, it seems to be taking me a long time."

"I suppose that time is something you feel you have a right to."

"You judge me!"

"I don't. I don't want to argue with you, either. If I wanted to argue with a man, I would have—" She was about to say, "stayed at home," but thought better of it and continued with the letter.

". . . some eleven years ago. Mrs. Pym was in education."

She would need the names of some places. "Arthur, what was the name of your mother's school, where she was mistress?"

"I don't remember."

"You talk like a little boy."

"Let's go back to bed."

"This is very important."

"I don't remember, honestly."

Who cared what the name of the school was? Let the detective find out.

"She was a well-known teacher," Charlotte wrote, "and she published articles and taught at a college. Some years ago, prior to her husband's passing, Mrs. Pym vanished from sight, and was never heard from again."

"Arthur, I want to know the address your mother had given you to write to."

By now he was back on the bed, behind her, and he was reading over her shoulder. He said nothing. She couldn't see his face. His breath was on her neck, winey, warm.

"Unfortunately the address is unknown," she wrote. "Please instruct the detective to make discreet inquiries regarding, first, the cause for Mrs. Pym's disappearance, and second, to make every effort possible to determine where she is, if she is still alive. If not, I should like to know where her grave is."

Charlotte thought that it must have seemed heartless of her to have put in that last bit. But this was a practical matter. One needed to transact a business arrangement without emotions. If she expected a reaction from Arthur, she didn't get one.

"There is one other matter. I wish to have inquiries made in reference to my husband. I wish to know with what woman he is involved, in a liaison. I wish to know her name, her particulars, and, in short, whatever there is about her to know. I realize, given the two separate situations, more than one detective will be needed.

"You must know, by now, I have left Hays. Please attend to this as soon as you are able. It is most urgent. Proceed without further word from me. I can give you no further information. I shall write again soon to see how it is progressing.

"Your niece, Charlotte."

She put the letter in the envelope, sealed it, stamped it. "I'll post it for you," said Arthur, trying to take it out of her hands.

"You will not. How does one ring for a maid?"

"You've been in here most of a week," he said. "I should think you already know."

"Whenever I wanted Eunice, she appeared."

There was a bellpull on the wall near the window. Arthur sat in the center of the bed and put the blanket over his head as if he were willing to be smothered. She pulled the bell for the maid.

"You've doubted me, Charlotte." His voice, under the blanket, was fuzzy and muffled. He sounded hurt. "I bared my past to you, and you wonder if I was inventing it, for I can't even imagine what reason. How could you do that?"

"I don't doubt you," she said.

She found her little purse with the Gersons' money and took out a dollar. It didn't take long for Eunice to come up, with a bucket of coal and another blanket. She'd been on her way anyway, not that Charlotte had asked for these things.

Charlotte opened the door just widely enough to take them. "Post this for me, Eunice, at once, please. And take this." She gave her the money. "Please go and buy yourself a cake somewhere, and tell the other maids I apologize for taking back the sweets they were counting on."

The little maid beamed. "This would buy three or four! It's too much!"

"Go on, and buy yourself three or four."

"Please, missus, I have to ask, is Mr. Pym with you?"

"He is. Why do you ask?"

"No reason. It's just that another lady had asked if he was any-where free."

"He's not free," said Charlotte.

She shut the door harder than she needed to. It was like talking about a cab. Or a hairdresser. Or a shop attendant. Or a doctor.

Suddenly she was tired. Suddenly the room was not quite as attractive, not quite as charming, not quite as comfortable. There was an aching, dull throbbing in both her breasts, from Arthur. Hays never, ever put his mouth on her breasts because that was what infants did, as if he thought that milk was stored there always and he didn't want to take any away, like it would need to be saved.

Her lips hurt from being kissed. There were probably indenta-tions from Arthur's teeth all over them. She was glad the room had no mirror. She didn't want to know what she looked like.

Everything between her breasts and the bottoms of her feet was aching, everything. She should never have written that letter. What did she care about Arthur's mother? What did she care about him? She never should have gone to the Gersons for help. She never should have come to Boston. She should have hitched her horses outside Uncle Owen's house and gone inside to look at him lying there dead.

She should have gone home to her husband. She really should have. Then everything would be all right.

What about the woman? Was she supposed to pretend she hadn't seen what she saw? Could she do that?

She couldn't have done it before she'd come to the Beechmont. That much was certain. But maybe she could do it now. Or, if not pretend, then just simply find a way to forget about it.

Or if not forget about it, overlook it. Could that be a possible thing, somehow?

"Charlotte." Arthur had come up behind her. His hands were on her hips, his face was pressed into her hair. "Your hair is all crinkly," he said.

"That's because it was in that awful braid all day."

"Come back to bed." He lifted the hair at her neck and kissed her neck, the only place that wasn't aching.

Well, now it was, but it was aching to be kissed a little more. He moved his hands to her breasts, lightly. She leaned back against him.

"Why did you do that?" he said.

"Do what."

"The letter."

"I don't know."

"You must have had some motivation."

"To help you?"

"Or to test me."

That was what Dickie had done in their interview. He'd tried to trick her into confessing that, when it came to the hotel, her word could not be trusted. Maybe people were always doing that to each other: I dare you to prove a big disappointment to me.

"You only say *test* because you're a student," said Charlotte.

"Perhaps I'll be one forever."

She didn't answer that. He'd just accuse her again of judging him in a negative light. She thought about the way Hays's face had looked when he came calling on her—a younger Hays, a nervous blushing suitor, in spite of his money and his position and his career—all those years ago, at that boring school in New Hampshire where she was spending her days teaching frightened little girls to go around in circles in goat carts.

He'd be waiting for her at the edge of the paddock, or by the stables, or in the reception room. And when she came toward him, there'd be a lift to him, a visible rising of his spirits, as real as if his sentiments were like one of those hot-air balloons when the ropes are cut and they soar, miraculously. There'd been no effort made at concealing that.

Funny how Hays could show affection in public in intimate gestures, taking her hand at a service in church, like a lover, or gently, absentmindedly, brushing his knuckles at the side of her neck in the middle of a drawing-room soiree with business associates from so many different countries, it would sound like the Tower of Babel in there, and he alone, Hays, her husband, would know what was what, would stand there with his feet planted squarely, sure of himself, fisting his hand as another man would do to cause violence, and then tenderly, sweetly, caressing her, in front of everyone.

And then in private he'd be secretive, guarded, speaking in camouflage, in riddles, coming to her like a hobbled old horse, like a horse so controlled and so spiritless, it doesn't know when its bridle is off or on, or if the paddock gate is shut or open. Where did that soaring balloon of the old Hays go?

Off into the horizon, out of sight, sinking into some ocean or crashing on some cliff, or running out of power in a clear blue sky and slowly, gracefully, horribly, descending straight down, as if it were meant to do that all along: it would crash and be pulverized to dust.

Maybe some fault of it was hers. She was willing to admit to herself that it was not all one-sided. Maybe when she'd got sick, at first, she'd given her husband the idea she did not want him near her.

Maybe she'd been a little too shrill in the way she lay there and shouted at him, yes, shouted, "Leave me be!" As if it were his fault that the fevers came, the numbing, the pain.

And what about that day in Aunt Lily's office, when it was revealed that something was wrong with her? She had never seen that look on his face before, and she knew it was only a shade of the depths of his feeling, because she'd seen his struggle to mask it. Fear. I'm the only thing he's afraid of losing, she had thought.

Arthur said, "I suppose I should thank you for your intentions."

"No need."

"What was in your mind?"

"I had thought of it, that was all."

"But why?"

"Perhaps," she said, "it's because the academy I went to was a Christian girls' school, and it was instilled in me to be useful."

"I don't think so." He was whispering into her ear, pulling her to him more closely. "I'm glad you can't see what my face is like."

"Describe it."

"No."

She turned around and he kissed her hard and she kissed him back even harder, clutching at him as if she were drowning. They went tripping over each other to the bed, flinging themselves down, kissing.

Someone was at the door. They realized that the knocking had gone on for some time. Arthur grabbed for the blanket, to cover himself.

It was Aunt Lily: a tense, pinched-face Aunt Lily, with tears in her eyes, tears down her cheeks. "Charlotte, my friend Miss Single-ton has died," she said. "Let me in."

∽ Thirteen ∾

A Beechmont bed that was big enough for two lovers was inadequate, Charlotte found, for someone trying to sleep beside her aunt, who was tall and broad to begin with, and kept tossing about and pulling at the blankets and flinging out her limbs, and muttering half-coherent things, repeated in pairs, like, "Clamp that! Clamp that!" And, "The ointment, the ointment!"

She considered going upstairs to the room Aunt Lily had abandoned, but she didn't want to take the risk of finding someone else in it, such as the beautiful math tutor, or some other man.

It was odd to be in a position of giving comfort to someone who had only seemed to exist to give comfort to you. "You aren't necessary at the moment." Those were Aunt Lily's parting words to Arthur.

Miss Singleton had died in her chair just after dusk. Terence and two other young men—two Italians, from the Italian tenements—were with her, and the lady pianist, and a lady who'd just checked in from Cape Cod, who painted seascapes and hoped to talk shop with someone more accomplished than she was, although she was pretty good herself.

A supper party was taking place, put together from what was scavenged from Mrs. Petty's abandoned kitchen. There were new candles, a lot of wine, champagne, and a festive air, for no particular reason except that Miss Singleton had spent a pleasant day, and was looking forward to a biscuit cake that Georgina had made her that morning, with no-sugar blueberries and blackberries from cans: berries for Berry, which she never ate.

Terence and the lady from the Cape had argued with the Italians about Rome. The Americans said, Oh, the paintings, the history, the statues, the Pope, the beauty, the hills, the glory; and the Italians laughed at them and said they were naive, they were innocents, they were like schoolchildren. "Roma, *puttana,* is not *bella,* is a whore!" they cried.

Miss Singleton sided with the Italians, great favorites of hers; they'd been with her all day, which was why her mood was good. She said, "Gentlemen, I should love to paint your faces, I've been thinking about doing it since this morning, and wondering if I'm up to it," and then she tipped back her head and gave a gasp, and her jaw fell open and she was dead, and they went running downstairs for Lily.

In a fit of temper, at the sight of the woman so utterly still, as if the polio had entered all of her, one of the Italians had seized Georgina's cake, rushed to a window, opened it, and hurled it, plate and all, to the street.

"Pity the detective's not down there to think it was meant for himself," observed Terence. He'd only arrived for supper but had been told that everyone else had monitored the detective with great interest; he felt he'd missed out on something.

Aunt Lily hadn't mentioned the detective. She'd waited until

Arthur was gone before she threw herself down on the bed and sobbed. Charlotte patted her hair, held her hand, poured her a glass of water, and gave her the rest of the wine.

When the burst of tears had let up, Charlotte asked her, "Were you Miss Singleton's physician?"

"Not officially. She'd lost faith in the medical profession. In fact I knew her for more than thirty-five years, and I don't mind telling you, for many of those years, we were singularly close to each other. And I've no more to say on the subject, Charlotte, if you don't mind."

For a long time, Charlotte sat in the one, narrow, straight-backed chair. She was fully dressed, in respect for Aunt Lily, who had anyway demanded it. She was wearing Mrs. Gerson's too-big dress; she had no nightclothes. Mrs. Gerson had forgotten to pack any for her, in the haste and confusion of that flight. "I have got to buy some clothes," Charlotte said to herself.

She watched her aunt sleeping. Arthur had left for the night train west, to go and see his dissection. Strange that a man who planned to be a physician, and was so eager for a body dug up from a bog, was so squeamish, so downright hostile, when it came to the proximity of known, brand-new death. He kept nervously glancing up at the ceiling as he dressed—and there was some awkwardness about that, in front of Aunt Lily, and with the tiny size of the room.

He shuddered to hear Aunt Lily's recounting of what had happened. He said, "That's so vulgar," and it wasn't clear if he meant Rome-like-a-whore, or the act of someone's heart, right there in the building, performing one last beat and then stopping, just stopping. "You can go up to see her before you leave tonight, if you like," Aunt Lily told him. By the look on his face, you'd think it would be torture for him to do so; he looked as though he would rather throw himself off the roof.

"Good night, Arthur," Charlotte said, at the door.

He tried to pull her into the hall with him. He wanted to kiss her, but she pushed back her shoulders and went stiff, and spoke to him formally, hostesslike.

"I hope you have a safe journey."

"Come with me. Come out to the Valley."

"Go, or you'll miss the train."

"Your old home. West, all those towns. You all but said it's your old home."

"I'm with my aunt now."

"No, come with me. You must realize you want to. Your aunt has so many friends here, she'll be all right without you."

"You're the second person in one evening to ask me to go away with them."

"You said no to the first to be able to say yes to the second."

"I think not," said Charlotte, and she smiled at him sadly.

And shut the door.

She pictured him out in the darkness, the snow. She pictured the journey of the train. The frosty windows, the steady beat, the sound of the whistle, the iron wheels, the sight through scrapes in the frost of black trees lit up by the moon, and looking like black, somber skeletons. She pictured the mountains in the distance, and the little stations—grimy, desolate, dirty lanterns on dirty poles, snow every-where.

It still felt good to know their names. Forge Landing. Wachusetts. Allenberg. East Derby, Derby River. Fairfield. Blackstone Junction, where Miss Georgeson's was. North Blackstone, Blackstone. Oak-ville, where Arthur was going. Chetterdon. Bigelow Mills Village, where her home was, before Miss Georgeson's.

Morton Falls. Cranfield. Westerville. Wall Gorge Township, with a tower of a mighty, astonishing waterfall, where you weren't allowed to go until you'd turned thirteen; it was your thirteenth birthday present—pure, raw watery power—and then you had to be with so many teachers and servants, who guarded you fiercely, every second, it was galling, and they said they'd tie you with a rope like an animal if you tried to get close, so close that the roaring of the water came into your head so loud, it would seem you'd be deaf forever, and think that the deafness was worth it; and the spray with its icy strength made you feel that if you threw yourself to the Gorge, just fled from every restraint, you'd be as light as a feather, borne up by all that water, pushed up into the air; and you could fly.

Then Lanbridge, at the end of the line, where the little lake was, where she'd tipped over in a sailboat and might have died if the water had not been so shallow.

She tried to picture herself beside Arthur on a train seat, her hand holding his. Her head on his shoulder. Her thigh pressed up to his thigh. "A newly married couple," other passengers might say.

"I hired him," she'd have to answer. She couldn't picture herself beside Arthur.

She put some more coal on the fire. She didn't know where the lavatory was on this floor. She was not in the mood to go searching for it. She relieved herself in the chamber pot, as quietly as she could.

She covered Aunt Lily with a blanket she'd thrown off. She cleaned up the remains of her and Arthur's supper. She balled up the wrappings and threw them into the fire. She brushed her hair, leaving it down. At about four in the morning, she ventured out into the hall.

She peered down from the second-floor landing. The gas lamps at every staircase and in the downstairs hall were lit—they were low and flickering, but they were on. A noise had got Charlotte's attention: a growly, nasally heavy snoring, which sounded at first like a door being blown open and its hinges creaking.

Moaxley, his cloak around him like a blanket, was asleep with his mouth wide open in an armchair. He must have dragged the chair out to the hall from one of the sitting rooms.

He was a rumpled, bedraggled-looking guard, and you had to wonder what he was sitting guard for, in the silence, with the door locked and bolted. But then you remembered: death.

The cloak had slipped off him here and there to reveal not his customary clothes, but something blue. In one hand was a blue cap, which was clung to in sleep like something attached to Moaxley's fingers.

It was the uniform of a Union soldier. He was the right age for it. It almost made you wish you were a man, and a soldier yourself, just to have something to put on when death came onto the scene, besides draping yourself in yards and yards of black, like ladies were supposed to. Charlotte's mother-in-law had about an acre's worth of black crinoline, folded up and stored in a chest, for the widow's dresses she felt sure she'd be one day needing to have made. All the ladies over forty had some. White when you're a bride, black when you're a widow, as if there were nothing worth mentioning in between.

Why should death be given the pitch of an empty-sky night? *Raise the colors! There is nothing ignoble in a pulse being stopped when the blood coursed valiant and true.*

Maybe it wasn't "pulse." Maybe it was "heart." She couldn't remember where those lines came from. Some history play: Richard, John, Henry? Some old king, played by some Heath, as out of place in an American town hall as a bustle at the tailbone of a young and vigorous American lady.

All the same, they were nice lines. Maybe the histories had their uses. If anyone's blood had run valiant and true, it was Berenice Singleton's.

Charlotte turned and climbed on tiptoes up the two flights to Miss Singleton's floor. She almost lost her footing as she neared the top and heard her voice called, in a small masculine whisper. She'd been so intent on watching the steps, one at a time, she didn't see

Harry Alcorn until she was right before him. He was sitting on the topmost tread, with his head in his hands and his knees bunched up. He was wearing a cream-colored linen suit and a white shirt without a tie. In the thin light, he looked ghostly.

"Hello, Charlotte, what are you up to?"

"You startled me!"

"But wouldn't one expect to be startled, walking about in the dead of night?"

She caught her breath. "I've come to look at Miss Singleton."

He waved his arm in the direction of all of the doors, shut tight, of her rooms. "A crowd's in there. They're not wasting any time. They're fixing her up. Did you know she's to have a burial at sea?"

Charlotte had a mental image of a gang of dark-suited men holding up a coffin in which lay Miss Singleton, and throwing it over some cliffs, like the cliffs at the summer place at Squab Cove. That couldn't have been what he meant.

Harry moved over and let her sit down beside him. A burial at sea? "They're going to put her in the *water*?"

"Her husband was an admiral or whatever it is that's close to the rank. He was on that infamous ship at Havana."

"They told me. That warship that was exploded. They said he was the commander."

"No. That would have made it more bearable, I suppose. He wasn't supposed to be there. He was inspecting things, and was given a ride, and was due to meet up with another one. Berry took it bad. She was already living here pretty much most of the time. So we brought in a lawyer and she put it in her will she wanted to be taken out by the Navy and put into the waves, so she could join him, which isn't allowed for civilians, ordinarily, but she paid the Navy in advance for their trouble, and they feel bad about that boat. And her husband was a powerful man."

"Did you ever meet him?"

"Oh, certainly. Berry's Pirate. That's what he was called. His name was Andrew, and he was the best-humored, most energetic man that ever put foot on a vessel. He really looked like a pirate, you see. Had these big mustaches and the torso of a giant, and short legs, bowed like. Could cuss like the worst of them. A good man. Dead."

"Does Miss Singleton have to be taken to Havana?"

"No," said Harry. "I suppose they'll just do it from here, and chug off from the naval yard over in Charlestown. Where's Lily?"

"In my bed."

"She's got to get in for early rounds, or the wards will fall to pieces, even worse than the shape they're in."

"I'll make sure she's up soon. I met your wife," said Charlotte.

"I heard."

There didn't seem to be anything else to say, at the moment, about that. "Can one go to the yard and watch the boat go out?"

"Indirectly, I would think. She's got a house, a grand one, right over at Bowdoin Square, empty as anything for the last two years, except for servants. It's her official, you know, residence. We're going to have her brought over there so the Navy can fetch her properly. Anyway, that's the address they've got. No reason to confuse things. And it's the Navy who's getting the house. The Pirate was particular about that, though I suspect he might have changed his mind if he lived to see what was done to poor Cuba."

"Was Moaxley in the States' War?"

"A sergeant or something. Decorated, and all that."

"I saw him downstairs. He's got a Union uniform on."

"Does he?" Harry seemed pleased. "Nice touch, that. I knew he'd meant to have a replica made and thought it unreasonably sentimental of him. But he was indulgent of the lady. Good Christ, so was I."

"Why a replica?"

"My dear Mrs. Heath, perhaps when you're of a certain age, outfits you wore at twenty will still quite fit you. He was twenty years old in his Union days. Pity the fabric's better now than it was for the war."

"I hadn't thought of that."

One of the doors opened. A gray-haired, short, plump woman came out from Miss Singleton's with a bundled-up pile of laundry under one arm. From the way she glared at Charlotte, this had to be the managing housekeeper, Mrs. Fox.

And a curt old sourpuss she was. "Harry, why is this lady out of her room, when it's against all the rules?"

"I believe, Mrs. Fox, she wants to go and pay respects."

"She can go to Bowdoin Square like everyone else. There's to be a laying out before the sailors come to fetch her. Is this the Mrs. Heath who brought the police, and caused poor Lily so much trouble?"

"I did not," said Charlotte, "do any such thing."

"Is she dressed?" said Harry, and Mrs. Fox gave a military-like nod of her head.

"What about the pictures?" said Harry. "Tell me you didn't touch them."

Mrs. Fox didn't care about the pictures. "That's your department."

"She left them all to me, you know," said Harry to Charlotte. "I don't feel grabby and greedy about it, talking about it now. I've known for ages."

Charlotte was curious. "What are you going to do with them?"

"Put them on my walls, and take down every tedious, stupefying thing I've got hanging anywhere that's not one of hers."

"Maybe they should go to a museum."

"Maybe they will, I suppose. Eventually. My own demise is not the subject, and I'm not going to think about it. But I'll tell you, when Moaxley got that suit made, it was likely to be for someone else's going. Specifically mine."

He stood up, groaning, and held out his hand to Charlotte. "Come on. This is my hotel and I can do what I like."

Charlotte fussed with her hair and straightened out the folds of Mrs. Gerson's dress, dangling off her so amply. Mrs. Fox disapproved of these gestures.

"You're going to look at a corpse, Mrs. Heath," she said. "Not to someone's drawing room Thursday afternoon."

"Give it a rest," said Harry, rising to Charlotte's defense. They went inside through the same door Mrs. Fox had exited.

The big wide-open space was lit by candles, not many of them, but just enough to give everything a yellowy glow. Chairs had been set up at the far end. The screen that had separated Miss Singleton's sleeping room was gone.

In the chairs, around the bed, were Beechmont servants: little Eunice and Georgina; a few maids Charlotte hadn't seen before; Terence; a young, blunt-faced, blond man; two curly dark-haired gorgeously handsome young men who had to be the Italians; the woman with the horsey face she'd met in her bath, who was supposed to have stayed in the hotel because the roads were full of snow, which they now were not, and a woman with a dark-blue turban tied around her head, who had to be the pianist, because her fingers were thrumming on the bed where Miss Singleton lay, as if playing a tune for her, and not a somber one: the fingers were moving in a quick, high-spirited way.

Charlotte whispered to Harry, "Where is her chair?"

"In the snow. They threw it out the window."

"It wouldn't fit!"

"First they took it apart. It's not as if she wanted to have it sunk with her."

No one looked up at Harry and Charlotte. No one was asleep. Quietly, in low, murmuring voices, they were playing some sort of a game, an alphabet game, one of those things Charlotte's father-in-law and mother-in-law detested, and said were for dilettantes.

"What letter are we on?" said the horsey woman.

"*P*," someone said, and Terence said, "What's the old name for Portugal?"

"Lusitania," called out Harry. Then he said, "Where's the Quarterno Gulf?"

"Istria!" said the two Italians, as one. Charlotte wondered which one had thrown the cake out the window.

"Where is the Rideau Canal?" said the pianist, and one of the maids spoke up.

"Canada." She blushed. "I come from Ontario."

"What connects the South China Sea to the East?" said the blond man, and Terence said, "We had that one last week," and the blond man said, "I wasn't here," and the horsey woman said, "The Strait of Formosa, and I wasn't here either."

"Miss Singleton," said Harry quietly to Charlotte, "was addicted to place-name games, and would say, when stumped for an answer, that the Pirate, who knew every spot on the globe, would whisper it in her ear, and I'll be damned if he didn't, because she'd come up with an answer every time."

"Shame we're not playing with shots of whiskey," said Terence.

"It wouldn't be right," said Georgina, "for a vigil."

"Well, we ran out," said Terence.

And another maid, as Irish-looking as anything, said, "Are we on *T*?" They were. "So then, where is Tralee?"

Everyone pretended that the question was too hard, but it didn't matter. You could tell she'd just wanted to say it, and she said it again: "Tralee." There were tears in her eyes, and she said, "I was just after thinking, it ought to be creepy, her being so suddenly gone. But she wasn't creepy alive, and she's not given over to being such-like, now that she's departed."

"She would have liked that. Not creepy," said the pianist, and one of the Italians demanded to know, what was the meaning of the word, and little Eunice said, "Like when you think there're insects crawling on you, or something's ugly. Or in other words, the opposite of how she looks."

"She is beautiful, she is *incantevole,*" said the other Italian, and he didn't have to say what that meant because his hands made gestures in the air to suggest, somehow, "like a very good statue in the middle of a fountain."

"Are you sure we're out of booze?" said the blond man.

"If we weren't, I'd be sitting here finishing it," said Terence.

"I have grappa," said one of the Italians.

Terence brightened. "Where is it?"

"It's in my room," said the pianist, "and he and I are not sharing it with anyone else."

"Don't look at me," said Harry. "Bar's closed."

Charlotte just stood there. Miss Singleton's body simply looked like Miss Singleton, exactly as she'd looked the other night, when she'd abruptly canceled out Charlotte and let her eyes close. She was lying down instead of sitting; she was on top of the covers in a purple and red satin gown with ruffles all over the bodice and at the sleeves. A few of the fingers on her good hand were paint-stained.

Maybe whoever had washed her had left the paint there on purpose. Where was the ice-garden picture?

Charlotte looked around. The paintings stacked everywhere on the floor, against the walls, had been backward the night she was here. But now some were turned out. She saw a couple of watercolors of rigid dark boats in an ice-crusted bay, and a watercolor of a man's battered brown shoe on its side near a dustbin.

What fixed her attention were the three big oils lined up against the wall just outside the sleeping area. No wonder everyone had kept saying to her, Did you see her pictures of Harry, of his wife? No one had mentioned Miss Blanchette, but there she was, too.

At the bottom of each one, unlike all the other pictures, there were titles, in narrowly drawn capital letters, in black.

"Harry Done In." She'd put him on a sofa, in of course a pale suit, sprawled out, not so much napping as unconscious, his mouth all slack, his lips a little flabby, his face so weary-looking, it would seem no amount of sleep could cure it. On a table beside the sofa in a glass of water were dentures. It was so real-to-life, you'd think that if you held your hand near those lips you'd feel his breath.

It was the first picture she'd seen of Miss Singleton's which implied in any way that something was actually moving. The teeth in the glass were so detailed, it seemed that if the table were bumped or shaken, they'd start clattering.

Harry noticed what she was looking at. She only now realized that the teeth in his mouth were artificial. She wondered if they hurt, if they fit right. It didn't seem right to mention it, and she didn't, but she remembered that Mrs. Petty—Rowena—had written that he suffered from gum decay. She'd had to cook special foods for him.

"I'm going to hide my picture," he said.

"I think it's wonderful."

"Do you like my wife?"

"Lucy Reading," it was called. Mrs. Alcorn sat at the same table next door where Charlotte had eaten her big, good, game-and-meat pie.

A book was open before her. Her neck was bent slightly toward it, swanlike, and there was something about the look of a swan in the paleness of her skin, the feathery white creases of her dress, a silk one; and it was like looking at a woman whose face you'd think you had seen in the moon, when you were a child and thought the moon had people's faces. You could tell by the glassy look of the eyes, she wasn't reading that book.

"She's beautiful, and it's so, so very sad," Charlotte said. "But how did Miss Singleton ever see her?"

"Moaxley carried her over."

"Miss Blanchette didn't mention that Miss Singleton was ever a visitor."

"She wouldn't. She's keen on privacy."

Harry didn't say anything about the one called "Miss Blanchette Napping." It was her, all right: brown, inscrutable, tough.

She sat in a ladder-back chair with her hands folded in her lap, her back straight, her feet flat on the rug, the same rug as in next-door real life. In sleep she was as stiff and wooden as ever, but then you noticed that one eye was partially open. There was a gold-brown glint to it and you knew it was not an eye filmed over with sleep. You knew it was fully, absolutely alert.

Another alive thing!

She got you, thought Charlotte, as if her words could float next door into the ears of Miss Blanchette. "But I think it's safe to say, you'll not be hung in any of the guests' rooms." Then she said to Harry, "I was hoping to look at a picture she made of a garden, in an ice storm."

"I never saw it."

"All the flowers are coated with ice."

Terence had heard her. He perked up his head and whispered, "Do you remember what came of your tarts, or whatever it was you tried to give her?"

Charlotte looked at him. "Are you teasing?"

He shook his head grimly.

"She burned it? She *burned* it? I wanted it!"

This was not appropriate for the situation. She didn't care. She lowered her voice, though. "I told Arthur I would like to ask her if I could buy it from her."

"He told her."

"And she put it in the *fire*?"

"I had to wheel her over myself."

"But I *wanted* it."

"She didn't," said Terence, "think that it was any good."

"It was! It was the best!"

Charlotte started over to the biggest of the fireplaces, where the fire was nearly out, as if she meant to get down on her knees and dig through the cinders and ashes. Harry grabbed her by the arm. "She burned lots of them," he said. "I'm sure she had a reason."

"The ice was too flat," said the pianist. "She told me so, and I looked at it myself, and I have to say, she was right. The glaze was a failure. Ice on a bud was trickier than chunks of it in the water, like with those boats. She scrapped it and called it practice."

Scrapped it! The one single thing! The one single thing she adored! She adored it, she'd wanted it in her room, she'd wanted to fall asleep at night with it there as the last thing she looked at, and there again in the morning, as the first. She knew that stomping her foot on the floor was something a three- or four-year-old would do, and she didn't care about that, either. It was criminal to have wrecked that picture. It was viceful. It was a sin.

How am I going to imagine it, she thought miserably, when I only saw it that one time?

But in fact it was already fading from her mind: the clarity of it, the solemn, icy stillness, the eerie glint, the silence. And she sniffed and started to cry: for the picture, for the painter, for all that terrible, sealed-up, locked-up, frozen immovability.

And she thought, What room would I have hung it in, anyway?

Not her sickroom; she was never spending another night in there again. Not her bedroom, next to Hays's, but separated from his by a desert. She could imagine what her mother-in-law would have said if she'd brought the frozen garden into the house. "Don't you think you've had quite enough of things that are paralyzed, Charlotte?"

There was a rap at the door. Moaxley loomed in the doorway, his cloak off, in his old-fashioned uniform with its brand-new texture and gloss. His cap was still in one hand. You wanted to salute him. "Hearse's here, quiet like, for the trip to Bowdoin Square. They say they'll get it done before sunup."

"At the back?" said Harry.

"At the back."

Harry said, "I have to ask all the ladies to go back to their rooms."

No one asked why, or put up an argument. Charlotte was the first one out. She went rushing down the two flights to the second floor, but when she got to the bottom, she found that she was sobbing so hard, she was blinded by tears, and she sank down on the step and put her head in her arms.

Damn this hotel! All it did was make her cry. Damn it to pieces!

She stayed there like that, like she was all folded up, crying and crying, until the hearse men asked her to get out of the way. She wiped her eyes with the hem of Mrs. Gerson's dress, just to be able to see, and then she cried on the way back to her room, even louder, and it didn't matter who heard her or whom she woke up. Death was in the building. It was allowed.

She crawled back into bed beside her warm aunt. She hadn't realized how cold she was. Harry must have worn heavy, winter-wool, masculine underclothes under that summery suit. Not her. Ladies didn't. If Hays had ever found out she used to put on his one-piece long underwear—union suits, they called them—to go out riding, he would have hidden them whenever he went away on trips in cold weather, or he would have taken them with him.

Aunt Lily stirred in her sleep. "Is it morning?"

"Not even nearly," whispered Charlotte.

"Have to get to the hospital."

"You will. It's the middle of the night. Go back to sleep." She liked the way her aunt rolled over like an obedient child. Charlotte pulled up the covers and snuggled closer to her.

Hays. There were plenty of things about her that Hays would never know. When he'd found her at Miss Georgeson's—and that was what he said, "I found you," as if she were a mushroom hiding under leaves and old brush in the woods somewhere—he seemed to have thought she only that minute began existing.

Miss Georgeson had told him two things about her: that she was an orphan, which wasn't true, and that she rode a horse like a man.

Miss Georgeson called all her girls orphans. She enjoyed the melodrama of it. "My orphans, alone in the world but for the Lord and my little academy." She said this even about the girls who had parents coming to visit on Sundays and taking them away for holidays.

Charlotte stopped crying. Thinking about Miss Georgeson caused her—whether she wanted to or not—to brace herself up. Miss Georgeson believed that a girl who couldn't be firm with herself was a girl who might as well have a backbone made of jelly.

And a girl with a backbone of jelly is a girl, she would say, who could never get onto a horse, because she'd slide right out of the saddle.

Every girl at the academy had to have a thing or two that mattered, so that the teachers could have something to threaten to take away. It was the basis of Miss Georgeson's teaching philosophy: allow for a passion, and then threaten it.

It didn't matter what the passion was. It could have been candies, dresses, magazines, books (but only for a few, who anyway never misbehaved), or the pet ducks by the barn ("We'll have your Mrs.

Quack for dinner if you don't attend to your Latin"), or swimming, or climbing trees (which was condoned), or speed and horses.

It was as if Charlotte had a middle name of it. Charlotte Speed-and-Horses Kemple.

Miss Georgeson herself had told Charlotte that as soon as she realized Hays Heath took an interest in her—that was exactly the way she put it, took an interest—she felt it necessary to tell him, "She doesn't ride a horse like a girl, but like a man, and I wouldn't esti-mate she'd be willing to change that, much as we've tried."

Poor Hays. He must have blinked at Miss Georgeson as if she'd told him that Charlotte had robbed a bank. Miss Georgeson admired the way he rose to the occasion. He felt that, if the rules of the school allowed it, that was that; he pointed out that ladies were beginning to ride the new bicycles without sitting sidesaddle, because their skirts would catch in the spokes. Why not extend it to horses, at least rurally?

"I admire your liberality," Miss Georgeson had told him. She was crazy about Hays; everyone was.

But never once did he ask if there was a pre–Miss Georgeson's Charlotte Kemple, a Charlotte Kemple who'd lived a life before, in a house with a mother and a father. You had to be at least five years old before the academy would take you.

Didn't he look around and see there weren't babies; it wasn't a nursery? Miss Georgeson wouldn't have lied about actually going to an orphanage and scooping up tiny girls, and bringing them to the school. She wasn't that inventive.

Well, Charlotte thought, when it comes to most people, if you find a mushroom in the woods, you don't ask how it came to grow there, or how it grew at all, or what it was made of, or why it sat on its stem so staunchly, with a little brown umbrella for a head, or a little beige thimble. You asked, Is this something I can eat?

At her wedding, a huge and lavish production on the lawn of the household, in late June, with white tents put up everywhere, and an orchestra, and every flower from every hothouse for miles, there were thirty-four guests from the academy: teachers, servants, girls, and Miss Georgeson herself, plus half a dozen more from the pony school in New Hampshire.

Everyone mingled with the Heaths, but there were over two hundred guests. It was, after all, the wedding of the family's youngest son, the wedding of the Heath who, at the age of thirty, was more successful in his career and his income than all the rest of them put together: he was their shiny emblem, their prize. "Hays is marrying an orphan from a school in the country, very polished." That must have been what they said. When they seized her arm and said they'd just been talking to her family, that very nice lady over there, that well-behaved girl, she didn't correct them.

He'd never, ever asked her anything. None of them did. Arthur did. "Tell me about where you come from." Arthur hadn't said that like it was part of the Beechmont process. He'd said it like he wanted to know.

Aunt Lily was stirring, grumbling. Charlotte slipped out of bed. She knew she wouldn't be able to fall asleep. She put the last of the coal on the fire and watched the embers flare up, and then she gathered up her things: her purse, her coat, Everett Gerson's big wool mittens.

Her aunt called out crossly, "What are you up to *now,* Charlotte? Are you planning to give me even more headaches than you've given me already?"

"I went to look at Miss Singleton while you were sleeping."

"Oh," said Aunt Lily, softening. "How was it up there?"

"It was all right. The hearse came."

"And now are you planning to go off to sea with her?"

"I am not," said Charlotte, "hysterical. Does everyone think I'm at your apartment, really?"

Aunt Lily heaved herself to a sitting position. Her eyes were bloodshot; her hair was a mass of tangles. "You should thank God the woman looking after my rooms is as good as gold. It would seem she's got you holed up in that back room, where all I ever did was store things."

"Has anyone gone looking for me there?"

"Charlotte, yes. Turned away every time."

"Hays?"

"Your father-in-law. Two of your brothers-in-law. I don't know who else."

"Then let them think I'm still there."

"Where are you going?"

"On a train."

"Tell me where or I'll—"

Charlotte smiled at her. "Forbid me to go to the stable? That's what Miss Georgeson used to do. The mistress of my school. She said if I wasn't good my spine would disintegrate to jelly and I'd never be able to get on a horse."

Aunt Lily was fully awake. She didn't care about spines right now, and she didn't care about Miss Georgeson.

"I'll take you by the hand to the hospital with me. I'll bring you into the wards, then I'll bring you into the receiving area for people who have rotten things the matter with them, and nowhere else to go. After half of one hour, you'll be as shocked as if your soul itself had been raked."

"That's the way you used to talk to me about morphine, but I don't remember anything you actually said."

"That's because you were on it when I talked to you."

"I got off. I got well. Why did you tell me I had a brain disease?"

"Brain, virus, spine, it's all the same thing. What does it matter what I called it?"

"That doesn't sound doctorly."

"I just woke up, I don't feel it. I had terrible dreams all night. And my friend is dead. Where is Arthur?"

"At his cutting-up."

"Are you going to Arthur? Charlotte, look at me. Tell me you're not doing that."

"I'm not. I wrote a letter to Uncle Chessy. He'll get it soon. I asked him to take care of some business for me."

"I don't need hearing about that right now. Going on a train where?"

"I want to see my mother and father."

Aunt Lily fell silent. She hadn't known a mother and father existed. She looked up at Charlotte for a long moment, carefully, then said, "You'll need some money."

"I have some. I have plenty."

"How long will you be gone?"

"I don't know. A day."

"When you come back, Charlotte—are you coming back?"

"Oh, yes, I would have to."

"Where will you come back *to?*"

Charlotte hadn't planned that far ahead. "Perhaps I'll come back here," she said, and Aunt Lily fell back on the pillow and groaned. Poor Aunt Lily.

∽ Fourteen ∽

The boy in the front room of the *Daily Messenger,* on the bottom floor of the only office building in Bigelow Mills, was working on the words for an advertisement for a cheese shop.

"Cheese, please," he murmured. The newspaper covered the whole of the Blackstone Valley.

The boy was about fifteen, scrubbed-looking, earnest, the kind of boy Charlotte's sisters-in-law called "dewy," as in, "Look at that dewy boy over there, couldn't you just go up to him and devour him?"

He paced about with a notebook and a thick pencil. His eyes were intent on the page the notebook was open to. "Cheese. Cheese, cheese. Please." It was obvious that this was the first assignment he'd been given, besides fetching things and general servitude.

It was a derelict room, freezing cold, with old desks here and there and a front counter. The only other *Daily Messenger* person there was a woman of about Aunt Lily's age, sallow-faced, unhappy, bundled up in a coat and a scarf at one of the desks. She was trying to make a connection on a telephone, which she appeared to loathe. The connection kept not going through.

The woman gave a kick to the little coal stove; it appeared to have had better days. It was smoky and almost useless. The ceiling and upper walls were sooty-grimy from it, and so were the windows, which had the look of having never, ever been washed.

"Excuse me, I want some information," said Charlotte, and the woman looked up and eyed Charlotte up and down and made it clear she wasn't having anything to do with what she saw.

"I'm using the telephone." But nothing was happening. The woman was merely holding it.

"Hang on, I'll come talk to you, soon's I try this out," said the boy. He cleared his throat for a recitation. His voice was in the act of changing over to a man's, so he was one minute squeaky and the next, an alto. "Got it, Miss Eckhart. It's good, give a listen."

"You got an illustration?" said Miss Eckhart.

"Almost."

"They want it with the picture. They want it already. An hour ago they wanted it. Who gets blamed you don't have it?"

"I'm a word man," said the boy. "But don't worry about a picture, I can do it."

"Me, that's who gets blamed. I'm the one brought you in. You want to be a reporter? You're far from it, far."

"I can describe it. Take me half a second to get it drawn."

"What's the words?"

The boy puffed out his chest. "A youth. A boy, nine, ten years old. He's asking for cheese."

"What's the words exactly?"

"Please, please, cheese. Good for the caterpillars, bad for the bees."

"That's it?"

"That's it."

"What do vermin have to do with selling cheese?"

"It's not vermin. It's the indirect approach. That's how they do it in the cities. You have to lure them with an angle."

"What's the illustration?"

"A boy, like I said. A backyard, big porch, nice people. Summer. Barefoot. A chunk of cheese in one hand. A caterpillar crawling over one foot, another one that just got turned into a butterfly. That's what he's looking at. A bee's in the air, near his head, big one. Wants to sting the shirt right off him. He holds up the cheese. It's a protection. It's a *shield*. The bee hasn't got a chance. Great, great things happen when you eat cheese."

"You were supposed to appeal to a married lady with a house to run."

"I appeal to her children."

"Children don't read papers."

"It's simple words. They can look over her shoulder. They'll beg for cheese sandwiches, when they never liked them before. They'll be flattered someone's operating at their level. They'll comprehend it. It's a story, see. With a hero." The boy looked at Charlotte. "What do you think?"

"I want to find out information about the shoe store on Market Street," said Charlotte.

"Go in there. It's open." Miss Eckhart appeared to have given up on her telephone call. "I wish they never invented these things. I wish they would stop inventing things that're supposed to make things easier, and they only make everything maddening."

"It's the snow and the wind," said the boy.

"That's all I've been getting in my ears all morning from this thing."

"I didn't find the information I wanted at the shoe store," said Charlotte. "It used to be a house. It used to belong to a family named Kemple."

"My ad," said the boy.

"I think," said Miss Eckhart, "we'll use the same one we used this whole month."

"It's a wedge of cheddar with two little legs and a mouth," said the boy despondently. "A walking, talking wedge." He came over to the counter and put his elbows on it, right in front of Charlotte. "Do you know what it's saying? It's saying, 'Randall O'Keefe has the best cheese in America, and I got that straight from a cow.' There's a cow down in the corner. Isn't that the worst thing you ever heard?"

"No, it's not," said Charlotte. "But maybe you should try something simpler."

"You in papers?"

"No. I want someone to tell me what happened to the people who lived where the shoe shop is. There must be someone here who would know."

"Artie would know," said Miss Eckhart.

"Who is Artie?"

"He owns the shoe shop."

"He's not there," said Charlotte. "I saw a woman who told me she's only been working there a few weeks. She told me the owner went to New York to look at new designs."

"That's just what he did."

"The woman in the shop didn't want to talk to me."

"Were you there to buy shoes?"

"I was looking for information."

Miss Eckhart gave Charlotte a look that meant something like, "Between you and me, we both know that someone like you would never buy shoes there." She got up from her desk and turned her back on Charlotte and strolled to the hall at the back of the room, signaling, with a bristling display of disdain, "Go away."

Charlotte wished she'd borrowed Mabel Gerson's coat as well as her dress, which she wasn't wearing anyway. She had changed into her own before leaving her room at the Beechmont. She was fully aware that her clothes cost a great deal more than Miss Eckhart's. She wanted to say, "I don't blame you for looking at me the way you do," but that would have made everything worse.

"Wait, please," said Charlotte. The woman paused in mid-step.

"Maybe Artie went to New York, but there's never new designs here, don't believe it," said the boy.

"My problem is," said Charlotte patiently, "I've been sending money, in the form of postal checks, once a year to that address, for nearly ten years. I have regularly received notices that the checks were cashed. I've just come by train, a long way, which took an age, and it was not a pleasant ride, and I have to ride it all over again, which I am not in a happy mood about. And now I've arrived to find that what I was looking for isn't there. I want to know why I've been giv-ing money to shoes, and I believe, if something is taking place which is not on the up-and-up, not that I'm saying so, it would possibly be an interesting story for your paper."

"I'll get Burke," said Miss Eckhart, and disappeared down the hall.

"Golly," said the boy. "Embezzlement." His eyes went bright with future headlines; his intensity made Charlotte think of Dickie, the old Dickie, not the policeman but the boy in the tannery.

Burke turned out to be a plump, bustling, nearly totally bald man at the furthest edge of adulthood. He smelled like printer's ink and cigars, and he was clean-shaven, unlike most men his age. His face was unlined and pudgy, and relatively youthful, but you had the sense, at any second, he'd be overwhelmed by his years, and be changed against his will into someone very elderly, all pasty and wrinkled and moaning, with every bone in his body complaining. He gave off an electric tension, and seemed to know this about him-self; he wanted to be admired for the fight he put up against decrepi-tude, which Charlotte was happy to do. She offered him a bright smile, which was not completely forced. The boy grudgingly moved out of his way as Burke approached Charlotte at the counter.

If Charlotte expected sympathy from this man, she was let down. He established his own vigor very quickly, and then the credentials of Artie of the shoe shop, who was his friend, his gun partner; they'd gone out in the woods and to the ponds every fall some forty, forty-five years. Deer, grouse, pheasant, turkey, duck, they stocked their own larders plus did their bit for charity: a whole ton of game, if you added it up through the years, for the feeble-brained asylum in Chetterdon and also for the hospital in Oakville. Was the lady inquiring about either of those places, seeing how the subject was the sending of money?

He didn't ask Charlotte for her name, which was just as well. She would have given a false one.

The Valley was as geographically intact as if it existed as its own state, and it was known to keep to itself, but there was a branch of the Heaths not far away, in one of the bigger, more prosperous towns. They owned the one bank and had a summerhouse out in Lenox, which everyone west of Boston would probably know about. It was called a palace, because that was what it pretty much was; it looked like a thousand-tiered wedding cake made for all the gods of Olympus and every French king put together. There was a painting of it in her father-in-law's study, which he only kept, he said, because he liked to be reminded of the base and vulgar road he had managed to avoid by staying out of the allure of the Berkshires, and closer to Boston, in his simple, by comparison, monastery-like little house, as if the household were nothing but a box. Her father-in-law and her mother-in-law had little to do with that branch, but Hays's sisters and their husbands were always going there for weekends.

She couldn't call herself a Heath and she couldn't call herself a Kemple, because who knew what that would imply personally?

"Anonymous," she might have said, for a name. Burke seemed satisifed with just "lady."

She'd been sending money for what purpose, if not charity?

"There was a family named Kemple who lived in the place where the shoe shop is," said Charlotte. "I—I represent someone who has an interest in them. An old interest, over the years."

"Like a benefactor?" Burke's interest was waning. He only seemed to care that his friend was not being maligned.

"Something like that," said Charlotte.

"They sue somebody? We had a family that hauled the paper mill to civil court for putting acid or something in their creek, and they got a settlement so big, they became investors. They put it all in the mill, and now they've got a fortune."

"It wasn't for anything like that."

"You looking for Kemples?"

"I am."

The boy wandered over to a desk, scowling at his notebook. He wrote down some words, crossed them out, wrote some more.

"Artie's got a daughter married to one. Gloria. The husband's Cyrus, Cyrus Kemple, works logging, a big guy. Artie never said anything to me about checks going into his shop."

"That's all right," said Charlotte. "Who are Cyrus's parents?"

"Don't know."

"Where can I find Gloria?"

"Can't, just now. Went to New York with him. Get her out, give her a little whirl. Nice girl, her. Doesn't get out much."

"Where can I find Cyrus?"

"Can't. He's out in the woods, where he always is."

"Are there any other sisters or brothers?"

"Artie's got nine, six boys, three girls, and they're every one of them living."

"Cheese," said the boy, sitting down in a battered old chair, which creaked in spite of how slight he was. He was reading aloud from his notebook as if he were alone, trying out lines. "Cheese on my toast, cheese on my roast. Cheese on my taters and cheese on my peas. Cheese on my baiters and cheese on my knees."

Burke looked over his shoulder. "You got a picture with that?"

"Give me two minutes."

"What's a baiter?"

"Uh, fishing," said the boy. "Guy fishing. Lunch sack full of cheese."

"Make him young. A boy," said Burke. "Make him a twelve-year-old. His mother packs his sack. I want to get rid of that wedge with the mouth. Put on the lunch sack, Randall O'Keefe's Best Cheese in America. I think he might go for it."

"Yes, sir!" cried the boy.

"Do Cyrus and Gloria have children?" said Charlotte.

"She's barren," said Burke, as plainly as if he were talking about an acre of land.

"Does Cyrus have sisters or brothers?"

"There's a sister out on one of the farms, outside Ware. Pretty place, Ware. No, wait. She died. Diphtheria. Was a spinster. Ran her obit, half a paragraph, oh, eight, ten months ago. You want it dug out?"

"Yes, please."

"It'll cost you."

Charlotte opened her purse, then changed her mind and snapped it shut. "I'll be happy to oblige with payment, after you give me what I need. I would also like to know if there were any other notices regarding Kemples."

"Weren't. Payment'll be two dollars."

"Is it actually?" said Charlotte. "I think that's quite high."

"Information's precious."

"But I won't have you rob me. I'll pay you a quarter."

"Half a dollar."

"Thirty cents."

"Up front," said Burke, sighing.

Charlotte had never bargained for anything before; she was careful to conceal the little shock of triumph it gave her. She dug into her purse for the right amount of coins, which Burke quickly put into his pocket.

Digging out an obituary consisted of this: Burke hollered out the name of Miss Eckhart and she hollered what did he want, and he hollered, louder, he wanted a back-paper search, and she came out to the front and asked, for pity's sake, she was busy, on what?

"Death. Woman named Kemple. Out the farms. Summer, maybe late spring, last year."

Miss Eckhart had a mug of something hot in her hands; she was using it more to warm her fingers with, than to drink it. She looked down at the floor as if that was where past copies of the paper were stored, right at her feet, and after a moment she said, "Brigid, forty-three, unmarried. I think it was all that diphtheria out there."

"What were the names of her parents?" said Charlotte.

Miss Eckhart consulted her memory. "Daughter of Mr. and Mrs. Kemple, and the address was here, Ninety-eight Market. That's all that was there."

"That's the shoe store," said Burke. He gave Charlotte a satisifed, end-of-transaction look, and you'd think she'd come into the office to find out the address of Artie's.

"Thanks for stopping by," he told her. He turned and went over to the boy at the desk. "Give me that thing, the picture stinks. I'll have them do it upstairs." He grabbed the notebook, and the boy followed him out, running after him. Charlotte put her purse back on her arm.

"Going back on the train now, are you?"

She nodded at Miss Eckhart.

"Want me mention to Artie you were around?"

"Perhaps I'll write him a letter."

"Feeling a little low down, not getting what you wanted?"

"I'll be fine."

"Cup of tea, before you shove off?"

"No, thank you." She could imagine what it would taste like, in that place. She got to the door, and had her hand on the handle, when Miss Eckhart called out—in a sudden mood for conversation, it seemed—"Powerful cold out. Frigid. Was warmer when we were dumped with all the snow, but now it's just bitter, don't you think?"

"Thank you for your help, and goodbye," said Charlotte.

"Seems merciless, the cold out there, for someone that's been standing on the sidewalk most of the whole time you've been in here. It's not someone I ever saw before. I'd say it's someone that's follow‑ing you, in case you don't know it, by the way. Course there's not anyone else here knows it, as I thought you might want to keep it quiet."

Charlotte froze. The composure, the patience, the outward show of steely reserve and self‑containment she'd maintained since she'd been in that awful shoe shop, and even before that, since the moment she stepped off the train, and had her feet on the ground of her old town—well, on the packed‑down snow of it—suddenly dissolved inside her into something as mushy as jelly. Her voice came out quiv‑ery. "You know that someone's watching me?"

"Know it when I see it like the hand at the end of my arm," said Miss Eckhart. "You need a back way out?"

The newspaper front door was solid wood; half of it wasn't a window, as you'd see in most offices. Funny what you tend to be grateful for.

She couldn't be noticed from outside. She leaned against the door.

She willed it to stay put, as if talking to it: Stay put, wood, please. She knew what could happen. It could crumble, like the wall in the hotel the night she arrived there. Like the ice-garden painting in the fire, the paint making hisses and sparks. Like her own body when she first got sick. Like the life she'd been living with her husband, all of it. Like the solid, crystalline knowledge, inside her like an extra, vital organ, that she could trust him as well as sunrises and sunsets.

You lean on something, chances are, it gives way. One shudder, then a silent implosion, then a silent collapse.

And *then* what? Wake up God knew where, with that man Burke demanding more money, and that boy writing more ditties about cheese? She remembered the snow-laden branch on the tree at the edge of the square, which Hays was ducking behind, to kiss the woman. She remembered that the branch could have broken off and crashed on their heads. She pictured it all over again, as if it really had happened. She felt a little stronger. She said to herself, "I wish I were Miss Blanchette. I wish I were a tree."

The door didn't do anything except keep on being a door. "Can you describe the person to me?" said Charlotte.

Miss Eckhart didn't waste any breath on adjectives. She set down her mug on a desk. She looked at Charlotte squarely, kindly. The lines of her face all relaxed. "He's a copper."

"A copper," repeated Charlotte. Well. "Does he look like one from these parts?"

"No. I would've recognized him if he was. He's city. Written all over him, the poor man. I'd venture he hasn't been at it for long. Like I said, we got a back way."

"I won't need it. I'm indebted to you for the warning." Once again, Charlotte opened her purse. She went back to the counter and placed two dollars on it. "Thank you for the back search on the obit-uary," she said.

"You already paid," said Miss Eckhart.

"Accept this for yourself."

Miss Eckhart's eyes lit up. "I couldn't."

"You must. I'm sure your salary is wretched. You can go and buy some shoes."

"Boots, would be more like it."

"Then go and buy some boots. And thank you again."

Dickie had chosen that moment, as Charlotte opened the door, to come barreling in, either to take hold of Charlotte bodily, or confront her, or just to warm himself at the weak, smoky stove. She was ready for him. He came in with a headlong rush: it was funny to watch him stagger and fight for balance, like someone on skates for the first time.

Charlotte laughed out loud. Dickie.

Her head went all bubbly, her spirits soared. It wasn't because of his presence, and she knew it. It was more like a case of absence. It was a matter of who he was not.

Not Hays. For the second time, not Hays. She realized she'd imagined him out there, almost magically, as if he'd picked up some signal from her, all those miles away, like birds of certain species were said to be able to do.

She'd hoped he was a bird. She'd hoped he had flown to her through the cold bright winter sky, and there he would be, her husband: "Charlotte, let's go home."

And she wouldn't care about Kemples. She would tell herself she'd lost her head in coming all the way here (but she would write the shoe store a letter, most definitely). In less than four hours she could be home in the big warm sturdy Heath house, not in the sickroom but upstairs, in her end-of-the-hall real bedroom, with her own dressing room, her own washroom. A bath. Lying in her bed. Hays in the doorway, in good humor, in his dressing gown.

"Charlotte, my dear, you've been gone pretty much of a week. Did you have a nice time of it?" Like she was the one coming home from a trip, not him.

Not Hays. Weren't husbands supposed to go and look for their wives, if they got home one day and their wife wasn't there? And then she wasn't there the next day, and the next and the next and the next and the next? And all he did to try to go to her was to follow her horse, back to the bakery? And write her a letter, one letter, which had sounded as empty as a hole? He would wait for her to send for him. That was what he wrote.

She pictured Hays at the Gersons'. The good Gersons, covering for her, their debt to her paid in full. "Oh, we drove Charlotte to the trolley, that was all we did." Hays going back home, exhausted. Going after the horse—it had to have been the mare; the male might even have nipped him—must have been an ordeal. Sherry in his room with some sisters. Eventually a letter: "My dear Charlotte," or whatever it said.

Wait for you to send for me. That was the only part of it she remembered. It was the only part that mattered. Into the fire it had gone. He would wait, he said.

That was funny, too. She couldn't help it. She threw back her head and laughed again, not in little giggles, like a girl without an inner core of firmness, but loud, with her mouth open and her shoulders shaking. Miss Georgeson had frowned on giggling, because it sounded like tittering mice.

You couldn't be married to a man for all those years and not know what he meant when he said something to you that was encoded; you didn't even need to stop and think of a way to decipher it. Like crossing the desert. Its meaning would be plain because you knew the code. You can't not know the code, even if you would like to.

It would have been funny if she'd let Aunt Lily read that letter. Aunt Lily didn't know him that way. She would have taken the

"I'll wait for you to send for me" as a sweet, respectful gesture. Every inch of him a gentleman. Giving his wife the next move. Thoughtful, wise, generous.

Hays didn't wait. Hays was not a waiter. When he said, "I'll wait for that," in some deal he was making, some factory he was trying to get shares in, some bicycles or stoves or carriages he wanted produced, some big thing he was trying to buy, he meant, "Take the deal or the factory, or the bicycles, stoves, carriages, or big thing, and do me a favor and throw it into hell, because I don't believe in waiting."

Every man he'd ever made a deal with—if that man got to know him even a little bit—must have known what it meant for Hays to say, when a shipment of something was late, or a payment was overdue, "Are you asking me to wait for that?"

She'd heard him herself many times, in meetings in his study—there were always processions of men in business suits coming to the town. Voices muffled on the other side of the door. Long minutes of silence. Then words from Hays like a proclamation: "If I tell you I would wait to see that happen, I would mean it is not worth having."

He wasn't like his mother, who believed in God taking his own good time in getting around to answering people's prayers.

That was pretty much it. She'd known this about him forever. At Miss Georgeson's, he'd come right back to see her, and Miss Georgeson was quick, at the very beginning, to speak to him about her age. "Miss Kemple is so young, and this school is the only place she knows, so why don't you wait to court her until she's at least gone off to her after-graduation new position?"

"I don't believe in waiting. Waiting is for people who have nothing better to do." You could admire it, in a way. Miss Georgeson certainly had admired it. It was honest. An emblem. A sign of a man who knows his desires and knows how to have them satisfied. A man who knows his own mind.

Maybe some of it had rubbed off on her. Maybe she ought to thank him for that.

And now here was Dickie, upright, his decorum reestablished, in the ugly rundown newspaper office. She held out her hands to him. She wondered if she would always, for the rest of her life, remember this, exactly the way it was.

"I'll wait for you to send for me." It had been embedded in her mind since the moment she'd seen it written on that page. She must have been waiting for it to come to the surface, to allow itself to be found. If it hadn't been her husband's handwriting, she would have thought that someone else had done it, in his name. Someone who didn't know the code.

She hoped she would remember it like something filed away in her brain, like Miss Eckhart's back-search of old papers. She hoped that in five, ten, twenty years, and more and more, she'd be able take out this memory, intact and solid, and say, "I was wavering on what to think about my husband, but when it came to me, when it really, truly came to me what he thinks of me, I had thrown back my head, and I was laughing."

"Hello, Charlotte," said Dickie.

She squeezed both of his hands, thick-gloved, but she could feel the cold in them. Her own self was a firm thing she could count on, after all. It wasn't as if she hadn't had practice in coping with complexities.

"Hello, Dickie. You know, I was only just thinking of you, and saying to myself, 'I wonder if I'll ever see him again,' and here you are, to answer my question."

Dickie was not in a jokey mood. He said to Miss Eckhart, "There's a tea shop at the end of the street that just closed its shutters. Does that mean it's closed for the day?"

"They do their business mornings, rule-like," Miss Eckhart

answered, with her chin out, her eyes narrowed. She was as wary as if this were an interrogation.

"Is it closed for business now?"

"It could open if you were to knock at the window and have a coin in your hand, like an admission price."

"Thank you," said Dickie.

And Charlotte was bustled out into the street, down the icy sidewalk, in the shock of the freezing air. Dickie didn't touch her, didn't offer his arm or put a gloved hand at her elbow, as if steering her, and he walked at his own fast pace, without taking slow steps like men were always doing with ladies. It felt good to trot, just to keep up with him.

The shop owner must have recognized Dickie for what he was; there was no need to offer money to get him to open up. It was a small place, dim, coal-smoky, with smells in the air of old cooking grease—lardy and oppressive—and stale tobacco, and that dank smell of snow brought in on people's shoes, which had melted into puddles and dried. Charlotte sat down with Dickie at the table nearest the hearth. The shop owner was a dour, pale, heavy-whiskered man without an ounce of congeniality in his body, or maybe this was only the way he behaved with policemen.

There was no menu; there was nothing left to be had except chopped-egg sandwiches and potato cakes and stewed tomatoes. We'll take it, the man was told. Dickie acted as if he and Charlotte had been going into restaurants together for years. The owner did nothing with the fire, which was down to charcoal, so Dickie disappeared into the back and returned with a bucket of coal and took care of it himself.

There was no waiter. The owner brought tea and milk and put it down grudgingly. Dickie's mood was like a nimbus around him of bad air, combined with what was there already. Charlotte saw the way he wasn't looking at her directly, not once. He knows, she thought. He knows about the hotel.

It did not seem surprising to her that he'd followed her. She poured their tea, a good hostess. Were they going to be polite, were they going to keep things proper, or would Dickie make a scene? It wasn't hard to picture him, having finished thawing himself, and putting some food in his stomach, turning on her with his old childhood intensity, his eyes flaring: Charlotte, I know everything, I know what you've been up to. Like a substitute for her husband, perhaps. I know, I know, I know.

As though she were guilty of something heinous. As though she couldn't say the same thing right back. She sat up a little straighter. It was decent tea, strong. A glow came over her when she thought about Miss Eckhart. I'm sorry I had misjudged you, and thought ill of you earlier, Miss Eckhart, she thought.

They were going to keep it polite. They were going to keep it proper. It was just like their first interview, except that this time they had a world of new knowledge behind them, and this time the food wasn't Rowena Petty's.

They looked at each other across the little table. The egg sandwiches were dry and the bread wasn't brand-new fresh, and the tomatoes had too much sugar, and the potato cakes weren't cakes at all; they were fried-up ovals of yesterday's mash, or last week's, with nothing else in them but lard and slivers of old onions, but she was hungry—again, although she'd eaten a big breakfast on the train— and she wasn't going to be fussy.

Charlotte took the first move. "Why are you here, Dickie?"

"I'm working."

"Oh, are the Boston police in the habit of sending men outside their . . ." She didn't know the word for outside the city limits.

"Jurisdiction," said Dickie. Somehow she already knew that he wasn't going to try tricking her this time; he wasn't going to be indirect; he was going to tell her the truth, uncoded, plain. "Actually, it's my day off. But it's not unusual for a man to take on a special off-duty assignment from a civilian, in his spare time, particularly a man at my grade, where the income, I'm not shy about telling you, is not high."

"Am I a special assignment?"

"You are."

"You followed me because someone paid you to?"

"It was awfully easy, Charlotte. In the dining car on the train I was at the next table, to your left. I sat there with a newspaper up to my face, but I kept lowering it. You never noticed."

She didn't even remember what she'd eaten in the dining car. She had taken no notice of anything at all. Chugging, rocking, shaking, a blur of motion and noise, all part of a background, blotted out, insignificant. Her mind had been possessed by other things. It was if, inside herself, she'd left the clear bright light of day and was some-where else, in a dim and shadowy place, where it was hard, but not impossible, to look around.

Of her parents, she remembered almost nothing. The broad shoulders of her father in a worn muslin workshirt, as he crouched over his plate at the table: his strong back, the ridges of his shoulder blades, the hair at the back of his neck, red-gold in firelight, and someone saying, "You have your father's hair," as if it weren't obvi-ous. Her father at the chopping block, splitting wood, the sleeves of his shirt rolled up, his powerful arms. The sound of the ax. The back of the cap on his head, sweat-soaked.

Her mother at the laundry tub. A hairnet on her head, some kind of brown mesh, brown on brown, but you could make out what was hair and what was not. Bending over the tub, smelling like lye herself. The back of her heavy gray apron. A smocklike apron, slipped over the head, with ties around the middle to be fastened in the back, always coming undone, dangling. Hair coming out of the net. Frayed hems of dresses, always coming undone. Kneeling over the tub on some sort of stool. The bottoms of her shoes. Always coming undone. Her stockings showing through shoe holes. Her stockings with holes, frayed threads. The skin of the bottoms of her feet, frayed.

From the back was the only way she saw them. It was like standing in a room with two people you've come up to from behind, and saying, "Turn around, please," and they would not.

Of her brother and sister she remembered only this: herself in a flat, narrow bed—a mattress, old horsehair, cold, close to a cold stone floor: not a bed but a mattress on a floor. Herself in the middle of two sleepers, bigger than she was, each one with their back to her. Herself lying flat. Looking up at the ceiling, at shadows. If she moved her arms just right, within the narrow corridor of their bodies, she could lie there and fall asleep with her palms pressed against them, each one, at the backs of their shoulders, like things to hold on to, and they didn't growl at her and push her away; they were too far gone into sleep.

Of her house: dark, sunlight in the cracks of the walls, fires that were always too weak, too cold; dampness, like something almost visible that would jump off walls and seep through your dress to your bones. A dusty front yard. The street, smelling of horse droppings. Clattering wheels. People. Motion. Horses, noise. Outside. Outside was always better than in. A voice. "We would be interested in taking the youngest." Was that Miss Georgeson? Had Miss Georgeson come to the house?

No, it was a thin lady in a dark brown cape and a dark brown old-fashioned bonnet.

Papers in her hand. Crisp, white papers. Gentle. A gentle lady, soft-spoken, not harsh, not hard. Kind eyes. The lines of her mouth soft, not rigid. Looking at her. "What a fine girl you are, then."

Going out. Across the little yard. Dusty. Looking back. Looking forward, a carriage, get into the carriage! High-wheeled in the back, lower-wheeled in the front, marvelous.

A double-seater with a roof. Leather cushions. She'd never been in one before. The lady. "Do you like it?" Oh, yes. "Do you know what it's called? It's called a cabriolet." Pronouncing it slowly. Cab. Ree. Oh. Lay.

It was as if she'd never known a single word before this one. Cabriolet. It was the first word she'd ever learned, like a baby. She remembered that. Riding in that carriage, away. She hadn't known yet that she would spend a long stretch of days and nights—just ahead—crying; just crying, with the sense she'd never come to the end of the tears; she'd be damp and sobbing forever; they would never dry up.

But they did. The plate of sandwiches was empty. Dickie had just finished the last of the potatoes. The owner came and took the teapot and brought it back, refilled, with more milk. It felt like a long time since they'd spoken a word. It was not uncomfortable. No one else came into the shop. It was closed. But no one was forcing them to leave, or even to hurry. A benefit of the company of a copper.

At last, Charlotte said, "I want to be told who hired you, Dickie."

"Well, I expected as much but I'm not at liberty to say."

So much for politeness. Charlotte was stirring milk into tea and flashed up the spoon as if she'd fling it across the table at him, which she quite possibly might have done. "Dickie! If you don't, I'll—I'll—you know what I'll do? I'll go to that horrible tannery, this very day, and I'll tell them that when that leather-stretching thing unbolted from the wall and fell on top of you and nearly *did you in,* it was *not* accidental; you unbolted it *yourself.*"

In answer, he grinned at her. He was proud of it! It was the truth! All those years ago, and he was as proud of it as if it had happened yesterday.

"Then let's agree to keep each other's secrets, Charlotte, shall we?"

"For the sake of old friendship?"

"Yes."

"Who hired you?"

"The hotel did."

"*Harry?*"

"I was there anyway. They'd wanted the main manservant, or whoever he is, to go off with you, tailing like, by way of looking out for you. But he was needed for the business with the hearse."

"Did he have on a Union army uniform?"

"He did."

"That's Moaxley. Were you watching the hotel again, Dickie?"

"It was just at the end of my hours. Call came in there was a hearse. If there's a hearse being loaded from a public-like building in the very wee hours of the night, it would behoove the Boston Police to take a look at it."

"That was a lady named Miss Singleton."

"We know."

"Her husband was a war hero. In the war with Spain. Not the States, Spain. Cuba," said Charlotte.

"We know."

"How much is Harry paying you?"

"A lot."

"Are you going to tell me it's not a, you know, a thing?"

"A bribe?" Again, a grin. "I am unbribable. I am a man with a job."

"And so what are you telling the Vice people?"

"I'm not telling them anything. I don't work for them, I work for the City of Boston. I investigated a complaint. I was asked what I observed. I told the truth. I observed ladies checking into a hotel, being guests of that hotel, and checking out. There are no complaints from neighbors. There are no disturbances of the peace.

There are no banks or creditors or suppliers owed money to. No gambling takes place in public rooms. Inordinate amounts of spirits are not consumed. It pretty much all tallies up with other reports."

"Others," said Charlotte.

"Oh, sure. Every couple of years or so, another one."

"Did Harry when he offered you all this money you're not telling me about mention to you where he thought I might be going?"

"My children need money for schools," said Dickie. He wasn't being defensive about it, just stating a fact.

"I thought they were babies."

"I'm thinking of the future. Who is Arthur?"

Ah, gaps in his knowledge, big ones! "A dead English king," said Charlotte. "Probably a made-up one, not historical."

"Mr. Alcorn mentioned that he would like me to deliver a message. 'Mrs. Heath, think twice about Arthur, please. Use your reason.' That is, I was to deliver it if you got off at Oakville, which you did not. That was the whole of the message. My instructions were to simply keep close to you. Mr. Alcorn's a city man. He thinks the moment one leaves Boston, one is naturally prey to forces beyond one's control. He was sure you'd be robbed, assaulted, kidnapped. Exposed to barbarians."

"And what did you think, Dickie?"

"I thought all along you were going out to look at the old school, you know. I thought you'd got sentimental."

"Miss Georgeson's been dead at least a half dozen years. It wouldn't be the school. I would never have done that."

"You're not sentimental."

"No," said Charlotte.

"Then why," said Dickie slowly, "are you looking for your mother and father, and why have you been sending money to them?"

"Dickie! You snooped!"

"Well, that's my job."

"How did you do it?"

"One of the print-set fellows came out to see what was what, with me out there. Offered him a half-dollar to go inside and use his ears for me. Do you want me to find out where they are?"

"I have a brother who's a woodsman, a tree cutter," said Charlotte. "And a sister who died on a farm, by herself."

"Do you want me to find your parents, Charlotte?"

"No. Yes. No." She drank the tea in her cup. She put down the empty cup. She picked up the cup as if it were full and tried to drink the tea she thought was still there. Then she said, "Yes."

"Wait here," said Dickie.

"What do you mean, wait here? Alone? With that horrid owner? That's not going to happen. Where are you going?"

"The police station, of course."

"You think they're *criminals*?"

"I think everyone's a criminal, Charlotte, I'm a policeman. But no, not in particular. The station will have addresses, they always do. Maybe not written down, but in someone's head, probably a beat-walking man, there's an address, with known-about residents. This is not a big town."

"All those rowhouses, though. Did you notice all those row-houses, out back of the station? They aren't even on actual streets. They're like pushed-together cinder boxes."

"It's mill housing."

"It's tenements."

"I thought you hadn't noticed anything."

"I noticed that."

"Because you think that's where they are?"

"Yes."

"Then we have something to go on," said Dickie brightly, and Charlotte said, "When I go back to Boston on the train, are you going to sit with me, or are you going to go back to your private-detectiveness and just shadow me?"

"I can sit with you."

"Does your wife know where you are?"

"Oh, yes. I telephoned to the sanatorium. It's quite near the house. They went and got her and she said, Is it on the up-and-up, this type of job? and I assured her, and she hoped I'd make it back for my next hours. Being trained a nurse, you know, she believes in routine. And she's glad for the money. And she hoped while I was out here, I'd go back to the tannery and make it explode or something."

"Does she know about the bolts in the wall?"

"One's partner in marriage does not need to know small details from one's past that don't matter."

"She sounds nice."

"Maybe you'll meet her one day."

"And your babies. I would like that, Dickie."

"So would I."

"Dickie?"

"What?"

"Thank you for not asking me any more questions about the hotel, even though it would be unethical of you, seeing that, at the moment, Harry's your employer."

"You're welcome."

"And thank you for not asking me any questions about my husband."

"You're welcome for that, too."

They got up and put their coats on. The owner appeared.

"A dollar," he said, with his hand out. Dickie reached in his pocket, but Charlotte already had her purse open. She had never paid a bill in a restaurant before. She handed over a bill, and Dickie put a nickel on the table.

They went outside. Dickie seemed to know where the police station was. "We can walk there. It's not far." The street and sidewalks
were empty; it was much too cold to stir about. "I forgot how cold it
gets out here," Dickie said. This time he held out his arm to her, and
she took it.

At the end of a block of shops, they turned down a side street.
The station was at the end of it. Across from the station was a lit-up
little dress shop, and Dickie pointed to it. He wanted her to go inside
and wait for him to do his errand.

Well, she needed new dresses. He left her just before the station
and watched her cross the road. He went inside before she did; she
wanted to look in the window first, to see what sorts of things they
had. If it was anything like the shoe shop, she was in for a depressing
time of it. She pulled up the collar of her coat and burrowed into it.
She had Everett Gerson's big mittens on, but they weren't doing
much good.

Inside the dress shop, a woman customer in a worn old wool coat
was holding up a brightly patterned shirtwaist, turning it this way
and that, studying it. It was not an attractive dress, but it wasn't
awful.

Suddenly Charlotte was aware of someone standing behind her.
Maybe because Dickie had told her about the perils Harry imagined
for her, way out here near the end of the train tracks, past the bounds,
in Harry's mind, of civilization, she found herself shivering, all the
way down her back, inside her clothes. She forgot she was in full
view of a police station. She almost didn't turn around. She had the
thought that if she dashed into the shop, she'd be laughing at herself,
in less than two seconds, for her fears. She'd probably imagined it.
She wasn't a coward. She turned around.

Hays.

"Good afternoon, Charlotte," he said gently. He looked away

from her, to give her time to conceal from him the degree to which he'd startled her. She appreciated that.

Then he nodded and smiled as if he'd only just parted from her that morning, as if they'd had breakfast together, and perhaps even lunch.

Hays. Flush-cheeked, not completely from the cold, in his handsome, heavy gray English greatcoat with the double set of pearly-gray buttons. His fine leather gloves. Black arctic boots. A muffler at his throat, the striped one she bought for him last November.

The striped one! Maroon and blue stripes, soft cashmere, about a hundred times more colorful than any other item of clothing he owned, which had been the whole point of buying it. She'd never seen it on him before. It disappeared into a drawer right after he opened it. She'd wrapped it like a gift. It hadn't been his birthday. It hadn't been anything special. He had hated it. His whole family had hated it.

Derby hat. The dark gray one, custom-fitted. She almost thanked him out loud for not fingering the brim and tipping it to her. He didn't believe in tipping one's hat to one's wife, unless your wife was in the company of another person, or with a group. There were no other people.

Code. Everything, everything coded.

She didn't mention the first-time muffler, although she knew he wanted her to. His breath made little white clouds in the air between them. He was nervous. She knew that. She could hide things better than he could. She didn't have a face that went pink with the least bit of feeling.

Next to the dress shop was an electrical-goods shop with the cleanest front windows in town. Displays were in the windows: batteries, buzzers, lighting fixtures, all sorts of gadgets, and those electrical belts that everyone said were so useful, with built-in batteries.

You wore them beneath your topmost layer of clothing. They were said to be good for backaches, ailments of the spine, muscle cramp‑ing, time‑of‑the‑month disorders, and general problematical nerves. Two of Hays's sisters had them. When Charlotte was in her sick‑bed, Aunt Lily had said she would personally introduce a secret, vil‑lainous strain of virus into the entire household if anyone tried to electrically shock Charlotte in any way, and she didn't give a damn what anyone said about juice from a battery being good for paralyzed limbs. If God wanted humans to be jolted with electricity, said Aunt Lily, God would have made it a nice thing to be struck by lightning. Everyone remembered what had happened to Hays's mother's per‑sonal maid, under that wreck of a tree—the lightning tree—so the threat was effective. Charlotte's sisters‑in‑law had stopped wearing their belts for a while, but they missed the tingly little sensations, they said, and put them back on.

This electrical shop stood by an alley. At the end of the alley, eas‑ing into the street, was a hired sleigh: two quiet spotted horses, wear‑ing blinders, and a muffled‑up driver. The seats were piled high with fur wrappings.

The driver had a silver flask in one hand and a whip in the other. He held both these things idly, like natural extensions of his arms, and Charlotte thought, If he so much as flicks that whip at those horses, I will run to their harnesses and set them free, and slap them on their hinds and tell them, Run.

Hays said, "Are you shopping, Charlotte?"

"In fact, yes, I am. I was just about to go in."

"Then may I stay here until you come out? I've hired a sleigh."

"I can see that."

"I offer you a lift."

"I already have one arranged."

"The policeman. Who's just gone into the station."

"He came with me from Boston."

"From Lily's apartment."

"Yes."

There was a certain type of lacquer which, when applied to some‑ thing perishable, stiffened it up, crustlike, with a colorless coating of resiliency. The Irish maids had jars and jars of it. They were always lacquering things for themselves and for Charlotte's father‑in‑law: seashells, flower petals, autumn leaves, birds' eggs, birds' nests, seg‑ ments of bodies of birds fallen victim to murderous cats. There were twiggy bits of feet all over a shelf in the yard shed. Tiny beaks. Feath‑ ers. The shallow shafts of wing bones. All lacquered. Resilient.

Charlotte imagined such a lacquer on herself, on all of her, from the top of her head to the bottoms of her feet. If Hays were to take off his gloves and touch the side of her face, she thought, he would think he was touching veneer. If he tapped on her forehead, he'd hear an echo. He did that sometimes. Coming home from a trip he'd wait until he found her alone in some room, and he'd go up to her and knock on her forehead: I am home, Charlotte, are you? It was another way of saying *Cross the desert,* but it was special for coming home.

But of course he didn't touch her. Of course he didn't take off his gloves.

"I should like to speak with you," he said.

Lacquer. Veneer. No, more than that. Glass. Thick. She imag‑ ined herself inside a jar, a canning jar, with some sort of opening so her voice could be heard. Steady voice. She was proud of herself.

"I should like to speak with you also. Why don't we arrange a time?"

"A time?"

"An appointment," said Charlotte. The horses were getting rest‑ less. The flask in the driver's hand was opened, was drunk from. The whip was not moved. Across the street, Dickie was coming down the steps of the station. She saw him. Hays didn't.

Somehow Dickie knew to go back inside. He walked up the steps backward, stumbled, didn't fall. He mouthed the words "Is that your husband?" but she could tell that he'd already figured that out.

Then she knew he was watching from a window. She didn't mind, not at all. She thought, being watched, being followed, this is getting to be a habit. She felt used to it already. What did Hays know, exactly?

That he knew *something* was undoubtable. She was making herself nearly breathless with the effort not to let herself erupt, gey/serlike, and flood him with questions, exclamations, everything pouring out at once into the frigid white air. Thicker glass!

The customer in the dress shop who'd been looking at the shirt/waist came out empty/handed. I wonder if they have that in my size, Charlotte thought. Maybe she'd buy it a little bigger than what she needed at the present time. She'd got to like the looseness of Mabel Gerson's dress. And anyway, she thought, all I've been doing is eat/ing; I've probably put on five pounds just this week.

"Are you telling me you would want me to walk away from you now, and have, as you say, an appointment, for a later time?"

"You wouldn't walk, you have your sleigh."

"I had hired it from the train station."

"And were you on the train I was on, early this morning? Hays, were you following me?"

"I don't know what train you were on. Early this morning, I was here. Did you see the hotel by the bank? The Blue Crest, it's called. Not a bad place. They say the hills to the west turn blue at dawn, but I don't think it happens in winter. I slept there last night."

She hadn't seen any hotel, she hadn't seen any bank. Slept there last night in the company of *whom*?

No questions! Thicker and thicker glass, thickest of all possible glasses!

"There are private dining rooms. I would like to arrange for one. I'd find it suitable."

"You mean today, Hays?"

"Certainly I mean today."

Charlotte shook her head. He looked at her at last, for a long, long moment, as if he meant to penetrate the veneer. She could tell he was giving her credit for it, a lot of credit. And she felt she had to return it, so she let him know, with a look, she did not find him to be, more or less, repulsive, which was pretty much the way she'd been looking at him up to now.

This is business, she thought.

"I think we'll wait," she said, "and meet in a place completely, you know, neutral."

"This town is neutral."

"Not to me."

"It's cold," he said.

"It was warmer when it was snowing," she said.

"Then meet where, Charlotte, and when?"

"Boston, perhaps." She looked down, thinking. It wasn't as if she could invite him to meet her at Harry's.

He didn't put up an argument. He said, "All right. Boston. How about the Tremont Arms?"

"It burned in a fire, Hays, four or five years ago."

"I'd forgotten."

She didn't know what she was going to say until she said it. "The Essex," she said. She didn't look at him. She willed herself not to. She felt she wouldn't be able to bear it if he didn't remember what that meant. He wasn't the only one, she thought, who knew a few things about codes.

She looked at him. He remembered. "The one we didn't go to on the night we didn't go to the play about the fellow trying to kill the other fellow with the sawmill blade?" He said this somberly, professionally.

The night we didn't go to the play. Not the night we first knew how sick you were.

Business.

"Oh," said Charlotte. "Is that the same hotel? I'd forgotten."

"I would have enjoyed that play."

"You would not have, Hays."

He gave her that. He said, "When?"

"What is your schedule?"

"I have to go to Albany for two days."

"More bicycles?"

"Yes, and automobiles," he said.

"You're branching out."

"Yes."

"In three days, then," she said.

"What hour?"

"I don't have a preference."

"Five?"

"Five."

"Shall I arrange for a dining room?"

"Please."

Dickie came down the steps again and this time he crossed the street, coming toward them. Hays turned. The two men did not shake hands, but merely eyed each other, not in an unfriendly way, but the way men size each other up, when neither of them is interested in conversation, and neither feels the other is a threat. They would probably get along well, Charlotte thought.

Slept here last night *why?*

Hays nodded in Dickie's direction, acknowledging him. "Then I'll retake my sleigh," he said politely. He held up his hand to the brim of his hat. "Goodbye, Charlotte."

"Goodbye."

"I've got it," said Dickie, the second Hays walked away. Hays didn't look back.

"Got what?"

Dickie was purely one-track. "The *location*."

"Oh."

"Come on."

She was not to have a new dress after all. Maybe she'd go back there. Dickie was bearing her away again, all blustery and police-manish. They were headed in the opposite direction of Hays's sleigh. She heard the driver call out to the horses. No whip. She heard the tinkle of their bells, just a few of them, but their sounds were shiny and bright in the cold, cold, bright air.

∽ Fifteen ∽

They left the shops and streets of the center of Bigelow Mills and headed toward the next village. She knew they were going east: the sky they were facing was gray with dusk. It did not feel right to be walking away from the sun.

A train whistle blew in the distance. A train she wasn't on.

A white wasteland. Little houses here and there, huddled down, dark, shuttered, looking like they suffered from spasms, from fatigue. Thick coal-dark smoke huffing up out of some chimneys. Thick wood-gray smoke huffing up out of others. Ice-crusted snow, so hard and dense you could walk on top of it without sinking.

A crowd of children, mostly boys, in too-lightweight clothes, passed by, headed back to the town. A few of them had sleds, but most had flattened cardboard boxes or barrel slats. They weren't bubbly and cocky and noisy like the Boston children who sledded on the Common. A grim silence was like a thing they carried with them. They were cold. And maybe their instincts told them who Dickie was. They barely looked twice at them.

Something howled from the direction of the woods to the north; the sound seemed to clutch at her heart. Wolves!

"Dickie! Wolves!"

"Dogs," he called out cheerfully.

Dickie seemed to have tapped into a concealed other self, an alter-native personality: a fearless, excited adventurer. A man obsessed with a mission. He also seemed to be immune from normal require-ments of sleep. Where was he taking her? It was a criminal act, committed against one's self, to be out in this frigidity. She'd give anything she had for a horse.

"I want a horse!" cried Charlotte, and she felt like King Richard on that battle plain, even though this wasn't a war for the ruling of England, and Richard was a twisted, evil man, with a vat of poison for a soul, and so many crimes on his record, including killing those princes in the Tower, and disposing of his wife, no one could feel a drop of sympathy for him, except for the scene where he was unhorsed, staggering about, reduced to whining.

The Town Players had put on *Richard III* while Charlotte was in her sickbed. Hays had wanted to have her carried over for the show, but his mother had felt it would look improper, as if Charlotte, a pale, sick lady in the audience, tied to some chair to keep her upright, would steal all the attention, like a doomed, innocent princess; and anyway the Heaths didn't want anyone to wonder if they were har-boring a victim of the dreaded polio. Hays hadn't put up a fight against his mother, but he'd found it necessary to be away on a trip for the two nights the play was running.

Her father-in-law had played the lead. Everyone said he'd done it brilliantly. She felt she knew Richard better than any of those other kings because her father-in-law had rehearsed his lines in her doorway. She was the one who'd coached him, urging him to play up the wicked wit, the knife-sharp retorts and observations.

It was true that of all those royal types, in all those histories, the one who was the worst of all villains had the best of all lines, the way that the Old Testament Satan, when you thought about it like this, had the single most interesting part. It wasn't very interesting to be God or an angel, because everything they did was predictable, and purely for the sake of being good, which was praiseworthy, but not interesting.

There were shadings, gradations of "good." This was a fact.

People with complexities were people who never bored you. Who was the least boring character in the whole Bible? Charlotte had said so to her father-in-law, and he had looked at her with eyes blinking hard with surprise, as if he'd only just realized that his daughter-in-law in a sickbed had a brain in her head, which she now and then actually used. She had opinions, theories.

He'd listened to her (in the greater whole of preparing for his role; it was just that once). He'd agreed with her about the inherent higher interest of evil, and said, winking at her, Richard-like, "But let's keep that a secret between us two."

He allowed her to help him think of interesting ways to have his Richard look twisted onstage. He hadn't wanted to stick a pillow up his shirt and be obviously a hunchback like other Richards he'd seen on other stages, and like Shakespeare had wanted: a deformed body to correspond with a deformed soul. So he gave his Richard a sideways slant, as if he were always about to fall over, which may have been inspired by the way Charlotte looked when she stood up at the side of the sickbed after some of the paralysis wore off. He hadn't needed the prop of a hump.

Arthur. Arthur the first time she saw him, in the green jacket, that little cushion stuck up his back. She'd thought he was crippled. He'd told her he was posing; he wanted Miss Singleton to put him into her ice garden as a troll. Arthur the troll. Could she think about him like that, shrink him down? Every time the thought of him came into her head, shrink him down a little more, until he was so small she could picture him standing in the palm of her hand, like a tiny ceramic figurine? That would certainly make things easier.

Terence: "He's studying deformities."

Arthur: "You're a magnificent woman."

Rowena Petty: "Arthur Pym! What are you doing with this lady! You stay away from this lady! You leave this lady alone!"

Arthur: "Delicacy is for snobs, Charlotte. Let's not be snobs."

Aunt Lily: "Look at me. Tell me you're not going to Arthur."

Arthur: "You can use your lips. You can use your mouth."

Harry, via Dickie, if she'd got off at Oakville: "Think twice about Arthur, Mrs. Heath."

Arthur: "Come with me."

Arthur: "On the night my mother walked away from me for forever I rolled over and went right back to sleep. I was eleven years old. Then everything fell apart."

Arthur: "Come closer to me."

Arthur, having looked over her shoulder as she wrote to Uncle Chessy to get a Pinkerton's man: "Why did you write that letter?"

Arthur: "I'm glad you can't see my face."

Arthur: "When I touch you right there, just like this, do you feel you would like me to never, ever stop?"

Stop, Charlotte thought. He wasn't tiny. He wasn't a troll.

"Dickie!" He'd sprung ahead of her; you'd think he was wearing a pair of skis. "Where are you bringing me!"

"It's not much farther." He flashed her an encouraging smile over his shoulder.

"Let's find some horses."

"You need the exercise," he called, doctorlike.

"I won't if I fall down dead from the cold."

The air was as sharp as pointed icicles. Her eyes kept watering. She felt that the insides of her eyes were being frozen. She felt that if she touched her nose it would fall off. She thought of all those furs in Hays's hired sleigh. What was that hotel? Crest Something.

Blue sunrises. Far, far back now. She felt like an exile. Slept in the hotel exactly why?

She was getting all fuddled. Wasn't that something that happened when you were about to succumb to death by freezing? Hays knew something. He *knew* something. He didn't know about Arthur. He didn't know about the inner workings of the Beechmont. Or he knew about the inner workings but not that she'd been there. Or he knew she'd been there but not that she had taken part in the inner workings.

Was he going to interrogate her at their meeting, was that why he wanted it, a business meeting, everything just so? "So, Charlotte, I've learned you were not as faithful to me as sunrises and sunsets. And I learned that in your unfaithfulness you were quite in a holiday mood. You were happy."

He knew everything.

No, he knew nothing.

Wait, she was the one who'd had the idea for the meeting. To postpone the inevitable. "I want to divorce you on the grounds of adultery." That was what he'd say. No, she'd say it first.

She'd forgotten to stipulate that they meet alone.

Maybe he'd bring one of his business-associate lawyers or some Heath one, or two or three, or he'd bring along his sisters, their husbands, his brothers, their wives, his mother, his father, a brigade of Heaths, and there was only one of her and it wasn't as if she could ask Uncle Chessy to come and stick up for her; he was a Heath, he'd say, "It's a conflict of interest," even though he'd sworn to be her friend.

Right at this moment, Charlotte thought, Hays was drawing up whatever sort of papers one drew up to dispose of one's wife, which he anyway had started to do, correct? Emotionally. Physically. The woman at the edge of the square. Or he'd drawn up the papers already; he'd had them in the sleigh.

What about the striped muffler? Oh, that. That was a—what did Hays call it when you went into a business meeting having planted incorrect information in the minds of the people you were negotiat⁄ing with? Subterfuge. Necessary subterfuge. Not tipping his hat to her when he found her alone? Same thing. As if he were saying, "You're still my wife but not for much longer."

She never should have thought of meeting him in the Essex Hotel. Mistake! Sentimental! A crack in the glass, a big one!

The sawmill play. The teeth of the giant saw. The heat of a packed⁄in audience. Nothing polite like at the types of plays her husband would rather go to. Shakespeare had not been polite. Those histories in Town Hall—even *Richard*—had been done too politely. What about Juliet? What about Cleopatra? There was nothing polite about mooning on a balcony because you want your new lover to come up to your bed. Or that dagger into Juliet's chest: her own hand seizing it like a deliverance.

And there was nothing polite about a snake in a basket, brought in to you so you could murder yourself with it. What part of Cleopatra's body did the snake bite, actually? Probably somewhere at her chest. Her breast, which one? In a spot her lover had put his mouth? To poison whatever traces of him remained?

After the sawmill play, they'd planned to have dinner at the hotel. With the type of wine Hays liked. She had partly planned what to say, and she'd partly been all right about just letting it run its course. The right moment. "I want us to have our own house. I want us not to live in the household. I want to buy furniture."

Then flat on her back in a sickbed.

She should have agreed to speak with Hays immediately. She shouldn't have made it a condition that he wait.

She should have got it over with. Wherever he was now, he'd be warm. He wouldn't be walking in the middle of nowhere, toward darkness, on a mile-high ice pack of miserable, rotten snow. Blisters were sure to be forming on every one of her toes, her heels, the soles of her feet. The blood in her veins was getting sluggish, as if chunked up with ice. The food from the tea shop sat uneasily in her belly. Lard. Lard made her queasy. She felt a cramping, midsection. Like a punch. Another, another. Left side of her stomach, low. Not the food. Not the effort of walking on ice-packed snow. Her time of the month. Cramps started one or two days before the blood came. There'd be preliminary spottings in a couple of hours.

A terrible desolation hit her. She realized that at the back of her mind she'd been (secretly, in spite of her better judgment) working up the hope that she had conceived. *Conceived*. And this time of course it would work, it would stay. And everything would be beautifully simple.

Charlotte: "Hello, Arthur, I've something to tell you. Something wonderful. You and I are going to have a child."

Arthur: "Super! Let's get Harry to give us a celebration supper!"

Charlotte: "I suppose now you'll have to finish your studies."

Arthur: "You're absolutely correct! We'll be together for always!"

Crunch, crunch, crunch. The sky growing darker. Every one of her bones, chilled. It hurt to breathe. She said to herself, "I'm so empty. And everything I do, comes out wrong."

Suddenly Dickie turned around, hopping from one foot to the other. "Here!" he shouted. "The location!"

They'd come to an outlying neighborhood of the next village, if "neighborhood" was what you could call it.

They were approaching a low, rough-wood, flat-roofed building, which stood between the edge of wintry nothingness and a jumble of rowhouses—a maze of them—that looked something like the bungalows of the Hollow but all pressed together, without the natural relief of the pretty Hollow pond and its grasses and trees. And there was no central focus, like the Gersons' bakery, which functioned in the Hollow like a yeasty hearth.

The building must have once belonged to some church. A faded, chipped sign above the door said "Bethel Congregational Meeting House." There were few windows—just two, one on each side of the door—and the glass was so steamed up you couldn't see inside. It was well-lit in there: lots of gas lamps and no one skimping on fuel.

There was no sign of a church, but just to the east, on a little mound of a hill, were piled-up stones in a rectangular pattern, which might have been a church's foundation. Yes, it was: what looked like a stack of rubble was actually five or six pews on top of each other, laid flat, like benches that have fallen over backward. In the dim light they looked eerie; they were scarred with burns.

The church had burned down. The remarkable thing was that the stones and the pews were clear of snow: either someone took care of them, like graves in a graveyard, or it just simply, irrationally, didn't snow on that mound, as if God chose to spare it, and had reached down into the sky, just right there, to protect it with a giant hand, umbrellalike.

The roof of the building was clear of snow, too.

The sounds coming out from the building were not churchy. There was a muffled, raucous sort of din, in inconsistent waves. You could tell the place was packed with people. The walls seemed to be oozing out warmth and sweaty vapors. The path to the door was so trodden, the snow was down to last year's top layer of earth: a path of frozen mud. No horses, no sleighs, no anything. Whoever was in the building had walked here.

"Let's go to the train station, Dickie," said Charlotte.

"Don't tell me you're nervous."

"I most certainly am not. I'm ready to go back on the train, that's all. The last one east is at seven. We won't have to go back to Biggie M, we can get it down the line. The next station's not far from here."

"Biggie!" said Dickie. He was just like a little boy on a treasure hunt, within grasp of the treasure chest of his dreams. You'd think the parents he was looking for were his own. He was taking this hugely personally. "I remember. That's what the locals called it. Biggie M! You used the old name."

"I did not. I said Bigelow Mills," said Charlotte. Her teeth were clattering. She was shivering.

"Remember that stinking, ugly little paper mill that used to be here, and everyone tried to pretend it wasn't? Like if you said just M, instead of Mills, it wasn't there? And the 'Biggie' was sort of affectionate?"

"I remember your stinking tannery."

"So do I. Let's go in."

And he pushed the door open with one hand while clinging to her arm with the other. A gentleman would have stood to the side and let her enter first, but this was not the time for those kinds of considerations. He went inside ahead of her, shieldlike, a good copper, pulling her behind him.

The noise hit them like a blast. It seemed at first that some sort of festive thing was going on, some wedding or important party. But no one was dressed up. No one appeared to be celebrating anything. There were no decorations. There was, instead, a feel of the everyday.

Dozens of conversations going on at once. Shouting, bellowing, harsh laughter, screechy laughter, tittering laughter, old people, young people, people in the middle of young and old, babies, children—a lot of children. Thrown on the floor just inside the door were the sleds and cardboard carried by the children who'd passed them earlier.

Commotion. Running about. Everyone in some kind of motion, even if it was only with their mouths, or raising their arms in the acts of eating and drinking and making wide, dramatic gestures. Tables of all different sizes. Chairs. A blustery wood fire in a hearth that took up most of one wall. Good chimney. Excellent draw.

Low beams. A smell of beer, cigars, tobacco, cooking oil, lard, sweat, wet clothes, babies' soiled diapers, animal fur. A dog sleeping under a table. A couple of cats by the fire. Heat. Tempers. Pleasures. Intoxications. A cleared space on one side, like a dancing floor. No music.

Fifty people, sixty, a hundred. Hard to tell. A riot of faces. No one took note of Charlotte and Dickie.

Some eight or nine people were involved in setting up some sort of corral-like scheme in the clear space. For some kind of game? People near the edges pushed back their tables and moved their chairs to enlarge the area.

Several planks were being placed on the floor on their sides, lengthwise, like sideways chutes, with the distances between each one measured carefully. The insides of the planks were completely lined with bumpers of white cotton batting, which appeared to be glued or tacked on. The batting was far from clean, but the effect of softness was obvious. The planks were supported at each end by blocks of wood that looked like small chopping blocks. Grooves had been cut in the blocks so the ends of the planks could be inserted. Four lanes began to emerge, each one about thirty yards long.

"Looks like they're setting up lanes over there," said Dickie, leaning toward Charlotte to be heard. He was acting like an expert on the place. "For some racing."

"Racing of what?"

"Don't know. Something small. But I'd make a good guess if I said there'll be some fairly serious wagering."

"Gambling, you mean. Is that legal?"

"I am not," said Dickie, "on duty. Are you looking around? Are you picking out your mother and father? Have you planned what to say?"

Was he teasing her? No, he was serious.

"How do you know they're here, Dickie?"

"Everyone is. This is where everyone comes at the end of the day. The end of the day starts early around here, I was told. Especially in the dead of winter. Don't you think this is tremendously exciting? I wonder if they have ale. I bet they do. I wonder if I ought to have some ale. I wonder which two are your parents! Hurry, Charlotte, and point out which ones they are."

He seemed to think that a deep-rooted instinct would flicker to life inside her, and she'd be led by it, like one of those pigeons people trained to fly away, then return to the exact spot it had left. Or those big reptilian, ancient-looking, Hollow female turtles that wandered all over for miles, but went back to Hollow Pond to lay their eggs. Even if you caught one, put it in the back of a wagon, and drove it to the edge of Kingdom Come, people said, back it would go, regardless of distance and dangers, as though the muck of its own private territory was sacred, and imprinted forever in its tiny turtle brain.

Maybe if she stood still, they'd spot her. What did she expect? She didn't expect anything. Or maybe . . .

A tall broad man in an old sheepskin jacket was testing the slotted-in planks to make sure they'd stay put. He had red-orange hair, not slicked back, but curly and wild-looking. He looked in her direction. Gave her a wary glance: the look of an insider, directed at an outsider. He was only about forty. A smile. He seemed to be saying, Nice hair color you've got there, missus. She had taken off her hat and unbuttoned her coat; the room was too hot for them. She felt she was on display.

From the opposite corner appeared two policemen in uniform, hurrying toward the door, as if they'd received some signal. Dickie had been looking about for waiters or for the bar; it was difficult to figure out how things got served.

"Brawl!" someone shouted. "Fight outside! Fight!"

Up went Dickie's hackles. The two uniforms were just passing, and Dickie quickly spoke police talk to them, identifying himself; did they want help? They did.

He was going to leave her in here alone? "Dickie, you said one minute ago you're not on duty," said Charlotte.

"I am now!"

There were shouts from outside, loud, a mob. Something pounded against the other side of the door. It sounded like a man's heavy body, thudding against it, as if he'd been catapulted.

It took the officers and Dickie awhile to get outside. No one seemed to think there was anything unusual going on.

Charlotte backed against a wall and tried to flatten herself like a board. Maybe she should have worn a sign: SPEAK TO ME IF YOUR NAME IS KEMPLE.

She'd never been any good at sorting things. Pictures and mementos for scrapbooks, her own jewelry, shells collected from a beach, books—it didn't matter what it was: she'd lose track of what went where, then she'd end up all thumbs and have to call for a maid. Her father-in-law had found this maddening. He'd point out a tree in which birds were perching and tell her to look at the finch, the little one, with the yellow; wasn't it perfect? All the birds would look the same; she'd see yellow in every one of them. But she could try. Like eyes that take some minutes to get adapted to the dark, when you've just left a bright place.

She decided to sort out faces by age and by arithmetic. It was almost twenty-four years ago that she'd left home. So add twenty-four years to her parents' ages from the last time she saw them. How old had they been, twenty-four years ago? Old. What were their faces like, twenty-four years ago?

Stupid question. Their faces were like masks on which faces had not yet been drawn. They were turned in another direction, away from her.

The crowd around the set-up lanes was getting bigger, noisier. Someone lifted a metal lunch pail into the air and banged on it with what seemed to be a hammer: a moment later, all through the building, things quieted down.

Now at one end of the lanes—the finish line—something else was being arranged. Four big plush cushions, like things stolen from an enormous divan, were placed within the confines of the planks, and on each cushion appeared all sorts of bright, gaudy baubles: playing balls, rag dolls, cooking spoons, small wooden horses painted orange, purple, and green.

Dickie—where *was* he; things had quieted outside, too—had been right about the gambling. In the hush you could hear the jingle of coins.

Bets were being placed, all right. Impossible to tell quite where or by whom. But there was a system at work, an intricate one, Charlotte thought. Nothing seemed to be written down. It occurred to her that whatever had happened outside might have happened on purpose, as a diversion. "Clear the house of police" might have been part of the system. People farthest away from the lanes stood on chairs, which looked like they'd break apart, but did not.

Charlotte forgot about her mission. Four young women, barely out of adolescence, or perhaps still in it, emerged from somewhere at the back. They were carrying babies who were all about one year old.

Four mothers. Their babies—girls, boys; impossible to tell—were dressed in little smocks, and on the back of each was a pinned-on sheet of paper with a number on it.

In all the world in all of time there could not have been babies, thought Charlotte, who were more exuberant, or more wildly consumed with baby joy and baby greed, than these, when they spotted those playthings on those cushions. When they were set on their feet and let go in those lanes, no one would need to advise them what to do.

The four men shifting their weight from one foot to the other near the start line were obviously the fathers. The man in the tall black squared-top hat that said JUDGE in white paint positioned himself with his back up straight on a high-legged stool that had materialized near the finish line. It was a good thing that everyone nearest the lanes sat down or crouched so as not to block anyone's view: Charlotte had been standing on tiptoe and she couldn't maintain it, and she'd never in her life stood up on a chair in public. She knew she wouldn't be able to even consider it.

The mothers placed their babies at the starting line, crisscrossing their arms in front of them, like harnesses, awaiting some signal. A man had come up close beside Charlotte. She saw the black wool sleeve of an overcoat, patched above the wrist with a shinier fabric. And a heavy black wool glove with patches of leather in the palm. Horse-smelling. A horse man. When she turned her head, she saw that the face of the man was Hays's face.

It wasn't a trick of her eyes. She hadn't been thinking about him so fully that she was seeing him in strangers. She wasn't hallucinating; she hadn't been brain-impaired from the cold, although the possibility of these things crossed her mind.

He'd switched coats. Hays had taken the sleigh driver's coat and gloves. Charlotte looked at him. He seemed pleased with himself. Did he think a local man's coat would make him *blend in*? He probably did. He probably really thought so.

"I hope you gave the cabdriver your coat, Hays. I hope you didn't leave him half naked in the cold."

"I loaned it to him. He's not getting to keep it. I've paid him quite enough," he said quietly. "Number Four, I've been told, is the odds-on favorite." He bent down toward her, as if everyone was still shouting, as if the noise level had grown higher instead of lower. She could feel his breath in her hair.

"You can't tell if they're boys or girls," said Charlotte.

"Four's a girl. She finished second last month, I heard them say, and she's been getting in practice in her grandfather's barn, where they set up a lane for her, just like these."

"Did you place any money on her, Hays?"

"I don't," he said, "gamble, you know."

"Then what would you call what you're doing here?"

"That's been more of an instinct."

"I want you to stop following me."

"I didn't follow you in the way you think I did. I've been out in this valley on my own. You'd seemed so surprised when you saw me. Didn't you think, Charlotte, that this part of the world was where I'd come to look for you?"

"You should have looked for me at Aunt Lily's."

"I had figured," he said, "if you were camped at Lily's, it would be an intermediate step, until the roads cleared."

"I think," she said, because her brain just couldn't—or didn't want to—make sense of what he was saying, "I want you to stop following me. I'll *not be kind* about it, if you ever follow me again."

"I went to your old school," he said. "Yesterday."

"I would never have gone back there without Miss Georgeson. You didn't know that?"

"I was looking for information. If you ask me the names of towns for a radius of, oh, fifty miles from the academy, I'll wager I could name them."

"If you don't stop following me, I shall cancel our meeting."

"I don't need to stop doing something I haven't done, unless by follow, you mean look for. Or you mean, go to a place where I think you'll turn up."

"I don't care what you call it."

"But you seem to care, Charlotte."

"I don't."

"You do."

"Hays, let's be polite."

The signal for the start of the race came just then: a tinny child's whistle, blown by the judge on his stool.

There was a noticeable discretion about the cheering and encouragement rising up from the spectators: this was a subdued audience, enjoying what it felt like to hold back cries, so as not to startle the racers. Two babies immediately tripped over their own feet, and then everything had to be started over again because someone (an unseen, anonymous saboteur) tossed a small bright-red spinning top into the lane of Number Three, who promptly dropped down and crawled toward it.

Wailing when the top was taken away. Discussions. Bubbles of noise, rising, falling, and then the father of Number Three got the offending obstacle placed on Number Three's cushion, which the judge allowed. The wailing stopped. You could tell that this was the baby who'd win, because his (or her) finish line now had the most toys.

"Number Four, in spite of the odds and all her practice, hasn't got a chance," said Charlotte politely.

"I tend to agree, but the outcome depends on what she's after."

Again the whistle, and this time no one bothered to hold anything back; you had to worry for the eardrums of the babies. Number One went down early and punched at the floor and started crying. Numbers Two and Four gave it all they had, but Two took a stumble and plopped down backward on its behind and just sat there, giving up, with a sad and baffled look. Number Four was looking the best, but then, within reach of the cushion, she suddenly turned around and ran back to the other end. All she wanted to do was run, and who needed to be bothered with baubles? Her parents looked heartbroken.

Four was clearly superior but Three was the winner, to wild cheering. Three flung itself on its loot with a shriek of pleasure that overrode every other sound. But it was drowned out by the louder crying of losers One and Two, who were picked up and carried to their cushions by parents. Number Four just kept on running back and forth, and every time someone tried to grab her, she slipped away like an oiled little pig.

Charlotte thought, I wonder if that baby's related to me.

Then she said to her husband—in his ear; he'd leaned down to her even closer—"Number Three, boy or girl, is going to grow up to be in business," and he said, "Your father's name is Cyrus John Kemple and your mother's name is Helen, originally Helen Roland son. They are sitting at the small square table nearest the fire, eating their supper."

The judge called out, "Now the two-year-olds. Bring out the two-year-olds!"

Like a day at the horse races. New sets of playthings were being arranged on the cushions: this time everything looked like something that could be chewed. The one-year-olds were whisked up in their mothers' arms, and they were all itching to get back into those lanes, and wiggled and howled. What made Charlotte pick up her foot and stomp it down hard on the toes of her husband, she didn't know; but it certainly, to her, felt good.

He gritted his teeth. He showed no expression when she said, stonily, "That's not fair, Hays. You spied on my life? You spied on my life and didn't tell me?"

"But Charlotte, I just now did."

"Before!"

"But I didn't know anything, before. I've only just succeeded in tracking things down today."

"Tracking *me*."

"Only to find you. When I learned of your parents, I'd thought you'd go to them."

"I don't *know* them."

"I'm sorry," he said.

"You *should* be."

"If I had known you were sending them money all these years, I would have added to it, Charlotte."

"You know about that, too?"

"The shoe shop," he said. She wanted to stamp on his other foot. But she didn't.

A new set of racers was being brought out. A whole new level of noise. The two-year-olds, it seemed, promised activities in the lanes which the babies couldn't even dream of. Charlotte didn't look at the lanes. She looked at the square little table near the fire.

The man and woman at the table were seated sideways to her. She didn't doubt her husband's word, but even if she wanted to—was he certain, was he truly certain and, if so, how?—it wouldn't have done her any good to ask. Hays was leaving. She saw the back of the sleigh driver's coat, going through the door. She did not go after him or call to him.

The man and the woman were placidly finishing their meal. The woman wiped her mouth with the hem of her apron. The man had a half slice of bread in his hand. He broke off the crust and ate it and offered the soft inner part to the woman, who smiled at him and shook her head no, and he popped it into his mouth. They sat there like two people alone on an island—a silent one, where nothing was moving, where nothing was happening at all.

What if they never got the money she'd been sending all these years? What if the shoe-shop man stole it? Or his daughter who was married to the woodsman, the tree cutter?

Charlotte reached into her purse, hoping she still had some coins. She did, but she didn't bother to count them: one of the boys who'd passed her and Dickie before, with a sled, was just now walking by, his fist in the air, apparently going after another boy.

Charlotte took hold of the raised fist. Dirty face. Brownish teeth, the two top ones chipped. Runny nose. She showed him the money.

His eyes grew wide instantly. "If you do exactly what I tell you, I'll give you these."

Solemn nod. Anything. "Did you see that man who went out the door a moment ago, a stranger?"

"Rich fellow, in a poor fellow's getup?"

"The very one. He asked me to do a secret errand for him, but I find myself too shy."

"I'll do it, miss."

Charlotte discreetly pointed out the table near the fire. "Do you know the names of that man and woman?"

"Kemple."

"Those are the ones. Tell them a gentleman wants to know if everything's all right with what arrives once a year in the mail to their old address. If so, he apologizes for being late this year, but it will come."

He was off in a flash. He was crafty; he didn't want his friends to know he was up to something. He sidled about this way and that, and when he got to the table, he made it look as if his shoe had come untied and he had stopped to tie the laces.

She couldn't make out their expressions as the boy spoke to them. They were crafty, too.

They had to be about sixty. They looked much, much older. The man was orange-gray in his beard; his head was nearly fully bald, except for a fringe of orange-gray around the back of his head, ear to ear, like pictures of the friar in the Robin Hood stories she'd read at Miss Georgeson's. Not the Sheriff of Nottingham, which was how she used to picture him.

The boy returned to Charlotte with his hand out. He made it seem he'd accidentally bumped her, or he was trying to pick her pocket. He said rapidly, out of one side of his mouth, "They get it just fine, thank you very much, does the gentleman want to have a word with them and I don't have to go give the answer if it's no."

"It's no," said Charlotte. The coins had barely reached his palm before he dashed away, as if he feared she'd try to take them back.

The man and the woman did not appear nervous or bothered by the intrusion, but that might have been their desire to maintain their privacy in the company of all their neighbors. They looked around and seemed perfectly willing to cope with whatever came their way. Placidly. Like they were past all feeling. Like that was the way they wanted it.

Charlotte thought she detected, though, a bit of relief in both of them when no one appeared to bother them further.

The man's face was thin, pale, almost gaunt—not sickly, just haggard. Not a mean face. Sad. He said something to the woman and she nodded, and he got up and went over to the lanes and tapped a man on the shoulder. Hand in his pocket. Hand out of his pocket. He was placing a bet on a two-year-old.

The woman was white-haired, with patches of gray. A sad face. Not the face of a complainer, or of someone who's all fisted up inside with bitterness. Charlotte realized that she must have expected bitterness, sourness, signs of a nasty disposition. The woman's face was deeply wrinkled, deeply worn. It was ruddier than the man's, as if she was outdoors more than he was. A plump chin. A small nose, small eyes. What did they do with the money, besides betting on babies? Was it enough?

Never a word. That was her own fault; she had no one else to blame. It was money sent to an address, not to people, not specifi- cally. The clothes on their backs would have been bought with it. They weren't badly dressed: nice, decent clothes, Sears-like. Noth- ing frayed, nothing visibly falling apart.

The first time a note, just that once, to Mr. and Mrs. Kemple. No mention of herself. No connection. "A man from your part of the Valley who knows of your old distresses has come into an inheri- tance and wishes to remember the people of his own home by offer- ing you some steady small assistance."

She'd imagined herself to be Uncle Owen, the *late* Uncle Owen, that Falstaff. Uncle Owen was always sending money to people. The reason she knew this was because not long after she married Hays, he asked her if she wanted him to make a contribution to her old school, or to her orphanage, or to both, and she'd said that just the school would be fine; and he'd paid for a new cooking stove for the cafeteria, and funded the tuitions for two new girls, straight through, anonymously, which must have made Miss Georgeson (in private) swoon.

She hadn't said anything to Hays about Owen. Or about missing the funeral. Well, if she'd stayed in her sickroom like everyone wanted her to, she would have missed it anyway.

She made a note to herself to remember to mention it at their meeting. It might be a good opening.

"I'm sad about Uncle Owen, Hays."

"So am I, Charlotte."

"I liked him."

"So did I, though I'd never said so before."

Something they had in common. Hays always said it was the best way to start a meeting. It would be better than just sitting down across from him and coming right out with something too blatant or too strong, like, "I asked Uncle Chessy to hire a detective to find out who that woman is, you'll know who I mean, the one you were trying to kiss in public but I interrupted it and your hat fell off." Or, "I suppose you want to divorce me, even though Heaths don't divorce."

The man Hays said was her father had placed his bet. He went back to the table, to the woman Hays said was her mother.

Pandemonium at the lanes. A desperado-type two-year-old had got loose, and came up with the idea that the lane dividers needed to be knocked over. Down went a couple of wood blocks, down went some planks. A gang of older children—four-year-olds, five—who must have been disgruntled at being too big to race themselves, rushed in to help out. Anarchy!

A long blast of the judge's whistle to settle things down. Should the bad-behavior two-year-old be disqualified? Arguments back and forth. Lanes reset. The child was allowed to stay in.

Whistle to start the race. As if on cue, like they'd planned this, runners Six and Seven immediately reached over their divider and starting swinging at each other's heads. Number Eight must have witnessed one-legged races at some fair or schoolyard: it bent up its left leg, took hold of its foot, and started hopping, and would not be dissuaded from this task, which it performed very well, until stumbling halfway to the cushion.

The winner was Number Five, by default. Five had a head of golden curly hair that poured down its back and obscured the top of its number. It was a chubby, extremely round child, waddling happily down its lane like a fatted goose, and when it got to its finish line, it lifted an edge of the cushion and crawled under it, head first, as if it meant to stay there forever, with its fat pink legs poking out.

The race was a disappointment. There was a wave of deflation all through the building, and a sense that people were saying, All right, now there's nothing to do but drink, so let's do it.

But people who'd put money on the fat child to win must have made out very well. Probably it was only its parents. Charlotte thought, I bet the man Hays said was my father didn't bet on Five. I bet he went for the hopper.

The entertainment was over. There was no change in the man and woman at the table by the fire. Did they sense they were being watched? They were probably satisfied that their anonymous man was not present. They wouldn't have been looking for a woman.

Charlotte couldn't tell if their eyes met hers—across the wide expanse of the room, through all those people—or if she were simply a stranger in their midst, who happened to be standing at a spot they happened to gaze at. "There's a lady stranger over by the back wall," they might have thought. Maybe they'd mention it to each other later: "Did you see the well-dressed copper-haired lady stranger by the back wall?"

Or maybe they wouldn't say copper, they'd say orange. Or they'd say orange-reddish. Maybe they'd say "attractive." Or, "smart-looking." Or, "healthy-looking."

Or they'd just talk about the message from the boy: "He wanted to know if it was all right, he'd come checking, and what do you think of that?"

"Charlotte!" Here was Dickie, red-faced, breathless, as happy as the one-year-olds when they'd burst out down the lanes from their starting line. "Charlotte, I've just chased a man nearly a mile and I believe he had a knife."

"What happened to him?"

"It was dark. He headed for the woods and got away."

"We're going to the train now," said Charlotte.

"But I want to see the races. I bet they're racing chickens. There's a town near the mountains where they're breeding chicks for it, special feed."

"You missed the races."

"Then I want to have an ale. The local coppers are buying. And I want to find your parents, say hello."

She took hold of his arm. "They're not here. I've looked everywhere. You were given incorrect information."

"Let's go find their house."

"That's not what I want to do. You have to follow me, Dickie, because Harry said so, and it's your job. We're going back to Boston. We're going *now*."

∞ Sixteen ∞

Eunice fussed, fidgeted, spilled water from the washing bowl, dropped coal on the floor. How could anyone sleep through two days and nights and come out of it fully alive, functional-like, without permanent damage to the brain?

Charlotte reassured her. "I already had a brain disease, and it's unlikely I'll have another. May I have a tray, with whatever meal's correct for whatever time of day it is?"

It was just about lunchtime and it had snowed again, not as bad as before, but heavier, wetter: the kind of snow, Eunice said, that came down like overcooked oatmeal, and made you want to cry. Outside, it was not a pretty day.

"What's the matter, Eunice?"

"I was so terrible worried for you."

"I'm fine. Hungry, but fine."

"Do you want a bath?"

"I want to eat."

She was back on the second floor, but in a different room, larger than the last one. A handsome, black-and-red Chinese rug. Shutters on the window, painted a dark shade of blue. White walls, bare, with markings in the places where pictures had very recently been removed. Charlotte thought of Miss Singleton.

"Did the Navy take away Miss Singleton, Eunice?"

"They did, already, yesterday."

"Did people go and sit in her house with her?"

"Heaps, it was lovely. All the maids and I stopped over at Bowdoin Square."

"Poor Miss Singleton. I wonder what will happen to her rooms."

"They're to be re-split up into regular ones."

"You're so nervous, Eunice. Was it from looking at someone dead?"

"The dead don't bother me, as it's the living I'd be all worked up by."

"Why don't you just tell me what's wrong."

"Nothing's wrong."

"Then please may I have a tray?"

No, she couldn't have one, apologies. There wasn't a new cook yet and Georgina was over her head. She was saying the most dreadful things about Mrs. Petty for abandoning her. Georgina had canceled meals in rooms. She closed the public tearoom, and she was keeping it that way until the new cook came in—a man, a Frenchman, coming over by boat, and it would take him ages and ages. Georgina was a little bit on strike.

"Can you get me a sandwich from somewhere? Or some biscuits? Or an entire loaf of bread, which believe me, I could eat?"

No meals in rooms. If you crossed the rule you were crossing a strike line. But the tearoom was only closed to the outside public.

Charlotte could go down there and have anything she wanted, as long as it was cold meat sandwiches, the only thing on the menu, for now.

Poor Eunice was in a bad way. She couldn't hide it. It couldn't be just the snow, and it wasn't Miss Singleton, and it couldn't be just a question of having hovered near Charlotte, on and off, all those hours, not knowing if she should be roused, and being alarmed the whole time that parts of Charlotte's mind were disappearing forever in some abyss, some quicksand-like hole of sleep. And it couldn't be just problems of the kitchen.

Charlotte sat up and pushed back the covers. She'd slept in her underskirt, nothing else. The little maid stood by anxiously, chewing on her bottom lip.

"Don't tell me," said Charlotte, "that anyone expects me to put on that hideous dress." It was laid out waiting for her on the little chair by the window.

It was actually a suit. The long, dull-gray wool skirt was more than abundant in its material: it was the type of sweeping multifold thing often worn by her sisters-in-law, which the Irish maids called a broom skirt. When you walked down a sidewalk, no matter how high the heels of your shoes, you swept up everything in your path— litter, dirt, dust, mud, slush, all sorts of disagreeable, indescribable things—and the wool would make everything cling, and you'd come home like something nasty, which the most low-standard cat in the world would refuse to drag in. The blouse was even worse: shiny glossed satin, dark green, like wet, soggy grass, with beige and gold diamond-shaped patterns in vertical rows, tiny white buttons—far too many of them—and a collar so high it would not only cover her neck but could cover her up to her eyes. And beige lace around the cuffs. The jacket was hanging on the back of the door, a gray wool lump, brand new like the rest of the outfit, but as shapeless as a box that someone's been kicking around.

"I think it's perfect, missus. The doctor sent it over, from one of her nurses who was sent out to buy it special for you."

"The doctor," said Charlotte, "wants me to look like I'm wearing something people drape furniture with, in spring cleaning. Did she send over anything for underneath?"

She did. On the bureau were heavy stockings, a white underskirt, drawers without ruffles, a white flannel under-vest that was simply pulled over the head, without buttons, and a corset cover, also flannel, that could be worn as a second, shorter underskirt. No corset.

"I'll be warm, at least. Is my aunt here?"

"At the hospital. There was a fire yesterday morning by the docks, a bad one. We don't expect to be seeing her anytime soon."

"Where are my clothes?"

"Being cleaned. It's a fine, grand suit. Cost a fortune."

"Then you're the one to have it," said Charlotte. "I'm sure it will fit, but if it doesn't, I'm sure you'll think of a way to alter it."

"Oh, missus, I couldn't. I never could. The doctor'll have my head off."

"It's a gift," said Charlotte.

"Oh, missus."

"If you don't accept it as a gift, I'll tell my aunt you stole it from me, which will put you in all sorts of trouble. But you can't have it till you get me my own clothes."

"I can do that. I'll just pop down now for them, oh, thank you, missus!" And Eunice covered her face with her hands and burst into tears, and Charlotte thought, There's certainly been a lot of crying in these rooms. Maybe Harry should start collecting tears in buckets, for the next time the plumbing freezes up.

She went over to the little maid, took her by the shoulders, and made her sit down, sobbing and shaking, on the bed, and so what if Harry had a rule about maids not sitting on things in a guest's room. Charlotte sat down beside her.

A knocking. It came so close in the wake of Eunice's breakdown, you had to wonder if whoever it was had been listening in the hall, with an ear pressed up to the door. It wasn't bolted. The knocker didn't wait to be invited inside.

"Good morning, Charlotte," said Arthur. "I'm back."

He looked freshly bathed, freshly trimmed, freshly dressed. Quiet clothes, no green jacket. A brown tweed suit, brown vest, somber necktie. He looked at her. Everything about him said, "Ask the maid to leave us alone and then let me come over and kiss you."

She looked away first. There was no chance of getting in a word. Eunice had peeked through her fingers and, seeing who it was, turned and flung herself across the bed, sobbing so hard, the bed shook.

"Those look like convulsions," said Arthur.

"Arthur, for the moment, please, go away."

"You should let me look after her. I'm almost a doctor."

"No, you're a student," said Charlotte.

"Like Hamlet," he said. His smile was a little too weak, a little too forced. There was a look on his face that made Charlotte feel suddenly heavy, as if she'd been standing outside all morning in the mush of the snow. He's as nervous as Eunice, she thought. And as worried.

A voice outside the door. "Everything all right in there, Mrs. Heath?"

The man was a genie. He was just like a genie. "Thank you, Moaxley, it is, as Mr. Pym's just now leaving."

"I'm right out here," came Moaxley's voice.

"Yes, I can hear you. Do you think you could arrange for a favor to be done for me?"

"Tell me what it is and you'll have it."

"I want my clothes. I'm told they're being cleaned. Eunice has found herself too under the weather to get them for me. It would be lovely if I could get dressed."

"Just give me five minutes."

Arthur had backed toward the door, holding that strange little smile. He was giving her the chance to change her mind. She tried to smile in return, but her face felt too heavy.

"He's gone, Eunice. Now sit up and dry your eyes. And tell me quickly what's the matter, because, if I don't have a meal very soon, I'll be unhappier than you are now. And you can't lie here all day blathering."

The little maid did as she was told, wiping her eyes with the inside hem of her apron. She calmed down enough to speak. "You've been so very kind to me, missus, and I don't deserve it."

And a new burst of tears, more sobbing. Somewhere between hiding her face in her apron and looking up at the ceiling as if she wished it would fall on top of her, Eunice uttered the words "Mr. Pym" with such a strangled-sounding sob, Charlotte went cold inside, as if she were back on that long walk with Dickie.

And then a deep breath, and a shudder, and it came out. Eunice's voice was flat now. She was miserable. "It's the letter I didn't post, Mrs. Heath."

"The letter to Brookline, do you mean?"

"The one."

"You gave it to someone else to send?"

"No, missus. I kept it in my pocket and I've got it here right now."

It was true. She fumbled for it, drew it out, handed it to Charlotte. Chester Heath in Brookline. Unopened. Worn-looking, crinkled. Eunice said, "I don't expect you'll forgive me. I don't deserve it. But I just couldn't keep silent about it, no more. It's still postable but I'd expect you'd send it yourself this time, not trusting me."

The letter in Charlotte's hand felt as heavy as a brick. She couldn't think what to do with it, and as she'd already started a pattern of tossing letters into a Beechmont fire, she went over to the coals and dropped it in, and didn't watch it flare and burn. No help on the way from Uncle Chessy! No Pinkerton's!

"I want to know why you did this," said Charlotte.

"It was Mr. Pym. He sent me a message not to when I'd come up and you gave it to me."

"But he was with me. He never left the room."

"He didn't have to."

"But he didn't say anything. I would've heard him. I would've remembered."

"He didn't have to speak. He could send a message, with his looks, of what he wanted me to do, secret-like."

Charlotte sighed, a long, heavy sigh. She lifted the outfit from Aunt Lily off the chair and thought, for a second, she'd throw it at poor Eunice; but then she placed it gently on the bed beside her and went and sat on the chair. "You can still have the dress, Eunice, and don't tell me you don't deserve it, because I hate it, I really hate it, when maids talk like that."

Sniffing, more sobs. Charlotte said, "Tell me about Mr. Pym."

"I can't."

"Are you Catholic, Eunice?"

"I am."

"Then pretend I'm a priest and this is confession time."

That seemed to help. The little maid nodded her head and patted herself on the chest, as if trying to slow down her heartbeat. "It's all like he told you," she said, "with the things that happened in the past. Except he reversed it, like."

"You know what he told me?"

"Oh, yes."

"He lied to me?"

"Not exactly, not for most of it, unless you count it a lie that he was the one it all happened to."

"And who," said Charlotte slowly, "would be the actual one?"

"It would be me, missus."

You think you're ready for anything. You think you can make

yourself sturdy for the bearing-up of information someone's giving you, which you don't want to hear. Funny that the coating of lacquer she'd imagined all over herself with her husband, out in the Valley, had worked, more or less, as a fairly decent shield. There was no such thing now. Charlotte felt small and raw and exposed, and it wasn't just because she was only wearing one piece of lightweight underwear.

What was it Aunt Lily had said, when she was making a threat about dragging Charlotte to the wards with her, and letting her see what it was like in the hospital? You would feel that your soul itself had been raked.

"Please don't have me lose my position," said Eunice, in a tiny voice. "Please don't speak to Mr. Alcorn about having me got rid of."

"I'll do no such thing."

Had five minutes gone by? Moaxley was back. He didn't knock, but made sounds of clearing his throat, like he was trying not to cough. Charlotte opened the door a crack. She wanted to wrap herself in a blanket but all the blankets were on the bed, under Eunice.

"I hope you'll accept apologies for your own clothes being too wet to put on," said Moaxley in the hall, carefully not looking in. "But one of the ladies is a traveler for a company what makes clothes. She was willing to be parted with one of the samples."

Through the door crack came Moaxley's arm, passing her a new dress. "Thank you very much, Moaxley."

"Hoping it's your size."

"It'll do just fine."

She expected it to be even more appalling than the one from her aunt. But it wasn't half bad. It would fit her loosely, but it wasn't overly big. The sleeves were ugly, and even worse, the dress was red—a solid, deep, maroon red, like dark wine. She'd sworn to herself the last time she was pregnant that she'd never wear any shade of red at all. How could anyone want to wear red who'd been through what she'd been through? Maybe it was mentally abnormal of her to automatically associate red clothes with blood, but men who'd been in wars probably felt the same way.

This wasn't a time to be picky. She'd have to retrain herself when it came to that color, and she wouldn't think twice about the fact that it blended so badly with her hair, and made her look, she felt, like a sugar maple full-blown with autumn leaves, or a heated-up, red-glowing fire tong, with a hot orange glow at the top.

"Would the dress be all right, Mrs. Heath?"

"It's excellent."

Charlotte draped the dress on her arm, found her purse, took out five dollars. It had annoyed her, all those days ago, that the money the Gersons had given her—had lent to her—was mostly all in small bills. But now she was glad of it. The extravagant sum she handed Moaxley seemed all the more lavish. He refused it.

"It's gratis," he said. "Mr. Alcorn said specially, for Mrs. Heath, granted what a help she was with the police, gratis."

"It's not for the dress."

"Thanks very much for the thought, but no," said Moaxley.

"It's not for you. Please take this to Georgina. Tell her it's my contribution to her strike. A private contribution."

"If you insist. But just one of those bills will be enough, more than enough, to make your gesture appreciated, Mrs. Heath."

"Maybe so," said Charlotte, "but five of them will be unforgettable. And tell her, if she wouldn't mind, could she wrap up some sandwiches she's making anyway for the lunch, and send them up to me, immediately, please. It's not crossing a line because it's not on a tray. It's not a meal. It's sandwiches wrapped in a napkin."

"She might be obliging." Moaxley took the money. Charlotte heard him chuckling to himself as he walked down the hall. I'm going to miss him, she thought.

Eunice sat at the very edge of the bed with her feet pressed tightly together and her hands folded in her lap, like a child who's been sent to the dunce corner in a classroom.

"Do you like it?" said Charlotte.

More sniffing. "It's not near as nice as the other but it's nice enough."

"I'm going to wash my face and then get dressed," said Charlotte. She hadn't meant for Eunice to jump up and come over to help her, but there was no telling her not to. Charlotte took off her underskirt and checked it to see if there were any spots from her time of the month. There weren't, but she knew there'd be some, soon enough. It was likely to happen that as soon as she put on the dress, her body would be inspired to start bleeding.

She realized that it would take her awhile to make a clear separation in her mind between "red dress" and "that blood." Thoughtfully, without mentioning it, Mabel Gerson had packed some cloths for the very purpose in the satchel she'd prepared. Charlotte admired that. She never would have thought of it herself.

The little maid handed her the new undergarments one at a time, then helped her put on the new dress. It buttoned up the back. Eunice's fingers on the buttons were trembly, but she managed. She seemed glad to have a pause in her confession.

The dress didn't hang on Charlotte as if it belonged to a much larger woman, as loose as it was. The material was lightweight wool. The waist wasn't gathered tightly at all. Its seams sat nicely above her hips. The bodice was simple, without folds to conceal a bosom. There was no extra fabric in the back for a bustle. A fine tweedlike pattern of raised black threads was woven into the neckline, which was low, so her throat wasn't covered.

The sleeves, Charlotte felt, should really have been left alone. Above the elbows, they were satin, and ballooned out, crimped and puffy, as if someone had blown hot air into them.

"Very stylish, the uppers of the sleeves," observed Eunice. "Balloons, they call them. It's what all the ladies are wearing."

"I don't believe in wearing balloons. These sleeves look all swollen up." But the lower parts were all right. There wasn't any fringe at the wrists, just double rows of buttons.

"You look so beautiful. It's so apt for you," said Eunice.

Charlotte found her hairbrush. She went back to the chair. Sat back down. Brushed her hair slowly. Gathered it up at the back of her neck. Twisted it into a loose knot. Reached up to the bureau where her pins were. Put in the pins. Her hands were steady. Eunice sat back down at the edge of the bed in exactly the same position as before.

"May I ask you some questions?" said Charlotte.

"Please, missus, please do."

"Was your mother a schoolteacher?"

"She was, and more, like you were told."

"Did your father work for Sears, Roebuck in Hartford?"

"Same as you were told."

"Was he fat?"

"He was."

"After he died were you offered a discount for life on things from the catalog?"

"I was. They were powerful fond of my dad."

"And did you ever," said Charlotte quietly, "buy things from the catalog for Mr. Pym?"

"I've done so. But he doesn't like it to be known, so he takes out the labels. At his college they look down on the type of product from the company."

"Is Mr. Pym a student of Harvard College?"

"Oh, he is, he's been one for ages."

"And what would be the reason you and Mr. Pym are on such close terms, Eunice?"

She looked down at her feet. "That I would rather not answer, please."

"How old did you tell me you are?"

"Sixteen."

"Mr. Pym is older."

"Oh, but it doesn't feel it."

"Are you in love with him?"

More tears, welling up. Little rivulets down her cheeks. "Please, it's not allowed. Mr. Alcorn's so very particular with us. There was a maid what took up with one of the boys, not a college one, but a boy from a farm, out in Dover. Mr. Alcorn got wind of it and they were thrown to the street without their back wages, as a penalty, and it was awful."

"No one's going to throw you out," said Charlotte. "Did your mother go away in the middle of the night when you were a girl?"

"She did, the way he said it."

"Did she send you an address of where to reach her?"

"It was just as he said."

"Did you try to get on a train and some men accosted you?"

"They were brutes," said Eunice. "I was out of my wits."

"But you got away from them."

"I did, like he said."

"He told me that there was an old schoolfriend who was a betrayer."

"That was true. My friend Ginny. Her father was a man my mum knew, on the board of the overseers of the schools. It broke my heart how she turned on me, when it was broke already from what happened with my mum."

"And where did you go when you ran away from those brutes?"

"I was in service then, at the home of an awful cruel lady, but I went back there. It was my luck then, another lady was visiting. She was kind to me, like you, missus, and she got me to tell her everything what went on, as I was not in a fit state to seem normal-like. The lady was one of them get-the-votes-for-ladies people. She was on her way to Boston and she took me with her. I don't know what happened to her afterward but this was where she brought me. She was fond of Mr. Alcorn and was a guest here sometimes."

"And here you are."

"Yes, missus. That's the whole of it."

"I was told there was a physician. I think I remember the name. Gudjohnson or something. Something Nordic."

"Yes, but that was an added-on bit. Mr. Pym had such a neighbor and he was over to his house all the time. The doctor was an old tippler, a regular souse. Don't know if you're aware of it, but Mr. Pym's been always with a gift for what's medical. He was a kind of apprentice to that man."

"And where would this neighborhood of Mr. Pym's be?"

"In Cambridge near the college. Such a pretty street, you never saw the like. Everything grand and leafy. Quiet-like."

"You've been there?"

Eyes cast down to the floor. "Please if you don't mind, I'll not answer that."

"And who is Mr. Pym's father?"

"A professor at the college, like."

"In what subject?"

"The arithmetic, what he's always had so much trouble with."

"And who is his mother?"

"A lady. She's one of them have-the-votes, too. I saw a painting of her. She's very elegant, very what you might call upper in the classes."

"When Mr. Pym brought you to his house, his mother and father weren't at home?"

"Oh, they travel such a lot. They go to Europe, to all sorts of places."

The door. Discreet, gentle knocking. Eunice jumped up and Charlotte stopped her, in case it was Arthur. "Who is there?"

"Your lunch, Mrs. Heath."

It was Georgina herself, handing in an entire tablecloth folded up around a stack of sandwiches. "Is Eunice with you?"

"She is."

"Is she all right?"

"I don't know yet."

"Tell her to come down to me. I want her to help with the serving in the tearoom, soon as she's able."

"I'll do that. I'm sorry Mrs. Petty had to leave, Georgina."

"She's such an old cow."

"Oh, I know."

"Not actually."

"I know. Thank you for feeding me."

"You're welcome. It's not crossing my strike if I do it myself. Thank you for the, uh, contribution."

"You're welcome, and you don't have to say anything else about it. Would you do something ever so kindly for me, which I know is not your job, but as you're here right now, I've the need to mention it?"

"Mention it, Mrs. Heath."

"Please ask Mr. Alcorn to telephone to another hotel for me, and reserve a room for me, beginning about an hour from now."

"Mr. Alcorn's gone out. He's gone to see a framer-man about putting poor Miss Singleton's pictures into frames, and anyway, I'm not speaking to him, for making me wait so long for a new cook to come over the ocean, and a French one, that doesn't speak hardly a word of English."

"Then ask Moaxley."

"He won't use the telephone. He thinks it will put electrical shocks into his ears. He's stubborn about it. Perhaps I can mention it to the managing housekeeper."

"Mrs. Fox."

"If you don't mind my saying so, she'll not be sad to see you leav⸗ing. She's terrible prejudiced about things, sometimes. What hotel?"

"It's called the Essex, near Copley Square."

"I'll have it phoned to. Will you want a cab?"

"Are the streets clear enough for carriages?"

"They are. Sleigh runners wouldn't go in all the slush that's out there."

"Then I'll have a carriage. Please have it meet me at the corner of the Common, across from the Dome. I shall walk down there."

Georgina didn't think it was out of the ordinary for a Beechmont guest to want to be picked up outside of the hotel. But she said, "Your feet will get wet. It's deep as a river with that mess of snow that came down last night."

"I don't mind wet feet."

"But we don't have anyone to spare to go with you."

"I don't mind going alone. When you're on speaking terms with Mr. Alcorn again, will you tell him, I'm his friend, and I shall write to him?"

At the mention of the words "write to him," Eunice let out another round of sniffly, choky sobs. More tears.

"And tell him to tell Miss Blanchette I would like to visit her again."

"I heard she was fond of you."

"And I of her. Good luck, Georgina," said Charlotte.

She bolted the door. Back in the chair, she opened the cloth and let it spread itself to cover the dress. She didn't care how dry her throat was—she'd get some tea later. She ate three of the sandwiches in silence, with Eunice's eyes on her. Cold chicken, with a coagu⸗lated jellylike fattiness between the meat and the bread, which Ro⸗wena Petty would have screamed at in horror.

There were two left, and Charlotte offered them to the maid.

Eunice got up and took them, and the tablecloth too, and carefully rewrapped them. "I'll save them for later and bring this back to the kitchen, if you're finished with me now, missus. Are you finished with me now?"

"I want you to know I'll keep your secret," said Charlotte. "Do you want to find out what happened to your mum?"

"Oh, I'd give the world for it."

"What do you think happened?"

"I think someone was meaning to harm her. I think it had to do with something she found out about in the schools. I was so little, you know, it's all terrible mysterious. She was so much concerned with things like honor. Things like that. I heard her say to my dad once, you know, you think if someone's involved with education, they're good people, they're not criminal-like."

"Tell me anything else you remember."

"There was a pair of little girls that went missing around the same time as Mum. Nobody ever said there was a connection. They came from another part of Hartford, the nicer part. I heard it talked about in the house where I went into service. Twins, they were. About my own age. I think Mum knew them, as they'd be in a school where she had girls in teacher training, from her teachers' college. It was all such a terrible mystery, like I said."

"Don't tell me you think your mother was a kidnapper," said Charlotte.

"Oh, I never would. It would be more of the opposite."

"As if these girls were being harmed, by someone else?"

"They were the cousins of my once-friend Ginny."

"I'll tell you what," said Charlotte. "How would you like it if I wrote a new letter to my uncle, and this time, I changed the names of the persons I want to be investigated? What is your name?"

"Ingalls, missus. They were George and Mary Alice Ingalls."

"Those aren't the ones I was told."

"No, he changed that, like he left out the bit about the two girls. The names he would've given would be, of his own."

"Why do you think Mr. Pym took your life, and made it seem to me it was his own?"

"He liked it better than his," said Eunice simply.

"And does he always tell the story to, you know, lady guests?"

"Now and then only. Not all the time."

"And does it bother you, Eunice, to know that he—that he does what he does?"

"Please. I'll not be able to answer that. He'll be going soon enough as it is. His tutor what he went to do the bog body with wants for him to come and be with him in the hospital out there. The tutor says it's not worth his while to do any more studies. He won't have a proper certificate but they say, out there, it doesn't matter."

"Do you want to go with him?"

"I'll not answer that. And I couldn't ask you to do what you said, missus, get a Pinkerton for me."

"You didn't ask. I shall be at the Essex Hotel, but I think, Eunice, when I want to contact you, to let you know what's found out, if anything, I shall do it by the mail. And don't start wailing again because I've said that word. Don't say anything. But I want you to go out now and find Mr. Pym, whom I'm willing to suggest is somewhere nearby."

Eunice gave a gasp. "Oh! What're you going to do to him?"

"I'm not going to do anything. I don't want to see him. I don't want to look at him. Go to him and take him away somewhere. He'll be wanting to know what you've told me, and you don't need to tell him what I know. I meant what I said when I said I'll keep your secret. You won't believe me, but you might have done me a very great service by not posting that letter."

"That's not the truth. You're feeling sorry for me."

"Think as you wish. Did he tell you that in the letter to my uncle I had asked for my husband to be checked?"

"He said you had one that was with another lady. But you know, not that it's a help to you, lots of the ladies here, they have the same kind of them. Of husbands."

"I'm very sure of that. When I write to my uncle this time, I'll only speak of your case."

"You don't want to know of the other lady?"

Charlotte smiled at her. "I think," she said, "I'll be better off keeping things simple. Now go and do what I've told you. Take him to another floor, into a room somewhere. Don't come back to this room."

"Will I ever see you again?"

"Probably not," said Charlotte.

The little maid took hold of one side of her apron like she was about to make a curtsy, and Charlotte said, "Don't *do* that." Eunice came closer to her, and stood on tiptoe—she was shorter than Charlotte, by a lot—and kissed her on the cheek.

"Eunice?"

"What, missus?"

"Don't forget my aunt's dress."

"Oh, I wouldn't." She scooped it up off the bed.

"And tell Mr. Pym, if he attempts to establish contact with me, in any way, I shall go to Mr. Alcorn, and also to his college, and also to his mother and father, and I shall make things very unpleasant for him indeed, whether or not he's going off to his tutor at his hospital. I expect that Mr. Pym would not be interested in having me do what I would do."

"He'll wonder why you would say so, if I haven't told you all of the truth."

"You can say I'm very cross because I don't believe in stealing people's stories and passing them off as one's own, as a general rule. You can tell him you told me that part of it, because I had forced you to."

The little maid nodded. She tucked up the tablecloth of sand⁄ wiches under one arm and hugged the dress to her chest, as if she were already trying it on.

"Goodbye, Eunice, and if you thank me again, I will scream."

"Goodbye, missus."

Charlotte threw the bolt to let her out. No one was in the hall. He was probably waiting for Eunice on the stairs.

She gathered up her purse, her jacket, her coat. She left Everett Gerson's big mittens on the bureau; a maid could have them. She counted the rest of her money. Enough for a cab. Enough for a room, if the Essex required a deposit. Enough for tea, for lunch. She was hungry again already. Well, the sandwiches had been breakfast, not lunch.

She'd have a bath as soon as she could. She wondered what the tub would be like, and if the running water came out hot, or would have to be heated. She looked down at her shoes. They were going to be ruined out there. Maybe she'd go shopping in the morning. Buy new ones.

She opened the door and peeked out into the hall, and a voice said, "Better if you went through the tunnel to next door, Mrs. Heath, and went out into the street from over there."

"Why, thank you, Moaxley. Is there a policeman outside?"

"A lady from the Society. Got herself fixed up like she's selling hot apples off a cart. We know her pretty well, not that she's aware of it. You might want to go in a direction away from the apple cart."

"Is there going to be a carriage for me?"

"There is."

"I should have known you'd turn up."

"It's my job. Would you want for me to go with you?"

"I'll be fine. I know the way."

"Well, then," said Moaxley, and Charlotte said, "You looked splendid in your army uniform, the other night."

He took the compliment huffily, but he put back his shoulders and let his chest, very slightly, expand. "Least I could do for the occasion," he said. "Mind your step when you get to outside. It's rotten wet out there."

"I'll be careful." Moaxley held out his hand and she shook it. "I'll just stay by the top of the stairs till you're into where you need to be headed. And by the way, not that it's my place to say so, about the dress, it's as they say, you know, becoming, on you." She hadn't put her coat on. His smile made her blush.

"Thank you."

"You're welcome."

And she went quietly down the hall to the tunnel-panel. Pushed it open. Looked into that gray, lustrous light, like the light near the mouth of a cave. What time had he said he'd be there for the meeting?

Five o'clock. A private dining room. "I bet he'll get there early," she thought. "I bet he'll come alone. I bet his family doesn't know where he is. I bet his coat smells like horses from that sleigh driver."

There'd be plenty of time to draw up the thing she was just now beginning to plan. Hotel stationery would do just fine. This time it would have a letterhead.

She wouldn't need a lawyer. She'd act as her own. An affidavit, was that what it was called? A solemn legal document. She'd act like Uncle Owen and Uncle Chessy, put together. "I, Charlotte Heath, born Charlotte Kemple, hereby swear that I shall ask my husband no questions concerning behaviors of his," she planned.

Was "behaviors" a suitable word? It would do.

"I shall not receive information pertaining to those unasked questions, provided that the behaviors, aforementioned, are solemnly sworn, by my husband, to have ceased, in a way that would cause them to be ceased *permanently*. And I shall expect from my husband, in return, exactly the very same thing."

She'd tinker with the actual wording. Print her name at the bottom, then sign it. Sign it before or after he agreed to it? After. What if he didn't agree to it? He would. He wouldn't.

He would. He would have to. She thought about the way he looked at her when she hadn't mentioned noticing that he was wearing the striped muffler. He'd wanted her to mention it. He'd looked hurt.

I bet he's got it on when he comes into the hotel, she thought. I bet he won't expect me to be there ahead of him. I bet he doesn't know I understand what he was doing when he went out to the Valley, where he'd found me the first time.

"Godspeed, Mrs. Heath," called out Moaxley in a hoarse whisper, and Charlotte stopped for a moment to let her eyes get used to the light. Maybe, she thought, she wouldn't go shopping first thing in the morning. Maybe she'd send for her horses. There would have to be a stable near the Essex.

She propelled herself forward, at a trot, rounding the tunnel corners with ease, with her heart tensed up and her hair coming out of its pins and tumbling around her. She didn't stop to pick up the pins or fix her hair. She wouldn't care if she looked windblown. Her legs, as if acting on their own, picked up the pace and went faster, at nearly a run, like those babies in the lanes, the ones who didn't fall down.